Julius Matthias

MICHELLE MAZEL

JULIUS MATTHIAS
— HOPE REBORN —

LIBRARY OF CONGRESS CATALOGING-IN-PUBLICATION DATA
Julius Matthias: Hope Reborn
Authored by Michelle Mazel
ISBN: 9781734383591
LCCN: 2021943849

American soldiers from the U.S. 4th Infantry Division in front of the Eiffel Tower, after French firefighters raised the tricolor during the liberation of Paris, 25 August 1944.

PROLOGUE

SOME KIND OF CELEBRATION was going on in the Hotel de la Paix. An assortment of small crafts on Lake Geneva appeared to be bobbing and dancing in the evening breeze to the lively music from the ground-floor terrace where people stood laughing and talking. Leaning on the railing of the balcony of his top-floor room, a man past the first flush of youth, could not take his eyes off the scene. Tall, and with thick blond hair lightly streaked with wisps of grey, the long months spent on the road had left their mark on Julius Matthias' sunburnt face and haggard mien. He had witnessed a German soldier murder his wife and had barely escaped deportation. He had traveled on foot more than a thousand miles through war zones, at times falling in with groups of partisans harassing German troops and had crossed several borders with the help of smugglers or deserters. After enduring the stifling heat and torrential rain, he had mostly slept under open skies. It had been quite an ordeal for a staid, fifty-four-year-old Doctor of Medicine used to a fairly sedentary life. Though he wanted to reach Geneva as fast as possible, he had stopped in Torino for a few days to shake off the dust of his travels. A little more than four months after his flight from Nagyvarad, his Transylvanian hometown, he had hired a limousine to take him to Switzerland. Fresh from the barber and wearing a suit he had made to order during his short stay, he presented his passport to a Swiss border guard, who promptly let him through without a second glance.

That night, he did not know what to make of the sounds of revelry below, while peace was still a distant dream for millions of human beings. On this, the first day of Autumn 1944, in spite of the Allied landing in Normandy and the progress of their troops through France, heavy fighting was still going on in Europe. In Germany and Hungary, deportations were continuing, with new victims being sent daily to the death camps. Should he then resent the sounds of merriment coming from the festivities below? Or should he welcome them as a demonstration of vitality and hope? Were the celebrations proof that the old continent would weather this tragedy as it had weathered so many in its long history? He did not know. Fate, which had hounded him for so long, had snatched him at the last minute from the clutches of the Nazis. If the celebration was a sign that he could now look unconcernedly to the future, he was too much of an atheist to believe it.

1

THREE LETTERS

GENEVA, SWITZERLAND. An end to the nightmare. It had been his dream for months … no, for years … ever since war started and Transylvania was taken over by Hungary, and more urgently, with the arrival of the Germans.

Dr. Matthias could have bribed his way out after openly leaving to travel to Budapest, where his sister and her family were allegedly living. From there, he would have gone to Geneva using fake documents prepared at great expense for himself and Magda, his wife. She kept refusing, and by the time she realized the danger, it was too late. Flying was no longer an option. Though he had not lost hope, even in the darkest hours when all seemed lost, he had never dared envision his first steps in Geneva and his new life.

Switzerland was just a way-station on the road to France, his true destination, where before the war, he had sent his children to pursue their studies. It had been more than two years since he heard from them, and he was desperate for news. However, his bank was in Geneva. In his doctor's bag, he had hidden the gold coins that had been secreted in a cache in his flat, but only a handful were left after four months on the road. How much money did he still have in his account? There was no point in making any plans until he had the answer. Besides, letters were quite possibly awaiting him from family and friends who knew that should he manage to escape, Geneva would be his first stop on the road to freedom.

He went directly to the distinguished banking establishment on the rue du Rhône that he knew so well. Dressed in some kind of strange uniform that made him look like an extra in a Viennese operetta, the doorman saluted Dr. Matthias and let him in. He went through the impressive portal and paced uneasily along the vast hallway with its distinctive marble tiling. It had been eleven long years since his last visit, but nothing had changed. Portraits of long-dead bankers still looked down superciliously from their gilded frames, and rich velvet drapes continued to bracket the windows.

Behind the high counter sat the same receptionist, a little greyer, slightly more bent, and wearing the same black suit and golden chain. The man looked at him with uncertainty at first before smiling broadly. "Herr Doctor! Welcome!" he said while taking the visitor's card and leading him towards a small salon as usual. Julius Matthias sank into a deep armchair as his uneasiness began to fade.

In the hushed yet familiar setting, the receptionist who had recognized him immediately contributed to a welcome feeling of returning to normalcy. A door opened and a middle-aged woman wearing a dark suit invited him to come with her while mentioning that the Director wanted to meet him. Trying to hide his surprise, he followed her, and they rose to the second floor in a majestic, gilded, wrought iron lift.

"Dr. Hans Steuber, Director" read a small plaque.

Upon entering the room, a man seated behind a vast ebony desk stood up and came forward, his hand outstretched. "Doctor Matthias, it is a pleasure to welcome you again," he said, smiling pleasantly, as his guest took his hand. Then, turning to the secretary, he added, "Renee, two coffees, please."

Sixty or so years-old, of medium height, and with an almost bald head, the man wore a three-piece suit that was obviously made to measure. With a pocket watch tucked into his vest and his sharp eyes peering out from behind a pair of gold-rimmed glasses, he was the very picture of a Swiss banker.

"You probably do not recognize me," he went on. "Hans Steuber, at your service. We first met when you came to open an account with us some thirty years ago, in April 1913, I believe. I remember it well, because the amount you were about to deposit fell short of the usual requirements of our establishment. However, you had a letter of introduction from one of the younger Rothschilds, and we did not want to offend him by turning you down." The man then paused before continuing. "Dr. Matthias, do forgive me. Here I am, babbling, and you must be wondering when I will get to the point. The fact is that I have some sad news."

"My children? Something has happened to my children?" Dr. Matthias replied.

"No, no, not to my knowledge, at least. It is your relative, Madame Corvin—I mean, Countess von Thüringen. The late countess, I should say."

"Madi? Madi is dead?" He closed his eyes, holding the chair to steady himself, almost smelling the scent of violets that she loved so much. He could see her beloved face and beguiling smile which had captivated him from their first meeting. Despite the war, he had hoped against hope that she was safe in the opulent home her husband had left her in the finest part of Budapest. He also hoped that fate would let them meet again, perhaps here in Geneva, where she had an account in this very bank. But dead! She was dead!

Sensing his distress, the director looked at him anxiously when the secretary walked in with a tray bearing two coffee cups and some biscuits.

Julius took a deep breath and sat down.

"Forgive me. It is so unexpected! She was so young, barely sixty! What happened? How do you know? Did she visit Switzerland recently? Was she ill?"

"Not at all. I see that you have some difficulties speaking French. Shall we switch to German?"

"I have heard far too much German lately. I may be a little rusty since I haven't spoken French in quite a while, but it will come back quickly. Do tell me what happened to Madi—to the countess."

"As you know, the countess, then Madame Corvin, opened an account with us in 1916 and gave you the power of attorney. Following her wedding to the count after the war, she came to inform us of her changed status. We congratulated her and even opened a bottle of champagne to toast her. At that time, she made a point to stress that your power of attorney would still be in force and signed an attestation to that effect. Since then, she has made substantial and regular transfers of money, which regrettably came to an end when Hungary entered the war with Germany in 1939. A little more than a year ago, through a trusted messenger, she sent a duly notarized document making you the heir of all her assets in our establishment. It stipulated that should you predecease her, your three children would share that inheritance equally. Last May, the same messenger brought us a jewelry box with instructions to keep it in our vault for the countess. A short while later, we received a death certificate, together with a letter addressed to you."

Hans then opened a drawer and produced a large envelope. "That's all I know. I assume the letter will explain everything."

Julius, now speechless, stared into space. Had Madi left him not only her fortune but also her priceless jewels so coveted by the count's children? Yet, they had had no contact since the day she had told him she did not want to see him anymore, more than fifteen years ago.

"There are other letters for you. I have them here," the director went on before letting out a small cough.

"The countess had a large fortune, very large indeed, not counting the value of the jewels, of which I know nothing. It all belongs to you now. There will be some formalities, of course, and we shall have to draft the proper documents. My secretary will fix you an appointment when they are ready. Meanwhile, it will be my pleasure to put a substantial advance at your disposal; no doubt you will need it. Please be assured that I am at your service should you need anything else; for instance, legalizing your situation with local authorities. Switzerland is not always hospitable to foreigners, but have no fear. With the bank's backing, you will easily receive a residence permit.

Julius, who had just taken the last biscuit off the tray, was at a loss to understand such a display of kindness from a perfect stranger.

"Mr. Steuber, I don't know how to thank you. I am yet to make plans, though I intend to go to France as soon as possible, and there could be some difficulties. What I would like, if possible, is for one of your assistants to help me find a room in a very good hotel. I have very little by way of baggage and ..."

"My secretary, Madame Boucheron, will take care of that."

As Julius was preparing to take his leave, the director came towards him.

"Please accept my condolences," he said softly. "I have had the opportunity of meeting the countess several times, and she was a very charming lady. Let me also tell you how happy I am that you managed to escape your country and reach Geneva. You see ... I knew the young Rothschild who recommended you very well. We attended the same temple in Vienna. I had a different name at the time. Later, I married the only daughter of a Geneva banker, adopting his name and his religion. Had I not done so, I wonder what would have been my fate and that of my family. And I feel the sufferings of a people, who have remained my people, very deeply."

Those startling revelations were halted by the sudden entrance of the secretary. Wordlessly, the two men shook hands, and a few minutes later, when Julius found himself back on the street with his medical bag and small suitcase, he also had a handsome sum of money in his possession, together with a letter from the bank confirming his hotel reservation. Suddenly, he felt faint again. Was it the shock of discovering that Madi was dead and with her the end of a hope he secretly cherished? Or was it the unexpected windfall that made his future secure? Was fatigue catching up with him, or perhaps more prosaically, hunger?

Since leaving Turin at dawn, Julius had eaten nothing but the three small biscuits offered to him at the bank. There were a number of enticing restaurants on the rue du Rhône. After a moment's hesitation, he kept walking until he stopped in front of a menswear store where he went in and bought a costly suitcase, pajamas, and a dressing gown—things he had not needed on the road but would be expected to have in his hotel. He took the Mont Blanc bridge on his left to cross the Rhône, turning right along the quay of the same name to reach the Hotel de la Paix where he had spent a night many years ago.

It was as if time had stood still; nothing had changed. Thanks to the bank's reservation, he was whisked to a suite on the sixth and last floor that was richly furnished with deep carpets and flowing drapes—symbols of a world he thought was gone forever. A vast and luxurious bed offered him rest and oblivion. He succumbed to temptation.

When he opened his eyes, dusk was setting in. It was nearly seven in the evening. None of the usual nightmares had troubled his sleep. In fact, he could not remember a time when he had slept so well. Feeling safe from both the men and the elements must have done the trick. Torn between hunger and the wish to read his letters, he called room service and was assured that a cold meal would be promptly sent up to him. The large envelope handed over to him by the director was beckoning on the nightstand; however, some superstitious dread stopped him from opening it, and he went out to the balcony to wait. Only after he had eaten his meal did he pick it up, taking out the documents one after the other.

There was an official-looking envelope from Bank Newman and Sons, the establishment founded by his sister Anni's husband. Manny Nagy, as he was known then, had seen the way the wind was blowing and had left Budapest with his family after the first World War and settled in the United States, changing his name to Newman. Julius had not seen him since, but he had corresponded with his sister for as long as possible. Her contact was one he had cherished, and the thought that Anni, her husband, and their children were safe, had comforted him during his darkest hours. He put the letter aside and drew the impressive, black-bordered obituary notice that announced, in fulsome terms, that the Dowager Countess von Thüringen had passed away after having received the sacraments of the church and would be laid to rest in the family vault on Friday, May 26, 1944. He set the letter on the table with a sigh and turned to the remaining items: an envelope addressed to Dr. Julius Matthias still retained a faintly violent scent. Madi's last letter, undoubtedly; and another from the cosmetic surgery clinic of Dr. Gilles—Marie-Christine Gilles—addressed to Dr. Julius Matthias, with handwritten instructions stating that the letter be handed to him exclusively, and if unclaimed before May 1945, it was to be destroyed.

When had Julius given Dr. Gilles the address of his bank? He did not remember and made up his mind quickly. The letter from America could wait; he was not yet ready to read the last words written by the only woman he had ever loved. However, what he really wanted was to know the fate of his children, and only Marie-Christine could enlighten him.

Julius and Marie-Christine had a longstanding friendship. They had met in Vienna when they were both lonely medical students. Though Julius was already married, his wife had chosen to go back to live with her parents after the birth of their first child. Marie-Christine, the daughter of a rather vulgar but extremely rich tradesman, had married an Austrian nobleman who needed the money to restore the family fortune and had agreed to let her study medicine while he remained in his castle. They had enjoyed a brief affair and parted ways in 1913 after graduating, thinking that they would never meet again. However, after her count was killed during the war, Marie-Christine decided to return to her native France to practice medicine, thus leaving her castle and two young children to the care of her late husband's unmarried sisters who had never accepted her. Under her maiden name, she fulfilled her dream and opened a cosmetic surgery clinic. In 1933, their paths crossed again. Julius had decided that his two eldest children would pursue their studies in France, so he traveled with them to Paris, where Marie-Christine and Julius soon discovered that their old attraction had not waned ... Dr. Gilles had also agreed to mentor Julius' daughter Elisabeth, who was going to study medicine, and indeed gave her a job when she graduated.

In a letter dated June 20, 1944, Marie-Christine had written: "My very dear Julius, I want to believe that you are reading this safely ensconced in one of Geneva's finest hotels, sipping the brand of French cognac you find so irresistible. Most of all, I want to believe that you have done the impossible, crossed war-torn Europe, and that we shall meet soon. You have no idea the relief I felt when I received news from your neighbor, Dr. Kadar, informing me that you had managed to flee. He had the blessed idea to send two letters, one in Hungarian for your children, and one in German for me (I wonder what you told him about me). 'Your wife,' he wrote, 'has been murdered. Please accept my condolences.' He also said that you had been able to get away at the last minute. I haven't yet been able to give the letter to your children or to inform them. I have no fixed address for Elisabeth, let alone a phone number; she calls whenever she can. We talked some two months ago; she was still in the south of France with her husband and their little boy, Emile, and intended to return to Paris as soon as it was safe to do so. She had seen your son André at Easter. Regarding Gabrielle, your youngest, she said she had not heard from her in quite a while, but she knew that she was safe. As soon as she gets in touch with me, I shall give her the news and tell her to write to you in care of the bank.

The Allied forces have just landed in Normandy, but the war is not over yet. The German troops are still here in Paris and have not relinquished their hold on the south of France. Now, what I want you to do is first send me a telegram to tell me the name and phone number of your hotel. I shall call you immediately; who knows, by that time we might be able to speak freely. Meanwhile, if you are in need of money, go to see my Geneva colleague, Dr. Wilhelm Hofstad. He is the director of Clinique du Lac on the rue de la Terrassière. I have asked him to advance you whatever sum you may need. Don't worry; we have business relations. Be assured that there is still a job for you in my clinic. Be of good cheer, I can't wait to hear from you. M-C."

Julius carefully folded the letter, feeling relieved. His children had weathered the worst of the war; now that things were looking up, why would anything happen to them? He was also moved by the solicitude of his old friend, but not that old; she was barely two years older than he was, and during their last encounter—admittedly, more than ten years ago—she was the one who looked younger, perhaps due to the ministrations of the clinic, of which she was both owner and director.

He turned his attention to the letter from America. Three closely filled pages dated July 1st in his brother-in-law's precise script. It was, however, the enclosed family photograph that caught his attention, with Manny in the middle, standing ramrod straight. Julius noted his jet-black hair and smiled at the thought that, at close to sixty-five, the banker was still vain enough to keep dying his hair. But he only gave him a fleeting glance and marveled at his sister. She was six years older than he was and endearingly beautiful, slim, and graceful, with blue-grey eyes so similar to his own. He felt profoundly grateful to the benevolent fate which had kept her safe. The couple was surrounded by their children and grandchildren. He wasn't quite sure who was who, though most had inherited the blond hair and clear eyes that Gitte, his mother and that of Anni, had gifted their descendants. They all looked happy and healthy. Obviously, they had never known fear and hunger, never endured the Occupation and worse. They faced the future confidently in the country their father had chosen as he had been prescient enough to sense the perils ahead, and forceful and courageous enough to convince his wife and children to leave Budapest and go with him to America. However, he—Julius—had not been able to convince his family to emigrate. True, he had sent his children to France, but first his own father, then his wife, had died because he had not been able to convince them to leave.

Realizing there was no point in dwelling on his mistakes, Julius started reading Manny's letter.

Dear Julius,

I am sending this to your bank because Madi wrote to your sister to tell her that she had just heard that your wife was dead—she did not quite know how—but you had escaped and were making your way to Geneva. We are, of course, sorry about Magda, but incredibly relieved that you are alive and free after the horrors of the last years. We are kept informed by those of our bankers friends who can still work in Europe. If only half of what they write is true, then it is horrendous beyond belief. Anni worries so much about you that she has trouble sleeping.

Now, let's be practical. The minute you arrive in Geneva, go to see Paul Zerner. You may remember him; he was our representative in Geneva, and he and his family welcomed Anni with open arms when I sent her there with the children in 1916. Today, he is the director of the bank founded by his father, which bears his name on rue de l'Arquebuse. He knows how to get in touch. Phone us from there as soon as you can. I have instructed him to give you whatever sum of money you may need. Don't hesitate to ask. My dear little brother-in-law, we are depending on you to arrive safely in Geneva and give us some good news soon. Nothing would delight us more than to welcome you here in Chicago. Don't worry about a visa; we have the means to get you one on the spot. And as for work, we can find you a post in one of the many charitable institutions we support, and if this is not what you want, we will help you find another solution.

Let me also tell you that the family is doing well, and your sister is as lovely as ever, in spite of our four children and six grandchildren. Our eldest, Charles, now runs the bank with me and Isaac, his son, the baby who was a year old when we came for your son's Bar Mitzvah, has enlisted in the navy by lying about his age and is fighting somewhere in the Pacific. Anni pretends to be very proud of him, though she is terrified for his sake, and so am I. Charles has two younger children, a boy and a girl, safely in school. Tibor has officially changed his name to Tony, a name I can't get used to and he has divorced his wife.

We were quite fond of her, but she had become very religious
and that did not suit him. She also wanted children, whereas he
did not. He is a fighter pilot and has taken part in the Normandy
landing. I believe he is still in England. As you know, news is
hard to get. Myriam, a teacher like her husband, lives in Florida
with their three children. Julia, our youngest, who was named
after you, is following in your footsteps and will soon graduate
from medical school. She lives at home with us, and we are in
no hurry to see her wed. That's it. Please phone. Manny."

Julius, strangely moved, put the letter and the photograph
back in the envelope. His sister's family was doing well, and
another path was open to him. Even if he did not see himself
going to America, it was comforting to feel that on both sides
of the Atlantic, parents and friends were ready to extend a
helping hand with offers of money and work. Then, his mood
changed, and slowly, reluctantly, he picked up the last envelope.

Madi had meant so much to him. He had known her
almost all his life. The circumstances had led Madi to leave her
home rather abruptly. He found her again many years later;
calling herself Madame Corvin she was a milliner in Budapest
living under the protection of Count von Thüringen, who
had set her up in a shop of her own. They had started a pas-
sionate affair, though their meetings had been few and far
between. She lived in fear of the countess, who hated the fact
that her noble husband had taken a little Jewess of no account
for his mistress and had once sent men to do her harm. Madi
had emerged unscathed, but the count, who was a colonel
of the Hungarian army, sent her to Geneva in 1916 for her
safety in his luxurious Mercedes. Julius, Anni and her children had gone with her. Julius and Anton, the colonel's aide
de camp, had taken turns driving. After the war, the count,
now a widower, had come back for Madi and had married

her. Only after his death did the two lovers reconnect briefly, but she later broke up with him. She had her reasons, but he had found it hard and had never stopped thinking of her. Now, he understood that she had not forgotten him and had indeed left him her fortune. He took the letter and smiled to himself. The flamboyant writing suited her temperament perfectly. However, as he read on, his smile quickly faded.

"Yuli, my love, my only love. Do you know that this is the very first time I am writing to you? The first and the last as well. Yet, we were so very much in love … and I never stopped loving you. You are still angry at our parting; believe me, it was more painful for me. You are a man, so you have surely found solace elsewhere; but I was left alone with my memories; alone, with no strength left to fight. Let me tell you first that you are to have all my money, as well as my jewels, which are worth a fortune. I want you to sell them at some point since I would not want another woman in your life to wear them. You see, for too long I have told myself that the money and the jewels were my secret weapon, my lifeline, and that one day I would be able to leave Hungary and end my life peacefully in Geneva, the city I was happy to live in. However, I waited too long.

In spite of the war, life was good. The count's children and their wives were most attentive to me, with an eye on the inheritance no doubt. Two or three high ranking German officers were courting me. They knew nothing of my origins. For them, I was the dowager countess, widow of the illustrious count whose family is kin to the German and Russian courts. Yet, I was going out less and less. Age and unstable health made me stay more and more at home. I kept worrying about you, and you have no idea how happy I was when Dr. Hans Grunewald came to tell me that you had managed to escape deportation. I don't quite know why, but I feel absolutely certain that you will make it and arrive safely in Geneva; alas, I won't be able to follow you.

The count's eldest daughter, recently widowed, came back to Budapest. She hates Jews and hates me, just as her mother did. She never accepted me and remonstrated her brothers for treating me with the respect due their father's widow. She was just here to deliver an ultimatum. She wants the jewels, and she wants me to get out of the house, (which has been mine for nearly a quarter of a century) and move to a small flat somewhere in the city, which she will grudgingly put at my disposal. Should I refuse, she told me with cold cruelty, she shall denounce me to the German authorities and see to it that I am sent to the ghetto. She gave me until tomorrow at noon to pack a small suitcase and have the jewels ready for her. Of course, she is not aware of the fact that the jewels are no longer here, that they are out of her reach in Switzerland. I do not regret it. On no account would I have let her triumph. For too long I have been the dowager countess, only to be sent away like a kitchen maid.

So, I have made my plans. I have called for Anton, you remember him. He has gotten old but has savvy sons who know how to navigate the strange world of today. One of them brought the jewels to the bank. He was well paid and I knew he could be trusted because his father has remained devoted to me. I shall ask him to render me one last service: to see that this letter reaches you at the bank. For my mind is made up. I would rather die than submit to that woman, who is, unfortunately, her mother's true daughter. I'd rather die also than be sent to that sinister ghetto, where, in any case, nothing but degradation and death await. The servants have been told to leave and come back tomorrow morning. I have all I need here. Death will be swift and kind. I shall have the last word: that dreadful woman will have to go in mourning for me—and for the jewels. I can picture her following my coffin, dripping in black crepe—for the family will, of course, hold a funeral in style. Yuli, my love. Don't be sad. I have no regrets. Thanks to you and your sister, I had a great life. Who knows, we may meet again in the paradise neither of us believe in.

Madi.

Filled with blind rage, Julius put the letter down. He had accepted her death, thinking that it had been an accident, a long illness, a peaceful end. But not like that! Not the victim of a vengeful woman. Not alone in that big house, faced with an impossible choice. He, who never cried, who had never cried, felt the hot tears coming. He imagined her carefully getting ready, putting on her most elegant nightwear before swallowing the pills and lying on her bed to wait for the end while finding the strength to smile at the thought of the count's daughter's disappointment. What courage, what panache!

Later, in front of the window, listening to the strains of Blue Danube, his favorite waltz, coming from the crowds below, he had thought of Magda, his wife, the mother of his children. A woman who had never loved him, who had done him great harm. She had paid with her life for an unlikely heroic act, leaving him free to flee. Madi and Magda, both dead in May. Why was he still alive? A senseless question. Divine intervention was not the answer. Chance? A lucky set of circumstances? He shook his head. The time would come when he would be able to mourn properly, but not yet. Within a month or a year, another set of circumstances could lead him to his death. Meanwhile, he knew he had to make the most of the new lease on life he had been granted.

2

A SENSE OF FREEDOM

JULIUS MATTHIAS, who had slept dreamlessly in a great four-post bed, woke up to a new life. Coming down to breakfast, he had been saluted with a respectful, "Good morning, Herr Doktor." Fresh coffee and delicacies he had not tasted in years awaited on a corner table overlooking the lake. He was seized by a new and powerful emotion. Together with his newfound freedom, he was regaining his dignity. The yellow star he had been compelled to wear, and the way the Hungarian civil servants and German soldiers had looked down at him, longtime patients crossing the street so as not to acknowledge him—he had left all that behind. It was over. He was himself again: Doctor Matthias, a person of consequence. What troubled him was the thought that his friends, his neighbors, had not been so lucky. What had happened to them? How many would emerge unscathed? How many would die, just as his wife had died? Once again, he wondered why he had been singled out for survival. He sighed. The fact was that he had too much time on his hands. There was no patient to see, no new stage to cover on the road to freedom with its attending perils. True, he would have to go and see Paul Zerner, his brother-in-law's friend; there were formalities to be taken care of at his own bank, but today was Saturday, and nothing could be done before businesses reopened on Monday. Which meant he had two whole days in front of him. On second thought, it was not so bad. It would give him time to take care of more mundane things. He had nothing to wear, bar the tailored suit he had made in Turin in order to be presentable at the border and the bank.

After consulting with the concierge, he again crossed the Mont Blanc bridge to the rue du Rhône, first stopping at a barber shop the man had recommended. He let himself be talked into having his nails done for the first time in his life. Then, he visited the tailor, where he suddenly felt in a quandary. Not knowing how soon Marie-Christine would reply to the wire he had sent before leaving the hotel, he thought he would not have time to have suits made to order. "Do not worry, Sir," said the tailor reassuringly. If I may say so, whichever suit you choose will only need minor alterations." Shoes and other necessities followed. They too would be delivered to the hotel that very day. He lingered in a well-appointed bookstore, where he bought the latest Paris travel guide issued by Baedeker just before the war; then, on a whim, chose two mystery stories by a French writer called Gaston Leroux, which, according to the salesman, were all the rage at the time.

The following day, he slept late for the first time in years and had breakfast brought to his room. In the afternoon, he went for a walk, going nowhere in particular, content to bask in the pleasure of being able to stride with his head held high, encountering soldiers and policemen without flinching and, exchanging smiles with more than one pretty woman who had looked at him invitingly. Somehow, he found himself at the Grand Café du Lac and sat down, perhaps at the very table where he'd waited for Madi to join him twenty years ago. It was May. The trees were in bloom, and there was a sweetness in the air. Closing his eyes, he could see her, seated in front of him, one of the exquisite little hats that were her specialty perched precariously on her tawny hair, so reminiscent of the strawberry blonde locks immortalized by Venetian painters.

Madi, green eyes artfully done, the sensual mouth, and the scent of violet still troubling his nights. They had one unforgettable week together in a country inn. The happiest time of his life, albeit short, so terribly short. He did not know then that he'd never again hold her in his arms. Of course, both were aware that theirs was a hopeless love; yet she had been the one to send him away. He had never loved another woman. She'd been lost to him, but he wished her well, had believed that the illustrious name she bore and the powerful family of her late husband would keep her from harm. He blinked away the tears, threw a handful of coins on the table, and left in a hurry.

On Monday morning, he went to see Manny's colleague, someone he had not met during his previous visits. The bank was tucked away on the fourth floor of an impressive stone and marble building. Paul Zerner welcomed him heartily. Tall and slim, with his hair artfully slicked back to hide his incipient baldness, he wore a ready smile on his open face and did not look like a Swiss banker. On the other hand, Zerner's bank was private, and he probably saw only select customers, Julius thought before following him to an elegant corner office.

"I understand you want to speak to your sister? Sit down, my secretary will try to get her for you. It could take a while; transatlantic lines are busy round the clock these days. Would you like a coffee while you wait?"

Julius accepted the offer of a coffee, finding it to be of quality and the banker truly friendly.

"Our house was founded more or less at the same time as that of your brother-in-law in Budapest, you know, though my grandfather left his native Poland to settle here. I never knew why he chose Geneva," Paul continued. "He did quite well. In the beginning, all his customers were Jewish, and only Yiddish was spoken. My father studied here, but he went to Poland in search of a bride. It was an arranged marriage. My mother never learnt French, or even German, and she still can't say the simplest sentence in those languages.

"Meanwhile, the bank was thriving, and its reputation brought together some important businessmen who were not Jewish. Mother did not like it. She badgered me until I agreed to travel to what she still calls the old country to find a bride. I had the good fortune to find a young, pleasant, and intelligent woman, who learned French in no time at all. Nevertheless, while my father was alive only Yiddish was spoken at home. He died in 1918, just after the war. Now, we all meet at her house for Friday dinner. It's not always easy. She is unhappy with me because 'I have let my children drift away from religion,' or so she says. It is true that I am not very religious; I attend services at the synagogue out of habit and because I meet many of my clients there. Worse, I sent Simon, my eldest son, to Palestine to finalize an important investment, and he came back with a bride. A gorgeous girl with a brilliant brain and sweet disposition, but an Oriental Jew. Her parents emigrated from Yemen towards the end of the last century. My mother reacted badly. Luckily, my new daughter-in-law does not speak Polish or Yiddish, so she did not understand what was being said, but she could guess. The situation became so fraught that I decided to make Simon my permanent representative in Palestine, and the young couple went back. He is doing a very good job despite the war and local insecurity. I can't wait to go there and see my first grandchildren, a boy and a girl. Only Jacob, my second son, is in New York to get familiar with American banking. His hope is that I will follow in Manny's footsteps and settle in the New World. Simon is pulling me the other way; he wants me to go to Palestine. Mind you, I understand them. They both tell me that there is no longer a place for Jews in Europe, that we shall never again be able to put our trust in the protection of European countries. They could be right. On the other hand, who created the United States if not former Europeans? Did they leave their prejudices behind? Jews are not always welcome there; some clubs won't accept them, as Jacob discovered at his expense. Before the war the press was shamefully sympathetic to Nazi Germany. According to Simon, Palestine is the only country where Jews can be free. He may be right, but it would neither be plain sailing here. The British, who are Europeans, have barred the doors to immigration, denying salvation to the tens of thousands of our people fleeing Nazi persecution. London openly favors the Arabs. According to Simon, the country is preparing for battle, with every Jew ready to fight to the death, and the British will have to leave, and a Jewish state will be born. I wish I could believe him. But my dear Julius, I am boring you with …"

"Not in the least, please do go on. These are issues I too shall have to deal with," Julius replied.

"Yes. We are, so to speak, in limbo. The old Europe, the continent we grew up in, is no longer; a new one is in the making, and no one knows how it will turn out. My mother, unhappy because Jacob is still unmarried at thirty, would like him to go to Poland to find a suitable wife. She refuses to believe that her Poland no longer exists. Mind you, he might find a nice Jewish girl from Poland in America …" Paul said.

"Yet, I envy you. You still have a country, a home to go to at the end of the day. I, on the other hand, have nothing. I cannot go back to the city where I was born, where I grew up, where I know every street and every alley. Today, there is nothing left for me but phantoms. I have no idea where I could live, or where I would want to live."

"How is it that you speak such good French?" Paul asked.

"I took lessons when I was a medical student in Vienna, and later I practiced with a charming lady from Geneva. Then, I attended the lessons my children were taking in preparation for their departure; they were going to study in France at my urging. I can't believe I had the foresight to do so. Had I not … Anyway, it's been a few years since I last spoke it, and I am still a little rusty. I am happy to see how fast it is coming back. Listen, Paul. Don't you have more important things to do than to keep me company?" Julius asked.

"My dear Julius. On the contrary, I am delighted. Here, there is no one I can talk with. My colleagues, solid Swiss protestants for the most part, would listen politely with their minds elsewhere, or silently curse those Jews who always have something to whine about. With family or friends, discussions always end in confrontation, which reminds me … We celebrate Yom Kippur on Wednesday evening. Do you wish to attend services at the synagogue? And break the fast with us the following day?"

"Allow me to turn down your kind invitation. I have never been observant, and the events of the past years did nothing to change my mind. It would be hypocrisy, pure and simple."

Paul smiled ruefully. "I almost envy you. However, as one of the leaders of the community, at least nominally, I can't afford to speak my mind. Ah, here is my secretary."

"I have your call. Please pick up the phone," the woman said before departing, together with her boss.

Sounding like a man having woken up in the middle of the night because of the time difference between Geneva and Chicago, Manny answered the call, his voice still heavy with sleep but with the quick worry of a man with a son and a grandson in the army.

"Manny?"

"Yuli!"

There was a babble of voices, and then his sister picked up the telephone.

"Yuli! You are safe! You are in Geneva!" And she burst into tears. Julius nearly did too. It had been so long since they had spoken; in fact, since she had left for America in 1926, nearly twenty years ago. The connection was remarkably clear, and her voice had not changed at all; she sounded so near while being so far. The words came tumbling out.

There was so much to say. He asked about the boys in the army. Tony, the pilot, was still in London; Isaac was home on leave; he would go back to his ship in the Pacific the following week. Anni, in turn, wanted to know everything, including how he had managed to get away and how his wife had been killed; she also wanted the truth about the death of their father. The old man had been murdered during the 1927 pogrom in their hometown, but Manny had not told her. The three of them could have gone on talking forever, but after one hour, the costly transatlantic conversation had to end. Julius, who had said nothing about Madi, told his sister that he would write her a long letter and Zerner would see to it that she received it quickly. He also promised to do his utmost to come and see them, but first he had to travel to France and look for his children.

He left the bank feeling profoundly unsettled. He pictured his sister, serenely presiding over her brood, cocooned in her life as the wife of a prosperous banker in a town untouched by war. She had had the good fortune to leave in time, and yet she represented the last remaining link to his carefree youth, to the town he had called his home for more than half of a century; a place he found himself irrationally missing.

Everything is going so well, Julius mused a few days later while observing himself in the wardrobe mirror of his room. *Freedom does wonders for one's health. I have put on some much-needed weight; I haven't looked so relaxed in years. Indeed, I even look younger. A stranger might think I don't have a worry in the world. I sample a new restaurant every day, rediscovering the pleasure of a good meal in pleasant surroundings. I stand in front of shop windows knowing that I can buy whatever takes my fancy. True, I still feel faintly guilty when I see stores displaying a dizzying amount of food: fruits, vegetables, meat. The things we have been deprived of for so long; the things my fellow Jews of Oradea who are still alive so desperately need. They are dying of hunger while here people walk by indifferently, taking everything for granted and not understanding how incredibly lucky they are. At times, I have to resist the urge to pinch myself to make sure that I am not dreaming. One wonders whether Switzerland is part of that wounded Europe I come from, where war is still raging. Romania changed sides too late and has paid the price: first, bombed by Allied forces, and then laid to waste by the Germans; in France, those Germans are being driven out by the French but are still putting up a fight. What goes on in the sinister camps where Jews are led to their death is now openly discussed. Are the good people of Geneva aware of any of it? I have my doubts.*

Am I the only one to be ashamed of being safe? Safe and free of material worry? The bank could not be more attentive, and its director incredibly helpful, to the extent of talking me to put in a request for a short-term residency permit, with the result that I received it on the spot. Something unheard of in a country which had not shown itself hospitable to Jewish refugees during the war. Whenever I visit the bank, I am called to his office and we enjoy a leisurely discussion while one of the employees deals with whatever I need. I know that he is a widower like myself. His wife died four years ago; he does not appear to be close to his children or his grandchildren. In fact, he seems a very private man who demonstrated a real sympathy towards me. Is it because, as he told me quietly during my first visit, he is also Jewish? He has not mentioned it since. Could it be because I find myself at the head of a truly considerable fortune? Who would have believed Madi would be so lucky, or rather, that the bank would advise her so wisely? She invested funds that she brought with her in 1918 in real estate and never touched the capital, merely drawing on the revenue for living expenses. Following her wedding to the count, she stopped altogether and reinvested accrued interest while making quarterly transfers from Budapest, half of those being invested and the other converted into gold.

Then there are the jewels. If only she had had the good sense to leave in time, she could have ended her days peacefully here, in the style to which she was accustomed. Anyway, this can't be the reason: the bank must have far richer clients. Does it matter? If he has an ulterior motive, it will be revealed in due time. I would not give it another thought, except that it keeps me from dwelling on the past, on the people I loved and will never see again, and on the future. I am in a kind of limbo. The past is gone; Geneva is a way station before the unknown: France. My children. Gabrielle, my youngest, is 27. What is she doing, where, and perhaps, with whom? I haven't a clue. She has not gotten in touch since she arrived in Paris in 1935. André turned 31 last spring. He could have written care of the bank, where I had opened an account for him in 1933, but he did not. Elisabeth did tell Marie-Christine that she had seen him at Easter; but where and doing what, she did not say. She too knew the name and address of the bank and could have written. Of course, as long as the Germans are there, they have to be prudent, and yet …

He had a nagging feeling that his children were adults. They had their own lives with little or no place for him. So, why go to France? To accept his old friend's generous offer? After years of being his own man, would he become the medical director of an establishment where perfectly healthy individuals underwent surgery to get rid of real or imaginary blemishes? That was not medicine as he saw it. Then why not go to Chicago? Work in one of Manny's charitable institutions? Besides the fact that he did not speak English, he did not find the prospect appealing. He understood that they were trying to help and reproached himself for not being properly grateful. He wished he could figure out what he wanted to do, and what he could do. He reminded himself that there was no hurry, and that thanks to Madi, he could even embark upon a life of leisure, though he would probably tire of it fast enough. His first priority was still to check that the children were indeed safe, which meant that he had to go to Paris. Should he wait any longer for Marie-Christine to call? It'd been five days since he had sent her a telegram. Had it gotten lost? Not impossible, but unlikely. Was she away from Paris? Wouldn't she have sent a letter to the bank to warn him? Had something happened to her? Should he try phoning the clinic? She had not suggested it, though it would have been the quickest way. Send another telegram, or do nothing and hope she would get in touch?

He decided to give it another few days while preparing his departure. Traveling to Paris was not going to be easy. The Germans were retreating and making their way home through the east of France, perilously close to the Swiss border. Train service was erratic because of the threat of the Luftwaffe, which covered their retreat. Drive then? How safe were the roads? He would need a visa; how was he to obtain one? Hans Steuber would know, so Julius went to consult him and ask for some advice.

Madame Boucheron, the secretary, who seemed to have shed her forbidding aura, told him to wait a few minutes and went to see if her boss was free; he wasn't. She had been tasked to add that, if the matter was not urgent, Doctor Matthias would afford him the pleasure of having lunch with him. Julius agreed, adding that the pleasure would be his. It was thus settled that a car would pick him up at his hotel.

Shortly before one, Julius arrived at "La Perle du Lac" (The Pearl of the Lake), a prestigious establishment situated in the heart of Mon Repos park. A table had been booked in a private salon with a picture window overlooking Lake Geneva, and closer to the horizon, the snowy peak of Mont Blanc. The banker, who was already seated, stood up to welcome him. He was apparently well-known. The maître d' promptly arrived and extolled the merits of the day's specials: Tournedos Rossini and Turbot in Hollandaise sauce. They made their choices; the sommelier suggested suitable vintages to go with the chosen dishes. The doctor who had not participated in such a ritual in years left it to his host to decide, while trying not to smile at the hushed tones and serious mien of the wine expert. Here, life had gone on as if the war years had never happened. The consultation over, Hans Steuber turned to him with a smile.

"At last, we shall have time to talk without interruption; I am delighted at this opportunity to get to know you better. But first, tell me. How can I be of help?"

"I have decided to leave for France without further delay; I believe I will need a visa, but I don't know how to go about it. I am afraid it will take time, and I thought that perhaps ..."

"Say no more. That's something easily done. Let me take care of it." From his pocket, he withdrew an elegant notebook bearing his initials and checked it quickly before continuing. "Come to the bank tomorrow at eleven in the morning. We shall go together to the French consulate. I happen to have an appointment with the consul; while we conclude our discussion, one of his subordinates will grant you the visa."

"Dear Mr. Steuber ..."

"Please call me Hans."

"Then, I am Julius. Hans, your generosity puts me to shame. I did not know you, and yet, from our first meeting, you have treated me not as a client but as a friend. I am deeply grateful, however, to put it bluntly, slightly embarrassed as well."

The banker then took off his spectacles and put them carefully in their case. "I don't need them," he said, rubbing his eyes. "But they are part of the image a bank director strives to project. It was what my late father-in-law believed. He also told me that I would look less like a Jew with them. I should have told him to go to hell, but I did not. He has been dead for many years, and yet I still wear them. Force of habit probably … or the fear that he was right. As to your question, it is true that I have developed a liking for you; furthermore, by helping you, I am paying a debt. A moral one, but a debt which weighs on me.

"Julius, you remind me of the man I could have been if fate had not decided otherwise. We have so much in common! Like you, I come from a very traditional family, and like you, I studied in Vienna, my hometown. My father was a highly respected rabbi. A community leader. I was the first born, and according to tradition, expected to succeed him. Just before my eighteenth birthday, he called me to his study to inform me that a very good match had been arranged with the daughter of another prominent rabbi. I had never seen her, of course, but that was not the point. I felt I was too young to marry. To tell the truth, I was not religious at all, and only pretended to be to avoid offending my father. What I wanted most was to study law. In short I wanted neither to get married nor to be a rabbi like my father.

One of my brothers, barely a year younger than I, was only too glad to take my place with the bride intended for me. Although my father was furious, when faced with my determination, he agreed to the switch. He did it with poor grace and ordered me out of the house so 'not to introduce unwelcome values,' so he said.

"I was fortunate. An elderly great-aunt I had been fond of left me her savings, which was enough to pay for my studies and living expenses. It was then that I met Wilhelm Steuber, a young Swiss protestant who had come to study law in preparation to enter his father's bank in Geneva. Somehow, we became friends. Towards the end of my second year, he invited me to spend a few days at the villa his parents had bought on the Mediterranean coast. I accepted without asking for advice from my father, who would no doubt have objected. He was still bitter and had turned his back on me. Though I faithfully went to Friday services, I was very rarely asked to partake in the Shabbat dinner.

I traveled to Nice with Wilhelm. His parents, though not overjoyed with his choice of friend, received me civilly and did their best to accommodate my dietary limitations."

At that point, the banker stopped to glance at the cream of lobster served by the waiter while the sommelier reverently poured a vintage white wine into his glass.

"I know. Lots of water under the bridges of the Danube and the Rhône rivers since, and I assume you have freed yourself from the constraints of our education," Mr. Steuber said.

"You are right. In fact, I have completely forgotten why we are not supposed to eat lobster," Julius replied while exchanging smiles, and the banker took up his tale.

"Wilhelm had a sister called Sarah; a common name in protestant circles. Tall and graceful, Sarah was painfully shy, perhaps because of some smallpox scars marring her pleasant face. Julius, I am getting carried away, and our cream of lobster is getting cold. A pity for it is the restaurant's signature dish."

The turbot that followed was no less worthy of notice, and Steuber waited until dessert had been served to resume.

"I was invited again a number of times. I enjoyed my discussion with Helmut, my friend's father, who displayed a nearly encyclopedic knowledge of banking. Sarah often listened without saying a word. Wilhelm and I graduated in June 1901. The Steubers were going to Nice as usual for summer vacation, and I was invited. Though nothing had been said, it would obviously be for the last time. Wilhelm was an only son and was about to join his father's bank where he would be groomed for being his successor. There was talk of a match with the daughter of another banker. Me—I was looking for a job. I had not found anything yet and was beginning to despair when, three months later, a telegram informed me of my friend's death in an automobile accident. Helmut beseeched me to attend the funeral. As you know, Jewish tradition demands that burials be carried out the same day, but our Christian friends do not share our compulsion to bury the dead at all speed. I left Vienna immediately and found the family shell-shocked.

"Three days after the funeral, Helmut asked me to come to his study. Sarah was there. He then made me a stunning proposition. In a word, to take my friend's place at the bank—subject to startling conditions. You guessed it: I would have to convert, take the family name and ... marry Sarah. To say that I was speechless would be an understatement. Convert? I had been raised in the respect of our traditions and still went to the synagogue most Fridays! Become a Christian? I had not forgotten the outrage when Gustav Mahler converted four years before; if you remember, it was the price he had to pay to become the director of the Viennese opera. My father's comments had been scathing.

In short, it was so outrageous that I was ready to decline on the spot. That's when I saw Sarah looking at me. It came to me …" he then sighed and took a sip of wine before continuing. "… how much the proposal had cost her and the bottomless humiliation she would suffer should I refuse. I later discovered that it was her own idea, and that she had to fight to convince her protestant father, whose prejudices against Jews were no less potent than mine against Christians. Anyway, at that moment, I realized what my future would be should I accept. Less than a week before, I was wondering how long I would be able to manage without a job; suddenly, a miraculous solution was available. My mind processed all this in a matter of seconds. You know the rest. Herschel Salzberger became Hans Steuber. I did not even need to change my initials." He then sighed again, watching the snowy mass of Mont Blanc beyond the clear glass window.

"What was bound to happen, happened. People talked," Hans went on. "The news reached my father. My name was erased from the family bible, as if I no longer existed, and the family mourned me for seven days. No one would talk to me, neither my father, my mother, nor my brothers and sisters. When I heard that my father had died, I took the train to Vienna, but they would not let me in the house. It was almost a relief, and a door firmly shut on that aspect of my life. Relations with my father-in-law were cordial, although he never really warmed to me though we got on well enough professionally. I did my best to tune out some of his comments. More than once, I caught him scrutinizing the faces of my children—his grandchildren!—in search of some "Jewish" trait. It was profoundly insulting and hurtful for me. Sarah took note. She threatened not to see him anymore and not to let him see the children if he did not mend his ways. In the end, he became very fond of them and often boasted of their accomplishments. Our relations improved. I had a good life. I grew to love my wife, a worthy woman who gave me three children I can be proud of. She left me too soon. If she was still alive, I could never have spoken to you so openly.

"As time passed, the family bank was incorporated into a larger establishment, which induced me to stay. Helmut retired, while I climbed my way to the top. One son followed in my footsteps and is now the director of a local branch; another is a professor at Geneva University They have married well; I have several grandchildren. They know nothing of my past. Then, Hitler, that monster, appeared. I was quick to grasp the danger and sent emissaries to my brother, now head of the family. I offered to pay everyone's passage to America. My emissaries were cursed and turned away. They had been promised a big fat envelope should they succeed, so they went back again and again.

"However, my brother would not listen. Ultimately, the family was rounded up and sent to the camps. Are they all dead? Is anyone alive? I don't know. I got in touch with the Red Cross International committee whose headquarters are in Geneva, and they opened a file and promised to do their utmost to get information. I never said they were my kin. I feel ashamed, but not enough to tell the truth, which makes me doubly guilty. I have never told anyone what I am telling you today. Even today, my secret could do me untold harm, both professionally and personally. My children would not know how to cope, and yet I needed to talk about it. In fact, I already feel better. I sense that you don't judge me, do you understand? And that brings me to your question. In helping you, helping one of my people, I find a measure of redemption."

Hans Steuber then paused for a moment.

"Guilty, Hans? Why?" Julius replied. "Because you have not suffered and you are free? Come on, had you remained in Vienna, married the girl your father intended for you, and taken over his mantle, where would you be today?"

"I would have saved them, found the words to convince them to get them out of Vienna in time."

"You are not thinking straight. Hans might have found the words, but Hershel? You would have understood too late."

"Don't be so sure. Look at you. You resisted temptation, went back to your native city, and founded a Jewish home. You made a success of your life and were wise enough to send your children abroad to study. You even managed to escape, and that can't have been easy. You looked haunted when first I saw you last week, exhausted, both physically and mentally. Julius, I admire you."

The object of his admiration took a deep breath. Should he reply that he too had been unable to convince his own wife to flee when flights were still possible? That only her death had saved him from deportation and allowed him to flee? Probably not. To what purpose? "I did nothing to deserve your admiration," he replied after pausing in thought. "It was mainly chance. Hans, life is a succession of roads taken or not taken. You made the right choice. Your children, and even yourself, have escaped humiliation and terror. You feel guilty when you think of those you left behind, but I too bear the weight of being free while my wife is dead, murdered in front of me, while so many of my friends and neighbors have been sent to the death camps. Like you, there is nothing I can do about it, and there is no point in letting these thoughts torment us. 'Carpe diem,' as the Romans used to say. I assume that, like me, you learned some Latin at the university. Believe me, I appreciate this remarkable meal. I have had nothing like it in years. I am far from being a connoisseur, but this white wine is exceptional."

"It is indeed," replied the banker, accepting the change of subject. "It is a Puligny-Montrachet. The 1939 vintage we are sampling is proof that the vineyards have fully recovered from the mildew blight that decimated them a few years before."

"Hans, I have a last question for you," Julius asked. "I had opened two accounts for my son. One for funds that were his, and the other with money I deposited for him and his sisters. I wonder whether you might have an address for any of them? And whether you could tell me without violating the bank's obligation of secrecy?"

"The problem no longer exists. Your son came with his sister Elisabeth in September 1939, when France entered the war. They closed both accounts, fearing that they might not be able to access the funds should the situation deteriorate. They left no forwarding address."

The two men lingered over coffee and petits fours, talking desultorily as if loathing to end what had been an intensely emotional encounter. It was decided that they would meet the following morning at the entrance to the French consulate situated along the vast Bastions Park in the heart of the city, not far from the Town Hall.

Doctor Matthias soon discovered the difference between the way a man recommended by a prominent Swiss banker is received and the tribulations he had faced when he had applied in 1939 for a Swiss visa prior to a trip he never made, owing to the outbreak of the war. Here, it went without a hitch, and a visa was stamped on his passport in a matter of minutes. The vice-consul, one Jerome Andrieu, asked him idly how he intended to travel to Paris.

"I am not sure," he replied, surprised. "I am told the train is unsafe and I am thinking of driving."

"Ah! You have a car?"

It turned out that Andrieu was interested in selling his son's car. The young man had come to live with him in Geneva and was in no hurry to go back. The vehicle was a 1942 Renault Juvaquatre with barely 20,000 kilometers on the clock.

"It's a six HP model, won't go beyond 100 km per hour, but considering the seven liters to a hundred-kilometer consumption, it's not too bad in this time of rationing. You can have it at half price because my son needs the money. It has French plates, which is a bonus for traveling in that country. Why don't you check it out? It's in a nearby garage."

Why not? Julius thought. Despite never hearing about the model, he figured out that Andrieu would not try to sell a faulty vehicle to a man recommended by a personal friend of his boss. The garage was close by, and he walked there after parting with the banker. Andrieu must have phoned ahead; a mechanic in grimy overalls was checking a four-door sedan painted in dark orange. Doctor Matthias, who had driven

Mercedes practically all his life, looked at it dubiously. The garage owner, a fat man with fawning manners, enumerated its good points in French with a strong German accent. Not quite convinced, Julius asked for a test drive. This reasonable request had the man scratching his head (the mechanic who knew the car, he said, did not speak French). Upon hearing that his prospective customer spoke German, he told the mechanic to change into street clothes. Half an hour later, they were back, and Julius declared himself satisfied with the sedan. The mechanic, suitably compensated, had told him that it was sound and in very good condition.

Having first gone to the bank to withdraw the necessary funds, Julius went back to the consulate. A delighted Andrieu dealt with the paperwork and gave him a fairly recent road map. It was agreed that the vehicle would remain in the garage until Friday. The mechanic would bring it to the hotel in the late afternoon.

"Let me give you some words of advice if I may," said the Vice-Consul, in parting. Have money in small denominations ready and refrain from showing large bills. Stop at night in country inns rather than in big cities. Be on the lookout for planes, the Luftwaffe is still very active in eastern France. Take cover at the first sign of trouble; they shoot at whatever moves. Remember, in France, you won't find anything near the quantity of goods we have in Switzerland. Better buy everything you will need here."

3

A SETBACK

JULIUS WHISTLED HAPPILY while trying to plan his forthcoming journey. It would take at least two days, he thought, to cover some 700 kilometers on roads that were most likely damaged from the war years. Andrieu had suggested stopping for the night at the halfway mark, just outside of Dijon, a city of some hundred-thousand inhabitants recently liberated from German occupation. The best thing would be to leave on Saturday. Today was Thursday. On Friday, he would do some more shopping; he hadn't yet bought toys and clothes for Emile, the little grandson he was eager to meet. He would then go to the bank, withdraw money, and bid farewell to Hans. His last visit would be to see Paul Zerner and entrust him with the long letter he had written to his sister. It had not been easy. He knew how fond she had been of Madi, her childhood friend, and had glossed over the circumstances of her death.

There was a message waiting for him at the hotel. A Doctor Hofstad wanted to see him urgently. *News of Paris at long last!* he thought. Marie-Christine must have gotten in touch: how else would the man have known that he was in Geneva and at the Hotel de la Paix? However, Julius felt it strange that she had not contacted him directly. He shrugged and walked out as the taxi was depositing a client at the entrance. In less than ten minutes, he reached the Clinique du Lac, discovering that it was not at all on the lake, though the rue de la Terrassière, where the establishment was situated, was a short distance away. It was hidden behind high walls, as if to protect the privacy of its clients. The guard at the entrance checked his name on a written list and opened the gate. A well-tended garden led to an impressive villa. Surprisingly, it was designed in a Mediterranean style, fairly unusual in this austere town. A tall, thin almost completely bald man, his open white blouse flopping around a black three-piece suit, came out of the building holding a telegram. He fired a rapid series of questions without a word of welcome, and spoke French with such a heavy Swiss-German intonation that Julius found so difficult to follow that he suggested they switch to German.

"How come you speak German with an Austrian accent?" The man blinked.

"I studied medicine in Vienna."

The man blinked again, nonplussed.

"You studied medicine? In Vienna? When?"

"I graduated in June 1913."

"Matthias, Matthias … Yes, I seem to remember a student with that name. You look like him. A Protestant from Hungary, right?"

"From Hungary, certainly, but Jewish, not Protestant."

"Jewish?"

There was no mistaking his surprise as he went on.

"My dear colleague, I apologize. There seems to be a misunderstanding. Allow me to introduce myself: Wilhelm Hofstad, proprietor and director of the Clinique du Lac. Please, come into my office."

Julius followed, wondering what it was all about. The office was deceptively plain, with the subtle elegance fitting of an establishment catering to an elite clientele. His host offered him a seat while standing by his desk, apparently at a loss for words.

"Listen," he said at last. "I find myself in a very unpleasant and totally unexpected situation. I was not aware that you were a colleague. I need to ask you a few questions, so please do not be offended. I will explain later."

"Go ahead."

"Thanks. Where did you first meet Dr. Gilles?"

"Well, in Vienna; we graduated the same year."

"Are you sure? I was there too, in 1912. There were very few women, and I don't remember anyone named Gilles."

"At the time she was married to an Austrian count whose name she bore. He was killed towards the end of the war in 1917 or 1918. She went back to her maiden name and returned to France. I believe she took a special course in Paris before opening her clinic."

"An Austrian countess ... it does ring a bell, though I don't think I ever met her. The fact is that I did not recognize her when we met some years ago and she did not recognize me either. So you kept in touch after graduating?"

"Not at all. We went our separate ways. Many years later, I saw her name in a medical journal. It so happened that at the time, I am talking of the early thirties, Elisabeth, my eldest daughter was thinking about studying medicine in Paris.

Vienna was not an option; Austria was no longer safe for Jews. So, I wrote to Dr. Gilles, who answered promptly and not only agreed to sponsor her application but also promised to keep an eye on her. In fact, when my daughter graduated, Dr. Gilles was kind enough to offer her a position.

Hofstad, looking increasingly embarrassed, scratched his head. "I see. Let me explain. The political situation here is extremely ... volatile, shall I say. One has to be exceptionally careful, and a clinic like mine cannot afford the slightest whiff of scandal. For the past ten years, I have had a professional relationship with Dr. Gilles. We had been introduced by an eminent plastic surgeon who works in Switzerland and France. It led to a mutually profitable collaboration. We both have fairly well-known patients who prefer to have their surgery done in a neighboring country, where they are less likely to be recognized. We oversee their travels, sending a medical attendant to facilitate their stay abroad and supervise the care they need when they come back. It is a costly method but favored by some of our rich patients. When the telegram you sent from your hotel reached Madame Gilles' clinic, Gustav, my clerk who had gone there to close our account, was at the reception. Upon hearing the postman announcing that there was a telegram from Geneva, he claimed it, fearing it was from me, and wanting to avoid having to explain my involvement with Gilles."

"What do you mean?" Julius asked suspiciously.

Hofstad sighed.

"I am sorry to tell you that our colleague is in jail."

"In jail! That's not possible! Why?"

"She is accused of collaboration with the Germans. A very dangerous accusation these days. I don't know if you are aware that there is a very ugly mood in France. People are often accused without proof, and there have been some summary executions. I do hope that Doctor Gilles is a victim of a wrongful arrest and will be able to demonstrate her innocence as soon as possible; until she does, however, all her friends are suspect. So, you are very much in luck. First, because your telegram was not handed over to the police, which would have made them suspect you of complicity; and second, because Gustav brought it back to me and I was able to warn you. I was of two minds about it. Though I come from the German-speaking cantons of Switzerland, I do not like Germans and their collaborators. I can see that you are neither. You were planning to work at the clinic?"

"Not at all." Julius was in shock. "Marie-Christine in jail? Accused of collaborating with the enemy?" He shook his head.

"I have the greatest respect for cosmetic surgery and to the hope it gives the war wounded, but it is not my calling. I am a general practitioner, happy to be treating men, women and children. The fact is that I was hoping that Dr. Gilles would have some news about my daughter who had to flee Paris when the Germans arrived. They kept in touch, and Dr. Gilles, agreed to serve as a go-between between us in spite of the danger. She and I would exchange letters about medical matters, which were, in fact, a cover for passing news. I think it shows that she can't have been working with the Germans. I was hoping she could tell me where my daughter is today. Nothing more. Thank you for the warning. I shall now present myself at the clinic as a father looking for his daughter, not as a personal friend of the director, which would have landed me in hot water."

Having declined an offer of refreshments, he made his way back to the hotel on foot, thinking feverishly. There was no longer any urgency in leaving Geneva and reaching Paris alone, friendless and without a clue about the whereabouts of his children. At the same time, he knew he had to go.

That night, he had trouble sleeping. He felt adrift. Marie-Christine, his erstwhile lover and good friend, always so carefully groomed, was in jail, perhaps roughly interrogated. Could she have collaborated with German occupying forces? After all, the two sons she had had with her late husband were probably officers in the Reich's army. Whether they had been posted to Paris or not, they must have visited their mother more than once. Was it enough to make her a suspect? Given the "ugly mood" alluded to by Hofstad, it was quite possible. In any case, he could no longer rely on her help, nor her hospitality. It was not a question of money; he could afford the best accommodations, but he would be on his own.

He had hoped that Marie-Christine would guide him in the new France, which was not yet completely free. Of course, Theo Khan could still be in Paris. It was in his flat on the rue de Passy that Julius had stayed with his children in 1933. He had not had any news of his old friend since the beginning of the war. Had he and his wife survived the four years of German occupation? He had changed his name from Khan to Castan when he was granted French citizenship fifteen years earlier, but whether he was Khan or Castan, he must be eighty now. Still, the rue de Passy would be Julius' first stop. His last thought before finally succumbing to sleep was that he had not written to inform his good friend and neighbor doctor, Kadar, of his safe arrival in Geneva. He would do so in the morning and warn him not to reply at the clinic address, as had been agreed before his departure. Not having another address at the moment, he would advise him to send his letters care of the bank.

It had taken him so long to fall asleep that he woke up after ten in the morning. The letter for his sister was ready; he re-opened the envelope to tell her that he would be leaving Geneva the following day. He then took a cab to the rue de l'Arquebuse, where Paul Zerner warmly welcomed him once again and assured him that the letter would reach Chicago as swiftly as possible.

"By the way, here is a letter of introduction to a colleague in Paris, who knows your brother-in-law. Don't hesitate to call on him. Are you in a hurry? Would you care for a cup of coffee with a slice of my mother's famed apple strudel?" Paul asked.

"With pleasure. I overslept and left without breakfast." Julius replied.

"We have just what you need. Come with me."

As Julius poured himself a second cup of coffee, he also accepted another slice of strudel, which lived up to its reputation. Idly, Paul then asked him what his plans were.

"I am all set. I have my French visa and just bought a second-hand car with French plates. I am leaving for Paris tomorrow."

"Are you traveling with friends?" Paul asked.

"Well, no. I don't have any here. I shall be on my own."

"On your own? Could you ... No, it's too much to ask, though ..."

"Go ahead, if there is something I can do for you, I shall be glad to help."

"It would be to take a passenger. It would mean a lot to my mother and myself, but I am afraid to impose. It's a long trip, and you probably have no wish for company."

"On the contrary, it would alleviate the tedium of the journey."

"Yes but … it is a woman."

The banker appeared so flustered that Julius wondered whether the unknown woman was his mistress.

"She is a widow," Paul added as if he had guessed his thought. "The granddaughter of a childhood friend of my mother's. Perfectly reliable and respectable."

"Won't it be too tiring for an older person?"

"No, no, she is not old. Her grandmother was my mother's friend. These days, there are unfortunately too many young widows."

"If she is not afraid to travel with a perfect stranger, I shall be happy to take her. Can she be ready in time? I intend to leave by nine in the morning."

"Don't worry. She will be waiting for you in front of the Hotel de Savoie in Saint Julien, a little town five kilometers from the border on the French side."

Julius blinked.

"She has no papers?"

Zerner sighed.

"Let us rather say that her situation is … irregular. I don't know how she entered Switzerland, nor do I want to. She tells me that she has to go to France. I was able to find her some French documents perfectly authentic. They have to be considering the price I paid for them. The photo is not a very good likeness, but this is often the case with women. Her French is nearly faultless. She was going to travel alone. I found someone who will get her through the border and bring her to the Hotel de Savoie. She says she will make her way from there. My mother is very unhappy with this plan and demands that I find a better option. I can understand her. France is still unsettled. American military units have entered Germany, the city of Boulogne has been freed, and according to what my correspondents tell me, Calais will soon be next, but fighting still goes on along the Atlantic coast. The German troops are not relinquishing their grip on Holland and have inflicted heavy losses on the Allied forces. I would feel better if that young woman, who is under our protection, traveled with you. On the other hand, I would not want you to get in trouble. Should you be stopped at a checkpoint, and should the police suspect her, just say you met her by chance and don't even know her name. Listen, the more I think about it, the more I think it is not such a good idea."

"Why not? How could I refuse? You told me she was the granddaughter of a friend of your mother's. A young woman whom fate has already treated harshly, depriving her of her husband; she is an illegal refugee, and hence in danger. She has my sympathy. I have experienced some of what she went through, but for a woman, it must have been more painful and more dangerous. My brother-in-law holds you in high esteem, and I see no reason not to trust you. I am willing to risk it. I believe we should meet before. She will no doubt feel the same and may perhaps want to see the car so that she doesn't have to check every vehicle stopping in front of the hotel.

"You could be right. It's a very good idea, and even more so since I shall have to discuss it with her. Obviously, she knows nothing of a plan which only came into being when I heard about your departure."

"If she refuses, I won't be offended."

"She won't. It's the perfect solution. She was setting out alone because she didn't have a choice and must have felt uneasy about it. As to her story I can't say anything. She is adamant about the need for secrecy. She might tell you more when she knows you better. Listen, I will be at my mother's tonight for Shabbat dinner. Come, you shall be able to get acquainted with our young friend who is staying with her. It's on St. George's boulevard, close to the main synagogue. We dine early, and you will have a good night's sleep before embarking on your journey.

"How will she cross the border?"

"Don't worry. That part of the program has been settled already. It is far easier to cross from Switzerland into France than from France into Switzerland. You have no idea the amount of contraband going over the border. Just one more thing. My mother is very observant, as I told you in our first meeting. Since she lives in her house, the young woman must dress and behave accordingly. Tell me what your car looks like; she probably won't be able to go and look at it. Tomorrow she will wear thoroughly modern attire. Julius, I won't keep you any longer, you must have a lot to do in your few remaining hours here."

While on his way to his bank to withdraw a sizable sum in notes and coins, Julius began to have second thoughts about so readily agreeing to escort a mysterious widow with secrets to spare and false papers to boot. Would he have to spend hours making small talk with a perfect stranger? What would happen should they be stopped on the way? How would he explain her presence in the car? He had intended to break the journey at mid-point and spend the night in a hotel where he would surely have to show his passport. As for the Shabbat dinner at old madame Zerner's: it was another thing he could have done without. He sighed ruefully. Too late to back down now.

Warned of his arrival, Hans Steuber left his office and carried him away to a nearby brasserie in spite of his protests. The food was surprisingly good, and he left in a far better mood. Hans had listened with sympathy and had once again assured him of his support. He also had some words of advice.

"Julius, my friend. You are a free man, in good health, and with the means to live in comfort for the rest of your life. Your children have now grown into adulthood; you told me that the youngest is already 27. By all means, help them if they need you, but think of your own future."

Julius nodded his thanks and they embraced, vowing to keep in touch. Julius concluded their meeting by warning him not to use the address at the clinic and wait for his call from Paris.

When doctor Julius Matthias presented himself at Madame Zerner's house, he found the door ajar. Voices could be heard from within, and he pushed his way in. Men in black were conversing in Yiddish, waiting to be invited into the dining room where women were busy setting the table. Paul's mother, Dvora Lea Zerner, an energetic woman, in spite of her small stature, was briskly giving orders. When everything was done to her satisfaction, she invited her guests to take their places: the men at one end, on either side of her son, who sat at the head of the table, the women around her at the other end. Paul then stood up to deliver the traditional blessings, and the familiar ritual awakened a powerful wave of longing in Julius. His father's voice, his hands pulling apart the challah, the freshly baked ceremonial sweet Shabbat bread, heated discussions around the table about some obscure Talmudic issue being hotly disputed; memories of a world he had thought no longer existed. Yet here, in Geneva, nothing had changed, with the exception of the sweet wine used for the blessing which Simon Zerner had sent from Jewish vineyards in Palestine. Was there, after all, a measure of solace? Here was the stuffed carp, served cold with tangy horseradish, and the chicken soup with dumplings, followed by stewed meat and potatoes.

Only Yiddish was spoken. At first, the talk was all about local news: the outrageous price charged that year for choice synagogue seats on the evening of Yom Kippur; the weather, with rain expected in the morning; and, of course, community gossip. Soon, the mood shifted. All in attendance had friends or family members trapped in war zones, and the fear was that they could still be rounded up and deported in the convoys, which had not been stopped by the progress made by Allied forces. It was as if the Germans were eager to complete their sinister enterprise while they still could.

As Zerner explained, the Soviet troops were advancing, and the spearhead of American forces had entered Germany, but the fight was far from over. The Wehrmacht was scoring a number of successes in Holland. Then, there was the dramatic situation in Palestine, with the British navy prowling the Mediterranean, looking for refugee ships and turning them away from the coasts of the Promised Land. Julius listened, enthralled. These Jews, safe in their peaceful Geneva haven, were deeply concerned about the plight of their people, helping refugees who entered Switzerland clandestinely and those who had been caught and thrown in jail, collecting money to be handed over to emissaries coming from Tel Aviv, who would then risk their lives to bring it back to Eretz, a word that he was not familiar with. In French, his host then explained that the official name of Mandatory British Palestine was "Palestine-Eretz Israel" (Palestine—Land of Israel).

Julius smiled his thanks, trying to convey another question. The guests seemed to all know each other, and there had been no attempt at introductions, so Julius was not quite sure who his intended travel companion was. Paul caught on and looked pointedly in the direction of a woman not in the first flush of youth, who was listening with the intense concentration of someone who did not speak the language. He observed her with curiosity. She had very short hair of the palest blond, sharply contrasting with the golden, almost tanned hue of a determined face. He wondered if it was a wig when she raised her head. Her eyes were a clear color, between blue and green. She must have sensed his surprise and smiled fleetingly before turning her attention to her plate. How old could she be? She was probably over thirty and under forty. Not so pretty with that sharp, almost angular face, though she was not devoid of charm by any means. What could her story be? Had she, as he had done himself, reached Geneva after a long and difficult journey, finding sanctuary in the house of her grandmother's friend? He would have sworn that it was not the sun that had given her skin its complexion. Altogether someone out of the ordinary. Traveling with her might not be such a bad idea, but he felt her company might also stop him from worrying too much.

The rain did materialize early in the morning in the form of a steady drizzle emerging from thick low clouds, making the roads slippery. Driving a car he was unfamiliar with, in a town he did not know well and where road signs were few and far between, he lost his way several times. It was as if fickle fate would not let him depart from a place that had welcomed him so generously before handing him such a bitter blow. He checked his watch again. He was running late; his passenger would have to wait unless the bad weather had delayed her as well. At last, he reached the border and he was waved on after a short perusal of his passport. Behind him, Switzerland was fast disappearing under a blanket of mist, as if a door were closing. The unknown beckoned. Without Marie-Christine, how was he to find his children? When and if he did find them, what would he do? At 54, could he reinvent himself in France? The two Zerner boys, who had grown up in a country that had remained apart from the conflict, were telling their father that there would be no place for Jews in post-war Europe. Like Paul, he was neither tempted by America nor Palestine. He told himself he had to be patient. The war was not yet over. With the return of peace, he would be in a better position to decide where to go next.

He accelerated, forgetting that he was not driving his faithful and reliable Mercedes, but a far humbler vehicle, which skidded on a sharp corner and narrowly escaped ending up in a ditch. He managed to right the car in time and proceeded at a more sedate pace. No need to rush. Saint Julien and the Savoie Hotel were less than a mile away. The young woman was no doubt waiting comfortably in the lobby. He was entering the small town when rain started falling in earnest. Visibility was so poor that he stopped the car by the curb. The windshield wipers were swishing furiously, but he could not see a thing. Suddenly, the door opened and the woman, throwing off her sodden coat and tossing it in the back, sat down.

"Heavens! How nice and warm it is," she said, putting down her backpack, her only baggage. "I am sorry to barge in like that, but I saw an orange vehicle approach and stop, and I assumed it had to be you. The hotel marquee wasn't good protection, and I could not stand another minute in that pouring rain."

She had a slightly husky voice with more than a hint of some kind of accent.

"The car has a heater. It is the latest invention, I am told. I don't know how it works, but I am very happy with it," he replied, before adding: "but I don't understand. Why didn't you wait inside? I hope you weren't worried I wouldn't be coming!"

"Of course not. Paul told me you were very reliable. Besides, you are not really late. I was indeed waiting in the lobby when three gendarmes came in, probably to take shelter from the rain. They stared at me and whispered. At first, I took it for a compliment but then I worried that they would ask to see my papers. Not many women travel alone these days."

"Paul assured me that your papers are perfectly authentic, and even the photograph would pass muster if one did not look too closely," Julius replied.

"True. Pity he did not ask for my opinion before buying them at an extortionate price. I am allegedly called Ginette Lentier, aged 25—nice, but not credible. I live in Lille, a city in the north of France, a region I know nothing about. You may have noticed that I have an accent. I could perhaps pass for someone coming from the south of France, but no one will believe that I am from the north, and I would be at quite a loss if asked anything about a town I have never visited."

She shivered, and Julius picked up the plaid blanket he had thoughtfully put on the backseat. She smiled her thanks and wrapped it around her shoulders. It gave him an idea.

"Do you have a shawl or a scarf in that bag? Yes? Wrap it around your neck. Should we be stopped at a checkpoint, I shall explain that you have a cold and cannot speak. That should do the trick. You don't look dangerous. I do hope that you haven't caught a cold by the way. We shall try to find an open café and get you a hot drink as soon as possible."

"Thank you. That was quick thinking. And I am grateful to you for letting me travel with you. I was ready to be on my way alone, but I have to admit that this is a much better solution."

Julius thought her French was perfect, albeit with a lilting rhythm he could not identify. He wanted to ask her about it but remembered Paul's warning.

"Please, don't mention it," he said. "I am delighted to have company and happy to be able to help someone who, like me, had to flee to avoid persecution. We are living in dismal times and must help one another. Is someone waiting for you in Paris?"

"No. As a matter of fact, I am going to Marseilles."

"Marseilles! Why go to Paris then? It will triple the time!"

"Forgive me, I have my reasons."

As the rain slackened, Julius resumed driving slowly; the road was still slippery, and he was not familiar with the route he had chosen. When he had driven from Geneva to Paris with his two eldest who were going to study in the French capital, it was summer, 1933. They had traveled under the scorching sun through a Europe unaware of the tempest to come. André and Elisabeth had taken turns driving with him. They were in no hurry and chose the mountain road with its splendid views. Now, September was drawing to an end, and the vice-consul had advised him not to chance the weather on mountain passes; it was better to go through Nantua and Bourg en Bresse, and then turn onto highway 6 in Macon, a city liberated earlier that month. Andrieu had explained that highway 5 might be shorter, but retreating German soldiers had been reported there, adding that Doctor Matthias would still have to be careful and keep a lookout for stragglers and deserters along the way. *I wonder what he means by being careful,* the doctor had thought. *If I do encounter them, it will be too late to do anything about it!*

There was very little traffic and not many peasants working the fields that Saturday in September. Only a few people could be seen outside in the small villages they passed through. Around eleven, seeing the open wooden shutters, Julius stopped in front of a roadside inn.

"We are not open yet," a stout woman apologized, a vast apron emphasizing her ample charms. "Lunch is served at noon." She spoke with such a strong regional accent that Julius had trouble understanding her.

"Of course, of course," he said with an understanding smile, "but would it be possible to serve a hot drink to my wife? She has a cold."

She scratched her head.

"There is neither tea nor coffee. One can't get them these days, and we are out of chicory. What do you say to a nourishing soup? It's just been made."

Her proposition was immediately accepted. Thick and redolent with the large chunk of meat it had simmered with, it must have been very good since "Ginette" ate two bowls full.

"Good for you," said the woman. "You've got to put on some weight or your husband will look elsewhere!"

She laughed heartily at the innkeeper's joke. Indeed, Ginette was wearing a pair of trousers far too big and a thick pullover, which completely hid her form. She smiled without replying and stood up. They were making their way to the car after leaving a generous tip when a man, who appeared to be the owner and was as skinny as his wife was fat, yelled at them from the open door:

"Be careful! There could be some trouble on the roads, even …"

His accent was, if anything, thicker than that of his wife. *What did he say*, wondered Julius. *It sounded like 'boche*[1].*'*

"He probably meant *vaches*," hazarded his companion.

"Cows on the road? I suppose it's possible in this season. What are we supposed to do if we encounter them? Blow the horn? And if they won't budge?"

She giggled. It was a lovely sound.

"I take it you have never lived on a farm. Don't worry. If the horn does not do the trick, I shall get out of the car and shoo them away." Then, abruptly changing the subject, she added, "Paul told me that you come from Hungary, but you speak French practically with no accent!"

"Not quite. I was lucky to be taught by a distinguished French professor, but it was a long time ago. Later, I had Swiss friends, took some more lessons, and I used to read French medical journals. I must say, I am delighted to see that it's all coming back fast. By the way, your French is not so bad yourself! Don't explain. I understand from Paul that you have good reason not to reveal anything about yourself.

[1] *Boche*. Slang for a German soldier.

He did say that your grandmother was a friend of his mother. Am I right in assuming she came from Poland as well, hence those pale eyes and your blond hair. He also told me you lost your husband. I am sorry. There were no children?"

"Unfortunately. As for my French, I got it from my father. I am not trying to change the subject; I wish I could tell you more, Doctor Matthias."

"Julius, please."

"Julius it is, and I am …"

"Ginette?"

"No way. It's a terrible name. Call me … The hell with it. Call me Lily; at least I will understand that you are talking to me! Paul said … he said you are a widower as well?"

He nodded without answering and concentrated on his driving. Most of the clouds had disappeared by then, and the sun was beginning to shine. They were going relatively fast; the road was in excellent condition and practically empty. Strange. Lunchtime, maybe? There was not a single cow to be seen. The farmers must have rounded them up.

"We'll stop as soon as you see a restaurant. I am beginning to get hungry."

"Dvora Lea—Madame Zerner, Paul's mother, has made us some sandwiches. Now that the weather has cleared, can we stop somewhere? There is no traffic to bother us.

He thought it was a good suggestion and slowed down, looking for a likely spot. He soon spied a building somewhat off the road. It no longer had a roof, and one could see rooms filled with debris through its crumbling façade. The result of a bombing raid, no doubt. However, a stone table and two benches still stood in a garden that seemed miraculously untouched and somehow inviting. Julius turned into the dirt track and parked the car under the shade of an oak tree. The pair stretched themselves as they got out. There was no sound. The sky was a clear shade of blue, and it was getting warm on this last day of September. Lily picked up some yellowing newspapers on the ground and swept the table and two benches as best she could. She took the sandwiches out of her rucksack and spread them on the kitchen towel in which they had been wrapped. Before sitting down, she brought her sodden coat from the car and left it to dry on one of the benches. Under the harsh light of early afternoon, she appeared to be closer to forty than to thirty; Julius had not been far wrong the previous night. In spite of her extraordinary eyes, she was not beautiful; she had an interesting face, her sharp chin contrasting with the generous mouth, and lots of self-assurance. One could see it in the way she walked. She was tall for a woman, and far too thin for his taste. Though on second thought ... He shook his head. Now was not the time. He bent to reach the canteen he had filled at the hotel and poured water in the two pewter goblets he had bought along. They drank in companionable silence.

"We could be anywhere in Europe," she mused after a while. Everywhere is the same landscape of ruined homes. Think of the family who lived here, all the families who have lost everything? And yet, the people of Europe have had centuries of common pasts and share the same religion. It is incomprehensible."

"Centuries of common pasts? Where did you study history? There has been fighting in Europe since the dawn of time, with religion often inciting conflict between the warring factions. Today, communism and Nazism have nothing to do with religion!"

"Each to his own," she shrugged. "I was reflecting on the difference between what goes on here and in Palestine, the one land where Jews are standing their ground and fighting."

"I am ashamed to admit that I haven't been following the events there very closely. When I was still in Hungary, I would switch on the radio in secret to get the latest news and turn it off as quickly as possible to avoid being detected. On the road, news was scarce. I have a lot of catching up to do, but not now. First, I have to take care of my own problems and those of my family. When I know they are all safe, I shall probably show more interest in what is going on over there. I hope that this doesn't disappoint you."

"It is not for me to judge, and if I have offended, I beg your pardon. Here, Madame Zerner made bread just before Shabbat and garnished it with brisket pickled in brine and then cooked over a slow fire. She also added some homemade pickles. She once gave the recipe to my mother, who could never attain that level of perfection. Besides, my father did not care for it."

"I can't see why not. I have never eaten better. Madame Zerner is a superb cook, as I noticed yesterday. If Paul ever goes bankrupt, she could open a restaurant," he added lightly. "I assume that your father was not Polish?"

"Certainly not. He was Egyptian."

"Egyptian? There are Jews in Egypt?" He stopped short of continuing, feeling himself reddening.

"Without going back to Moses and Joseph," she laughed, "there were Jews in Egypt well before the first Ashkenazim ventured to Poland, or Hungary for that matter. You are a doctor and have never heard of the Rambam, Moses Maimonides, who was physician to the sultan of Egypt?"

"I forgot he was Egyptian."

"He was not Egyptian! He was born in Cordova and had to flee from persecution."

"I am sorry. I shall check the issue thoroughly at the first occasion." He smiled.

While devouring another sandwich, Julius remembered that his friend Theo had reproached him about the very same thing more than a quarter century ago, after being appalled to discover that though he knew the writings of that illustrious sage, Julius had not known that he was a doctor like himself. Julius drew a hand across his face. Suddenly, memories were crowding him. Other rustic lunches, clandestine meetings with Alix, his sometime-girlfriend from Geneva, in a sunny clearing, his gleaming Mercedes hidden under tall trees; the farm of his friend Sandor, the two of them leaving women and children to go for long walks in the great Transylvanian forest, so close. Both would then forget their everyday problems for a few hours. Eyes half-closed, he felt himself transported to the bank of the small stream where two little faces danced on the waves. A blond head and a darker one. Sandor and Julius tanned by the same golden hue by that year's endless summer. They had managed to evade the supervision of Julius' big sister, Anni, and had escaped into the forest. Having gorged themselves on berries, they busied themselves trying to catch little fish with their bare hands. Happy memories of a bygone era ...

He raised his head. His passenger, eyes half-shut, appeared lost in thought. He told himself it was time to get up and to take to the road again, but he did not move. What was the hurry? There was no one waiting for them at the end of that first leg of their journey. Why not linger a little longer, enjoy the peace and quiet in the day's hottest hours? In a matter of minutes, they both fell into a light slumber.

The steady rumble of an approaching vehicle woke them up and they exchanged the guilty smile of two school children caught napping in class. But it was not a car. It was a plane, and it swooped down closer as if to see them better.

"I wonder what the pilot is looking for," commented Lily, stretching. "It's a French fighter. I hope it does not mean that there are Germans in the vicinity."

"How can you tell it's a French plane?"

"Look at the tricolor roundel! It does not look at all like the sinister black cross on a white background of the Luftwaffe. The war years should have taught you that much. Being able to tell the difference between friendly and enemy aircraft often makes the difference between life and death. If it had been German, I would have immediately flung myself under that stone table to take shelter."

"All planes look alike to me, and they all meant danger when I was on the road. I would dive for the nearest cover—a tree, or a ditch—as did the people I was traveling with. You have to understand that although some of the planes we saw could be on our side, they would not know whether we were friend or foe, and would have shot us just to make sure. Here, of course, it is another story. We are in France and have nothing to worry about."

He checked his watch. They had been here for three hours! Time to go. Lily shook her coat, which was almost dry, and put it back in the car with her rucksack. Then, with a half-smile, she disappeared behind the house. Julius made do with a willow tree by the oak. He was on his way to his car when he heard confused noises from the dirt road. Open-mouthed, he saw two soldiers coming at him at a fast pace. He checked again, but no, he was not mistaken. They were wearing the hated greenish uniforms he had hoped never to see again. German soldiers, here! Officers! And they were coming straight at him; or rather, going to the ruined build-ing. For what? To hide? Behind them, two French soldiers were gaining fast.

Suddenly, one of them shouldered his weapon and fired a long burst, causing one of the Germans to tumble to the ground. The other was hit; he stumbled, but managed to turn around and fire, hitting both French soldiers, who also fell down. The man went on walking unsteadily. When he saw the car and Julius standing frozen there, a smile of pure glee crossed his face and he raised his weapon again. Julius realized that it was not fair to have escaped deportation and walked so many miles only to be killed in France by a German bullet when he heard the shot and tried to understand why he was not dead as the German was down.

Looking for the shooter who had just saved his life, he saw Lily, slightly out of breath but still holding a gun in two very capable hands ready to fire again. She did not have to. The German had been hit squarely between the eyes. A stunned Julius, his heart beating wildly, managed to compose himself and check the bodies on the path. Both Germans were dead; one of the Frenchmen, his head covered in blood, was trying to sit up, and a geyser of blood fused from the leg of the other one who had not recovered consciousness, a sure sign that the femoral artery had been hit. There was no time to lose. Doctor Matthias retrieved his medical bag from the car while picking up the water canteen with his other hand

and ran to the wounded man. Cutting his trouser leg as fast he could with his scalpel, he applied a tourniquet, stopping the flow of blood. The soldier did not move. Then, Julius stood up and went to the other Frenchman who looked dazed. He sponged the blood, searching for its source. The soldier had been lucky. A bullet had whizzed so close it had grazed his scalp, hence the bleeding, but that was all. Julius had just finished bandaging the head when the man eagerly asked him if he had been the one who had killed the German. He was about to reply "no" when Lily stopped him.

"Julius never misses, especially at such a close range," she said with aplomb. "He only needed one shot."

She focused on him with such intensity that he swallowed and stuttered that he had been lucky.

"Lucky! Don't be so modest. That was a crack shot. You also seem to know your way around the wounded. Are you a doctor?"

"Indeed."

"Then we are the lucky ones. A crack shot and a doctor!"

Turning to Lily, he added, "now that your husband has finished treating us, give him back his gun. Careful, the safety is not on."

"I wasn't sure if more Germans would come," said Julius, taking the gun from her. "There. It is safe now."

Suddenly, there was a babel of voices and a flurry of activity; more soldiers approached, all of them French this time. The next few minutes were full of noise and confusion. A lieutenant with a recent angry scar running across his face yelled for a doctor and an ambulance on a field telephone, while the soldier, who had been lightly wounded, reported what had happened.

Julius Matthias, slightly apart, watched the scene, happy to notice that his shock was wearing off. Never had death been so close. If the German had not been wounded and had fired faster, if Lily had arrived one second, a tenth of a second later ... He stole covert glances at the young woman, who had gone to the car, where she was now sitting. He had never seen a woman with a gun before, let alone a woman who knew how to use it with deadly results. This was one of the many changes war had brought. So, she had a weapon to protect herself! It went a long way to explain why she had been ready to travel alone. What was more astonishing was the fact that she had not been flustered, had not hesitated to shoot to kill and had done it. Why then not bask in the glory of that deed? Why did she have to hide her identity? Who was she? Where on earth had her Polish mother found that Egyptian father? So many questions ... Yet, the main thing was that she had saved his life. Everything else was irrelevant at that point.

When the field ambulance arrived, a medic attended to the soldier who was still unconscious, and a stretcher was brought out. The medic then exchanged a few words with the second soldier and went back, apparently satisfied, to the ambulance, which soon disappeared from view. The lieutenant with the scar, eyes reddened by a lack of sleep, was now berating Julius. Didn't he listen to the news? Wasn't he aware that there were stragglers on the road? Hadn't he seen the plane? Suddenly, he stopped.

"I am sorry. Forgive me. I was fuming at those two hot-heads. Instead of waiting for the rest of the group to catch up with them, they wanted to be heroes. If you hadn't been here, they would both be dead, and the last German would have had time to barricade himself in what's left of the house. He would not have lasted long; there were too many of us, but we might have had to pay the price. You were the hero, not them. And with just the one clean shot! Moreover, the medic tells me that had you not acted promptly, Antoine might have bled to death. He is my sister's husband! I can't thank you enough. Now, where are you going? Paris? This late? It will soon be dark and there are some bad patches on the road further on. My advice is to stop for the night. It will be more prudent. You can leave early in the morning. There should not be any more Germans. We were told of a dozen soldiers or deserters cut off from their unit and making quickly for the border. We've been tracking them for some days; a reconnaissance plane found them for us, and we thought we had killed them all, but these two managed to slip away. I don't believe there are others. Still there is no point in taking chances. I won't let you drive away alone. Two of my men will escort you to the town of Saulieu. No, don't thank me. It is you who will do me a favor again. I want Langlois, the other wounded soldier, to go home for the night. His wife is a qualified nurse and she will be able to watch over him. I am sending sergeant Bertaud with him. He too lives in Saulieu and will be delighted to see his wife and kids for a few hours. I shall give you petrol vouchers. No, no, don't thank me."

In the end, having left the ruined house well past four, they reached Saulieu after dark. Julius had let Bertaud take the wheel. The stocky sergeant was familiar with the road and, of equal importance, knew when to leave it to go in search of an open petrol station. He peppered them with questions, and in between, offered to sell them nylon stockings, cigarettes, and chocolates he "happened" to have found. Julius continued to politely decline his offers. He was itching to discuss with Lily, who was sitting in the back next to him, what had happened, but was stymied by the presence of the soldiers. She was pale and looked worried. He tried to reassure her with a smile. Putting his hand on her knee, he whispered, "Don't worry, it will be alright." He was nevertheless wondering how they would manage when they reached the hotel. Should they find one in Saulieu, a city he had never heard of, and would it have two rooms? That was not the only problem. If he kept pretending Lily was his wife, then they would have to share a room, which would embarrass her; if he did not, she would have to show her papers. Andrieu had told him travelers had to fill out several forms, collected by the local police. Salvation came in the form of Langlois, who asked him which hotel they were booked into.

"None at all," Julius replied ruefully. "Though we were not sure we would make it to Paris tonight, we did not know where we would eventually stop. Can you recommend a suitable establishment?"

"Don't worry, doctor, I can do better than that. You and your wife will do us the honor of being our guests for tonight. We have a separate flat on the top floor of our house; this is where my son sleeps when he comes from Paris where he lives. It will be far more comfortable than a hotel. No, it's no use arguing. My wife would never forgive me if I let the man who saved my life simply go away. Besides, one never knows: if I take a turn for the worse in the night, you will be there to save my life again!"

Needless to say, his offer was immediately accepted, and Julius made only a token demurral before letting himself be persuaded. He felt his passenger relaxing by his side. She must have shared his misgivings about their eventual sleeping arrangements.

4

LILY

TEN DAYS INTO AUTUMN, that Sunday still had a summery feel. By noon, the temperature had reached 25C degrees, and in spite of the open windows, it was very hot in the car. They were driving at a fast pace and would probably reach Paris before evening, though they had left Saulieu much later than planned, having only woken up slightly before ten. In fact, Lily had fallen asleep as soon as she settled in the Juvaquatre and was still lost to the world, a small, satisfied smile on her face. Julius Matthias was also smiling. It had been a spectacular evening. They had received a hero's welcome. Bertaud had called ahead when they left him at his home, and Marie Langlois, not quite reassured about his report on her husband's wound, waited anxiously outside a pleasant recently painted detached house, flanked by her sister and her brother-in-law who had come to give her moral support. While she fussed about "her Henri," the brother-in-law parked the car in the courtyard and her sister took them to the upper flat, telling them that dinner would be ready in an hour. They toured their new domain. Intended for a son who lived in Paris with his wife and their little girl, it was more spacious than they had expected: a drawing room, a master bedroom, and a smaller room with a modern bathroom between them. It was the perfect solution. He would leave Lily the bigger room and take the other. There was a jug filled with cold water on the drawing room table. They drank thirstily and sat down with some hesitation. Julius was the first to break the silence.

"I haven't thanked you for saving my life. I really thought it was the end. Any other woman would have been too terrified to act and would have run in the opposite direction. You were not even flustered. It was incredible."

"Nonsense. The war has gone on long enough for women to understand the need for weapons and to learn how to use them. If you can't shoot straight, what is the point of having a gun? In any case, you don't have to thank me. If it hadn't been for me, you would never have found yourself in such a situation. You would have stopped for lunch in a roadside inn, resumed driving, and reached Paris without incident. I have brought you nothing but bad luck, as I have done to all those I have loved and who've died. I should let you go on alone."

"Don't talk nonsense. You might as well blame Madame Zerner for having prepared sandwiches for us. And I am too much of an atheist to believe that someone can bring bad luck."

"What has religion got to do with adversity?"

"Not adversity, but the belief that someone is jinxed as if he was pursued by an alien force. I do not believe in alien forces. As to the loved ones you have lost, are you telling me that it was not because of the war, but because of you?"

She hazarded a smile. "Thank you for that interesting point of view. I shall try to adopt it. But first I am going to freshen up a bit before dinner."

"Wait, can't you tell me a little more about yourself? Who are you, in fact? Why the need for secrecy? Why not accept the compliments about the shooting that are rightly yours?"

"I can't … I can't. Please don't ask me. Besides, the less you know the safer you will be."

Her voice trembled and she blinked away tears.

Julius watched her go, sighing in frustration.

Dinner at the Langlois was a far cry from dinner at the Zerners. There was no priceless China and sterling silver, nor any starched and embroidered napkins, but there was a rustic cotton tablecloth dotted with stylized flowers and mismatched plates to accommodate all the guests. Family and friends had come to see for themselves that "our Henri" was truly alright.

None had arrived empty-handed. Wine, roast beef, and lamb chops, as well as a mouthwatering apple tart were doing a great job of supplementing the hearty stew and baked potatoes hastily prepared by their hostess. Twenty people were seated around the sturdy table, and they all spoke at once. Henri Langlois, sporting an impressive bandage, had refused to change out of his dusty and bloodstained uniform in spite of his wife's objurgations. He was basking in the general attention and ate heartily, stopping only to let the women who were getting up one after the other kiss him full on the lips. His wife looked on indulgently while monitoring him closely and not letting him drink wine or alcohol. He had vainly tried to protest, but she had stood firm with the support of Doctor Matthias, who had explained that although the wound was superficial, he had fallen, and his head had struck the ground. There might be some concussion, even if it did not seem likely. A great deal of concern was also expressed regarding the other wounded in hospital; however, his life was not in danger, "thanks to the prompt and heroic intervention of the doctor that divine providence had sent to both soldiers."

Julius himself had his fair share of admiration, and it was not solely due to his "heroic actions." Relaxed and well-rested after his Geneva stay, he cut a fine figure in the casual outfit he had bought for the trip. Women stole glances at the handsome doctor, his blue-grey eyes and face still tanned from four months on the road, his blond hair barely touched with grey. When Langlois started extolling his bravery, his coolness under fire and the way he had disposed of the German with one single bullet, Julius had no trouble playing it down, while avoiding looking at his companion. But then a heavyset man with a florid face, identifying himself as a weapon buff and collector, asked him about the gun he had used.

"Don't start him on that subject," Lily said cheerfully, once more coming to his rescue. "He can go on for hours, to the point that I know all the details by heart. It is a 9.65 caliber gun made at the Enfield Royal Small Arms factory in England for the use of his Majesty's troops. Its net weight empty is slightly less than 800 grams and can fire thirty rounds to the minute. Julius, have I forgotten anything?"

"No, and I could not have said it better." He smiled while the audience broke into applause.

"Where did you find that fine weapon?" The collector was not yet satisfied.

"All I can tell you is that I didn't get it from a collector like you and that the villainous-looking giant with a mustache who sold it for cash did not give me a receipt."

All laughed and the collector proposed a toast to "the doctor and his lovely lady." Marie then produced a bottle of pre-war champagne she had been keeping, she said, for a great occasion, and what occasion could be greater than her husband's miraculous escape? In her turn, Lily, who had been liberally sampling the wine, though not appearing the worse for wear, toasted the hostess and the host. She received her share of admiring glances. She was wearing a flattering green blouse and a matching headband, which somehow softened the effect of her truly awful haircut ("I cut it myself," she had told Julius earlier. "I was trying to pass as a boy; now that my hair has grown I shall have to find a good hairdresser in Paris …")

Soon, the conversation turned to other topics. A man in his fifties, whose three sons he said were in "Leclerc's army," complained about the worsening situation. At that point, Julius must have looked blank, for the man explained the differences between the so-called Leclerc army, the Free French Forces, and the French Forces of the Interior, made up of former Résistance fighters against German occupation now more or less organized in light infantry units. It seemed that all there had been involved in the Résistance; the younger among them had actually fought with the FFI. It had been hoped that after the Normandy landing in June, the war would be effectively over, but there were still large numbers of German troops, not only in the west, where they were trying to battle their way back to Germany, but also in the south of the country. There were casualties every day—dead or wounded—in small numbers, admittedly, but soldiers' families, and even civilians in areas not yet fully liberated still lived in fear.

The baker, seated across from Julius, complained of how hard it was to find flour, eggs, and pretty much everything he needed while the black market was flourishing, and the interim government born of the Résistance had trouble asserting its authority. Here and there, people took the law into their hands, raiding shops accused, rightly or wrongly, of having welcomed the Germans a little too warmly. Self-proclaimed patriots were busy denouncing real or imaginary collaborators. Happily, agreed the dinner guests, nothing of the kind had happened in Saulieu; however, letters from relatives or friends told of unacceptable violence: summary execution of so-called "traitors" without the benefit of a trial and sordid acts of revenge and score-settling. As for women suspected of having slept with the enemy, they were publicly shorn by vindictive crowds if they were not thrown in jail. Julius winced, thinking of Marie-Christine. Had she, too, suffered that indignity?

A little later, a glance at Henri Langlois reminded him of his duty.

"Marie, my dear," he said. "It's time to take your husband off to bed. He needs his rest."

There were exclamations of protests while Henri stood up with ill grace; however, he did look exhausted and let himself be led away, not before inviting his friends to come back for lunch the next day, Sunday, adding that there was still enough left to feed them all.

Soon, Julius and Lily found themselves alone in the top-floor flat. Julius deposited his suitcase in the smaller room while she entered the bathroom. When she exited, wearing a long and ample nightgown, he went in. She had already switched off the light when he walked out, a little self-conscious in the elegant pajamas bought in Geneva. He stifled a curse. He had forgotten to turn on the lamp in his room, so he made his way in the darkness towards the door. Suddenly, her voice stopped him.

"Julius, come here for a minute."

He made a few tentative steps in her direction and felt her hand grasping his.

"Why leave me alone in this great bed? No questions, please. Don't worry. As I told you before, I can't have children."

He found himself by her side, not sure what to do and fearing he was about to take advantage of a woman under his protection. He told her how he felt, adding that she may have had a little too much to drink.

She laughed softly. "You may be right, so what? I know very well what I am doing. Your wife is dead, so is my husband. We are both adults, and I am sure you want it as much as I do. Let's make the most of this night. Tomorrow, it shall be forgotten. You will go your way, and I mine."

There was a slight rustling noise and he understood she had taken off her gown. Then she took the matter in hand, so to speak; albeit not for long. Julius took over fast enough. It had been so long since he had had such a young and enthusiastic partner. Lily was not one for sophisticated games; she was full of joyful energy, to which he responded with a vigor he did not remember displaying. He and his wife had not shared a bed in decades, and during the long years of war and troubles, he had not been able to look elsewhere. On his way to Geneva, he had stayed on a farm in Italy for several days, made welcome by a woman far from the first flush of youth, whose husband had been taken prisoner by the Germans—but a far cry from the youthful body he was able to admire when Lily switched on the light and got up to get them each a glass of water.

"How old are you?" he asked, caressing her small firm breasts and flat belly.

"I was born in 1909. What about you?"

"In 1890; in fact, by 1909, my first child was born."

"You were only 19? You must have started early. Tell me, could we do it again despite your advanced years?"

He put the light out by way of an answer. This time it lasted longer and was more intense. He was getting his breath back when he noticed that she had fallen asleep.

His hands behind his head, he let his mind wander. At barely 18, he had indeed married young. Magda was older by seven years. A widow, she hoped a younger man would give her the children that her first husband had not been able to father. And he, well, he only cared about the medical studies his in-laws would finance. She had had the children she wanted; he had become a doctor, but the arranged marriage had never turned into a loving one. Marie-Christine, his fellow medical student with no inhibitions, had initiated him in the pleasures of lovemaking, but it was the vulnerable and tender Madi who had made him discover love. Lily, now that was a revelation. A demonstration that, at 54, there could still be wonderful surprises. That along the way it might not be too late to find someone not only to share his bed but also his life. What a strange turn of events. Lily was 35, as would have been Georgy, his beloved first son, so tragically dead by drowning in infancy. She was right: he had indeed started young. Too young? He had never considered that matter, but there could be something to it.

Light from a streetlamp filtered through the wooden shutters. He glanced at the lovely body so serenely framed and wondered what the secret was she was so afraid to tell him? She had killed a German officer and was therefore on the side of the angels; she was in possession of a British made weapon ... so what?

"You aren't asleep?" She asked in her warm, slightly husky voice. "Since they say: 'third time lucky' feel like another round?"

He hesitated briefly, fearing he was not up to the challenge, and quickly found that his fear had been groundless. He let himself get carried away again by a partner as inventing as she was sensual. Then, she turned on the light and went to fetch a pack of cigarettes from her bag. She looked at him inquiringly, and he shook his head. A fine sheen of sweat on her prone body, eyes half-closed, she smoked for a few minutes, stubbed her cigarette in the glass of water left on the night table, and kissed him lightly on the cheek.

"You have no idea how much I needed that. I was beginning to forget how one does it, and how good it felt. Now I shall be able to go on without it, at least until Marseilles ..."

This time, Julius was the first to fall asleep.

By the time they woke up, it was almost ten and they took to the road one hour later, after a hearty breakfast eaten while Marie was filling a basket with sandwiches, fruits, and a bottle of wine in spite of their halfhearted efforts to dissuade her. Julius had examined her husband, who did not appear the worse for wear after the events of the previous day.

They drove through sun-drenched roads without any further mishaps, and at around two in the afternoon, entered a prosperous-looking little town. A sign in a wayside café announced that travelers were welcome to bring their own food, so they did, avoiding the envious glances of other patrons. As the kilometers went by, they wondered how long the war would last and what would be the new Europe when peace returned, and whether Jews could go back to their homes in the towns and villages which had so willingly handed them over to the Nazis to be taken to the death camps? Julius hoped against hope that the countries and the people concerned would be suitably ashamed and open their arms to the survivors. Lily did not entertain similar hopes. The survivors, she said, would have to leave the old continent and look elsewhere for a safe future. By now, they were talking freely, as if they were old friends, though with the unspoken thought that they were entering uncharted territory. It was clear that they could not go their own way when they reached Paris. Lily had admitted that there was no one waiting for her there and that she would have to find a hotel. So, it was decided that she would go with him to meet the Castans, his old friends; if they were no longer there, they would go together in search of a hotel. In the morning, they would make plans.

Traffic began to build up as they neared the French capital. Families were returning home after a weekend in the countryside or a day spent in the splendid Fontainebleau forest. Marie Langlois had warned them: now that Paris was free, people were resuming their old routines. Lily pored over the map and guided Julius, who had quite forgotten the route he had followed more than ten years ago. The Castans lived—or used to live—on the rue de Passy, a choice location. Julius stopped in front of what used to be the carriage entrance, which now led to an inner courtyard where he had parked his Mercedes during his last visit. Was his old friend still there? Had he survived the war and the German occupation? The concierge, who had seen the car from his window, came bustling out.

"You can't park here, he said importantly. Move or I call the police."

"Just a minute," said Julius, getting out of the car. "Are Monsieur and Madame Castan still here?"

"Monsieur and Madame Castan?" The man peered closer.

"Monsieur le docteur! Forgive me. It's getting dark, and I did not recognize you. Madame Castan did not tell me you were coming. You have not changed, not changed at all! Go ahead, go ahead, leave me the key. I shall park the car in the courtyard and bring up your luggage."

Julius Matthias released a breath he had not realized he'd been holding. Taking Lily by the hand, he got into the lift and punched the button for the third floor. Then he rang the bell. Suddenly, Theo was there. Not as upright perhaps, but with the well-remembered sardonic smile which was immediately wiped out.

"Yuli! Is it really you? You are alive! Praise be to God! Come in! Come in!" He embraced Julius as if to carry him bodily into the room. Lily followed uncertainly. "Tell me, who is your charming companion?"

He must be pushing eighty, but he has not changed at all, Julius thought as he observed his friend with affection. *Once a skirt chaser … yet, shouldn't he be slowing down?*

Rapid steps were heard coming their way.

"We have company?" Zsazsa, holding a ladle, had exited the kitchen. She did not raise her head at once, and Julius took a long look at her. Still standing upright, still a little overweight, her white hair caught in a bun and a myriad of wrinkles on her face. Then, she saw him. She turned white and dropped the ladle. He caught her just in time and settled her in an armchair.

"Yuli, my little Yuli," she said, taking his face in her two hands. "We have been so worried about you. Now I can die in peace."

Lily, still standing by the door, murmured that if all was well, she had better be going if she wanted to find a hotel before night.

"Wait," said Julius. "I will go with you to make sure you are all right."

"Yuli, who is your young friend?" Zsazsa asked.

"Lily. Her mother is a relative of the Geneva Zerners, and they asked me to escort her to Paris."

"Zerner? Friends of your brother in law? Nice people. We got to know them well when we lived in Geneva. You can't let that child go alone in search of a hotel on a Sunday evening. The streets are not safe. We have plenty of room here and we shall help her find something suitable tomorrow. Don't argue, young lady and don't thank me. Come help me make the beds in the guest rooms, then we shall make dinner together. By the way, I am Zsazsa, and my husband is Theo. Come on. Yuli, wait until I come back to tell us what has happened."

She got up and the young woman followed her in a daze, trying to cope with the new situation; as for Julius, he was thinking that the many years spent in France had done nothing to tame Zsazsa's terrible Hungarian accent.

"The daughter of Zerner's friend, is she?" Theo commented with a knowing smile. "If that's the way you want to introduce her, without bothering to call her by her name …"

"Dear Theo, what a pleasure to discover that you haven't changed at all. Let me tell you that I don't know her name. She told me to call her Lily, and I have no other details. She has her reasons, and I promised Paul I wouldn't pry. These days, many people have reasons to keep their identity secret. However, yesterday, with great efficiency and without losing her composure, she shot a German officer who was about to kill me. That convinced me that she could be trusted. Don't look at me like that. I met her for the first time barely forty-eight hours ago.

"If you say so. Let's talk about it later. You have heard my wife; we are not to discuss anything before her return. Just tell me one thing. Magda?"

"She is dead, killed by a German soldier. I am ashamed to admit that's what made my escape possible. You will hear all about it when Zsazsa comes back. But what about you? How did you survive the war and the occupation? How could you go on living in Paris with Germans everywhere?"

"Let's sit down first. That's better. By the way, don't worry about your luggage. Duflot, the concierge will bring it up. He has a key to our flat. Would you like to drink something? A glass of the French cognac, the kind you used to enjoy so much?"

"Thank you, but no. After dinner, with the ladies."

"Do you want to know how we managed? Well, at first, with a great deal of apprehension, and even a touch of panic. Have you heard about what the French called '*exode?*' No? well, as the Germans were getting near—I am referring to June 1940—Frenchmen deserted Paris in droves; tens of thousands fled to the south of France, using every available means: cars, trucks, bicycles, on foot even. It was chaos. We

decided to stay. What was the risk? Two blameless old people
in a well-to-do area? We had been settled in Paris for more
than twenty years; those who had met us 'before' and were
aware of the fact that we were Jewish could be counted on
the fingers of one hand. We have both become French citizens; we changed our name to a bland French-sounding one.
We are at pains never to speak Austrian or even Hungarian
in public and even make an effort to avoid it at home. I am
generous to the concierge; I give liberally to local charities
and to the nearby orphanage of Sisters of the Assumption.
We were never stopped or bothered. Nevertheless, we could
not remain indifferent to the sight of German soldiers strut-
ting through the streets and the German flags on the Champs
Elysees. In the beginning, we told ourselves that it might
have been a mistake not to leave Europe altogether and go
to the States when we still could, as your sister did. It was
too late, of course. The government had taken measures
against the Jews. There were notices on Jewish-owned stores.
Wearing the yellow star of David became compulsory, but
we did not have to wear it since no one knew our true identity. The press attacked Jews daily; people were turning into
informers and denouncing former friends or neighbors. Jews
were being arrested. At first, their fate was unknown; very
little information filtered through regarding the abomina-
tions carried out in Germany and Poland, the death camps.
Little by little, the news got out, but many still refused to
believe. Not us. We had seen antisemitism firsthand; you
remember why we left Nagyvarad. I had been set upon by
a frenzied mob hell-bent on killing a Jew, any Jew. To this
day, I wonder by what miracle I was able to get away? At
the time, there was nothing I could have done ... Had I

complained to the police, I would have been turned away, as you were, more or less, when your father was killed during the 1927 pogrom. The murderers were never brought to justice. After the Vel d'Hiv roundup, the situation changed. People began to understand.

"What roundup?"

"Of course, you had your own problems, and you did not hear about it. It happened on July 16 and 17, 1942. Foreign Jews were arrested by French policemen acting upon the orders of the German occupying forces, but still! They were kept with little food and water for five days in the Velodrome d'Hiver, a bicycle racetrack and stadium. Around 13,000 people, including 4,000 children, were then deported. I can't begin to tell you how bad it was.

"Theo, I never knew! I did listen to the BBC in French, albeit furtively and for a few minutes to avoid being discovered. I was aware that France had been occupied, but somehow I was sure that the Jews there had been spared the anti-Semitic outrages that we'd encountered."

"Each of us was dealing with what he had to endure in his country. As for anti-Semitic outrages, they did not start with the German occupation. Well before, foreign Jews had been deprived of the French citizenship they had been granted; Jewish properties seized; Jewish children kicked out of schools. After the Vel d'Hiv, Zsazsa and I felt that we had to do something, but what? And how? So, we dropped a few hints to the concierge, a veteran of the 1914 war, to gauge his reaction. He caught on quickly. Turned out he was already active in a Résistance network. So we did our duty as good citizens and we helped the Résistance."

"Are you serious?"

"Totally. You have no idea how much we enjoyed it. No longer hiding at home, doing something for the country that had welcomed us so generously, but also doing something for us and for the future. Don't look so dubious. I didn't shoot anyone. I am far too old to play those games, but we hid several fugitives here, and my wife delivered messages for the network."

"But what if you had been caught? Had you thought about that?"

"Of course. What was the risk, after all? Dying a little sooner? You are a doctor; you know that at our age, death can happen at any moment. And had we been captured, we each had a cyanide pill."

Julius could only stare. At ease in his comfortable armchair, wearing a smoking jacket and slippers, his black hair once so thick now sparse and greying, Theo did not cut a heroic figure, yet the old man had taken incredible risks and was mentioning cyanide pills as if it was the most natural thing to have.

"You put me to shame," Julius sighed. "I did nothing."

"Don't be ridiculous. Me, I was not alone; I was part of a network that had the support of a large segment of the population. What could you have done in a country where antisemitism was accepted as a matter of course, where people couldn't care less about the fate of the Jews when they did not blame them for the ills that had befallen them? Who would have fought with you? For that matter, against whom? Did Romanians or Hungarians revolt against Germany? Have you forgotten that they had all passed the same legislation against the Jews? The only solution was to get away—for those who could, of course. You should have left ages ago. When my wife comes back, I suppose you will explain why you didn't. Here, I was not alone; we were not alone. We were working with Résistance fighters, men and women from all walks of life struggling to get rid of the Germans and restore the honor and dignity of France. I found a meaning for my life. I even made friends, and my affairs were in order. Yuli, we see you as the son we never had. You know it. We made you our sole heir, with the stipulation that, heaven forbid, something happened to you, your children would inherit. How are they, by the way?"

"I wish I knew. I have no idea where they are and what they are doing. Doctor Gilles …"

"Your handsome dark-haired friend …"

"If you wish. She used to pass on news covertly. But she is in jail, on suspicion of collaboration. I can't believe it's true. In any case, she is the only one who knows where Elisabeth is, and my daughter is the only one who knows where her brother and sister are. Tomorrow, I shall present myself at the clinic in the hope that someone knows something. The problem is that Elisabeth never told me her husband's name!"

"Don't worry. We were at her wedding. It's doctor Metzger. Benjamin Metzger. Your daughter swore us to secrecy because he is not Jewish and she was afraid you would disapprove. I attempted to reassure her since I was convinced you wouldn't care, but she would not listen. We kept in touch as long as she was in Paris. When her husband was called up, he urged her to go to the south of France where she would be safer. A card posted in Poitiers a year ago, maybe two, informed us of the birth of a little boy."

"Emile. Marie-Christine—Doctor Gilles—found a way to pass on the news. So Elisabeth married Metzger! I met him, you know, the first time I came to the clinic with her.

He was about to enter his fifth and last year at med school and was already working at the clinic. Marie-Christine asked him to help Elisabeth through the registration process. He seemed nice enough. Did they get married in church? His family did not object?"

"No, they just went for a civil ceremony. Both his parents are dead. He is indeed a nice man besides being head over heels in love."

"What about André?"

Theo made a face.

"We saw him a lot during his studies; he used to come for dinner on Friday evenings. After that ... he went out a lot, made new friends, met girls. We saw him less and less. I heard he had moved, and his visits stopped altogether. Mind you, if he had had problems, I am sure he would have contacted us. Don't look like that. A couple of old people are of no interest when you are that age. Anyway, it's nothing to do with you. Ah! Here is Zsazsa calling. Give me your arm and let's have dinner."

Madame Castan had done wonders at the short notice. It was a truly festive meal: traditional Hungarian cherry soup and roast chicken in sweet paprika sauce—both well remembered and well-loved by Julius.

"Zsazsa, you are a wonder! How did you ..."

She did not let him finish.

"Cherries I have the year round. I bottle them in the spring. And I happened to have a chicken in the refrigerator. Now, let's go back to the salon. I shall take care of the dishes later. We want to know everything."

They went to bed well after midnight. There was so much to be told! Lily had left them alone after dinner, saying that she was tired; besides, she believed Julius and their hosts would prefer to speak Hungarian.

Slowly but painfully, Julius had begun his tale, stopping at times to take a sip of the French cognac reverently opened by Theo. He was looking inwards as he revived the dark days ushered by the Hungarian takeover of Oradea in 1940. Jewish property seized, Jews forbidden to be civil servants, the humiliation of the yellow star. Clients he had known for years, whose lives he had saved, or whose children he had ushered into the world, crossing the street in order not to have to acknowledge him. The plans of escape he had made, and his wife refusing to leave. Her absurd conviction that they would be spared because of their standing in society. The faithful Sandor, his childhood friend, risking his life to supply them with food. The last weeks before the Germans arrived, led by a colonel whose sinister reputation spread dread through the community. Adolf Eichmann arrogantly paced the streets of the city. Jews were ordered to go to assembly points prior to being dispatched to an unknown destination. The last night in the flat. A frightened Magda who understood too late what was about to happen and who had begged his pardon. The morning. Magda intervening to protect a terrified girl molested by a German officer. Magda being shot dead by the officer. Julius, saved because he was not there, having gone back to his neighbor's flat, to give Dr. Kadar the address of the clinic and ask him to inform Dr. Gilles of what was happening so she could tell the children. Kadar physically prevented him from rushing to his wife's body; Kadar went instead and closed Magda's eyes. The little group of shocked Jews were shepherded by the Germans who had failed to notice that one of the men on their list was missing.

Later, there was the perilous journey through the town. Doctor Matthias, wearing a suit without the yellow star, was poorly disguised by an old felt hat and horn-rimmed spectacles, his medical bag in one hand and a wooden cane in the other, braving the nearly empty streets. No one stopped him. Then, the lengthy walk to Sandor's farm. Wrenching farewells and flight. Weeks of trudging through war-torn countries. Joining a band of gypsies. Then a month of fighting with partisans. Going through Italy. Finally, arriving safely in Geneva at last.

When he raised his head, Zsazsa was crying and Theo was looking every single one of his 80 years.

5

DOCTOR GILLES' CLINIC

THE SUN FROM THE DAY BEFORE was long gone, and driven by strong winds, angry clouds rushed south. The tweed coat bought in Geneva was doing a good job of keeping the cold out, and Theo's sturdy umbrella would take care of the rain if it came. Julius Matthias could not explain why he didn't take his car for that fateful meeting. Was it because he was afraid that he would get lost, or that there would be nowhere to park? So, he walked, using an old street map Theo had provided and thoughtfully marked the route in red, adding that it should not take more than half an hour. Julius felt unsettled, torn between the thought that either it would be a waste of time and that the clinic would be closed now that the owner had been jailed or though it was still functioning, no one in the clinic would know anything about his daughter's fate.

Dare he dream of finding Elisabeth back in Paris now that it had been liberated, perhaps doing her rounds? Not really. What was strange was that he felt apprehensive. He could not fathom why. His papers were in order; he had slept in a good bed, in the house of his oldest and dearest friends, who had assured him more than once that he was welcome to stay with them as long as he wished. He had not slept well, not because he was afraid of some unseen foe, but because Lily was asleep in the room next to him and he had to fight the urge to join her. He had woken up to the tantalizing smell of coffee and sweet and spicy Hungarian rolls that Zsazsa had just taken out of the oven. She had remembered how fond he was of that delicacy and had prepared the dough before going to bed. He embraced her, moved beyond words, and sat down. Minutes later, Theo came in, arguing with Lily, fully dressed and carrying her knapsack, who said she just wanted to thank him and his wife for their hospitality and leave. He, of course, wanted none of it. Julius asked what her hurry was, but it was Zsazsa who won the day.

"Child, you can't possibly go out like that. I shall make an appointment with my hairdresser; I am sure she can fit you in this morning. What? Your papers are not in order? Theo will get you a new set so that you can go anywhere without fear. It will only take a few days."

Lily exchanged a helpless glance with Julius and let herself be coaxed into a chair while the two old people fussed about her and made plans.

As he got ready to leave, the flat was turning into a very hive of activity. Theo was getting ready to call a so-called engraver, whose real specialty was providing, at a price of course, ration books, without which nothing could be bought, for his guests, as well as a new identity card for Lily; his wife was planning a visit to the hairdresser, followed by a trip to her seamstress. Theo would then accompany the young woman to the forger's workshop.

Julius took the old lady aside and uselessly tried to tamper her enthusiasm, reminding her that she and her husband should take it easy at their age.

"Take it easy! Dear Yuli," she exploded. "If you only knew! When we heard what had happened to the Jews of Nagyvarad, the shock was so terrible … you understand, we had been so sure that you would arrive in Paris one day in search of your children, and it was that hope that gave us the strength to go on. When it appeared that all was lost, that you had been sent to the camps with Magda, we felt that it was the end, that there was nothing left to live for. For two days, we stayed at home, not even eating. That's when Theo came to me. He was deadly pale. He said, 'Darling, I can't take it anymore. Let's die together tonight. We have our pills; the concierge has the keys. He will find us tomorrow. He will know what to do. I gave him instructions a long time ago.'

"Yuli, I was tempted, sorely tempted. But I could not. 'Theo, dearest Theo, we can't do that. Imagine that our Yuli managed to survive that hell. He will need us, need a home, need our friendship to start to live again.' Thank goodness he listened to me. Let us take care of you and of that charming girl. I see the way you look at her. Don't deny it. Don't worry. We shan't overdo it. What? Don't go all sentimental on me, Julius Matthias. We are alive and well and we shall enjoy having you and your young lady around. Besides, now we have a doctor in the house, right?"

There was no denying that the Castans appeared to be enjoying the excitement. Theo had dressed carefully, and Julius noted that he still inserted lifts in his shoes to gain a few inches.

He shrugged helplessly and left.

Suddenly, he was in front of the clinic, noting the impact of the bullets on the handsome façade and the imposing wrought-iron door, which was left open, with no one guarding to check visitors. The hall was dusty, and the place was strangely silent, not the quiet of a well-run establishment but one with a lack of activity.

"We are not accepting new patients," said the bespectacled and severe-looking woman at the reception. Busy checking files, she had not raised her head.

"Good morning. I am Doctor Julius Matthias and I wish to talk to Doctor Gilles," he said.

She looked at him with interest and picked up her phone.

"I have here a Doctor Matthias who wishes to see Doctor Gilles," she said. Then she wrote something on an open file and asked him to come with her. He followed, not a little surprised. Had Marie-Christine been released? He would have loved to believe it. What was more likely was since he had presented himself as a doctor, one of the medical staff had been contacted. Someone who might have information on the two doctors who had worked there before the war.

He was led to a small salon and asked to wait.

"You should have made an appointment, or called to announce your visit," he was told coldly. "Be patient, it may take a while."

She left without offering him a glass of water or a cup of coffee. He was about to take out the first of the two mysteries that he'd bought in Geneva when he had a second look at his surroundings. He was not mistaken. This was the very room he had been taken to when he first came to the clinic with his daughter in 1933. Then, he had been impressed by the understated elegance of what was, in fact, a waiting room. Today, it was shabby and dusty; the quality paintings had been taken off the walls, the handsome sculptures were missing. The gilt chairs had lost their luster and the drapes were in need of a good cleaning. The housekeeper must have been let go now that the place was closed. He sighed, remembering that first meeting with Marie-Christine since they parted in June 1913, the day they had both graduated from the Vienna School of Medicine. He was the youngest of the class; she was stunning in the deceptively simple black dress from the House of Worth especially ordered from Paris. During the graduation ceremony, she seemingly had eyes only for her noble husband, who had left his castle at dawn to arrive in time; seated in the front row, he applauded politely. Yet it was in the arms of Julius that the sultry countess had spent the preceding night.

Julius sat down. So his daughter had married Benjamin Metzger! Julius tried to remember what he looked like. Of medium height, with no remarkable features, he had not appeared overjoyed at the idea of shepherding a foreign-sounding young girl around. If truth be told, Julius had paid him scant attention. He gazed in wonder at Marie-Christine, the temptress, who had taught him new and daring ways of lovemaking … She must have felt the same way, since barely one hour later, they were in bed in her flat, which was conveniently close by. They had discovered that time had not diminished their mutual hunger and enjoyment. They had been lovers but love had never been a factor in their relationship a daring concept at the time. He found himself comparing Lily's juvenile silhouette with the more mature allure of Marie-Christine until a twinge of conscience reminded him of his friend's plight and of the reason he was there. More than a quarter of an hour had passed when he realized that whoever had been called was coming from somewhere else and settled down for a long wait. He was soon caught in "The Mystery in the Yellow Room," the improbable adventures of a journalist turned sleuth before the First World War. It was all very civilized, with no hint of things to come.

When the door opened at last, it was to let in two men—a police officer and a civilian. They chose two armchairs facing his and stared at him without saying a word. If it was an attempt at intimidation, it did not work. Julius observed them in turn. Tall and overweight, the policeman appeared to be in his fifties, with a hard face and a cynical sneer. At least ten years younger, the other wore a wrinkled suit too big for him and had the pale complexion and hesitant walk of someone just out of hospital. The former was the first to speak.

"I am Inspector Moreau. When did you last see the Gilles woman? And what exactly were you doing with her?"

His tone was as hostile as his words, reminding Julius of the way Hungarian officials used to address him. He sent a silent blessing to Dr. Hofstad, who had warned him and to his clerk who had somehow gotten hold of the telegram before it fell into the wrong hands.

"I saw Doctor Gilles for the last time in August 1933. I don't understand. Why isn't she here?"

"Don't play the fool," Moreau said, raising his voice. "Here, I ask the questions, and I did not ask when you met her, but when you last met her. Maybe you don't understand French? You would be more at ease with German?"

"I understand French well enough, thank you. And my mother tongue is Hungarian, not German. I repeat that I have not seen Dr. Gilles since August 1933."

"What happened? You quarreled?"

"Not at all. Give me two minutes to explain. It will save time for you and for me," replied Julius, who continued to speak without waiting for an answer. "I met Dr. Gilles at the School of Medicine of Vienna, in Austria, where we both studied. We graduated in 1913, and I went back to my hometown of Nagyvarad in Hungary."

"One moment. Your papers, please." The other man requested.

"And you are?"

"Call me Dupont; that will do." The officer then examined the passport proffered. "You pretend to be Hungarian, but this is a Romanian document!" he exclaimed.

Julius sighed.

"The world has changed, Mr. Dupont. I was born in 1890 in Nagyvarad, a Transylvanian town, part of the Austro-Hungarian empire. Hungary was on the losing side during the last war and was deprived of Transylvania by the Versailles treaty. Nagyvarad became Oradea. In 1940, Hungary, Germany's ally, took back the town."

"But you, though Hungarian, are not a supporter of Germany?"

"I am not."

"Let us see if I have it correctly," mused Dupont, though Julius was sure that it was not his name. "You went back home in 1913 and did not contact your erstwhile comrade until you are miraculously reunited in Paris? When and how did you discover where she was?"

His tone was more interested than hostile.

"A mere fluke. I noticed her name in an advertisement for her establishment. I believe it was in 1928 or 1929."

"So, you rushed to see her? Why?"

"Not at all. I sent her a polite letter of congratulations, she answered, and we kept an erratic correspondence."

"When did you decide to come after all, and why?"

"In 1931 or 32. My daughter Elisabeth wanted to study medicine; she chose Paris because bilateral agreements made it possible for Romanians to study in France. I wrote to my colleague, hoping she would be willing to help Elisabeth get accepted by the School of Medicine. She said she would do it gladly. My daughter was accepted; I accompanied her to Paris in August 1933 to settle her in. We went together to meet Dr. Gilles—as a matter of fact in this very room. She promised to take care of Elisabeth and indeed gave her employment when she graduated."

"I see. So now you are seeking a job too?"

"Absolutely not. I hope she can tell me where my daughter is."

"You do not have her address? You have quarreled?"

The policeman had taken his passport and was rifling through the pages, obviously not believing a word of what Julius was saying.

"We did not quarrel. My daughter left Paris for the south of France in June 1940, as did thousands of Frenchmen, I've been told. Putting her address in a letter would not have been prudent. Mail was being opened in my country as it was in yours, I believe. Dr. Gilles was kind enough to serve as a go-between. She would transmit messages from my daughter under the guise of information about a patient, and I would do the same. In fact, I was hoping to see Elisabeth here now that Paris has been liberated."

"Why didn't she write to you since there's no danger anymore?"

"No danger? Here maybe. My poor country is still ravaged by the war. Russia has not been able to defeat the Hungarian army; besides, when I managed to flee last May, the Allied forces hadn't yet landed in Normandy. Since then, I have crossed half of Europe on foot before reaching Geneva. Elisabeth had no way of contacting me."

"Mr. Matthias, I have been in charge of the Gilles affair for some weeks and have seen no mention of a Doctor Elisabeth Matthias in the clinic register."

"Well, she is obviously not back. She should be on the pre-war lists, either under her maiden name, or, since she married Doctor Benjamin Metzger, under …"

"That name is not on the list either."

"Not even on the pre-war register?"

"Don't tell us how to do our job, Matthias. This establishment does not employ a large staff, and I have a good memory of names." Dupont appeared to be losing patience. "Do you want to change your story, or shall we continue the discussion in the police commissariat?"

"I have told you the truth. Maybe Dr. Gilles erased the names to protect …"

"Enough!"

The policeman stood up.

"According to your passport, you arrived in France on the morning of September 30th. When did you arrive in Paris?"

"Yesterday evening."

"October 1st? Then you spent a night on the way?"

"Yes, in Saulieu."

"What hotel?"

"I stayed at a friend's house."

"He has a name, that friend? A phone number?"

"Langlois. Henri Langlois. I have the number in my wallet. Here it is."

Moreau and Dupont exchanged glances and the latter picked up the phone on the table and asked reception to connect him.

"Langlois?" Commandant Dutertre speaking.

I was right, thought Julius, consigning to memory the name and rank.

"Corporal Langlois at your service, Commandant. I know I was supposed to go back to the regiment this morning, but Captain Barois gave me an extra day to recuperate from my wound."

He was talking so loudly that Julius heard every word, as did the inspector.

"I am calling about another matter. Do you know Doctor Matthias?"

"Doctor Matthias? A hero! A true hero! He saved my life, Commandant. I hope he gets a medal. There was this German deserter. I was wounded, and he was about to finish me off when the doctor, a civilian, adjusted his gun, cool as you please, and shot him right between the eyes! And then he took care of my comrade who was bleeding like … I mean, he would have died if Doctor Matthias had not stopped the bleeding!"

"Corporal, could you describe this Doctor Matthias for me?"

"Describe?" Langlois was nonplussed. "Distinguished looking, smartly dressed, fiftyish or younger, tall, blue eyes, and blond hair with a touch of grey."

"Very well. What regiment are you from? Thank you and speedy recovery."

Dutertre turned back to Julius.

"Doctor Matthias, I am beginning to believe that you have nothing to do with what has happened. The registers may have been tampered with as you suggest. Thank you for your patience. You are free to go."

Julius breathed more easily. Lily, who had saved his life two days ago, had rescued him again.

"Listen, I still don't know where my daughter is. Could it be possible for me to see Dr. Gilles and ask whether she has some information," he risked.

"Out of the question!" The policeman, who was about to leave, was adamant. "You don't seem to understand. The woman has been charged with collaboration with the enemy and could get the death penalty."

"The death penalty!"

"My friend," said Dutertre, "you tell us you have not received any letter from your daughter since the war started; what news you had was from Gilles. I am afraid she was lying. She may have betrayed your daughter immediately, as she betrayed others."

"It is not possible! There must be a mistake!"

"Come on. In times of war nothing is impossible. People who seem to lead a blameless life are suddenly doing unspeakable things."

"Maybe, but not Doctor Gilles. I have known her for too long. How can you be so sure that she is guilty? I have barely been in France two days, but I have already heard that the situation is sometimes being used for settling accounts and many unfortunates are being falsely accused."

"Indeed. That is not the case here. We have evidence. Irrefutable evidence. Doctor Matthias, I have seen with my own eyes the proof of her betrayal and was nearly caught because of it."

Turning to his colleague, who hovered impatiently by the door, he added: "Moreau, we are both satisfied with the doctor's explications. There is nothing more for you to do here. Nevertheless, I shall stay a few more minutes. Matthias has come far enough to be entitled to some explanation, and even more so after what Corporal Langlois told us."

The inspector shrugged.

"If you want to waste your time, go ahead. I shall catch up with you later."

The commandant rubbed his eyes before beginning. "Doctor Matthias, like most Frenchmen, I was drafted, and I fought as best I could. I had the good fortune not to be taken prisoner and was sent home when the armistice was signed. Once back in Paris, it did not take long for me to see that it was my duty to keep on fighting the enemy. I was able to clandestinely reach the so-called free zone, the southern part of France not under occupation. You may have heard about the Résistance. We were not many at first, and we lacked weapons. Soon, however, more and more volunteers joined us. We did what we could, sabotaging railway tracks and passing information to the allies. After 1942, when the Germans took over the south as well, we ambushed them whenever we could. Our people were familiar with the terrain. Anyway, after the Normandy landing last June, we could afford to move more openly, and we harassed the retreating German troops. We suffered heavy losses, of course. They had reconnaissance planes and were helped by a few die-hard collaborators. In August, something went wrong with one of our operations. They knew we were coming. Our own doctor was badly wounded. He called himself Louis Lenormand. That was not his real name, of course. We were all using aliases for safety.

Louis told us that he had been able to break out of the *stalag*—the German prisoner camp where he had been taken after his capture. Somehow, he made it back to France and to the free zone where his wife had settled after fleeing Paris. You have heard about the *exode*, right? He knew the Germans were looking for him, so he visited her secretly, whenever he could. One day, two or three years ago, he told us he had not been careful enough, and seeing how worried we were, he added that what he meant was that his wife was pregnant and that it could not have happened at a worse time. I told him jokingly that, being a doctor, he should be able to deal with it, but he replied that his wife was dead set against abortions and that he was not too keen on them himself. I asked whether she was a devout catholic, but he laughed loudly, without answering, and never referred to the subject again. Anyway, he was badly wounded in August, as I said, but managed to get a message through to her, so she came to the place where we had him hidden. That's when we heard that she was a doctor as well. He called her Donna, but it couldn't have been her name."

Julius stopped breathing. A small child, two doctors, one calling herself Donna, his aunt's name who had married his father after the death of her sister, the mother of Julius and Anna, and who had raised the two of them; Donna whom their children called grandmother ... no, it could not be true, just a strange coincidence! Dutertre, who had not noticed his shock, was still talking.

"Donna saw immediately that he had to be taken to hospital without delay or he would remain paralyzed. The problem was that there were Germans everywhere and they were checking all the hospitals of the region. So she decided to call on a colleague in Paris she felt she could trust: your doctor, Gilles. I was present when she phoned her, heard how they were planning to transport him. Gilles would send her own driver, in uniform, by train to Lyon with the necessary documents to take charge of the wounded man. Only the two of them knew all the details. I can see her, smiling despite her apprehension and assuring me that it would be safe, that she had worked for that woman and that she was completely trustworthy.

"In the morning, we set out for the train station. Louis was in a wheelchair, dressed as a priest, a huge bandage covering most of his face. She was pushing the chair, dressed as a nurse. She was not supposed to go with him; it would have been too risky. A driver was indeed waiting. She did not recognize him, but he held up a big sign with the name "Father Christopher" the agreed password known only to the two of them. Donna said that the sign was written in her friend's writing. She walked up to him, pushing the wheelchair. Suddenly, he let go of the sign and grabbed her. A German officer joined him as a black van careened in. She was pushed inside, together with Louis, while a second officer who had seen me with the couple started firing at me. I was hit—two bullets in the chest and one in the leg. I shall never understand how I managed to turn the corner at a run before collapsing. I don't remember what happened next. I woke up in a convent's infirmary two days later. The Sisters told me I had been left at their door. Apparently, I had been very lucky. There had been no internal damage, and the bullet had gone through the fleshy part of my leg. I was nursed back to health, and a month later, I returned to my unit. Someone told me that the Germans must have been in a hurry because they had not tried to chase me. We kept on fighting. There was no point in finding the Gilles woman as long as the Germans were in Paris; besides, we only knew her last name, and I wasn't sure whether her establishment was in her name.

Nothing was done until Paris was liberated in late August and I came to investigate with some of the men from our unit. You can't imagine the number of "Gilles" in the phone book. It never occurred to us that the place we were looking for was a beauty clinic. We found it by mid-September. We interrogated the driver first, but he was not the man I had seen in Lyon. He said he knew nothing, but later cracked under pressure and admitted that he had been arrested by the Gestapo as he was about to board the train. They took the sign from him. He was released in the evening and warned that he was to say that there had been no one at the Lyon station. Should he say anything else, he would be rearrested and deported. I assume it was done to protect the woman, since she was the only one who knew about the operation. When we confronted her, she tried to pretend that she had no idea what we were talking about. I pressed her with details, and when she understood that the game was up, she fainted. When she came to, she refused to say anything.

Julius closed his eyes, his worst fears realized.

"Did you learn what happened to them? To Louis? To Donna?"

"I am afraid I did. Our poor comrade died three days later. They had tortured him in vain to get him to speak. Donna was deported in the last convoy to leave Paris on August 17, two days before the start of the battle for the liberation of the town. You look upset, my friend. You can't believe the woman could be capable of such a monstrous betrayal?"

"Just one more question," said Julius, reeling from the shock and wondering if he was about to faint for the first time in his life. "Do you know their true names?"

"Unfortunately, I don't. In the Résistance, we learned not to ask questions and to try to know as little as possible about the background of our comrades. Under torture, even the bravest can sometimes succumb. He was taken in as "Louis Lenormand," the name on his false documents, and it was under this name that he was buried. I understand that they had her down as "Donna Lenormand." Gilles won't reveal their true identity."

Julius shook his head despairingly.

"Commandant, please listen to me. I have to talk to Dr. Gilles, urgently. I am afraid that we are talking about my daughter Elisabeth and her husband, Doctor Benjamin Metzger. No, no please, listen. Both worked at the clinic before the war. Both were convinced they could trust Doctor Gilles. Do you seriously think there could be another doctor couple in the same situation? Wait, I have a picture of my daughter here."

He withdrew a yellowing photo from his wallet, taken in 1933 as they were about to embark on their voyage to France. Standing next to her smiling older brother in flannel trousers, Elisabeth, wearing a calf-length summer dress, looked radiant.

"My God! It is her! Dutertre was dumbstruck. My friend, I am afraid that you are right. Why then do you still wish to see that woman? What can she tell you about the fate of someone she betrayed so cruelly?"

"Nothing. My son-in-law is dead; my daughter ..." he blew his nose and continued. "My daughter has been deported. There remains one thing I can and must do for her: find her son. My grandson. He must be about two. It is for his sake that she would not reveal her name. Now, on that day she was taken by the Germans, she was expecting to be able to return home in the evening. What happened when she did not? Who is taking care of him? I am all he has, Commandant. I have to find him, give him a home. If Elisabeth is alive, she depends on me to do it; and if she is dead, it is my sacred duty to do so. Doctor Gilles has to know something. I have to believe it."

"Doctor Matthias," there was real compassion in Dutertre's voice. "First, I have to receive confirmation that the Lenormands are indeed the Metzgers. It could take time."

"On the contrary, it should be simple. They both studied at the Paris School of Medicine. They have a file there, photos. You have seen them both. It won't take a minute."

"My friend, today nothing is simple. Finding the files will take time. I shall start the ball rolling today. Then, I shall set about arranging a visit. The odds are not great. Dr. Gilles has not been tried yet, but they will ask for the death penalty. What makes you think she would talk to you?"

Julius drew his hand through his hair. "Are you sure you are not making a terrible mistake? If it was Dr. Gilles who betrayed my daughter and her husband, how is it that the Germans did not know their true identities? That she was deported under a name that is not hers? Donna told you she had worked for Doctor Gilles. Why wasn't her name on the register as Elisabeth Matthias or Elisabeth Metzger? I am convinced Madame Gilles erased her name and that of her husband to protect them. I am convinced that she fainted when you confronted her because she did not know what had happened until you told her. I am convinced she was betrayed."

"Why not say so, then. Why not claim she is innocent?"

"I don't know. Maybe she was afraid she would not be believed. She will tell me."

"I understand you desperately want to believe your friend is innocent, but tell me this: if she did not betray your daughter, how come she was not arrested by the Germans? They had already arrested her chauffeur, they knew about the plot, knew she had agreed to help two Résistance fighters—two terrorists, in their view—and was sending her own driver to bring back the wounded 'terrorist.' At the time, people were arrested and deported for far less!"

"I have been wondering about that. What if they had tapped her phone? What if they wanted to keep on doing so in the hope that she would lead them to other terrorists or provide them with useful information?"

"My friend, you are clutching at straws. I shall do what I promised you, with no great hope of success. That woman has been incredibly lucky. Especially since, according to what we were told by the staff, German officers and their women used to avail themselves of her establishment. That alone would have been grounds for a long sentence. She could have been executed without a trial. It has happened before."

"All I ask is a chance to see her for a few minutes. Nothing else. If she knows something, she will tell me. You may have someone accompany me in order to make sure we are not trading secrets."

"Leave me your address and telephone number, but don't hold your breath."

"Can't I call you?"

"I am sorry. I have no fixed office yet. But I will get in touch if I have news."

"Thank you."

"I wish you luck, doctor."

Julius walked out in a daze. His son-in-law was dead, his daughter deported; yet, he could not believe that Marie-Christine had acted so vilely. About to say that her two sons from her late Austrian husband served under the German flag, and they were probably the "German officers" who visited her establishment, Julius had wisely kept silent. He had also not told the commandant that he had another reason to believe that his friend was not guilty. "Donna Lenormand" had been deported as a Résistance fighter. The Germans had no reason to suspect her of being Jewish. Marie-Christine, who was well aware of the fact, could have refused to talk in order not to divulge that information. An indiscretion, a leak, and the Germans would learn the truth. It could seal the fate of his daughter. Meanwhile, he must not lose hope. An allied victory appeared to be close; Elisabeth could survive. He would not let himself contemplate in what condition she would come back, even less what she was enduring. What had Zsazsa said? She and her husband had pledged to be strong to help him should he come back. Well, that's what he had to do, Julius told himself, be strong to help his daughter. But first, find the child.

6

THE TWO POPES

A GREY DAY FILTERED THROUGH a window opening onto the courtyard. Seated on the sofa in the small room Madame Castan called her boudoir, Lily was waiting for her hostess to come back from whatever she was doing next door. Lily felt adrift and not a little embarrassed by what she had done. She had slept badly, waking several times, wondering how she could have behaved in such a way with someone she had met barely 24 hours earlier. It was true that she was still in a state of shock. She had killed a man and kept on reliving those fraught few minutes—no, seconds. Instead of going into hiding when she heard shots, gun in hand, she had foolishly rushed over. There was Doctor Matthias, frozen as a deer caught in the headlights, while the German aimed his weapon. She had fired first, deliberately going for his head and killing him on the spot. It hadn't been her first kill, but this time, she hadn't had a choice. It had brought back memories. She had drunk a little too much to drive them away. It had not quite worked and so … to think that she had been wary of the man at first! He was too rich, too sure of himself, too "old Europe," too old even. She could try to tell herself that alcohol had dimmed her inhibitions, but she knew what she was doing and had taken the first step. Of course, there had been no one since David's death.

In the end, it had happened. Squirming in her narrow bed, she had wondered what he had told the Castans. Had he boasted of his good fortune? In the morning, fully dressed and ready to go, she had been made to sit down and Madame Castan had put a bowl of steaming coffee and two fun-ny-looking rolls in front of her. She had been reluctant to meet Julius' eyes, fearing she'd see contempt or indifference; instead, there was sympathy, but also warmth. And so she had let their host persuade her to stay a little longer. No one was waiting for her in Marseilles, and she did not know what kind of welcome she would get from her brother-in-law. It did not stop her from wondering what she was doing in this comfortable flat that her husband, a dedicated commu-nist, would have called sneeringly "bourgeois," or worse, "petit-bourgeois." Why such a huge place for a couple of old people living alone? Monsieur Castan—she could not bring herself to call him Theo as he had asked her to do— had explained that he was still working when they bought it. Needing an office and a waiting room, he had taken the two flats on the floor. Now that he was retired, the smaller flat had become a nearly independent unit used by visiting friends. It comprised two bedrooms, a bathroom, a sitting room, and even a small kitchen. She sighed. Yes, she would not mind staying a little longer to try to figure out what the future held in store for her. Her parents were both dead; strangers were now living in the house where she had been born and had grown up. Her uncle had wisely left in time and had settled in Argentina, a country which did not appeal to her. Would she ever be able to go home? Would she want to now that David was dead? When the war was over and the country free? Questions, questions … Strange how her life had been turned topsy-turvy.

To fulfill her husband's dying wishes, she had gone to rescue Rosa, her mother-in-law. She reached her town barely ahead of the Germans. Fleeing had become impossible. Jews were being rounded up and ordered to assemble in the main square. Rosa had pleaded with her to hide, and seeing her hesitation, had embraced her.

"May God bless you for coming so courageously," she had said. "Now you must think of yourself. I will be leaving with my friends, my neighbors. Whatever awaits us may not be too bad. But you—you are not from here. You do not speak the language. Nobody knows that you came. You aren't on the community register. Save yourself."

When the Germans arrived to take the old woman, they had looted the house but failed to see the visitor hunkered down under a pile of rubbish in the basement. Gripping her gun and determined to fight to the end, she had heard them moving from room to room. Then, the door had opened; a shadow briefly appeared on the wall before receding. The soldiers left. She waited two days, thirsty and starving, before the intense quiet had lured her into leaving her hiding place. Everything had been ransacked and there was nothing to eat. Leaning over the kitchen sink, she drank and drank from the faucet. Then, she took a makeshift shower in the tiny bathroom, shivering under the bitterly cold water. As night fell, she picked up her knapsack and stepped outside. Creeping in the shadows, she crossed the desolate Jewish Quarter where a few dogs were still waiting for their masters to return. She had been lucky. As she was leaving the town, she spied a table laid for supper through an open window. She was so hungry that she ran across the street, vaulted into the room, and grabbed two big loaves of bread and a hunk of cheese. No one heard her; there had been no disturbance. Nevertheless, she ran and ran to put the greatest possible distance between her and the site of her theft. At dawn, she stumbled upon a shepherd's hut, empty in that season, and had pounced on the food. She slept blissfully and woke up when dusk had fallen. Hiding during the days, walking at night through a region she was not familiar with, she marched steadily, looking to the stars to chart her way, blessing the years spent in youth movements which had taught her that skill.

Her original plan had been to bring Rosa to Marseilles, where David's brother, Simon, lived with his family, and it was there that she was going for lack of any other option. She intended to travel through Macedonia, not the fastest route, but probably safer since partisans controlled most of it. The smuggler who helped her cross the border attempted to molest her after having been paid; she brandished her weapon and he ran away, cursing wildly. It took her nearly a year to reach Geneva, after months of trudging through roads filled with fugitives and deserters. More than once, she had to use her gun to discourage a man who thought that a pretty young woman would be easy prey. At one point, she had cut off her hair and started dressing as a man.

One day, she encountered four women marching together and joined them. Who were they and what their story was, she never knew. Nobody asked questions, and no one volunteered details. They traveled for several weeks, foraging through a countryside devastated by the war or buying food whenever they found some for sale. The harsh winter of 1943, with its icy rains and biting winds, forced them to take shelter in a deserted village partially bombed to rubble. Huddled in one of the few houses which still had a roof, they burned furniture to keep warm and ate whatever they could find. Every morning, they went through deserted living quarters in search of anything that could be eaten. The villagers had not been able to take everything, and each discovery was hailed by cries of happiness: tins forgotten at the back of a kitchen cabinet, sacks of potatoes miraculously untouched in a cellar. On one unforgettable morning, they heard four hens and a rooster that must have fled during the bombing and come back, settling in the roofless church.

The women lived in remarkable harmony, perhaps because there was no man to fight over, or because they lacked a common language, and therefore, never quarreled. They left the village when the thaw set in. One woman quit shortly after, soon replaced by another who appeared out of nowhere. Days became a blur. At the end of June, Lily caught a cold that soon turned into pneumonia, perhaps as a result of months of deprivation. Her comrades left her at the entrance to a convent in northern Italy where she stayed for a month, nursed back to health by the Sisters who thought she was French.

Getting back on the road was hard. A smuggler got her through the Swiss border in exchange for the little money she had left. Tired and desperate, she remembered her grandmother's old friend Dvora Lea Zerner, who lived in Geneva. The two had corresponded for years. Lily had informed the woman when her grandmother had died and had received a touching letter of condolence. She thought Dvora Lea's house was situated on rue Saint Georges. Somehow, she found the street, and the impressive Zerner mansion located opposite a synagogue. Yet, it took every ounce of determination she still possessed to ring the bell. A glance at a shop window had revealed a bedraggled young woman in wrinkled clothes, a rucksack on her back.

She never should have hesitated. The first surprise over, Dvora Lea welcomed her with open arms and offered to host her as long as she wished. She "loaned" her more suitable clothes, pretending to have found them in her wardrobe, though they appeared brand new, and bought her two pairs of shoes. Sleeping in comfort and eating her fill for the first time in nearly a year, Lily had let herself be cocooned in the banker's house. Meanwhile, her hostess submitted her to a discrete form of inquisition about her family situation and what she intended to do. She had answered readily, having nothing to hide. She should have caught on sooner. As soon as she was fully back on her feet, Madame Zerner, all smiles, had told her that she no longer needed to fear about her future; a suitable match had been found for her. Thunderstruck, Lily had mumbled that she was a widow with no money and could not bear children; Dvora Lea had replied that she came from a good family and spoke Polish, and that was all the man wanted.

"My son, Paul, and I will give you a small dowry so that you can buy your bridal gown, and we shall pay for the wedding. We've told our widowed friend Moshe about you, and after he saw you last Friday at the synagogue, he declared that it would be enough. He is extremely well-off. With six children already, he does not feel the need for more. Don't worry, he is barely fifty and not bad looking; you met him the other day when he came by to return a book I had allegedly forgotten at his sister's.

Lily turned her down on the spot, without trying to soften the blow. Dvora Lea had been upset. She'd thought she was doing her best for a penniless refugee and was offended by Lily's blunt refusal. It was too late for Lily to make amends; the time had come to leave that hospitable house. The son, Paul, had been more understanding and had insisted on not only giving her enough money to get by until she arrived at her brother-in-law's house, but also providing genuine papers, which did not come cheaply. All was set when fate intervened. Instead of finding herself on the road alone again, she was traveling with a man she did not know. Instead of being on her way to Marseilles, she was lingering in Paris, where complete strangers were treating her like a long-lost daughter. It was embarrassing. Her behavior—their behavior—in Saulieu had created a new situation, and she did not know how to cope.

"Here you are. You will look great in those when the seamstress has adjusted them for you. What do you say?"

She realized that Madame Castan was talking to her and came back to the present with a start. The old lady was showing her several elegant and pricy dresses.

"Madame, I cannot accept ..."

"Of course you can. You are Julius' friend, who is like a son to us, so you are part of the family."

"But Madame, I barely know him!"

"Don't call me Madame. If you can't manage Zsazsa, think of something else. Aunt maybe?"

Lily examined her hostess. Under a cap of well-cut white hair, two penetrating eyes made up for a rather indifferent face, crisscrossed by a thousand wrinkles. Slightly overweight and not doing anything to hide it, she still held herself with a straight back, despite her advancing years. She also wore flats, perhaps because she was taller than her husband.

"Calling you 'aunt' will not change the fact that I met Doctor Matthias less than three days ago!"

"So what? Yesterday you called him Julius. I shall be frank with you. Theo and I find you charming, and when Julius said he wanted you to stay a few more days, we immediately agreed."

"He asked you? Did he say why?"

"Well, he explained that Zerner had entrusted you to him and that he felt responsible for your wellbeing. He added that he felt deeply for someone who, like him, had gone through hard times. He is not happy about the idea of your setting out alone for Marseilles, where he feels you are not sure you'll be welcome."

"But Madame, I can't ... He doesn't owe me anything. I can't take advantage of your hospitality."

"I told you not to call me Madame. As for the rest ... Julius has not said a word, but Theo and I noticed that he likes you and you are not as indifferent to him as you would have me believe. Don't blush. You have both been widowed. Besides, we are happy to have some company. So, what do you think about these dresses?"

"Madame—aunt—it's too much. They are far too expensive and nearly new."

"Expensive, no doubt; new, far from it. I am too old to wear them anymore. Too old to show my legs. Come on. Help me put them in the suitcase. The taxi should be here any minute. It's a pity that you can't drive. We could have taken Julius' car."

"I can drive, but I don't have my license here. In any case, my papers are fake."

"Don't worry. The pope will take care of that. We have already made an appointment to get ration cards for you and Julius. He will see to the rest."

"The pope?" Lily thought she had misunderstood.

"That's what we call the forger. I mean, the engraver. He looks like a Russian orthodox priest. We call them "popes" in French for some reason. He does not like to be called a forger. Be careful, he is not Jewish and does not know that we are. These days everyone is hiding something. He is a White Russian who passed himself off as an orthodox priest during the war. Ration cards are his specialty; they are in great demand and are his main source of income. He also does fake documents, more authentic than real ones. Though I don't understand why you can't use your name now. Here, you are safe."

Lily took a deep breath and looked at her steadily.

"Madame Castan I can't because I am wanted for murder. I killed a man."

It was out. She had said it. She was getting up to leave when her hostess put her hand on a shoulder. Far from being shocked, she gave her a smile of encouragement.

"You killed a man! That must have taken a lot of courage. This is not about the German Julius told us about, I assume. Were you defending yourself? Fighting for your country?"

"It's not that simple. The man I killed had been one of ours. A childhood friend of David's, my husband. I knew him well. He was caught, taken prisoner, roughly treated, and even threatened with hanging. To save himself, he swore he was innocent, gave them my husband's name, provided details … They must have believed him since they let him go. Then, of course, they came for David, who refused to speak. He was the one they hung like a common criminal. I came face to face with that traitor one night. I had a gun. I fired. My only regret is that he didn't suffer."

She closed her eyes, replaying the events of that August night in slow motion. It had been very hot; there was a full moon in a cloudless sky. One month had gone by since David's death; that day in the morning, a little band of friends assembled at his grave for the traditional prayer. One of them told her the truth. David had not fallen into a trap as she'd been led to believe. He had been betrayed by one of them, who was conspicuously absent. She was assured the traitor would not escape retribution. It was just a question of time. That night, sleep had eluded her. She went out and started to walk aimlessly, thinking of her husband, a stocky young man, not very tall, and not precisely handsome, but certainly full of life. Always ready to plunge heedlessly into action without caring about consequences. The day before his arrest, they had had a terrible quarrel. She had urged him to stop his clandestine activities, or at least act with greater caution. He had reacted badly, lashing out at her.

"Had you given me a child, I might have been more prudent. But you haven't been able to, so just leave me alone, will you! At least I have some meaning to my existence."

He left, slamming the door behind him without giving her a chance to answer, without giving them a chance to make up. She never saw him alive again.

On that August night, as the first rays of dawn appeared, bone tired, she'd turned towards home as she heard someone coming, recognizing the man who had betrayed David, who did not know that she knew. He asked her where she was coming from so late, commenting with a coarse laugh that she was lucky to have found someone to warm her bed so quickly. Without thinking, she drew her weapon. (Perhaps he had opened his mouth too late to call for help?) When she fired, he fell heavily to the ground. In spite of the danger—the shot must have been heard in the quiet of the pre-dawn—she crouched over the body, taking out his fat wallet and expensive watch. Hopefully, the crime would be considered a robbery gone wrong. She burned the papers at home after throwing the watch and the empty wallet in the sea, but found herself unable to discard her weapon as prudence dictated, but it was David's—the 9.65 caliber gun made at the Enfield factory. He had been immensely proud of it and had been keen to teach her how to shoot and to take care of it. She cleaned and oiled it, oddly soothed by the thought that, by avenging him, she had made her peace with him. Two days later came the knock at the door. A kid out of breath told her that two officers were looking for her. She did not wait. Plans had been made long before, and in a matter of minutes, she disappeared through the secret well-camouflaged way out that David had devised. Then ...

A handkerchief was being pushed in her hand. She opened her eyes, surprised to feel the tears flowing. Madame Castan looked at her anxiously.

"My poor child! Are you sure the police are still after you? Won't they give you a medal?"

"It's only in France that the war is over. Where I come from, if I am caught, they could hang me like they hung my husband. Aren't you shocked?"

"Shocked? After a life of fleeing antisemitism and persecution? Five years of war—I mean the present war, not the other, though I also lived through that. After what the Germans did? What are they still doing? I wish I had killed one or two, believe me. Enough! Take the suitcase; the taxi must be waiting."

"Very well, but I shall pay the seamstress."

"Don't be ridiculous. Besides, there's no question of money. I shall give her nothing, not even ration tickets. She will get more on the black market from the evening dress I am bringing than the cost of the alterations she will make."

"Why on the black market?"

"That's what sells these days. Eggs, butter, cheese, meat, fruits, vegetables, and more. If you want to get good stuff, or stuff at all, you have to be ready to pay. Otherwise, you will be regretfully told that the grocer, or the butcher, or the clothier, has nothing left. You have no idea of the number of people who have gotten rich and will keep on getting rich as long as complete order is not restored. My seamstress has a select clientele of women who have money and don't ask questions."

Indeed, tenderly extracted from its three layers of tissue paper, the evening dress in simmering flame colored silk drew cries of admiration from Madam Gertrude, a plain woman in her fifties who assured Madam Castan that she would be happy to alter her clothes to fit her young niece. For the next hour, this young niece found herself forgetting the past, the present, and even her uncertain future. The two women turned her this way and that way, conferring, measuring, and sticking in pins while Lily let herself succumb to the forgotten pleasure of trying on elegant designs. When they left, she was wearing a dark blue dress of fine wool cinched with a large belt that had needed no alteration. Their next stop was a tiny tearoom where the owner, a lean Hungarian lady, rushed to embrace Madame Castan, and speaking Hungarian all the while, led them to an empty booth. The leather seats were cracked, the tablecloth mended in places, but the hot chocolate was thick and creamy, and the cake melted in the mouth in spite of its weird sounding name.

"You never had children?"

The question came as a welcome surprise. So Julius had not told everything to his friends!

"No. We were in no hurry when we got married; when we thought it was time to have a family, I became pregnant, but miscarried at six months. My fault. I was still going riding, took a bad fall, and nothing could be done to save the child. It was a little boy. David never forgave me. We were advised not to try again for at least two years. In fact, we waited too long, and it didn't work. We quarreled end-lessly, which did not help. David's brother told him to get a divorce and marry someone who would make him a father. It was horrible. If it hadn't been for the war ... You probably understand, having no children yourself."

"For me, it was different," replied the older woman sadly. "I desperately wanted children, but Theo did not, and made it clear that if I refused, there would be no wedding."

"I can't believe it!"

"He had his reasons. He comes from a rich family—very rich. His father was a well-known philanderer and was imprudent enough to let himself be caught publicly with a married woman. There was a terrible scandal, and his wife divorced him when Theo was still in infancy. She got cus-tody. His father died when he was only 12. In his will, he had stipulated that his son would only inherit his fortune when he married, much to the chagrin of his former wife, who thought she could lay her hands on some of the money. When Theo was 18, he fell in love with a girl of sixteen, a lovely child with the face of an angel. I saw the photo. Instead of telling him to wait a year or two, his mother pushed for a speedy marriage. The girl came from a humble home, and her parents enthusiastically welcomed such a splendid match. She must have gotten pregnant on her wedding night. She went into labor far too early. There was no one to assist her, and she died with her unborn child. Theo never forgave himself or his mother. More to the point, he swore that he would never have another child as a way of atonement. When I met him many years later, he told me the story, saying that he loved me and would marry me—if I agreed to his conditions. Lily, my dear, he had a great deal of charm, my Theo, and could have had any woman, or so I thought at the time. And I—well, I was madly in love with him. I wanted children, but I wanted him more. I said yes, and he told me how grateful he was and that he would make it up to me. We have been together nearly sixty years, and I never regretted my decision. Well, almost never. We have Julius, and he is like a son to us."

"That means something. I have no one. I have no child and will never have one; I have no husband either."

"Come on. You are young, you are healthy, you are free. Pretty as you are, you will catch yourself a good husband."

"Perhaps." Lily was suddenly smiling. "In fact, I already turned one down." She then proceeded to tell the story of the "good match" arranged by Dvora Zerner.

"You didn't like him?"

"He had a wart on his nose and a flabby bottom."

"The wart would not have been too bad, but a flabby bottom?"

They both burst out laughing. By then, it was time to keep the appointment made by the old lady at the hairdressing salon who tut-tutted when she saw Lily's hair. The only thing to do, the hairdresser said, would be to give her a good cut and wait until it grew a little longer. Once again, Lily let others take care of her. When it was over, she scarcely recognized the modish person with a gamin haircut peering at her in the mirror. Here again her "Aunt" had not let her pay, and the stylist had refused to take her money. There was something unsettling in the sheer normalcy of it all. As if she were an ordinary denizen of Paris, a nice middle-class girl having emerged unscathed from the war and was now running errands with her doting elderly parent, instead of being the penniless refugee who despaired of ever being able to return home.

According to the plan, Theo, who had remained at the house to wait for Julius, would then be driven by him to meet the two women in a bar at the corner of the rue de Passy, near the salon.

Theo was there, but he was alone and got up as they walked in.

"Julius neither arrived nor phoned," he said worriedly. "So I came on foot. As soon as I got here, I phoned home but there was no answer. I thought for a minute that he had come here directly, so I phoned the concierge. The car is still in the courtyard."

"Really Theo, what are you afraid of? That he has been run over?" scolded his wife. "He just crossed half of Europe on foot, and you think he can't handle the streets of Paris? He has obviously been delayed, unless the news he has received has driven the fact that he was supposed to meet with us out of his mind. He will apologize later."

Since they were now in danger of being late, it was agreed that they would all go back home. If Julius hadn't arrived, Zsazsa would stay to wait for him, while the other two took a taxi to the forger's place of business.

Theo's uneasiness was rubbing off on his young companion who seemed to feel her earlier happiness draining away. "I knew I was bringing him bad luck," she tormented herself during the short ride, not even distracted by the sight of the fabled Eiffel Tower that she had never seen. The taxi left them in front of a rather ugly building on the Left Bank of the Seine. A modest plaque on the ground floor announced the offices of "Vladimir Malenkov, Engraver, by Appointment." The man who opened the door was tall and thin, a black fur cap covering his greying hair and a face half-hidden under a bushy beard. Though he was wearing a tired-looking suit two sizes too big, it was easy to see why he'd gotten his nickname. With his somber mien and vaguely crazy expression, he could indeed have passed for an orthodox priest.

He welcomed them politely and gestured to two armchairs before resuming his seat behind his worktable. "How may I be of use to you today, Mr. Castan?"

Theo briefly explained that he wanted rations books for his nephew and niece who also needed a "new" identity card and a driving license; Lily would give him the authentic documents Zerner had bought for her to cover part of the cost. Malenkov—if that was his real name, which Lily seriously doubted, considering that there was nothing Russian-sounding in his accent—took the Ginette Lentier papers she was extending and used a magnifying lens to check them thoroughly.

There was a curious sound, and a wheelchair came into view.

"This is Boris, my associate. He is the true artist."

He was a quite younger man, with pale blond hair matching Lily's own.

He stood up with the help of two canes, threw a seemingly indifferent glance at the visitors before sitting down on a chair.

"What does the Jew dog want today?" he said in a deceptively friendly tone.

She gave a start. He was not speaking Russian but Polish. His partner answered in the same tone of voice and the same language.

"So he has found himself a little whore who could be his granddaughter and wants us to help?" Boris continued, smiling amiably all the while.

"He always pays on the spot, and besides, he brought us some valuable documents," Vladimir protested.

"I don't like working with Jews, and …"

Lily did not give him time to finish. She stood up, red with anger.

"So, you don't like Jews," she said, speaking in Polish. "You piece of filth! You must be sorry that the Germans have left. They must have been your friends after having made such a good job of cleansing Poland of its Jews. Of course, they destroyed the country and massacred some brave Poles, who were Christians like you. Wasn't it fortunate that you were safely living in France? I wonder how many French patriots and how many Jews you had to betray in order to be left alone by the Gestapo?"

"How dare you!" The so-called Boris was foaming at the mouth.

"Why? You insult my uncle, you call me names, and yet you are surprised by my answer? Wait, you haven't heard anything yet." Lily started cursing him with all the frustration and helplessness she felt while the two men stood frozen. When her rant had run its course, she turned to Theo, "Let's go, I don't want anything to do with these two monsters."

Then she burst into sobs.

Castan, who had followed the exchange uncomprehendingly, got up and extended his hand to take back the documents he had given the pope.

"Wait a minute, please. Boris spoke in French. "I believe I was wrong, Mademoiselle. I apologize wholeheartedly. Sir, your niece is accusing me of having betrayed Jews and Résistance fighters."

"Lily, I don't know what he told you, but I have always found him trustworthy. He was taken prisoner and tortured by the Germans in Poland. You see what they did to him. He never said a word. His comrades got him out and smuggled him into France."

"He called you a dirty Jew," Lily replied.

"I have heard worse, especially from Poles. I assume these two are Poles, not Russians. I should have guessed, the way Boris looks. Mind you, I never heard them speaking Polish before. Why pretend to be Russians?"

"Camouflage, my friend, camouflage," answered Boris with a twisted smile. "Germans are less suspicious of White Russians; after all, they are fighting the communist regime, which forced us to flee. I never called you a dirty Jew. Just a Jew."

"A Jew dog!" Lily had stopped crying.

"True, and I apologize. You called me worse, a piece of filth, right? I was wrong. I'm sorry. I just came back from the hospital where they pushed and pulled at me for one hour before the surgeon, just back from London where he spent the war years, told me that not only wouldn't I get better, but I'd probably get worse. The surgeon is called Grinstein—a Jewish name. I was feeling mad at the whole world, but especially at the Jews, and more precisely, one coming in with a beautiful girl. That's why I forgot myself and said things I sincerely regret. Please forgive me. Can we start again? My name is Zbignew Komowski, at your service, even though I call myself Boris and have the papers to prove it."

He smiled, with more warmth this time, adding, "please sit down. Turning to his companion he said "Vladimir— that's his real name, his father was Russian, but he was raised by his Polish mother—do bring us a bottle of schnapps to thaw the chill."

"How come you speak French so well?" Lily demanded.

"I taught Latin and French at Warsaw University."

"How did you get here?"

"As your uncle told you, I fought, was caught, tortured; there was an assault on the prison; some friends, including a number of Jews, helped me out and nursed me till I was well enough to travel, which I did dressed as a Russian orthodox priest. I loved to draw and was an amateur photographer, and that's how I started my new métier after I met Vladimir. He went to the Kraków seminary but changed his mind and became an engraver. We opened this studio together and have been busy manufacturing fake documents—a way of fighting the enemy while earning a living.

"So, which one is the pope?" Lily smiled.

"Whoever you want. My Latin is better. He knows all the prayers."

Vladimir returned with an ice-cold bottle and some glasses, and they all drank to victory over the Germans. Then it was back to business.

"I assume you don't want your real name on the papers, no? Boris asked. "What shall I put down?"

"Lily, if possible."

"No problem. Date of birth? Shall we say 1914? August 5? In Bordeaux to explain the touch of the south in your speech? I have just what you need. What about your family name? You want something sufficiently ordinary so that you do not risk meeting someone who is going to ask you whether you are a relative of X or Y. Lily Martinez? Lily Martineau? You like Martinez better? We have a very good camera, a brand-new Leica bought from a German officer who was recalled to the Front. I shall take a few pictures. Your documents and driving license will be ready tomorrow morning."

Lily took out her wallet, but he waved it away.

"Your uncle will pay for the ration books as usual; for the rest, we are taking the very good papers you brought us. Please, I owe you an apology; then do not deprive me the pleasure of helping a Polish girl—and a beautiful one at that. I haven't seen one in a very long time, and it has been years since Vladimir and I heard someone cursing in Polish with such fluency and verve."

"Very well, then. Thank you, and I apologize as well. I am sorry if I offended you. We are all on edge these days. May I ask you another favor? Could my uncle use your phone to call home? We have a small problem."

"With pleasure. The telephone is on the corner table."

Theo got up and put on his spectacles to dial. There was a short conversation in Hungarian. He stumbled and had to hold onto the table to steady himself. Lily rushed to his assistance.

"Has something happened to Julius?"

"Not to Julius, no. It's his daughter. Elisabeth. Her husband has been killed. She was arrested by the Germans and deported in the last convoy to leave Paris. Julius doesn't know what happened to their little boy."

7

DESPAIR

BACK IN RUE DE PASSY, Julius Matthias took small sips of the heavily sugared tea his hostess had made for him, adding a generous dose of alcohol without asking. He was desperately trying to make sense of what had happened. In the letter she had written on June 20, Marie-Christine had assured him that his three children were safe; she wanted him to contact her. Had she been lying? To what purpose? To hand him over to the Germans as soon as he arrived in Paris? Why would they arrest him? No, at the time the letter had been written, everything was fine. What happened between June 17th and that accursed day in August? According to Commandant Dutertre, and there was no reason not to believe him, Elisabeth and her husband had been betrayed. Someone who had known about the meeting, known where and when it was due to take place, had informed the Germans who did the rest. Could it have been Marie-Christine? He found it highly unlikely. She had fainted at the news—the shock of being found out, according to the police. Besides, she had refused to answer their questions. Julius did not agree with their assessment. The shock must have been first hearing what had happened to Elisabeth and to her husband, then understanding that she had been betrayed.

He wondered why she had not said a word—after all, she must have known who could have found out and betrayed her. Was it one of her sons, both officers in the German army, present in the clinic at the time? Could he have heard something? Perhaps talked with the driver? Had he, furious at what his mother intended to do, decided to act without implicating her? She must have thought about it when the police explained what had happened, thought about it and let herself be arrested rather than denouncing her son. In any case, would she have been believed if she had given him up? Probably not. I have to see her, thought Julius. She would tell him the truth. She had to know where Emile was, the grandson he'd never seen, not even in a photograph, who had lost his father, and was bereft of his mother. Before rushing to the help of her husband, had Elisabeth left him in the care of someone she trusted? Her sister Gabrielle maybe? Or her brother André? They used to be very close. Had she left instructions in case she was taken? Probably not. He had no idea where these two were living. Marie-Christine, who was in contact with Elisabeth, might know. Julius felt that had no other path to explore.

He tried to tell himself that there was no reason to fear that the child was in danger. Surely his mother had seen to his safety. But had she thought about her own well-being? He dropped his head in his hands, remembering his friends, his neighbors, huddled on the pavement below his windows before being harshly driven towards the so-called assembly point on the road for deportation. Remembering all he had heard about the camps. How would she cope? A well-loved child—his favorite if truth be told; a carefree student, a doctor, a wife, a mother ... But no. She had been the wife of a Résistance fighter, and she probably helped the Résistance as well. She had a cool head, which would stand her in good stead. Moreover, the Germans were not aware of the fact that she was Jewish.

His shoulders slumped. Who was he fooling? What were the odds of her emerging unscathed from that ordeal? And it was all his fault, he told his friends. Yes, he had had the good sense of sending his children away from Romania and from those central European countries increasingly hostile to Jews. What he had not wanted to see was that the danger would not be contained and that the flames of hatred would consume the whole continent. It was to America that he should have sent them. To America, and more precisely, to Chicago, where his sister and her family were safely entrenched and where, according to his brother-in-law, was located one of the best schools of medicine of the country, one of the first to open its doors to women. As for his son, he could have had his pick of some of the finest engineering schools in America. Their aunt and their uncle would have been there to hold their hands and guide them on their path. Fool that he had been, he had only thought of France and had sacrificed his children for a dream!

His old friends were suffering with him, too stunned to interrupt his monologue. It was Lily, the outsider, the newcomer, who stood up suddenly.

"Enough. Julius, you are not thinking straight. What happened to your daughter is a terrible tragedy, but it has nothing to do with your choices. Had she contented herself with raising her child and seeing to her patients wherever she was living, in all likelihood, nothing would have happened to her. Didn't she go through four years of war without mishap? It is because she took part in the Résistance, or because she came to the rescue of her husband, a militant, that she was arrested. You say that your sister is safe in America. Haven't her children been drafted? Are they not in the army? They are. Do you imagine that they are not facing danger too? Come on. You acted for the best, according to what was known at the time. You sent your children to safety more than ten years ago when no one, absolutely no one, had the slightest inkling of what was going to happen. Stop blaming yourself."

"She is right, you know," said Castan. "And you forget André and Gabrielle."

"I haven't forgotten them! I am worried about them too."

"Well, you shouldn't. Had they been in trouble, they would have tried to get in touch directly or indirectly, by writing to your bank, as did Dr. Gilles and your sister, for instance."

"André and Elisabeth perhaps. They were there together in 1939 to close the accounts, but I am not sure about Gabrielle."

"They could have written to your sister in America. Don't tell us they don't have her address," added Theo. "Even if they didn't. All they had to do was to send a letter to the bank." Just write 'Manny Newman, Bank Newman, Chicago.' André never wrote to us, or even phoned to ask how we were doing. Yet we welcomed him here, helped him throughout his studies; I was the one who got him his first job. Why? Zsazsa and I, we are convinced that there is no place for us in his new life. He is what, today? Thirty-one? It isn't likely that he is married, but perhaps he has children with a nice little Christian girl who is unaware of his past, or more to the point, unaware of his religion? And he was not keen to apprise you of the fact? Now, Gabrielle. She never came to see us after she arrived in France. André wouldn't tell us anything about her. Here again, isn't it possible that she has made a new life for herself as well? How old is she, 25? 27 you say? You were forever telling me that she was extraordinarily beautiful. André once said that your wife arranged for her to study in a prestigious convent school in Budapest where she passed herself off as catholic. You knew about it, right?"

Julius nodded, and he went on.

"She probably did the same here, and no one knows who she really is. What are the odds that she is happily married, has one or two children, and has no wish to have her past exposed? Elisabeth never said anything about what her sister was up to, right?"

"Right, but …"

"But what? Do you believe that if something happened to either of them, Elisabeth would not have informed you? I tell you, they are both well and they haven't contacted you because they have no wish to do so. Furthermore, I would not be overly surprised to learn that your grandson is with one or the other. You want to make sure? It is perfectly understandable. Just don't let it keep you awake at night. You have enough worries about Elisabeth."

"Theo, my friend, when I managed to escape the Germans and flee from Nagyvarad, when I trudged kilometer after kilometer for months, I had one thought only: to be reunited with my children, hold them close. Today, I am here, and the first thing I learn is about what happened to my darling Elisabeth … and the second, if I follow your reasoning, that the other two could not care less about me. It's enough to drive a man insane."

"I have never been so glad to not have children," Theo replied while getting up. "Please forgive me for that thoughtless remark. Come to the dining room. Zsazsa remembered how fond you are of spicy goulash and has made the dish for you."

Julius, who did not feel like eating, embraced his hostess, who hugged him with tears in her eyes. He accepted the hand that Lily was offering and followed her to the table.

That night, Lily came after midnight, after being woken up by his tossing and turning. She silently got into his bed and covered his mouth with a kiss when he protested that he would not be able to … and proceeded to show him how wrong he was. His last thought before falling asleep was to thank a god he did not believe in for having sent her to cross his path.

In the morning, Theo came with him to the offices of the Red Cross where they waited for what seemed hours in the middle of an anxious crowd. People were desperately seeking news or means to send letters and parcels of food to loved ones. Now and then, a man or woman left in tears. When their turn came at last, a tired volunteer, looking like he was in his sixties and seated behind a desk overrun by papers, noted down all the information Julius had given him about his goddaughter, "Donna Lenormand," and shook his head wearily, saying that if she had indeed been deported in the last convoy from Paris, it was, unfortunately, more than likely that she had been sent to Auschwitz. He added that he would do his best and would contact the head offices of the Red Cross in Geneva to see if they had any information.

On the way back, Julius told himself that he was an idiot. What he should have done was to immediately call Hans Steuber who knew everyone there.

Once contacted, the banker was horrified at the disaster that had befallen his friend's daughter. He would, he said, without delay get in touch with his contacts and urge them to leave no stone unturned in order to know where nurse "Donna Lenormand" was being held.

And then there was nothing left to do but wait.

Days went by without news or hope. In the rue de Passy, a distraught Julius was comforted by his friends as best they could. Madame Castan had unearthed her old, heavily annotated cookbook and held an animated conversation with him as to the best French translation for some of its most exotic items. Theo would share a glass of his favorite cognac with him after dinner. At night, Lily was there with him, but what they had was no longer the unbridled passion of their first encounter. He reached for her with the despair of a drowning man, marveling at always finding her ready for him. Early in the morning, leaving her fast asleep, he would go to the kitchen where Theo, who was always up by five-thirty, was already seated. They would make themselves a pot of coffee and slices of bread with homemade jam, and, speaking softly so as to wake the women, start reminiscing about their former lives. The friends, the "Austrian Circle," of which both had been members, a dedicated group of Viennese-born Jewish lawyers and architects who had settled in Nagyvarad, then part of the Austro-Hungarian empire. It was through the group that they'd become acquainted some thirty years ago. Then would come the "do you remember" phase, an evocation of happier times, dinners among friends, and philosophical discussions into the small hours of the morning. Sometimes, Theo would wonder what had become of an old friend or a former flame. Julius would sigh, unwilling to delve into the last, terrible months, the last days, and trying to shut off unwanted images.

Theo listened, empathized, now and then covering his friend's hand with his own. Neither believed there would be a happy end to the war. Fighting had not abated in eastern Europe; deportations went on and trains still carried people to their deaths. The heroic but doomed uprising of the Warsaw ghetto in 1943 had not saved the tens of thousands of Jews who still lived there. The sole and thin sliver of hope was that at long last, the Red Army had decided to invade Hungary. Would the Russian troops drive out the Germans in time to salvage what still could be salvaged of the Jewish community? There had been fierce fighting around Debrecen, the country's second largest city, and Admiral Horthy, who had signed a separate peace agreement with the Soviet Union, was promptly arrested by the Germans, and the Hungarian army kept on fighting the Russians.

At the end of their morning talks, the old architect would shrug and tell his friend that these questions did not appear to greatly concern the French; when they were not complaining of the restrictions and the lack of so many things, they were turning to politics: infighting in the provisional government of the French Republic, the settling of scores against individuals rightly or wrongly accused of having collaborated with the enemy, and the drafting of a new constitution, which would, for the first time, let women vote—a bitterly divisive move.

By then, the women were up, and it was time to tackle more mundane tasks such as the daily chores in a household of four adults. A maid came twice a week, but it was Zsazsa who took care of the shopping and cooking. In the beginning, Julius had been loath to go out, for fear of missing a call from Dutertre or from the clinic where he had left his name and phone number. It was ridiculous; he was well aware of the fact that his friends were competent enough to take a message, but after four months battling nature or flesh and blood enemies, he found himself helpless, waiting for a hypothetical answer from someone who had done his best to dampen his expectations.

A week spent moping in the flat finally brought him to his senses. Armed with a letter of introduction to the director of the main offices on Boulevard Haussmann near the Opera, he ventured out to open an account at the Bank Société Générale, recommended by Hans Steuber on the ground that it was a solid establishment with branches throughout the country. His second foray was to accompany Lily to retrieve her new identity card and driving license from the engraver's studio.

Boris appeared to be in a great deal of pain and let the doctor examine him and make some helpful recommendations. Now that she had proper documents, Lily offered to drive on the way home, and he readily acquiesced. She handled the car through the busy streets with such a great deal of assurance that he declared that henceforth, she could chauffeur Madame Castan in her quest for supplies. It was soon apparent that Lily had a natural talent for bargaining, a skill popular in her native Egypt, and would often go shopping alone. Everyone had apparently forgotten that she had intended to leave as soon as she received her new papers, and she no longer mentioned it. She had her reasons. She told herself that she could not abandon Julius when he so obviously needed her. However, that was not all. A few days after her arrival, she had gone out "to buy some fresh bread" and had made a call from the post office, less than a block away. Her call to Marseilles had gone through almost immediately. Her brother-in-law was still at home. His tone had been icy. Not a word of sympathy; worse, he had made it clear that she was not welcome.

"David is dead because of you," he ranted. "You and your ideas. In 1938, I invited him to come live with us here, to be my associate. I found him a nice house with a small garden because I knew how much he would like it. He was ready to accept, but not you. It was not good enough. He stayed because of you. Now he's dead and you are alive. Had he had a son, a daughter even, I would have had no choice but to offer you shelter as a matter of respect to his memory. But you haven't been able to give him a child. Mother had been against the wedding and she was right. It did not stop her from asking me to help you. You were supposed to fetch her and bring her here, but you left too late and she was deported. Had she departed without waiting for you, she would have been saved. I don't owe you anything anymore. My brother is dead, my mother may be dead too, and you are no longer a part of our family. Do not come here. If I find you at our door, I'll call the police."

Back on the street, she'd let her tears flow. What would have been the point in telling him that she hadn't been the one who didn't want to come to France; David had been the one. David, who was afraid of nothing, would take the most frightening risks, but he had never been able to hold his own against his brother's arguments. David, who did not wish to find himself back in the role of the little brother who dutifully does what he is told. That's why he'd lied. She could see him again ashamedly explaining that he had turned down Simon's offer. He'd explained to her:

"Listen, he was pushing, pushing, and I was afraid once more he would browbeat me into agreeing. So, I said that it was because of you, that you were dead set against it and had threatened to leave me if I went to Marseilles. It was the only way. He got mad, started saying things about you so I just hung up. You are not angry?"

She had kissed him and there had been no more talk of departing for France. Who would have thought that this stupid quarrel in which she had had no part would have such disastrous results? As for her mother-in-law, had it been Lily's fault that she'd arrived late? Didn't he know what traveling in times of war was like? Besides, why hadn't he gone to fetch his mother himself? What was she to do now? She had been so sure of finding shelter with her brother and sister-in-law until she could return home.

She dried her tears, squared her shoulders, and went to get the bread. No one commented on her reddened eyes.

Days and weeks went by, and it would soon be a month since Julius had arrived at the rue de Passy with Lily. Whenever Julius floated the idea of moving to a hotel to stop imposing on his friends, they protested vehemently.

"Yuli, how many times do we have to tell you how much we enjoy your presence and that of your young lady, exclaimed Theo after one more discussion. In fact, you coming here was nothing short of a miracle. A dedicated atheist all my life, I have to resist the urge to rush to the nearest synagogue to render thanks. My wife looks as if she has shed ten years and bustles happily from morning to evening. We have started making plans, not for the immediate future; no, for when you leave, which will happen one day unfortunately. Take your time, stay, stay as long as you want, or as long as you can. That will give us happy memories to last to the end of our days.

Julius embraced him and said no more. The truth was that he had no wish to leave the flat, to confront the unknown, to make decisions. In Geneva, he had already found himself navigating between two worlds. There was the past, fifty years of a nearly ordinary life made of joys, sorrows, love, and tragedy, until the final horrors. There was now, with a dark and uncertain future. What was the hurry? He was loath to admit that he was reveling in this cozy atmosphere, something he had never experienced in the years he had been married to Magda.

Of course, there was Lily. He would sometimes wake up in the middle of the night and extend his hand to check that she was still there, still next to him. "To think that I had regretted taking her with me, that I might never have met her!" he marveled at times. It was strange how well they got on; they were yet to even have their first quarrel. She was beginning to relax, too, while she also smiled more and would often burst into a carefree laugh which delighted him. She would not, however, mention her past. Once or twice, she had been on the verge of talking about it, but something always stopped her. She must have had her reasons, and he would not have minded if he had not wondered: didn't she trust him enough? Was the past still too raw to be aired? He told himself that he would have to be patient and satisfied with her presence.

The Castans did not share his doubts and had wholly adopted her; Zsazsa introduced her as their niece, would not let her pay for anything, and would have showered her with presents if Lily had not strongly objected. One evening, Lily told Julius that it had to stop.

"I know they are doing it for you, to convince me to stay. You should tell them that they don't have to. You need me; there is nothing urgent for me to do as long as the war lasts. Please explain that it makes me feel as if I'm taking advantage of them. They are so afraid of offending me that they take care not to speak Hungarian so as not to make me feel excluded."

Julius nodded.

In the morning, when the young woman came to the kitchen where the men were already seated, Theo asked her if she could drive him to an errand he had in town, assuring her that it would not be long. She readily agreed. She was becoming quite fond of the elderly gentleman who paid her fulsome compliments with a twinkle in his eye.

She parked where he indicated and was surprised when he asked her to follow him. As he led her to a coffee house and begged her to sit.

"Lily, I have no errand to run. I just wanted to have a frank discussion with you. Julius has told us of your worries. You have misunderstood the situation. We took you in at the beginning because you are his friend, but you soon became our friend as well. No, don't interrupt. Listen. You cannot imagine what your presence has done for us. We used to stay at home for days on end, not bothering to dress; the concierge would do our shopping. I am not complaining; we are in relatively good health, and we have the means to live quite well. However, there was no joy in our daily life. We are delighted to have Julius and to be able to help him, but without you, we would be wallowing in gloom. Yesterday, I found myself humming a Viennese waltz for the first time in ages. Zsazsa, as I told Yuli, looks ten years younger. You make her enjoy life. If you could see how happy she is to take you out, to pamper you as if you were the little girl she never had. Don't worry. We know you will leave one day, perhaps with Julius as we hope, but at our age, we have to grasp the happiness that falls into our hands. As for the idea that we refrain from talking in Hungarian, my dear, ever since the arrival of the Germans, we have been at pains to use nothing but French, even at home. Should I feel an irresistible urge to switch to another language, nothing stops me from doing so when I am alone with my wife, as I do during my treasured mornings with Julius. Please, Lily, stop worrying, and don't deprive my wife of the pleasure of taking care of you."

As October drew to a close, the people of Paris were enjoying an exceptionally fine spell of weather which prompted Julius to suggest to Lily that they go on an outing. He made a stop at his bank, leaving her idly turning the pages of a magazine in the lobby, and disappeared inside. He came back looking preoccupied.

"Is something wrong?"

"No, no, the man was amiability itself. Listen, there is something I want to tell you, but not here. Let's go back to the car."

He drove without speaking until they reached a still verdant square near the town hall. Without getting out of the Juvaquatre, he drew a thick envelope from his jacket and gave it to her.

"Dear Lily, here are four thousand francs. They are for you."

She stared, taken by surprise, and visibly upset. "You want me to leave," she said flatly.

"Lily, no! That's not it at all. The other day, while listening to you, I came to understand how badly I have behaved. The feelings I have for you blind me to the extent that I have taken advantage of your kindness and sympathy. What I am trying to say is that I am conscious of the fact that you are almost twenty years younger than me and that your whole life is still in front of you. The money I am giving you is the key to your freedom. I don't want you to stay with me because you don't have a choice. I want you to stay because you want to be with me. The day will probably come when you will wish to leave, to go back home, wherever that is, and be reunited with your people once more. But if there is a thing that these terrible years have taught me, it is that one has to live in the moment to the fullest without asking questions. Why are you crying?"

"I thought you were sending me away. I don't want your money. I don't know what the future will hold, and I don't want to think about it. You know nothing about me. Listen, I want to stay with you too. I don't want to leave. You were kind enough to tell Theo about how I felt, and he reassured me. So, take back your envelope and let's not talk about money."

"No. It is more important than ever. As you can imagine, Zsazsa shared with me what you had revealed about your past, and you have my sympathy and understanding. You can tell me more when you are ready, but it will not change my sentiments. About the money: the war is not over, and no one can guess what will happen to us, or what will happen to me. You will be safe with that money. Consider it a form of insurance, please. I shall sleep better at night knowing that whatever may happen to me, you will not be without resources.

He gently pried the envelope out of her hand and put it in her bag. She turned to him, tears in her eyes. How could he have not thought that she was beautiful? Under the new and flattering haircut, her face appeared subtly rounder, and there was something mysterious in those curious eyes, forever shifting from green to blue. She smiled, and his heart contracted. Was he falling in love with the unknown waif that fate had thrust in his way? She was so young! Had his firstborn lived, he would be her age. Was fate toying with him again? Having dealt him a near mortal blow, was it luring him with the false promise of a fresh start? He hoped not. What he could not have known was that, at the same moment, she was asking herself the same question. Observing this mature man, with his determined face and still-athletic build, she was surprised by the emotions he stirred in her. The strong physical attraction was doubled by something else—affection? Tenderness? She was not sure. What did it matter? They had met barely a month ago. His gesture had moved her beyond words. With the money, she could confront whatever the future held. She put both hands on his shoulders and kissed him. Now, it was his turn to smile.

They returned in such good humor that the old couple exchanged knowing smiles. Their friend was over the worst.

Indeed, that very afternoon, Julius decided that he had waited long enough; he had to make plans. The day before, a phone call from Geneva had brought nothing new. In spite of Hans' efforts and the promise of a reward he had made, the Red Cross had found no trace of Donna Lenormand.

"Hans, tell me what you really think. Is the lack of information due to the fact that she is no longer alive?"

"Julius, I would never lie to you. And so no, I do not think that your daughter is dead. Why would she have been killed? It is a well-known fact that the Germans are meticulous in documenting each detail of their sinister enterprise. Don't lose hope. It may take time, but my contacts at the International Committee will retrieve the information we need. Dear friend, you may trust me. I shall call you immediately if I hear something, even in the middle of the night."

Not wholly convinced, Julius gave in to the inevitable. There was nothing more he could do, he told his friends. Nothing, that is, except find the child. Marie-Christine might help; only Dutertre had not gotten in touch. That left André and Gabrielle. Should either contact the bank, Hans had been instructed to inform them immediately and read the letter over the phone. Theoretically, finding André should have been easy.

"Theo, I shall leave that to you. After all, you facilitated his admission to the engineering college where he studied, and the director is a friend. Have a chat with him; he is sure to have a list of former students and might have kept in touch. If that fails, you found him his first place of work; a call there might be helpful."

Gabrielle would be harder to track down. Her father had no clue about what she'd been doing ever since she joined her brother and sister in Paris in 1935. She didn't write, except for a few hastily scrawled lines at the end of one of Elisabeth's letters. He knew from these letters that she'd been enrolled at the university for some unspecified program and was not living with her sister. There might, however, be one way to find her. When, at the suggestion of her mother, she hoped to be accepted into an elite convent school in Budapest, Gabrielle had written to Monsignor Octavius, an Italian prelate Julius had met in Nagyvarad. The two became good friends, and since the last time they met, Monsignor Octavius had risen in the Vatican hierarchy in Rome and had agreed to help, in the mistaken belief that this was what Julius wanted. In fact, the two women had acted without consulting him.

Julius had not seen his daughter since she'd left for Budapest in August 1933, but she had phoned once to apologize for the deception; she had also said that Monsignor Octavius was still helping her. It was not unreasonable to assume that they were still in touch. Of course, the prelate might no longer be in Rome. Julius would visit the Vatican envoy in Paris in the hope that he would be able to tell him the whereabouts of such an eminent cleric and would even be ready to forward a letter to his attention. There was another task for him, something he had been postponing day to day since his arrival.

He had to call his sister and tell her what had happened, only he was afraid that he would not be able to explain without bursting into tears. He swore to himself he would pick up the phone in the morning. Once more, he turned towards his friends.

"Enough talking. Our dear Zsazsa has been slaving for weeks over her stove to prepare delicious meals. Why don't we go to a restaurant this evening? My treat? She will have a well-deserved rest, and we shall endeavor to forget our problems and enjoy ourselves. Theo is the expert here. After so many years in Paris, I'm sure you are familiar with all the best places. I leave the decision in your capable hands!

His friend almost laughed at the idea.

"It could be a mistake. In the past, we did go out a lot, almost every night in fact. Not so much lately. It's been at least two years, and not only because we are not getting any younger. We could no longer stomach the sight of German officers throwing their weight around, escorted, more often than not, by their women—French women—with servile waiters fawning over them. Still, I do have a few good addresses. I will have to check how well they weathered the war.

He stopped and shook his head ruefully. "I am an idiot. How come I didn't think of it sooner?"

"Going to the restaurant?"

"Not at all. You and me. We can phone, write, but it will take time. The only way to progress faster is to get you to see Doctor Gilles. Since Dutertre does not appear in a hurry, let's try something else."

"Theo, get to the point!"

"When I was still working, I concluded that there were two ways around a problem: through official channels, or through unorthodox ones, which meant finding the person who could unblock the system and would agree to do so for a little gift. This has not changed."

"And you believe that you know such a person?"

"Not quite, but I know someone who might be able to help. During the Occupation, I met many people. Not all Résistance fighters were heroes with unblemished pasts; quite a few were not in the same category. I happened to save the life of one of them. He told me his name was Grandin, Jerome Grandin. I was walking home one evening when I saw him turn the corner in haste despite limping heavily. I have never seen such terror on a man's face. Then, I heard heavy footsteps and shouts in German. I grabbed him, pushed him into the hall of our building and into the lift. When I think about it, I realize that it was pure folly. I was incredibly lucky; we were incredibly lucky because they could have seen where he went. He had been shot in the leg, but there was no blood because of the heavy trousers he wore. Zsazsa cleaned the wound as best she could and bandaged it. We then settled him a recess in the wall in the passage leading from the original flat to the second one. We'd put a plain cupboard there when the war started leaving just enough room for a chair. This was where our radio was hidden. Grandin remained there for two days. Moving the cupboard was noisy and cumbersome, so we only did it at night to let him go to the bathroom and get food and drink. He never told us why they were looking for him, not that we wanted him to; in situations like these, the less you know, the better. It must have been serious. The Germans were determined to find him.

The first evening, they searched all the buildings on that stretch of the street, from cellar to attic. Not having found anything, they left two soldiers to keep watch all night and came back in the morning for another thorough search. I saw them looking at the cupboard and nearly died: *if they open the doors*, I thought, *they are bound to realize that the cupboard is not deep enough*. Fortunately, they half-opened one side, peered through, and kept going. It was even more fortunate that they didn't bring dogs. We were lucky. I'm speaking of him, of course, but us as well. Had he been discovered, Zsazsa and I would have paid the price, a heavy price. He was well aware of it. You should have seen how fervently he thanked us when the soldiers finally went away and he was able to leave at nightfall. I chanced upon him not so long ago after the Liberation, but he was not the same man. Fancy suit, cigar, big car. It couldn't have been during his Résistance work that he made all that money, but that is not to say that he had not been fighting courageously as well. He rushed to embrace me, pumped my hand, and assured me of his ever-lasting gratitude. Now is the time to check if he meant it."

"What can he possibly do?"

"I have no idea. But with the right contacts, it should be possible to find someone ready to take a few risks in exchange for some nice large bills. Transmit a message, ask your doctor if she has some information? Convince a guard to let you in?"

"We don't even know where she is being held!"

"If you know whom to ask, it shouldn't be too difficult to find out. The odds are she is in the Fresnes Penitentiary. It's a women's prison. It may not work, but what have we got to lose? If he declines to help, we won't be worse off than we are today. I thought of him just now, because he is the owner of a fancy restaurant off the Champs Elysees. He has invited us there several times, but we were not in the mood. I am going to call to reserve a table and mention his name so that he hears we are coming. Worst case scenario, we shall have had a great dinner."

There's a decidedly festive mood on the Champs Elysees this evening, thought Julius, who was driving and, as best he could, negotiated the Place de l'Etoile, where a policeman was perched on something looking like a highchair, doing his best to channel the flow of cars. On this Saturday, October 28, the great avenue undulated with people. Cafes and restaurants had set up tables on the sidewalks; US soldiers, in large groups or with young women on their arms, mingled with ordinary Frenchmen reclaiming, so to speak, their beloved thoroughfare. It was as if France wanted to erase the memory of the German conquerors who had, for so long, strutted there, and of the hated flag floating under the Arc de Triomphe. As if, he mused, they could not wait to turn the final page of the war years. What did they care about what was still going on in the rest of Europe? Maybe they were right? Maybe they had suffered enough. And their army was still fighting.

Following Theo's instructions who was seated next to him, Julius turned right into a side street and parked in front of a brilliantly lit building. Though the Juvaquatre was no match for the ostentatious and obviously brand-new vehicles lining the street, its passengers had taken great care of their appearance. Out of moth-balled wardrobes, the Castans had dug out clothes that were so well cut they gave them an aristocratic look. Lily was radiant in her midnight-blue outfit altered for her by the seamstress, and Julius, who, for the first time, was wearing the most elegant of his Geneva purchases, was not the only one to admire her. There were some thirty patrons seated around a number of tables covered by bright white cloths and sparkling cutlery. An army of waiters diligently attended to them.

"The new moneyed aristocracy," Theo whispered about the black-market barons with their heavily made up fancy women showing too much cleavage and wearing too many jewels. "Yet, some of those men did fight courageously against the Germans. Go figure."

On a raised stage, a dark-haired and rather plump girl in a skimpy dress was belting out the latest hits, moving suggestively, and fighting to be heard above the conversations and occasional raucous laughter, as well as the clatter of dishes.

Soon, they were happily sampling a succession of succulent dishes: goose liver, lobster, and filet mignon, accompanied by wines of exceptional vintages.

"It's just as I expected," Theo said. "I won't ask where they get the stuff in spite of the rationing."

Julius tactfully refrained from mentioning that he had eaten as well, if not better, at the Perle du Lac in Geneva. They were wondering whether to try the cheese platter or content themselves with the dessert when a hard-faced man in his forties entered the restaurant and made straight for their table, a waiter hastening to bring him a chair.

"Good evening, Madame Castan. Good evening, Theo. I wasn't expecting your visit. You are most welcome here. I am delighted to see that you are looking well. Who is this lovely woman with her handsome companion?"

Introductions were made. With some amusement, Julius noted that Grandin lifted Lily's hand to kiss it, lingering a little too long but leaving her unfazed. They made small talk until Grandin had ordered; then he leaned back in his chair and looked at Theo inquiringly.

"As you can imagine, we came here tonight because I wanted to talk to you, and I thought that it would be the quickest way," the old architect said.

"You wanted to know how I was doing?"

"That too. Let's be serious. You told me that if you were ever in the position to do something for me, you would do it."

"I did. You are my guests tonight."

"Don't insult me. I don't need your money. It's your help I seek."

"I always keep my word. If I can do something for you, I shall do it."

"Doctor Julius Matthias, my nephew from Hungary, is like a son to my wife and me. He barely escaped being caught by the Germans and has crossed half of Europe on foot to reach France where his three children live. He was wise enough to send them here to study before the war. His eldest daughter, Elisabeth Metzger, herself also a doctor, fled Paris in June 1940 and settled in the south of France, where she opened a clinic under an assumed name. Her husband, Doctor Benjamin Metzger, an officer, was imprisoned, but after a daring escape from his stalag, he was able to join her. He went on fighting in the Résistance, as she was doing. In August, they were betrayed and captured. Metzger, who had been badly wounded, died under torture. Elisabeth was deported in one of the last convoys. We don't know where she ended up, and Julius hasn't been able to get any information."

Grandin wanted to say something but Castan stopped him.

"Wait. As bad as it is, he has a contact in the Red Cross, and they are doing all they can. What is urgent is finding Emile, Elisabeth and Benjamin's son. He is barely two years old. My great nephew, if you wish. His father is dead; his mother ... all he has is Julius, who is desperately looking for him. His daughter was extremely cautious, and sent news through a third person. We don't know where she lived, and under what name. Hopefully, the child is being cared for by a maid or a nurse, so long as the money lasts but we can't be sure.

There is, however, someone who probably has the details we need, Doctor Marie-Christine Gilles. She is the owner of the medical establishment where Elisabeth met her husband and where they both worked before the war. The problem, and the reason we need your help, is that she was arrested at the Liberation and accused of collaborating with the enemy and treason. She is facing the death penalty. Julius, who has known her for more than thirty years, is convinced that she is innocent. I don't have to tell you that in today's world, it doesn't take much to get someone thrown in jail. In any case, Julius is convinced that she would tell him what she knows about the child's whereabouts. He asked to see her, which got him a lengthy and nasty grilling since he was suspected of being her accomplice. He managed to establish his innocence and even to get a measure of sympathy from his tormentors, though they stopped short of letting him meet with her, merely promising to try to arrange it.

But the days are passing, and he is worried about the child. What if the money left by his mother runs out? Will the kid be thrown in the street or sent to an orphanage? That's why I thought of you. With your contacts, can't you find out where she is being held, and perhaps arrange a meeting or transmit a message? Julius and I are ready to pay what it takes."

"Don't talk to me about money," Grandin replied. "I would feel ashamed to ask for money after what you and your wife did for me, and even greater shame at making someone who has already suffered enough, whose family has suffered for France, pay for a service that should have been readily rendered by French authorities. I will see what can be done. Finding where she will be easy; she is almost certainly in Fresnes, the women's prison. The next step will be spotting the person willing, in exchange for a nice sum of money, to facilitate a meeting between your nephew and the prisoner. It may take some time. Jot everything on a piece of paper, including your nephew's address and phone number in Paris. If he lives with you, don't bother writing down the address, for I am not likely to ever forget it. I still get a cold sweat when I remember the two days spent behind your cupboard. I just have one question. This Elisabeth must have known the risks she was taking. Isn't it more than likely that she has seen to it that her son would be in good hands should anything happen?"

"I hope, no, I think, you are right," Julius intervened. "But I have to make sure. Besides, she couldn't have imagined that both she and her husband would be taken, nor imagined what happened. The solution she chose could be short term. Even if Emile is safe for now, I have to think of his future."

"You have my word. I will try to arrange a meeting as soon as possible." Turning back to Theo, the Frenchman added, "I do have a condition, and it is non-negotiable. Dinner is on me."

While they all relaxed, he submitted Julius to a barrage of questions about Hungary, a country he only knew through the gypsy bands which were in great demand in the new-ly-liberated French capital. At the time, the doctor found it difficult to understand what he was saying. Later, his friend explained that the man had dropped out early and received most of his education from the streets. At some point, the singer, who had left the stage to a jazz ensemble playing lively tunes, came over to ask Grandin to dance. Obviously, they were more than just friends. Theo and his wife joined them.

Julius observed them with a smile, marveling at the smooth way they were moving and at their obvious enjoyment when Lily got up, and deaf to his protests, dragged him to the dance floor too. Doing his best not to tread on her feet, he let himself be carried away by his enthusiastic partner.

It had been so many years since he had last danced. Had he even ever danced with Marie-Christine? With Madi? He did not remember. Lily was something else. Was it a question of age? He looked into the depths of those very pale green eyes and tightened his grip. To think that they had only known each other for a month! A month of sharing the same bed, of feeling her next to him at night, always ready to accept his advances even if she did not initiate them. He found himself looking at her with a new tenderness. She smiled, and he suddenly understood that that month had changed his life ... and hers as well, he hoped.

8

LUNCH AT FONTAINEBLEAU

IN THE EARLY MORNING, the ladies were still fast asleep while the two men drank coffee in the kitchen as usual and discussed the previous evening's events which had surpassed their expectations. Theo was in a great mood, reminiscing about past revelries in happier times; his friend listened indulgently. Julius had been comforted by the meeting with Grandin. The man had been sincere; he had also said that he did not think that the child was in imminent danger. That's what Julius had been trying to tell himself, but hearing someone else say it, a total stranger, was infinitely reassuring. Lily had just joined them when the phone rang in the salon. They exchanged surprised glances, and Julius swiftly got up to answer it.

"Julius, it is I, Hans," said the banker. "Is there anything new?"

"No, unfortunately. And at your end?"

"Nothing yet. I have contacted a number of people at the Red Cross who are offering substantial rewards ..."

"Thank ..." The banker did not let him finish.

"Please! Listen, it's been almost a month, and there has been absolutely nothing. Not a whisper. It is as if your daughter had disappeared from the surface of the earth."

"She could be registered under another name. Her husband's name, her maiden name …"

"Julius, the damned Germans make lists. They are meticulous. They record who was deported, when, and from where. According to you, she was deported from France as Donna Lenormand; there is no record of a woman of that name arriving anywhere. That's what made me call you this morning. There has to be an explanation. Either her name was wrongly transcribed on a register, which is highly unlikely, or …"

"She was murdered as soon as she arrived or killed on the way."

"Julius, Julius. Think, man! In either case, it would have been recorded!"

"So, there's nothing to do?"

"Not quite. I wonder if you could have been misled about the day she was deported and that she was in a different convoy."

"You have lost me. She would still be on their lists, no?"

"Tell me, does your daughter speak German?"

"Of course. She speaks Hungarian, Romanian, Austrian-accented German, and French, as do all my children. Where are you going with that?"

"I heard something yesterday that got me thinking. Last August, a few days before the convoy you mentioned, there had been another one. I was told that the train went off the rails shortly before reaching the town of Weimar in Germany. One of the wagons fell on its side and the doors burst open. Several prisoners attempted to escape. According to the Germans, they all were recaptured the same night. What if the Germans were wrong? What if they didn't want to admit that one or more prisoners had gotten loose? Your daughter, for instance? Does she speak the language well enough to pass for German?"

"German, maybe; Austrian easily."

"What does it matter? If she did manage to escape that night ..."

"With no papers and no money? Where could she hide?"

"Julius, I have no idea. If she tried to escape and was retaken, if she was in a camp, her name would appear somewhere. The fact is that it does not. What can I say? It's a theory. It offers a glimmer of hope. Very faint, perhaps, but still. So, I decided to mention it. Don't worry, it won't stop me from pursuing my investigation. At my request, the Red Cross is compiling a list of doctors and nurses deported during the relevant period. So far, they have found no one corresponding to her description."

"Thanks for sharing that glimmer of hope with me. I would dearly love to believe in it and will continue to hope. Hans, I have just realized how selfish I have been. I have been so focused on what was happening to me that I completely forgot about your family. Please forgive me. Have you learnt anything?"

"Alas, what little has transpired about the fate of my brother, his wife, and their children leaves me with very little hope. As for thanking me, let's wait for news, or for the end of the war, and let's have lunch in Paris. Oh, and one last thing. I met your friend, my colleague, Paul Zerner. He told me your brother-in-law from America called him, worried about the lack of news since you left Geneva. I also took the liberty of telling him about your daughter. I said that's why you had not called. I added you were with friends in Paris and that I would get in touch to inform you. I was going to call from the office tomorrow."

"I had been dreading that call. What am I going to tell them? But I will do it today. I shall also call Zerner. I should have done it earlier, but there were some issues."

"He did say that he was worried about the young woman who was traveling with you. She had promised to inform him of her safe arrival."

"I will call immediately. Hans, if you don't come to Paris after the war, I shall visit you in Geneva and take you to dinner at La Perle du Lac!"

In Rue de Passy, after the despair of the preceding weeks, the banker's theory was offering a glimmer of hope.

"I for one will believe it," said Madame Castan. "As long as no one disproves it. If Elisabeth did get away, she will manage. She has a head on her shoulders; she is a doctor. After all, we clung against hope to the thought you would be safe, you would come back to us. And you did. Listen, it looks like it's going to be such a beautiful day, why not drive to Fontainebleau and lunch there? There is no point in staying here brooding."

It was such a good idea that all parties agreed. While the old lady went to dress, Julius picked up the phone again, this time to call Paul. Lily stood near to give him moral support. How would the banker react to the fact that they were still together?

"Just give him the news and let me speak to him," she told him.

They found Zerner at home, it being Sunday. Julius explained that he had not yet called his sister because he didn't have the courage to tell her about Elisabeth. Paul expressed his sympathy and understanding. Then, he asked about Lily. That was Julius' clue to hand the telephone to her. She spoke Polish, but it was clear that the exchange was a heated one. It did not last long. A rather sheepish Julius looked at her for details, and she burst out laughing.

"He started by yelling at me, demanding that I put you on again. I explained that it was I who had taken the initiative, that in spite of the age difference, I was no longer a child, and that we were both widowers. I added that I would be forever grateful for what he and his mother have done for me, but that he was neither my father nor my brother. He mumbled something and wondered what he was going to tell his mother. I suggested he just explain that I'm staying with the Castans, a very respectable family. He admitted that he had seen Theo and Zsazsa several times when they were living in Geneva years ago." She laughed again.

"I believe he is jealous. He is far too proper to have tried anything when I was under his mother's roof, but it was not for lack of wanting to. I would catch him looking at me at times ... Have you met his wife?"

"No. She wasn't feeling well."

"Well, I did," interjected Theo, who had heard. "It was more than twenty years ago but she can't have improved!"

While the young woman hastened to her room to get dressed, Julius turned to his old friend, speaking softly in order not to be overheard. "Theo, is there anything in that theory of Hans?"

The architect shrugged. "It is not impossible. Now, is it likely? I have no idea, and neither do you. Stranger things have happened. Why don't we assume it's true until we are proven wrong as my wife suggested? Come on, let's hurry up the women and get started."

It was in an unusually merry mood that they got under way. There was very little traffic. It was distinctly chilly despite a pale autumn sun, and people used their precious petrol coupons sparingly. How on earth did Theo, who had sold his car shortly after his arrival in France, daunted by the Parisian traffic, manage to get his coupons? This was a question that his friends refrained from asking. He did, however, know the way to the Fontainebleau Forest and gave directions to Julius who was driving. They took Route Nationale 7 at the Porte d'Italie. An animated Zsazsa was happily pointing at familiar spots, bemoaning the state of the secondary roads after years of war-induced neglect, sighing at the still boarded-up inns where her husband used to take her until they gave up the car.

They eventually found a pleasant establishment at the Carrefour de la Belle Epine. Though there were a few tables on the terrace, they opted to sit inside. The menu had scant options, but the wine cellar was well-stocked, and there was a roaring fire in the huge chimney.

They opted for the day's special, deer filet in *grand veneur* sauce, enhanced by a heady red wine. For the first time since his arrival in Paris, Julius Matthias, sitting close to the fire, felt himself relaxing. Theo, in a faded velvet jacket, waxed lyrical about the history of the place; his wife, looking like a benevolent grandmother in an attractive burgundy dress, nodded her approval from time to time, and Lily, wearing something soft and flowery, ate with gusto. It was all so ... normal. A family Sunday outing complete with a discussion of the relative merits of the chocolate soufflé and the Tarte Tatin.

Suddenly, Lily shivered. "Julius, would you mind trading places with me? There is a draught coming, and I am freezing."

When he immediately got up, she sat down.

"I thought I would never get warm again," she said with a relieved smile.

"Tell me, child, how did you manage in Poland? It must be far colder," wondered the old lady.

"I never lived there."

"How old were you when you left?"

"I have never set foot in Poland."

"But ..."

"I was born in Cairo."

"Cairo, as in Egypt? So you are not Polish?"

"I am, I am! Half Polish if you want. Wait, I shall explain. It may take a while so why don't we order first? I want the Tarte Tatin."

A few minutes later, as they looked at her expectantly, she sipped some of her wine, put the glass carefully on the table, and took a deep breath.

"I have to start at the very beginning. In Warsaw. Three-quarters of a century ago, Thaddeus Borenztain, my grandfather, my mother's father, was some thirty-years-old. He was a well-to-do businessman. His specialty was importing crystal glass and chinaware from Bohemia, then part of the Austro-Hungarian empire." She stopped to sip more wine before continuing.

"Widowed two years before, he was childless, and his elder sister, who never married, came to manage his household while searching for an eligible bride for him. Cautious negotiations started with a young widow who had a little girl and a respectable fortune. Her guardians were being difficult about the marriage contract, and discussions reached an impasse. At that point, fate intervened, according to my grandmother, Eva. It was, in her words, no less than a fairy tale. Grandfather had returned from a business trip and was dozing in the back of his new Mercedes (he had a driver, of course) when one of the tires picked up a nail at the entrance of a poor village. While the driver was busy changing the tire, a wild little thing, as my grandfather described her, running barefoot and in rags, stopped to admire the car. She was not yet sixteen, with blonde braids that fell over an angelic face and a body to die for. That's how my grandfather used to tell it to my mother, who repeated them to me many times.

Eva must have been beautiful indeed, since he fell in love on the spot. Her family was nothing to boast of. Her mother, a Jewish orphan, had been seduced by the local landlord who got her pregnant and convinced one of his Jewish tenants to marry her with the help of a secret dowry. My grandmother was allegedly more beautiful than her mother, that was something she told me herself. In any case, her parents were only too happy to give her to Thaddeus in marriage as he not only did not ask for a dowry but even gave her family a large sum of money. They did not even demur when he carried off his young betrothed on the spot. I am not sure they believed he was indeed going to marry her.

My grandfather then very properly handed her over to his sister, giving her a month to make his bride "presentable" and prepare her for her new status. I have often wondered what my great aunt thought of such a match, though she may have taken comfort that the young bride would not challenge her position the way the rich widow would certainly have done. As for Eva, dazed by the car and her future husband's opulent house, she raised no objection, though my grandfather was far from an Adonis. I never knew him, but I saw the wedding photograph. He was not very tall, already turning to fat and nearly bald.

It goes without saying that the wedding was a very private affair. My uncle Nathan was born exactly nine months later. Vicky, Victoria, my mother, was born two years after him, and they had no more children. Thaddeus was delighted with his offspring and proud of his wife's beauty, who, by the way, let her sister-in-law rule the roost. The sister died just after Nathan's Bar Mitzvah."

Lily stopped and drank some of the tea ordered with her tarte. "I am not boring you with my story? I can shorten ..."

"Don't you dare," said the Castans in unison, with Zsazsa adding that they were in no hurry, and that it was far more exciting than a novel.

"Very well. My uncle Nathan had no mind for studies and started working in the family business at 18. At least a head taller than the father he resembled, he was far better looking. He turned out to be an astute businessman. The firm now named "Borenztain and Son" expanded and had an impressive list of customers, many outside Poland. And so one fine day, a Monsieur Nissim Mizrahi appeared in its Warsaw offices. He was from Cairo. See Julius, we are getting to Egypt. He presented himself as purveyor to the court of Fouad Sultan. The Borenztain father and son had never heard of that Fouad, did not quite know what a Sultan was, and were not exactly sure where Egypt was located.

However, Monsieur Mizrahi was ready to pay in cash half of the amount of the considerable order he was placing. Nathan decided to deliver the goods to Cairo himself and get the balance owed. Despite the length of the journey, this was the first of many mutually profitable visits to Egypt.

"Meanwhile, Vicky had become an accomplished young lady, speaking not only Polish, but also French and Italian, as well as playing the piano and doing fine embroidery. Additionally, she was very pretty. Blonde, where Nathan was dark, azure eyes … She caught the eye of a young nobleman whose sister attended the same musical academy and courted her—but not because he intended to marry her in spite of her considerable dowry. She was Jewish after all. He made unwelcome advances and she turned him down three times. So, one day, he waited for her and tried to carry her away by force as she left the academy. He would undoubtedly have succeeded if by chance Nathan had not arrived to take his sister home. They came to blows. The Pole fell, struck his head on a stone, and died two days later. Nathan did not wait around. The same evening, he left Warsaw with his mother and sister.

"You probably guessed that they went to Cairo where they intended to stay until the affair blew over. By then, the firm had opened an office there, and Thaddeus, worried by the rise of antisemitism, had started sending gold ingots and foreign currency with his son on each of his trips, to be secreted in a very large safe imported at great cost from England. What happened next should not surprise you. Nathan married Nissim's sister, and Nissim himself asked Vicky to be his wife. She was reluctant. He was not handsome and was swarthy enough to pass for an Arab. There was no going back to Poland, however. The family of the young noble had taken the law into its own hands. The offices and premises of the firm were torched a few days after Nathan's departure; Thaddeus was found dead in the rubble. The courageous friend who saw to his funeral wrote that he had been beaten to death. Needless to say, there was no investigation of the arson, or the murder."

She wiped a tear and drank more of her tea.

"My poor child! How dreadful! If it's too painful, you don't have to continue."

"Thanks, Madame ... wait. Instead of aunt, why don't I call you Tante, as we do in Egypt? What I am telling you now are things I heard many times when I was growing up, but have never told anyone. I don't know why I am crying. I never knew him. My grandfather died before I was born. My grandmother would mention him often. She worshipped the man who had rescued her from poverty. Deep down, she was angry at my mother. More than once she complained that had she turned down the young man more diplomatically, the family would still be living happily in Warsaw. She died well before the rise of Hitler and the horrors that befell the Jews of Poland.

"But back to my story. Vicky, not really having a choice, accepted Nissim's proposal and never regretted it. He was enormously proud of her beauty, treated her like a queen, bought her sumptuous jewels and filled the house with servants that obeyed her slightest whim. He even went as far as letting Eva live with them instead of with Nathan.

"My grandmother never mastered French, the language spoken by the Jewish elites in Egypt, so we always spoke in Polish. Mind you, it was my uncle Nathan who taught me to curse in Polish in order to shock his mother and sister. He has a wicked sense of humor, and, so I was told, quite an eye for the ladies. He left Egypt for Argentina—but I am getting ahead of myself. I made my appearance on the scene in 1909 and was raised like a princess. I grew up in a magnificent villa surrounded by a well-tended garden in Zamalek, Cairo's fashionable district, as befitted the only daughter of one of society's leading couples. French was taught there. I learned Arabic from the servants.

"In 1927, I enrolled at Cairo American University, one of the first institutions of higher education in the Middle East to admit women, after the Hebrew University of Jerusalem which opened a year earlier, by the way. I graduated three wonderful years later, the best years of my life, speaking perfect English and with an impressive diploma that didn't lead to anything. My proud parents didn't care since it didn't occur to them that I would have to work a single day. I was living the life, riding around the Pyramids by moonlight, learning to shoot in a Jewish sports club ..."

"That's why you are such a crack shot!" Julius, who was fascinated by the story, exclaimed.

"Leave her alone," Theo grumbled. "This girl should be writing novels! She can spin a tale!"

"Be patient! I was even invited to a reception at the palace of Fouad Sultan, now King Fouad, because my father was a great friend of his Finance Minister, Joseph Cattaui Pasha. You may not know his name, but the Cattaui are among the great Jewish families of Egypt."

"Come on. Even I know that," the old architect replied.

"Maybe you do, but Doctor Julius Matthias here wasn't aware of the fact that there were Jews in Egypt and was quite surprised to hear that my father was Egyptian. Anyway, in 1932, I graduated, and we celebrated the event by taking the train to Jerusalem."

"There's a train between Cairo and Jerusalem?"

"Indeed, and it goes on to Damascus."

"Wait," the old lady said. "You weren't married then? You were 22, no? Sorry. None of my business."

"Perfectly legitimate question, on the contrary. I was not married. It was one of the reasons for that trip. There were two problems. One: I was not a beauty. Shut up, Julius. I was much thinner than I am today, too thin I was told; two: as you may see, I have my mother's blond hair and clear eyes and my father's complexion. It made people uneasy, and even more so since my Mizrahi grandfather had passed his swarthy look to his son and daughter. Uncle Nathan's children favored the Mizrahi side. There were those who thought my mother and grandmother 'did not look Jewish.' Are you sure I'm not boring you with this?"

"Dear Lily, not only is it part of your story, it's also part of a fascinating world we are not familiar with. But if it is too painful, you don't have to go on. Eat your tart; it's getting cold."

"It's not painful. I want Julius to know what happened to me, and I find it easier to explain in front of you all after having drunk a little wine to give me courage. I had indeed nearly gotten married to someone I met at university. Gaétan. A tall, young man, rather shy, and with the eyes of a dreamer. Though he sent me a new poem every day, we did not go any further. We were both too innocent for that, though we were always together. It lasted two years. But Gaétan was not Jewish. He was French and a Catholic, being the son of the French ambassador.

His parents were far from delighted at his choice. His mother, a remarkable woman, welcomed me or pretended to. I was received as if I was already a member of the family, but it was understood that there would be no engagement until he graduated, which he did in June 1931. The family was about to leave for a lengthy summer vacation, so decisions were postponed until their return. It suited my parents just fine since they were not keen on the match. They didn't want their only daughter to leave Egypt; besides, they were not religious, but would have preferred a nice Jewish boy, as they say. It was fairly obvious that, sooner or later, I would have to convert to be accepted by his parents.

In the end, the mother's strategy triumphed. The ambassador was posted to a different country and did not return to Cairo. She had known all along; they had conspired to hide the truth from Gaétan. They told him they would never agree to the match. Either to exert pressure, or out of a broken heart, he enlisted in the navy. Many years later, I discovered that he married a suitable girl, had a stellar career, and died heroically at Mers el Kebir."

After Julius professed his ignorance Castan recounted the tragedy that had cost the life of a thousand French sailors. The British Navy had attacked the French Fleet at anchor at Mers el Kebir in July 1940, fearing that it would be taken over by the Germans after the capitulation of France.

Lily took advantage of the interruption to finish her tart and drink her tea.

"Looking back on that sad episode, I have to admit that such a union would not have worked. We came from far different worlds and had little in common. But at the time, it seemed like a mortal blow, especially since it was widely expected that I would marry the son of the French ambassador. People assumed that I had been jilted, and I got my share of pitying glances. That's how my parents came up with the idea of taking me with them to Jerusalem. They thought it would cheer me up and that by the time we came back, the gossip would be about someone else."

"Why go to Jerusalem?" demanded the old lady.

"My parents were officially invited to the opening of the King David Hotel, a magnificent palace facing the walls of the Old City of Jerusalem. The project had been paid for by a consortium of Egyptian Jews led by Ezra Mosseiri, director of the Banque Nationale d'Egypte. My father was part of the consortium. The program included a series of lavish balls and receptions, the likes of which I shall never see again. I had had gorgeous dresses made for the occasion, and my parents hoped that I would meet someone suitable." She smiled ruefully.

"It did not work out the way they wanted. At the time, Jews from Palestine would go to Egypt to ask their brethren for money, and I imagined a land where Jews lived in absolute poverty. I discovered a different reality. We toured the country with my father's cousin who took us to his kibbutz. It was there that I met David. My husband."

"And that was love at first sight," Julius added, taking her hand.

"It's what I believed then. It took me a while to understand that I had fallen in love with the country, and that David, was just a pretext. We came from Tel Aviv. A modern, lively city with wide avenues and white houses. Theo, there is a whole neighborhood built in true Bauhaus style! Above all, a city inhabited by Jews—only Jews. In a place where one spoke Hebrew as in biblical times. Can you understand? You know, in Cairo, we could be rich, educated, welcomed at the royal court—two of the queen's Ladies in Waiting were Jewish, but we were still made to remember that we were Jews. Of course, it was not like in Poland, but we felt it.

"To come back to David, he was not especially handsome, but I had never met a Jew like him. Sturdy, exuding health, very sure of himself, and seemingly afraid of nothing. To top it all off, he spoke decent enough French. He did not leave my side during our short stay in his kibbutz and came with us for the rest of our trip. On the eve of our return to Cairo, he asked me to marry him, and I said yes. My parents were opposed to the match. They said it was too soon, that we didn't really know each other, and that life at the kibbutz was not for me. It was my mother who was the most vocal. I came to realize that by marrying him, I would have a valid reason to leave Cairo and forget Gaétan and my humiliation. David and I kept on exchanging letters.

It took me two years to wear down my parents. More accurately, it was the changing political situation in Egypt that tipped the scales. Jews felt threatened; the newly created Muslim Brotherhood was openly anti-Semitic. Egyptians did not try to hide their sympathy for Germany, which quietly backed them in their fight against Great Britain. My uncle Nathan, who still remembered what happened in Poland, was among the first to grasp that the rise of religious fanaticism, coupled with a new nationalism, would have catastrophic consequences for the Jewish community. He took his family with him to Argentina, but my father wouldn't consider it; he was too viscerally attached to Egypt to live elsewhere. After Hitler's takeover in 1933, my father came to the conclusion that I would be safer in Palestine so he relented. I married my David in a moving ceremony in the kibbutz.

"You lived in a kibbutz? Lucky girl!"

"Tante, it's not as romantic as it sounds. It took me a while to be accepted. I had to learn Hebrew. Later, I gave French lessons at the local school, but in the beginning, I worked in the fields. It was very difficult for someone like me who always had servants to do her bidding. I wouldn't have minded if I had David's support, only it didn't take long for me to discover that we had nothing in common. He had only two passions: his work and politics. He was a dedicated communist. I had met communists in Cairo, Jews mostly, and intellectuals. They had neither the same drive nor the same determination. Anyway, I came in a poor third, and it became worse after he found out that I would not be able to give him the children he wanted so much and who would have cemented our union.

"When the war started, I considered leaving him and going back to Cairo. But then my parents were killed in an automobile accident as they were returning from a weekend on the Mediterranean coast near Alexandria. I went home for the funeral. The mood in Cairo was bleak. Rommel's Panzers were closing in on El Alamein; Egyptians rooted for them against the hated English. There were awful anti-Semitic articles and drawings in the papers. I sold our villa and converted the price into pounds sterling. The family lawyer handed me a box with my mother's jewels and a lot of money. David had refused to accompany me on that painful trip, and I didn't tell him about my inheritance. I knew I would need that money if it came to a separation. I took a day off and went to Tel Aviv, bought ingots and gold coins with the pounds, and rented a safe in my name in the vaults of the Anglo-Palestine bank.

"In Cairo, no one was interested in taking over my father's stock of china and crystal, so I sold what I could and shipped what was left to the apartment my parents had bought in Tel Aviv that I had inherited. The apartment had three sunny rooms and a terrace on the top floor of a building along the seaside, but my parents had also acquired a one-room apartment on the ground floor where they stored some of their wares since they were considering expanding and entering the local market.

"I returned to the kibbutz. Life went on. I made friends and started enjoying of a mode of living so different from what I was used to. It was a good thing because David became more and more distant. He went out in the evenings to attend political meetings, or so he told me. I accused him of lying, of going to another woman, someone who could give him children, but I was wrong. He had his faults, but he was an honorable man. The truth was that he had joined a clandestine movement fighting the British. Bomb attacks, ambushes …

"I know, here in France, it feels wrong to see the British as the enemy. You have to understand that although Jews in Europe were facing deportation and death, England would not let them come to Palestine, the one country where they would have been safe. London openly favored the Arabs, who attacked Jews wherever they could. In 1929, they massacred whole families in Hebron and Safed in operations which were nothing short of pogroms.

"The British troops did nothing to stop rampaging Arabs. You should have seen how they treated us. Officers in particular would talk down to us as if … I felt it keenly because

I understood them only too well. Yet, the real threat came from the Arabs, and in the kibbutz, we all had weapons and knew how to use them, thanks to clandestine training. Anyway, to cut a long story short, even if a little late, David was betrayed by one of his comrades who had been caught and was looking for a way out. He was arrested, convicted in a travesty of a judicial proceeding for a crime he did not commit, and then he was hung. I was not informed in time and could not even bid him farewell. The whole kibbutz attended the funeral. I never wept so much in my life. Stupid, isn't it? I was no longer in love with him; he did not love me either and yet I only remembered our hopes, our happy times. He didn't deserve to be hung like a common thief. I soon discovered that he'd been betrayed and also found out who had done it. I was told that David's murder would be avenged by the members of his group. They would have done it, I am sure. Fate decided otherwise. I met the traitor one night as I was coming back from a solitary walk. He was drunk and … I had a gun. I fired. I killed him.

"At night, sometimes I remember how he looked, how his eyes widened when he understood. I have no regrets. I owed it to David; it was my way of making my peace with him. There was an inquest. Someone must have mentioned my name. Two British officers came to the kibbutz looking for me. A kid was sent to warn me. I hid for two days with friends and then fled, disguised as an old woman. I didn't know where to go and had no one left in Egypt. Then I remembered that David had intended to travel to Thessaloniki to bring back his mother, who returned to live there after the death of her husband, but that's another story. I managed to get on a ship bound for Greece, still dressed as an old woman and using my mother's Polish passport. I arrived too late to save my mother-in-law. David had a brother in Marseilles. I thought he might let me stay there until the end of the year. I was wrong, but again, that's another story. Anyway, the Germans were everywhere, and it took me months of walking at night and sleeping by day to get to Geneva, and to the Zerners, where I met Julius. I can't believe I have been talking so long. Let's go before they throw us out!"

It was Theo who asked the question Julius was afraid to ask.

"Just a moment. Do you know what you want to do?"

"I know very well but it's not possible right now. I want to go home, not to Egypt. There is nothing for me there anymore. No, I want to live in Palestine, the only country where Jews are free and no one can insult them. When the war is over, we shall get rid of the English, and have our own state. It will not be easy; we'll have to fight, but it will happen, which does not mean that I want to leave my new family. You, Tante, Julius. I hope I'll be able to convince you to follow me. Julius, we need doctors, and someone like you who speaks French, Hungarian, Romanian, and German can start working right away without having to wait to learn Hebrew. Theo, Tante, you will love the cosmopolitan feel of Tel Aviv. Start thinking about it!"

9

A CALL FROM THE CLINIC

THAT NIGHT, JULIUS SLEPT WELL; it was not only the seed of hope, however tiny, that Hans had sown. The questions he asked himself about Lily had been answered. Listening to her tale, he discovered a courageous but vulnerable woman who spoke quietly and without complaint of the tragedies she'd lived through. More than once, he felt the urge to embrace and comfort her. The thought that they might part one day now appeared both intolerable and impossible.

The long day had ended with the dreaded call to his sister. It had gone better than expected, thanks to Paul Werner, who was incensed enough at the news that he had taken advantage of a vulnerable young woman—his words—to phone Manny Newman. He must have been disappointed. Manny told Julius that far from sharing his indignation, he had burst out laughing, adding that he was jealous; as for Anni, she was delighted to hear that her brother had found a charming young woman to keep him company; both demanded details. He did his best to evade their questions. It was far too soon, he explained, as he'd known her barely a month. Swiftly changing the subject, he asked about their children. Tibor—who wanted to be called Tony, was now squadron leader and had received two commendations for undisclosed feats of bravery—no doubt related to raids carried over Germany that he'd only hinted at. His parents were proud, though living in a state of perpetual anxiety. Isaac, their grandson, fighting on the Pacific Front, had been promoted. Karol-Charles was now a full associate at Newman and Son, the new name of the bank, and supervised most of its operations while his father mainly dealt with foreign trade and overseas correspondents. Julia, their youngest, was being courted by a nice Jewish boy, Julius, who could have kept on listening forever, took a deep breath and interrupted her.

"Anni, my darling sister, I must tell you about Elisabeth."

By the time he finished, she was sobbing. Manny, who was listening on another phone, immediately asked for details and offered to see what could be done through his contacts.

"Thank you, but there's no point at this stage. Don't worry. I won't fail to call for your help if it becomes necessary."

He also turned down his sister's offer to come to Paris to be with him, saying that it was too soon. She had insisted, arguing that she very much wanted to see him and his new girlfriend. In the end, she reminded him that when he found the child, he was more than welcome in Chicago and could even come with the girl if he wanted.

Sighing, he poured himself a glass of water. Yes, it would be nice; in fact, wonderful, to see Anni, he thought. But live in Chicago? Accept a post in one of the charitable institutions his brother-in-law's bank helped? That was not what he wanted. What he wanted was to practice medicine the way he always did; open a clinic, treat patients there, and make home visits. Was it a hopeless dream? He missed it so much. What had Lily said? That he could practice in Tel Aviv? Find patients who spoke his language? Of course, it was far too early. There was Elisabeth, and Emile, but it was with a lighter heart that he resumed his inquiries in the morning. He wasn't even too disappointed when Theo admitted he wasn't able to trace André. Apparently, the young man was no longer in contact with his old school or first job.

That left Gabrielle. Time to try a long shot. He would write to his old friend, Monsignor Octavius. Even if the prelate didn't know where she was now, he might know where she lived before the war or what she was doing. With the letter in hand, he walked to the elegant building on President Wilson Avenue, which housed the Papal Nunciature, as the embassy of the Vatican was called. Surely someone there would know the whereabouts of such a prominent cleric.

Indeed, as soon as he explained the purpose of his visit, he was ushered into an office, given a cup of excellent Italian coffee, and told to wait. He took it to mean that his friend had weathered the war, and was proven right when the Nuncio himself entered and with a smile, explained that Monsignor Octavius was no longer in Rome but in Buenos Aires where he headed the Vatican embassy adding that he had done such sterling work that there was talk of his being in line for elevation to the rank of Cardinal. Meanwhile, he would personally put the letter in the diplomatic pouch due to be dispatched in the morning, though things being what they were, it would take at least a month to get a reply. Julius nodded, thanked him profusely, and made his way home.

It was as if a cloud had lifted. He had done all he could; there was nothing left for him to do but wait for news from

Geneva, for Grandin to arrange a visit to the jail, and for Monsignor Octavius to answer. A bit of the feeling of well-being he'd experienced in Geneva was coming back. He was recovering his freedom and dignity; his papers were in order, he had money in the bank, and he was living among friends. He had also taken it upon himself to show Paris to Lily—a bittersweet endeavor. Ten years ago, with his two eldest children, he'd discovered the city he'd dreamt about for so long, and that he saw for the first time. To think that at the time he would have given everything to be able to start anew along the banks of the River Seine! Of course, it was August, and the streets and monuments basked in the golden glow of summer.

Under the dreary October skies rarely lightened by the sun, Paris looked alien, and France a different country he knew very little about, a country waking up to the euphoria of renewed freedom after five nightmarish years, though the fighting was not over yet. German soldiers still occupied major towns in the east and were holding their own against the French and allied forces. Basic necessities were still in short supply and ration books ubiquitous. Then, there was the pervasive sense of unrest. The reality of what had happened, what Frenchmen had let happen during those years was sinking in. The brave Résistance fighters and their extraordinary heroism could not erase the shame of the many ordinary people who had collaborated with the enemy. France, like Hungary and Romania, had passed awful measures against Jews before helping Germans find and deport them.

Julius wondered whether there was a single country left in Europe where Jews would be welcome and could live in peace, and remembered Paul Zerner saying, "The old Europe, the continent we grew up in, is no longer; a new one is in the making and no one knows what it will be like." Nevertheless, the provisional French government had rescinded all anti-Jewish legislation and ordered Jewish property returned to its owners.

"That's assuming that the owners are still alive, and able to come back to claim their due," Theo bitterly commented. "Mark my words, it won't be easy to wrest property out of some greedy hands. Besides, it's not enough. What I want is to see the men who passed those laws stand trial. Mind you, I doubt it will happen."

Julius had nodded, wondering if similar measures were adopted in his native town, how many survivors would be able to take advantage of them?

That thought brought him back to Elisabeth. Hans still called every day. Not that there was news; yet for the banker, the very lack of news was encouraging. Julius wasn't sure he believed it. Fortunately, he had Lily. Watching her looking wide-eyed in wonder at one of the many monuments for which the French capital is famed, never failed to bring a smile to his face. He let her drag him to the Grand Palais where the Salon d'Automne was held. She discovered the prestigious yearly exhibition of contemporary painters and sculptors in the pages of the popular daily *L'Aurore,* which she read assiduously to follow the war. The star of that year's show was someone with the curious name Picasso, a communist, whose paintings were decidedly not to the taste of Julius.

"Don't you see that those fractured figures reflect the fractured world in which we live, and that the violence of the colors reflect the violence of our times?" she argued.

He shrugged helplessly, and they had both burst out laughing.

As they came back one day, Theo had news.

"There was a call from the clinic. A letter has arrived for you. And please don't feel guilty because you weren't home and could not rush to fetch it. The instructions were to come tomorrow morning at ten because the police want someone on hand when you open the envelope. They wouldn't tell me more, not even where the letter was sent from."

"Shall I come with you?"

"Lily, on no account should you come with me!"

When she flinched, he hastened to explain.

"Even if your papers are as good as the forgers said, there is no need to test them by presenting them to the police. Believe me, the policemen I met there were not friendly. I don't want you to risk it. Stay here and be safe."

"Then, let me accompany you," Zsazsa suggested with a smile. "My papers are perfectly authentic, and I shall be your elderly aunt wanting news. Don't argue. You will feel better with someone at your side."

"What if they decide to arrest me?"

"Arrest you? Whatever for? Don't be ridiculous. Besides," she added, contradicting herself, "if they do, someone must bring back the news, no?"

He relented, secretly glad to have her company. Of course, it meant taking the car, since she couldn't have walked that far.

Luck was with him, and he found a parking space across from the building. In the few weeks since he last visited, the clinic had come into its own. One could feel a discreet buzz hinting at work behind the closed doors. A soothing music was filtered in from unseen loudspeakers. A different woman was at the desk. Not young, but a picture of supercilious sophistication. Obviously, she knew they were coming since she stood up, and without a word of welcome, indicated that they were to follow her. Inevitably, or so it seemed to him, they were led to the room where he had waited for so long when he first arrived in Paris. Here too, change was everywhere. Costly paintings were back on the walls, marble sculptures sat on small tables, and new drapes framed the windows.

He remembered having been impressed by the under-stated luxury of the place on his first visit so many years ago. Today, neither Inspector Moreau nor Commandant Dutertre was there; instead, two perfect strangers stood up as they walked in. Julius thought that it was more in deference to the white-haired old lady leaning on a cane than to her companion. The first man offered her an armchair and asked whether she wanted a hot drink; the other demanded civilly to see the doctor's papers. Julius only had eyes for the thick official-looking envelope covered with Hungarian stamps and seals, slightly the worse for wear after probably weeks or months en route.

Having hoped for news of his children, Julius was bit-terly disappointed, although it didn't stop him from being curious. The envelope was addressed to Dr. Gilles, and he assumed that it had been sent by Dr. Kadar before receiving the letter mailed from Geneva, instructing him not to write to the clinic anymore.

"I am inspector Gentoux," said the second policeman. "Do you know the sender of this letter?"

"I believe it is my former neighbor in Nagyvarad, Doctor Kadar."

"I see. The reason you are here is that although it is addressed to Doctor Gilles, a number of documents have been enclosed which appear to be intended for you. They are written in Hungarian, a language that Inspector Lemuel and myself are unfamiliar with. I understand you speak it, but considering the nature of the crimes Dr. Gilles is accused of having committed, it is our duty to have them checked by a suitable expert to make sure there is nothing incriminating. We have to wait for the translator, if you don't mind."

The door opened, and a man wearing the uniform of a British officer entered and looked at Julius contemptuously, demanding in Hungarian-accented French to see the documents.

Madame Castan stood up with the help of her cane.

"In my days, officers knew how to behave," she said in Hungarian, with the distinctive intonation of the old elites of the defunct Austro-Hungarian empire.

The officer blinked and clicked his heels. "Forgive me for not introducing myself. You may call me Mr. Interpreter, if you wish. Where are the documents I am to check? Ah, here."

He picked-up the envelope, knitting his brow. "It appears to be an official letter from the Health Ministry in Budapest to a Doctor Kadar in Nagyvarad who forwarded it to the clinic."

"Who is this doctor, and what are his links to this establishment?" Gentout asked.

"Ladislas Kadar is a Hungarian doctor, now retired," replied Julius. "That's probably why he still gets mail from the ministry. He doesn't know the clinic and its director. We were neighbors in my hometown of Nagyvarad, and when I had to flee the Nazis, I gave him the address of the clinic where my daughter used to work. I knew Doctor Gilles, its director, because we both studied medicine in Vienna. I assume Doctor Kadar used the envelope to send me some information believing that its official-looking appearance would ensure that it would not be opened. He seems to have been right."

Nodding, the interpreter first picked up a photograph he showed Gentout before passing it to Julius, who held it with shaking hands. Taken in the Jewish cemetery of Nagyvarad, it was of poor quality, but he immediately recognized the tomb of Georgy, his first son, who had tragically died when he was five and was buried next to Donna, the woman who had married his father after the death of his mother and had raised Julius and his sister Anni. There was a mound of dirt marking a freshly dug grave with a simple wooden sign: Magda Matthias, 1883-1944.

"A relative?" the policeman inquired.

"My wife. Murdered by the Nazis."

"Why is he sending this? You weren't there when she died? You escaped in time?"

All three men looked at Julius accusingly.

"I was there when they killed her, but you are right, I fled immediately afterwards. You see, German soldiers rounded us up to send us to their camps. Magda went down first. I had lingered at my neighbor's house to give him the address of the clinic so he could tell our children what happened. I heard a shot, rushed to the window, and saw Magda fall. I then saw the Germans shoot her again as she lay on the ground. I wanted to go to her, but Kadar stopped me, saying there was nothing I could do for her and that it was my duty to try to escape. He went downstairs and closed her eyes. I hid in his flat and managed to get out of the city later. Not very brave of my part, I know."

"I apologize." Gentout appeared sincere.

The officer who now looked upon Julius with sympathy, picked up a second document. Written on Kadar's professional letterhead, duly signed and stamped, it was Magda Matthias' death certificate, with the hour and date of her death. Wordlessly putting it on the table, the officer reached for a short letter dated September 15 and translated it: "My very dear Julius, I hope this letter finds you safe and in good health. I am sending you a certificate you may need in your new life. Try to give some news when you can. Remember, you are not forgotten. Yours, Lotsi."

"Who is this Lotsi?" the nonplussed policeman inquired.

"It's … how do you call it—the nickname for Ladislas in Hungarian," the interpreter replied as he unfolded the last document.

"It is signed by someone named Sandy. Who is Sandy?"

"Sandor Toth. My foster brother, a Hungarian farmer. A protestant."

The man nodded again and translated as he read.

"Yuli, my dear friend, my brother, I am hoping with all my heart that you made it and that you are reading this in France surrounded by your children. Here at the farm, we are alright. None of my sons were wounded in the army, and it looks as if the harvest will be good. I want you to know that I kept my word. With the help of your friend, Dr. Kadar, we found the body of your poor Magda. These days, if one is not Jewish, one can do almost anything with money, and you left me more than enough. I even managed to have her buried next to your little boy and our dear aunt Donna. The cemetery guards let me dig her grave and even lent a hand. It was at night, and I gave them two suckling pigs. I am sorry I could not find anyone to come to a small ceremony or say a few blessings on her tomb. I am afraid that the Germans have deported all the Jews. If there is anyone left, they are in hiding. But I asked our pastor to write something. At first, he refused; you know how he feels about Jews. But even he was shaken by what happened. He is ashamed, as are your neighbors, and many others in town. So, he gave me a little prayer and I read it over her grave: "God of Abraham and Jacob, please welcome your faithful servant Magda and grant her eternal life among her people. Amen."

"I went back in the morning and took this picture which I gave to Doctor Kadar. I promise you that when the war is over, when the Jews are back, your wife will have a splendid ceremony. Yuli, I think of you when I go to the river to fish. I think of the days in our youth and I cry for you and for our country. Kadar has sworn he will inform me as soon as he gets some news of you and it gives me strength to go on.—Sandy."

Zsazsa sobbed quietly as Julius attempted to compose himself. The officer then stood up and addressed him in Hungarian.

"Doctor, accept my heartfelt apologies. I was ordered to translate material pertaining to collaboration with Germany. Obviously, it is not the case, and you and your family are the victims of the despicable regime that ruled our beloved country."

Turning to the two policemen, he added in French: "I assume you won't need a report."

Then he went out without waiting for an answer.

Gentout, who had risen, also apologized.

"I am sorry, Doctor Matthias. Please forgive us for that painful moment. Take the documents; they are yours. They are deeply personal and should not have been read in public. Unfortunately, as you know, Gilles is in jail, and it was our duty to check material coming from a country which allied itself with Germany."

Wordlessly, Julius put the letters and the photograph back in the envelope and helped the old lady stand. Together, they shook hands with the policemen, slowly went back to the car and drove a few minutes in silence. Suddenly, he stopped by a small park, deserted at the time, since children were in school. "Listen," he told his companion, I need to think. "Want to sit with me on a bench, or would you rather wait in the car?"

"I am coming, I am coming," said the old lady. "Just give me your arm. The letters have shaken me."

It was rather chilly despite the feeble sunshine. Julius took out the picture. Closing his eyes, he could see the vast dark cemetery and hear the sloughing of the wind through the tall trees, as it blew on the night he carried the body of his small son who had drowned in the Crisu river. So, this is where Magda had been laid to rest! Not where she would have wanted. Between Georgy and Donna, so close to a woman she had hated for so long and whom she had refused to mourn. Magda had died bravely, and it was her death that had made his escape possible. It had not been her intention, but it did not mean he should not feel grateful. All at once, he found himself wracked by sobs, yet he could not explain why. Zsazsa silently stroked his hand, and when the worst was over, she gave him her handkerchief.

"Yuli, stop tormenting yourself!"

"She didn't deserve to die like that!"

"Perhaps, but it's not your fault!"

"How do you know? Had I been with her, she wouldn't have tried to help the girl, maybe it would have been me who was killed?"

"You would have died instead of her? Then she would have faced the horrors to come alone, in the camps? Or you would have been 'lucky' enough to go together? You do know that they separate men and women in those dreadful places. You did what you could. She is the one who refused to flee when it was possible. Now, thanks to your two friends, your wife is decently buried near your firstborn. You can think of her in peace, forget how much she hurt you. Turn the page."

"Dear Zsazsa, we are not talking about the same thing. Yes, when I think of the woman to whom I was married for nearly forty years, the woman who bore me four children, I try to focus on her last, hopeless act of heroism, blanking out everything else. After all, ultimately, she saved my life. But what I cannot bear is the sheer indifference of my neighbors, my patients, the whole town, who did not try to ... Yet, I find myself at times yearning for the past. Our life. My friends from the Austrian circle. A world where I felt at ease speaking Hungarian, Romanian, or Austrian. I had my children, my home, my profession—my place in society. My wife hated me, but I could find solace elsewhere. That world doesn't exist anymore outside my memories. I don't even know if I shall be able to practice medicine again, my one passion. I shouldn't complain; thanks to you, and Theo, I feel I have found a true home."

"Now it's time to turn over a new leaf. Time for a new beginning. And thanks to the blessed initiative of Doctor Kadar in sending the death certificate, you can marry again!"

"Marry again! What are you talking about?"

"Lily, of course."

"Are you out of your mind? For me, Lily was a wonderful surprise, and today gives me both unexpected happiness. She is fond of me, of that I am sure, and yet so much younger! She was born in 1909, like Georgy! What kind of future is there for me, for her, for us, today, tomorrow, when peace returns? I have no idea where I shall be living, not even where I would wish to live. My wife died less than a year ago. I am desperately anxious about my daughter and grandson, and you talk about remarrying? What would my children say? Lily would turn me down anyway."

"Are you so sure? Why do you think she no longer talks of leaving? You have given her money, a lot of money, she told me. Your wife hasn't been dead long enough? Do you really believe it matters in these troubled times? As for your children, they have their own lives. Elisabeth didn't ask for your consent when she married Metzger. Gabrielle could have contacted you when she arrived in France. So could have André."

"Yes, but what of our future together? Lily wants to go back to Palestine. Will it be possible? I don't want to leave you. Could we go together?"

"There's nothing I want more. Stop worrying about the future. Who knows what it holds in store for us? Your father was fond of saying that the gift of prophecy was granted solely to fools or young children! Since you are neither, make the most of what you have today, and what you very well might have soon. Don't look at me like that. You know very well what I mean. Just go ahead and ask her."

"What happens if I ask her and she says no?"

"If she doesn't want to stay with you, she will leave anyway. Tell me, why didn't you ask those policemen to arrange a visit with Doctor Gilles?"

"There was no point; they would only have gotten suspicious again. I have the feeling that your friend, Grandin, will find a way."

"I agree. Let's go, Theo and Lily must be wondering what happened to us. It's too cold to remain here any longer anyway."

10

VICTORY PARADE

THAT NIGHT WHILE LILY SLEPT, Julius silently got up and walked aimlessly through the deserted streets. He'd done it before, kept awake by worry and uncertainty. This time, he arrived in front of a hospital, a hub of activity despite the late hour, and fought the urge to go in, to be in the familiar setting he'd spent so much time in so many years before. He shook his head hoping to drive away unwelcome memories and turned to go back to what had become his home. He was finding inaction harder and harder to bear and wished he could do something, but what? The diploma awarded by the Viennese School of Medicine did not grant him the right to practice in France.

When he'd arrived in Paris in 1933, Marie-Christine had offered him the post of medical director of her establishment, hinting that through her contacts he would be able to obtain the necessary certification. At that time, family obligations prevented him from accepting her help. Today, he didn't regret having turned the post down, but wished he'd received the precious paperwork. Nevertheless, he hadn't succumbed to the temptation of acquiring fake documents that had been hailed as: "better than the real thing."

Jerome Grandin had not forgotten them. Less than a week after their meeting in his restaurant he called to say that Doctor Gilles was indeed incarcerated at Fresnes and that the visit would be arranged in a matter of days. Soon after that, Grandin came to the rue de Passy for a quite different purpose. He wanted to invite the Castans and their friends to watch the commemoration of the November 11, 1918 armistice which marked the end of WWI and the Allied victory. It was to be held on the Champs Elysees on November 11. The event, the first since the beginning of the war, would be particularly festive. Grandin explained that he had bought commercial premises for his new offices above a clothing store near the Arc de Triomphe on the famed avenue. Its two spacious balconies would afford a great view of the parade.

Since there would be no parking available on the avenue and Madame Castan could not walk very far, Julius dropped his friends at the Passy metro station and joined them after parking the car. It was a short ride to the Arc de Triomphe. They came out to a grey morning; rain was expected later in the day. Thousands of people were already lining the avenue, making their progress more difficult. Matching their steps to those of the old lady, it took them ten minutes to reach their goal. An ancient lift brought them to the second floor. A shiny brass plate on the door marked the offices of "Grandin Export-Import." They entered a vast space, mostly bare of furniture, with the exception of a long trestle table covered with a starched white tablecloth laden with a variety of mouth-watering delicacies, and some chairs. Two French windows gave access to balconies where comfortable arm-chairs awaited the guests. It was a curious bunch. The two "popes", Boris leaning heavily on crutches, the singer from the restaurant sporting a dress in the blue-white-red colors of the French flag, an officer in a British uniform, and three conservatively dressed men in their fifties.

"I brought together people who have won the right to watch the parade," their host explained while urging them to pick up a glass of champagne and toast the victory. "People I owe a lot to. I can't get further into it. I shall mention our friend in uniform, just back from London; Theo and his wife, an elderly couple I had never met risked their lives to save mine; my Russian guests whose artistry has helped rescue many; my dear Lena"—he stopped to exchange a fond look with the singer—and went on "who took incredible risks to transmit vital information to the Allies and was arrested by the Gestapo; somehow she played dumb so well that they released her, not dreaming the extent of what she knew. Then, there are our two foreign friends who fought for freedom in their countries, and the three distinguished gentlemen who asked to remain anonymous. Enough said. Help yourself to the food and get acquainted before taking your seats outside. The parade will start soon."

While everyone was busy filling plates, the officer made a beeline for Lily. Her reaction startled everyone; she'd deliberately turned her back."

"Mademoiselle does not like the British, maybe she likes Germans better?" he hissed between clenched teeth. "Let me introduce myself. Lieutenant Bertrand de Lahousse, a Frenchman who was among the first to join General de Gaulle to save the honor of France."

"I had a friend on the 'Bretagne," Lily said, without turning around.

"The what?"

"She means one of the French vessels sunk by the British fleet at Mers el Kebir," one of the civilians explained quietly.

"You can't make an omelet without breaking eggs," the officer expostulated. "It was of paramount importance to prevent the French fleet from passing under Vichy control. It was England that saved France."

"1600 seamen died that day, ordinary Frenchmen faithful to their country. And it was not England that saved France, but American troops that saved the country. Besides, if the British had not shamefully capitulated at Munich, Hitler might have been stopped in time. As for the Germans …"

"As for the Germans," Julius intervened, "a few weeks ago, I was privileged to see how she dropped one with a single bullet. Enough said, we are not here to fight among ourselves."

"Come with me," Lily added as she let him to the balcony.

"You aren't angry?" she whispered.

"Not even jealous." he smiled.

"Jealous?" She made a small grimace. "It was such a youthful, innocent love. One of his last letters was from when he enlisted in the Navy. He was so proud then! He joked that he would have his first command before the age of 40. How could never have imagined that he would die when his ship was sunk by English bullets."

"Yet you are crying."

"Not for him. For those carefree bygone days where there was no thought of war and the future appeared so bright."

They lapsed into silence, idly picking up the powerful binoculars provided by Grandin to make it easier to recognize the world leaders due to arrive. Indeed, the other members of the group, happily eating smoked salmon, goose *pâté*, and *vol-au-vent,* would stand up every few minutes, alerted by the hurrahs, when a better-known personality appeared. Julius tried vainly to let himself be carried away by the general enthusiasm. The rotund gentleman with a cigar—was that Churchill? The fierce-eyed man towering above the crowds wildly cheering, was that General de Gaulle? Who were all the others with unfamiliar names who were welcomed with thunderous applause? In spite of the darkening clouds overhead, it was as if everyone there was caught up in the same fervor.

When the parade started, he closed his eyes, recalling another parade, so many years before: Nagyvarad's main square filled to capacity by cheering people waving farewell to the town's youth going to war. How handsome were those young soldiers in their colorful uniforms! Blue tunics for the lancers, red pantaloons for the hussars, and dragoons in their long coats! How could one not admire the shakos with their jaunty feathers, their boots polished to a mirrored shine, their drawn sabers dazzling in the noon sun! But for him, it had been heart-wrenching to see those healthy young men walking so bravely towards the unthinkable. Every day he had to deal with the true reality of the terrible fighting going on: broken bodies, youngsters barely out of their teens, disfigured, maimed, crippled. And how many carried home in wooden coffins?

He opened his eyes. Today, as then, hurrahs and cheers accompanied the marchers, but it was the only thing the two parades had in common. Well, almost. Here too, war was not over yet. Not only in France, where the legendary

"2eme DB," the company led by General Leclerc, a true hero whose feats redeemed in the eyes of many the shame of the collaboration, ably seconded by General Patton and his men, as well as by the FFI, was about to launch an all-out attack to liberate Strasbourg, the last German stronghold. The battle was expected to be fierce. Of lesser concern to the French, fighting was still going on in Germany and Eastern Europe—and deportations were accelerating with the death machines in the camps working overtime.

On the Champs Elysees, there was no sunshine, and it would soon rain. The pomp and colors of yore were missing. Rows upon rows of French regiments, including one formed exclusively of Africans—Tirailleurs Sénégalais, according to Grandin, whatever that meant. Scottish soldiers, marching to the tune of their weird music coming from weirder instruments, wearing-pleated skirts leaving their legs bare but for knee-length socks, afforded a welcome relief to the drabness of other uniforms. It was left to the warmly applauded American contingent to bring the one note of gaiety from their rousing band.

Civilians then took the place of soldiers, Résistance organizations, delegations from the provinces, as if the whole country wanted to be there. The mood was far from festive. Few smiles, and a deep, all-pervasive emotion mingled with patriotic fervor. The doctor from Nagyvarad felt neither. The victory being celebrated was not his victory, and he had had no part in it. The men and the women had fought and suffered. Now, they could look forward to building their lives anew. Truth be told, he envied them. He no longer had a homeland, a country to call his own. His thoughts turned to Madi who had serenely welcomed a death she had chosen.

She had thought about him to the end; her generosity had made his new life possible, and yet he was beginning to forget her. What had Lily told him the day they met? That she brought bad luck? What should he have said, he, who owed his freedom and fortune to the death of two women? He shook his head wearily. Around him, conversation was flowing. Lily was talking animatedly with the two forgers and nobody appeared to notice that they were speaking Polish and not Russian. Theo and one of the civilians had discovered they shared the same interest for Bauhaus architecture; the two others were trading Résistance stories. Zsazsa and Lena discussed fabrics and fashion. There was no sign of the officer. Julius got up and went inside, where Grandin was busy replenishing the buffet.

"I hope that Lily's outburst did not spoil the mood," he said quietly in order not to be heard outside. "I see that your officer friend has left."

"Don't worry. She put into words what many believe in France. Mers El Kebir was a shock for practically everyone. There were other options. Mind you, regarding the responsibility of Great Britain in delaying a firm response to Hitler, I am afraid France was also represented at Munich, and Daladier is no less at fault than Chamberlain. You have to understand that we are emerging from five dreadful years. People in France have endured fear, cold, and hunger. Not everyone was a hero, but there are some, including here, and I am proud to say myself, who fought with the underground, risking denunciation, torture, deportation, and death. You know it only too well since it has been the fate of your daughter and son-in-law. Your parents, the Castans, did more than their share. I shall never forget your aunt, that sweet white-haired old lady, telling me with her funny Hungarian accent—forgive me—that I did not have to worry about her; should she be caught by the Gestapo, she had her cyanide pill. What panache! Now the men who went to London are coming back. I admit it took guts to leave everything and undertake the dangerous journey to England to enlist. There were true heroes among them, men and women who dared to parachute into France to help the Résistance. Not all survived, but the majority became soldiers in a regular army, protected by war conventions, should they be caught. They never knew hunger, the ever-present risk of capture, torture, and deportation. They nevertheless belittle the Résistance and our contribution to the victory. It is sure to lead to heated political debates."

The Frenchman looked at Julius and added meditatively: "I may have made a mistake by inviting you today. For you, the war is not over, and all this is foreign to you. You have other worries."

Slightly surprised by such a perceptive remark, Julius smiled. "My friends are enjoying themselves," he replied. "It's good enough for me. I find the parade interesting. I've never seen Scottish soldiers before, or Africans with their strange headgear. Also, I shall be able to tell my grandchildren one day that I saw Winston Churchill and De Gaulle in person, even if I did not approach them."

"How many grandchildren do you have?

"I have no idea. There is Elisabeth's son, of course. I also have a son who is thirty and a daughter who is 27. I have had no news from them since the war started. They could be married and have children. I hope they do. We are living in strange times."

"Indeed. I have a son myself, and like you, I don't know where he is. His mother is German, a journalist. She was working for a popular magazine in Paris. We met before the war. I had a bar on rue de Lappe, near the Bastille. There were risqué shows, and she loved them—loved slumming, as she was fond of telling me. I was dumb enough to assume she was joking. There was a bedroom upstairs and she followed me there two or three times a week. She was insatiable. We took precautions, of course; she made sure of that, yet somehow she still got pregnant. I offered to marry her to give the child a father, but she turned me down. She told me bluntly that she was not interested in a low-life like me. She dropped me and promptly married a fellow German who worked for another paper. I saw the birth announcement in her magazine. It was a boy. She called him Adolf. Adolf! My son was named Adolf, can you imagine! There was no picture. War started, and she went home with the baby. I have had no news since about what happened to them or what Adolf looks like. I still see the priest, who prepared me for my first communion many years ago when I give him money for the poor of his parish. He tells me that those are the wages of sins." He shrugged. "I am boring you with my story, don't deny it. Have a glass of champagne."

"Wait, you don't bore me. I understand."

"Thank you. What makes this sorry mess worse is that I don't even know whether I want to see my own child. He must be nearly three by now, and I am a complete stranger to him. However, I can't stop thinking about it. It drives me insane at times."

"Listen … it's none of my business, and yet I wonder …"

"Go ahead."

"Well, when she dropped you as you said, she was already showing?"

"I am no expert, but yes."

"So, her colleague must have known?"

"Probably. So what?"

"You were not surprised to hear that he was marrying a woman bearing another man's child? It never occurred to you that she was taking precautions only when you were together, and that the child could be his?"

Grandin looked at him open-mouthed and gave him a hearty slap in the back.

"To think it took a man I barely know to make me see what was staring me in the face! I should have asked myself why she didn't get rid of the baby. You have no idea the service you just provided me. Let's shake hands!"

Dusk was deepening into night when the crowds thronging the avenue began to disperse. Grandin's guests, who were also beginning to leave, stood on the pavement as one of the civilians turned towards the small party.

"Take a look at those two with their fur coats and their supercilious attitudes! You shall see," he said bitterly. "The time for heroes has passed. Good people are going home. Now that they don't have to fight, you can be sure that the Jews will be coming back in droves."

"They have already been freed from the concentration camps?" Julius' tone was barely polite.

There was a painful silence. The man blushed and turned his head without saying a word. A chauffeur came to fetch Lena, the forgers and Grandin, who told him to first take back the Castans and the engravers; he, himself, and his girl would go down the Champs Elysees to their restaurant and wait for the car to return for them. Julius and Lily chose not to attempt to ride the metro, which was probably overcrowded, so they walked all the way to the Passy station where the car was parked.

"Did you hear him? The war is not yet over, and it's starting anew. The man looked nice enough; Grandin told me that he was a true hero. Don't people know what happened to the Jews? Or what is happening still? I could never live here," Lily said.

"Me neither."

"Where, then?"

"It's too early, I have too many unanswered questions. Will my daughter come back? What state will she be in? The child … Anyway, I won't go to America. I don't know the country, don't speak the language, and I would find it hard to practice my profession."

"What about Palestine?"

"There is that, but I have no knowledge of the country and what goes on there."

"It's not so hard, and you would be most welcome; you could practice as soon as you get off the boat!"

He turned to her and kissed her soundly in spite of the people around them.

"Darling Lily, be patient a little longer."

She smiled and they went on walking arm in arm, not hurrying, despite the rain which had started at last. He bought her a *crepe* from a street vendor about to close, and she ate it with relish under a doorway, licking her fingers afterwards. He kissed her again, tasting the sugar on her mouth.

At Rue de Passy, Theo and his wife were waiting for them in the drawing room where a cheerful fire blazed. No one was hungry after the plentiful buffet, so they decided to skip dinner. The venerable silver teapot with a rounded belly that had had pride of place in his friends' home in Nagyvarad now stood on a side table. From time to time, Theo would get up to refill the engraved glasses in their silver holders, which had also followed the Castans in their travels, from Vienna to Nagyvarad, then to Geneva and Paris.

Yawning, Lily said she was so tired that she wasn't sure she could get to her bed without falling. Julius was about to give her his arm when the doorbell rang. It was almost ten.

11

FRESNES PRISON

IT RAINED IN EARNEST and the slippery roads glistened under the glare of the headlamps. They had left Paris through the Porte d'Orleans and were travelling through small suburbs and poorly lit streets which forced Grandin to drive even more slowly than he had intended. Julius followed in his Juvaquatre, grateful for the presence of Theo next to him. The journey seemed endless, leaving him too much time to ponder the risks he was about to take. Could he be discovered, arrested? He hoped not.

"I apologize for coming so late," explained Jerome Grandin, after the concierge, who had escorted him to make sure that the unexpected visitor was welcome, left. "There was a message waiting for me at home from my go-between in Fresnes. I asked him to contact me if there was news. I went to see him. 'The Gilles woman is sick,' he told me, 'and was transferred to the infirmary this morning.' He had had 'a few words' with the duty nurse, a Madame Martin, who agreed to let Doctor Jules Mathieu attend to the prisoner. We have to hurry because her shift ends at midnight and it will take us nearly an hour to get there. Be careful. I'm not sure you will be left alone with her, and even if you are, someone may very well be listening behind the door. Follow me in your car, I shall leave you when we reach the prison. Just tell the guard that Nurse Martin is expecting you."

"Do you want me to come with you?" Lily had asked Julius.

"No. You are dead on your feet. Go get some rest."

"Then I am coming. I never go to bed before midnight anyway," Castan replied.

"If you must." Grandin was obviously unhappy at the suggestion. "But be careful. Don't wait for him in the car. Sit in the café opposite, just in case. Don't look at me like that. There shouldn't be any problem, but one never knows, and I wouldn't want my friend Theo to get in trouble. Come on. There's no time to waste. No, don't thank me. I shall call tomorrow to make sure that it went well. "

Five minutes later, they were on their way. Julius wasn't worried. Grandin appeared to know what he was doing. In any case, he had to take whatever risks necessary in the hope that Marie-Christine had the information he so desperately needed about Emile. After a while, Castan turned to him.

"Are you dreading the meeting with your dark enchantress?"

"Dark enchantress? Theo, you won't change. I can see it. But yes, I do dread it despite looking forward to it. She always pretended to be my age, though we both knew she was at least two years older. In 1933, when I saw her again in Paris, she was already 45, but with all the resources of cosmetic surgery at her disposal, she looked much younger. Today … she has spent two months in jail. You have heard how people who collaborated, or are suspected of it, are treated."

"It seems that the old prison guards have been reinstated."

"I saw that. I am afraid that they are keen to make up for their attitude during the occupation and will be doubly harsh. Marie-Christine is ill. I wonder what her condition will be like. Will she be thinner? Has she lost her looks? Is her hair cut? Is she scared—afraid for her life? She may not be very pleased to be seen in such a state. She also may rightly suspect that I came to get news of the child—not of her."

"There is Lily as well, right?"

"In a way. I was never in love with Marie-Christine, nor she with me. I am sure you understand. We enjoyed each other's company, and not only in bed. Nothing more, which does not mean I don't feel guilty."

"Guilty? Whatever for?"

"I've known her since 1908. She is part of my youth. I believe I told you so when I came to Paris in 1933."

"At which time you slept with her again."

"I was there for a week, and it was more than ten years ago. There was no commitment on either side, just the transient pleasure of reliving a past so full of hope. What happened next is that she took my daughter under her wing during my daughter's medical studies and gave her a post in the clinic after she graduated. That is not all. During the war, under the cover of bogus medical letters she gave me news. It was Marie-Christine who told me of Emile's birth. Wait, there is more. When she saw what was happening in Hungary and Romania at the beginning of the war, she managed to get me an official invitation to attend a medical congress in Geneva. On the strength of that invitation, I was able to get a visa for myself and Magda. It was almost a miracle. Although Magda wouldn't hear of it, it was that visa, which gave me access to Switzerland after my escape. Lastly, Marie-Christine wrote to me on June 20, care of the bank, offering to help and promising to find me a post in her clinic.

She has shown herself a true friend, and I cannot believe that she betrayed Elisabeth. I, on the other hand, did nothing for her. Worse, when I heard she had been arrested, I was stupefied, distressed even, but my first worry was what I was going to do since I could no longer depend on her hosting me in Paris. I didn't know how you had fared during the war and was not sure if I would find you still safe and sound at rue de Passy. But you were there, and from that moment, I no longer thought about Marie-Christine—except as a means to get information."

"What else could you have done?"

"I have no idea. Attempt to discover her lawyer? Ask whether I could send her parcels? Write a letter? Something held me back."

"What?"

"Theo, I told you how I met Lily, about our lunch in that ruined farm. I had never met a woman like her. By killing the German, she started an extraordinary chain of events. She saved my life, saved the lives of two French soldiers—and we ended up spending the night in one of their houses. Now, imagine what would have happened had Marie-Christine not been jailed, or if I had not heard about it while I was in Geneva. I would have left the town earlier, probably not have agreed to take Lily with me, and done my utmost to get to Paris in one day. We would not have had that night in Saulieu …"

"So what?"

"Can't you see that my new happiness, the new beginning Zsazsa and you keep talking about happened because of Marie-Christine's tragedy?"

"Julius, my friend, you are out of your mind. Let's say that there is some truth in what you've just told me. How does it make you responsible? You might as well feel guilty for having introduced your daughter to her! I have always considered you a most level-headed man, and all of a sudden, you get the most extravagant notions! Of course, you keep telling me how ashamed you are to be alive and free while all your friends were sent to the camps. As if it was your own fault. I suppose you are beginning to feel even more guilty for being happy?"

"You are right as always," Julius sighed. "But for whatever reason, I dread our meeting."

"Are you afraid that she will cling to you?"

"She is not like that—though after two months in jail and whatever she went through … I see that Grandin is slowing. Do you know the prison?"

"I visited it once. Professional curiosity. Poussin, the well-known architect that you probably never heard of, drew up the plans using a revolutionary concept: cells perpendicular to a central corridor. New York allegedly adopted that concept to build its largest jail on Rikers Island. I can tell you more if you wish when you come back."

Julius was no longer listening. He'd parked the car alongside the café, which was miraculously still open despite the hour. Grandin had blown his horn before, making a speedy U-turn. Theo had looked at his retreating back with concern, walked into the café, and ordered a double cognac at the counter. Warned by the horn, a woman wearing a nurse's uniform stood at the entrance of the dark building opposite. Neither young nor old, she appeared forbidding. He came to her, carrying his medical satchel, all thoughts of his companion forgotten.

"Madame Martin?"

"You are Doctor Jules Mathieu? Follow me," she answered briskly. "You are late. It's past eleven."

He nodded without a word. The emotions that choked him were so intense that he was unable to speak, as if he were back in another town, but in the same dark night. So many years ago, tucked in a huge, canopied bed with the lovely French student who had taught him how to make love. He followed the nurse as if lost in a dream, passing through long corridors in semi-darkness, going through one steel door, then a second, and a third, bolts clanking. They then reached a brilliantly lit courtyard with a grey pavilion in the middle.

"Here is the infirmary. Say nothing and come with me" she instructed.

More bolts. Suddenly, that never forgotten hospital smell, the permeating odor of disinfectant ineffectually trying to cover other unpleasant smells, and, in the background, a confused medley of sounds—hacking coughs, moans, groans, and calls …

"One never gets used to it," commented the nurse, a smile softening her severe countenance. "Don't linger. For now, she is alone in the Contagious Diseases Department."

"What does she have?"

"It's for you to determine."

Another door, a window with bars, another key. Under the feeble glow of a low-intensity bulb, a woman raised her head from the bed.

"Doctor Mathieu is here. Ten minutes."

The door shut with a bang behind the nurse.

"Doctor Mathieu?" Marie-Christine, who had recognized him, appeared surprised.

"Good evening, madame," said Julius, coming closer to the bed and putting a finger to his lips.

"I thank you for coming in spite of the late hour."

"Let's have a look at you."

Mindful of eyes watching through the window, he checked her pulse and then took out his stethoscope while she observed him gravely. She had a cold, nothing more serious. In fact, she appeared none the worse for wear. A slight fever was giving a rosy tint to a face that might have been too pale otherwise. There were a few strands of grey in her short— too short ?—otherwise sleek black hair. Had she suffered the indignity of being shorn publicly, like so many women accused of collaboration? He would never ask her. The new cut suited a face still smooth and wrinkle-free. She was not overly thin. While he bent over her, she whispered she was glad he was safe and asked if he had news about Elisabeth.

"Nothing."

As she gasped her shock, he added.

"Do you know where the child is? I must find him."

"No, but he is safe. Write to pharmacist, Georges, poste restante Montrichard, with your address and phone number. Georges shall contact you."

They were still whispering.

"Is there anything I can do for you? Do you need money for a lawyer? I want you to know that I am sure you had nothing to do with her arrest. Maybe one of your visitors …"

She paled and threw a panicky glance at the window. "No more," she hissed.

"Madame, let me reassure you," he said, straightening up and speaking clearly. "You have caught a cold. Try to rest and drink abundantly. You should be better in a matter of days."

"Thank you, doctor. I have reason to believe that I shall soon be set free."

She too was speaking loudly for the benefit of whoever might be listening.

"My fiancé, an air force general who was part of general de Gaulle's staff, just returned from England. He immediately testified to my Résistance activities. Two English airmen I sheltered and treated also came forward. It has become clear that the Gestapo suspected me and put a listening device on my phone. I can't wait to be out, forget those nightmarish months and resume my duties at the clinic."

"Excellent. I am delighted for you. Fresh air will do you good."

"Thank you again. She took his hand and examined him uncertainly. You are not jealous, dear Yuli," she whispered.

"I wish you all the happiness in the world, and even more so since I have to tell you that I have met a charming widow, albeit quite a bit younger!"

She let go of his hand and started laughing so hard that she coughed.

The sound of bolts being drawn heralded the nurse's return. "Doctor Jules Mathieu," repeated his instructions and wished better health to his patient and followed Madame Martin who took him back to the entrance. With a lighter, almost jaunty tread, he walked out. Fifteen minutes, barely fifteen minutes: that is what it had taken to deliver him of his dread and his feeling of culpability. Marie-Christine—he would have to call her Dr. Gilles, in order not to anger her husband—had weathered her ordeal with head held high. Why had he doubted her? Was he perhaps fonder than he thought of a woman who had once meant so much to him?

It was no longer important. The address was. Would the pharmacist know where the child was?

It was raining harder outside and the café was dark. He heard Theo hailing him as he ran towards the car where his friend was already seated.

"That was quick. It went well?"

"Yes," said the doctor, starting the car. "She doesn't know where my grandson is but says he's safe."

"That's good news."

"A great relief, you mean. I shall sleep better tonight. I have to contact one 'pharmacist named Georges' by sending him a postcard. Poste restante in a place called Montrichard. Know where it is?"

"A small city in the Loire Valley, some two hundred kilometers from Paris. I stopped there with Zsazsa many years ago."

"I shall write tomorrow and hope for a quick answer."

"I doubt he is indeed a pharmacist. This type of address was primarily used by Résistance fighters to preserve their identities. Tell me about the meeting. Was it difficult?"

"Difficult?"

Julius started laughing so hard he had to stop the car. Theo laughed with him without knowing why. When the old man had recovered his breath, the doctor turned to him.

"Dr. Gilles has a mild cold and does not seem to be affected by her prison stay. She appears rather well and looks forward to soon being released, the testimony of her fiancé, a general just back from London, and of two British airmen she hid, will clear her. Apparently, she was active in the Résistance. The Germans suspected her and were listening in on her calls."

"You believe it?"

"The Résistance part, yes. After all, she was in contact with Elisabeth, a dangerous thing to do. For the rest—of course not. I'm sure that one of her sons, present at the clinic at the time, heard her conversation with my daughter."

"And denounced his own mother?"

"That's not how he saw it. He was denouncing terrorists sought by the Gestapo. He must have found a way not to implicate her, since she was not interrogated by the Germans."

"And that's why you're laughing?"

"Of course not. After she announced that she was engaged to her general, she wanted to know whether I was jealous. You should have seen her, worrying about me, imagining me pining ... I wished her happiness and reassured her by saying that I had met a charming woman. She was not expecting it. I wonder who, between the two of us, was more put out. Nevertheless, I am sincerely happy for her. Theo, my friend, when I think of what I was telling you on our way here tonight! Men can be rather blind at times."

"Is that what you will say to Lily?"

"Come on. I shall say that we have the needed information at last before mentioning that Doctor Gilles is happily engaged to be married. Let it be a lesson to me."

"Which reminds me, the only thing Lily didn't tell us is her name, I mean her real given name."

"What does it matter? Who remembers that your Zsazsa is, in fact, Zsuzsanna, and she could very well have chosen to call herself Suzanne, the French version of her name."

"It's not the same thing. Tell me, what do you make of Lily's story? Are you seriously considering going to Palestine with her?"

"That's what she wants, but we are not there yet. I haven't begun to consider what my future will be. In theory, why not? Practically-speaking, I can see obstacles. I know absolutely nothing of the country and do not speak Hebrew. Many years ago, I thought about joining the growing Jewish community in Palestine, where Jews from Romania have settled by the tens of thousands. I believe I mentioned that to you. I quickly gave up that plan. I thought then, as I still do, that there was something admirable, heroic even, in this return to the land where our forefathers lived free so many centuries ago. But it would have been irresponsible to uproot my parents, who in any case would never have agreed to abandon their home and their quiet life. As for Magda, she wouldn't have heard of it and wouldn't have let the children go.

Today, the situation is different. I am free. So, should I take the chance? In any case, it would not be right away. I cannot leave France without having ensured that Emile is safe and provided for—and without knowing what happened to Elisabeth. Lily agrees. We'll have to wait for the end of the war. Afterwards, yes, I could make my life there. With you. I haven't found you again to lose you. Don't pretend you are not curious to see how the Bauhaus style you so admire has fared there."

"Yuli, my boy. Not so fast. The fighting over there shows no sign of abating, and between the hated British and the murderous Arabs, I don't see how we can resolve the issue. I agree, in theory, it is tempting, but is it feasible? Aren't we too old to contemplate such an upheaval? Don't answer. We may be healthy enough now, but one has to be realistic."

"You can't think that having convinced you to come, we would abandon you there!"

"That's just the point. I wouldn't want to become a burden for you."

"And you think I could leave with a clear conscience knowing you would remain alone?"

"Let's keep that discussion for another time. Right now, you have no idea how happy for you my wife and I are. A new life, a young and beautiful woman who appears very much in love—and if Zsazsa is right, you could find yourself a father again in a matter of months!"

"She said that? I'm afraid she takes her desires for the real thing. Not that it is impossible, but it is still premature."

"Come on. If my wife noticed, Lily must be asking herself questions."

"What your wife noticed is that in the month—make it six weeks—that we have been together some natural events have not occurred. Lily hasn't given it a thought."

"But you have."

"Yes."

"How would you explain such a pregnancy? Lily and her husband tried in vain for years!"

"First of all, I am far from sure. We need to wait at least a month. Then, medicine cannot explain everything. I have seen perfectly healthy women who could not get pregnant and found themselves with child when they had given up. I remember being called to assist a forty-year -old woman suffering from what she called violent stomach cramps, when, in fact, she was about to give birth. She had attributed her sudden weight gain to "the change," as she put it. One of my Viennese professors mentioned possible psychological causes. I am not sure I agree. On the other hand, what if it had been Lily's husband who could no longer father children? He could have had an illness, or a wound, affecting his fertility."

"You don't appear overjoyed at the prospect of being a father again."

"It is not that easy. Not only is Lily 19 years younger, but I would be 55 at the birth of the child. Not too old perhaps, and yet … What about Lily? Would she be happy or devastated? I would gladly make her my companion for life, but I'm not convinced she feels the same. I met her when she was at a low point in her life. Did she see in me some kind of refuge? Five, ten years from now, or even less, won't she be sorry she did? On the other hand, if there is a baby, we will have to get married right away. I wouldn't want our child to be a bastard. Which brings me back to my grown-up children. My son was close to his mother and will accuse me of having fled without seeing her decently buried. I can't imagine his reaction if he hears that, barely six months after her death, I am getting married to someone four years older than he is—and pregnant already! He won't be the only one. Remember how Paul Zerner reacted."

"Yuli, my boy. You are not making sense. For years you have been unfaithful to Magda. You had good reason since she would not sleep with you. We used to talk about it, remember? I never heard you mention that it troubled your conscience. Today your wife is dead, you are free, and you are ashamed to want to start anew with another woman who is also a widow?"

"What can I say? It's happening too fast. I told you I feel adrift, worse, manipulated by fate. Take the day we arrived in Paris. If you hadn't so spontaneously welcomed Lily, I would have led her to a hotel and she might have departed in the morning without leaving an address or even a real name. Theo, I can't lie to you. I do feel rejuvenated at the prospect of being a father again. I am tempted to go to Palestine and open my own offices to treat patients who come from my part of the world and speak my language. But you are right: I feel guilty. What did I do to deserve all this? Of course, there's no hurry. Until it turns out that she is indeed with child, we don't have to marry. Which will be another hurdle. Finding a rabbi is not something your friend Grandin can arrange."

"In France, you first need to go through a civil marriage, even if you are a foreigner."

"A civil ceremony! You can't be serious! Her papers won't bear scrutiny."

"Don't worry. I have the very lawyer to set it straight. I have been considering it ever since I heard her story. First, even though your papers are in order, you will need an identity card as a temporary resident enabling you to remain in France for two years. I shall ask the man who dealt with my naturalization process when we decided to settle in France for good. At that time, he was just starting out, but you could see he'd go far. I remember his secretary. She was from Senegal, or some other place in French Africa, and was a long-distance runner. You would not believe the legs she had ... she boasted of being able to crush nuts, no pun intended, between her thighs. What temperament!"

Julius laughed in spite of himself.

"Theo!"

"What, Theo? Are you losing your sense of humor? Relax. I have fond memories of the girl. At my age, I don't have much left in that domain. He fired her when he got married. Sometimes I wish ... Forget it, I am digressing.

Today, he heads one of the leading firms in his field. Not exactly cheap, but with so many contacts, he is well worth it. Yours will be an easy problem to solve. Regarding Lily, from her story, there is nothing to indicate that she has lost her Egyptian nationality. If she has her old passport with her, it should not be too difficult. We will discuss it tomorrow. As for a rabbi, have no fear! My wife and I contribute generously to at least three synagogues. For us, it was not a question of religion, but of solidarity to our people. With the death certificate so fortuitously established by your doctor Kadar, there won't be a problem."

It was past one in the morning when they arrived back in rue de Passy. Lily had not gone to sleep but was anxiously waiting with her hostess. When he entered, he saw such an apprehensive look on her face that he rushed to gather her into his arms.

"All is well, darling. Come to bed, I shall explain everything in the morning."

12

MADEMOISELLE MIZRAHI

LILY RUSHED OUT OF THE KITCHEN where they were eating breakfast. She was going to be sick again. When she returned, she shook her head at her friends who were looking at her with a knowing smile. Ten days earlier, Julius had, at long last, cornered her as she undressed in their room, telling her baldly that she was pregnant. She had reacted violently.

"Stop it. Since my fall and the loss of my baby, I can't get pregnant. God knows we tried enough. I'm late, not for the first time. All these months on the road have disrupted my cycle. I am sure it's a question of days now."

"Lily …"

"No! I tell you it can't be!"

"Won't you listen? I'm a doctor and I can see what you won't. Just look at yourself! Isn't it obvious?"

"No! No!" she was crying so hard her whole body shook.

"You don't want it, this baby?" he asked softly, reaching out to her.

"I can't think. I am so ashamed!"

"Ashamed? Afraid of being left alone to cope? Lily!"

"Not that. The child David wanted so desperately, and that I was unable to give him, I am having with someone else. It's as if I'm betraying him beyond the grave."

"It's not you who were unable to give him a child. He had the problem."

"He did it the first time."

"So did you."

"My fall ..."

"What about *him*? Was he sick? Had he had the mumps, for instance?"

"How did you know? He had the mumps after visiting a friend whose son ... but what does it signify?"

"Mumps have been known to cause sterility in men. Don't stare at me like that; it's a scientifically recognized fact. Lily, wipe your tears and give me your hand. Yes, like that."

After taking a small blue velvet box from his pocket, he opened it, revealing a diamond ring.

"Mademoiselle Lily Martinez, will you do me the honor of becoming my wife?"

She was back in Madame Castan's "boudoir" looking at herself in the wardrobe mirror. There was no denying that her face was rounder, even if she "wasn't showing yet," in the words of her hostess. She was having trouble coming to terms with her pregnancy and felt as if she was being carried along by a rollercoaster towards an uncertain future. Her fate was now being determined by people who, until recently, had been total strangers. She didn't mean Julius. Julius was ... she was not quite sure. Theo had spent a lot of money and achieved nothing short of a miracle. She recovered her identity … her former identity. He had taken her to a Mr. Dumoulin, a prosperous lawyer he appeared to know well, and they exchanged jokes she didn't understand. One by one, the lawyer checked the pages of her old Egyptian passport, still in her maiden name. She had kept it for sentimental reasons, as a reminder of a happy youth. He then returned it to her with a smile, saying that the matter would be settled in a matter of days. At what cost? Theo had adamantly refused to answer, telling her blandly that it was an engagement present from him and his wife; Julius professed ignorance. Soon enough, she was told to go to the Egyptian Embassy where the consul would receive her.

The embassy was located in rue La Perouse in the Sixteenth Arrondissement, not too far from rue de Passy, so she opted to walk there alone. It took her close to half an hour since she dawdled on the way, dreading an encounter with an Egyptian official and repeating to herself the story concocted with Dumoulin to explain the lack of a French visa on her passport, which was not valid anymore, or the absence of any stamp indicating that she had used it to enter the country. According to this story, she had left Egypt using her Polish passport (the first lie, because she never had one) to travel to Warsaw (the second lie, she had never gone to Poland), where her family—allegedly—still had property, and there was talk of a match with a distant relative. Though the match had fallen flat, she would explain to the consul, or his representative, that it had taken her two years to liquidate the family assets, by which time war had started and she had been unable to leave. Old friends of her grandmother had hid her and later provided her with false documents that enabled her to flee at the beginning of 1944. She understood that the official she was going to see had been paid enough not to try to pick holes in her tale and had been warned by the lawyer that on no account was she to mention money.

When she turned into rue La Perouse, she was struck dumb by the sight of the green flag with three small stars inside a white crescent floating over the building hosting the Egyptian Embassy. She still remembered the celebrations marking the independence of Egypt in 1922. Sultan Fouad—later King Fouad—had chosen that flag, the three stars standing for the kingdom's three provinces—Egypt, Sudan, and Nubia. She had been thirteen at the time, and had not forgotten how happy her father, a fervent patriot, had been. There were some in the then-flourishing Jewish community whispering that the stars were there to represent the three religions of Egypt: Islam, Christianity, and Judaism. However, independence was nothing but a dream, of course. The rejoicing had not lasted long. It soon became apparent that England did not intend to relax its grip and let the king rule as he intended. The first attacks on the Jews came, fueled by virulent anti-Semitic articles. The writing was on the wall.

She shook her head and entered the building where a concierge in traditional Egyptian garb escorted her to a small waiting room. The place literally "breathed" Egypt. Ornate furniture, heavy drapes, and a portrait of a turbaned Khedive Mohammed Ali, side by side with Khedive Ismail, wearing a tarbush, faced a faded portrait of the late king Fouad. There was also a life-sized reproduction of a bust of Queen Nefertiti and another of the mask of Tutankhamun. The air was scented by the warm sweet smell of a thousand heady perfumes which was the smell of the great houses in

Cairo. She closed her eyes and let herself be carried away to the vast salon of the impressive family villa where the sun, kept in check by magnificent lattice windows, never entered. She could hear the rush of the waters from the marble fountain in the garden mingling with the rustling of the foliage of the centuries-old trees. At times, Vicki's voice could be heard singing a traditional Polish song accompanied by the notes she played on the expensive Austrian piano her doting husband had imported at great expense.

Lily banished those bitter-sweet memories and dried her eyes and picked up one of the newspapers arrayed on a side table. It was *Al Ahram*, the venerable, most respected Egyptian daily. Despite being several months old, she found such unexpected pleasure in perusing its pages and reading about the people and places she once knew well that she lost count of time and was quite startled when the concierge asked if she would like a drink. Somehow, she found herself answering in Arabic, to his slight surprise—a surprise he must have communicated to his superior since when she was finally admitted into the consul's office, he asked her where she had learned Arabic.

"Your Excellency," she replied. "I was born in Zamalek and we spoke Arabic at home."

A few questions elicited that the consul, a pleasant man of some sixty years, had known her family, even met her father at a palace reception, and been impressed by her mother's beauty, adding gallantly, if not truthfully, that she had inherited it. From a drawer, he extracted the pictures of his own children; she thought she had met his youngest daughter, now married with children, who had also studied at the American University. They went on to talk about the Cairo horse racing track, now closed, and the heavy-handed British forces whose numbers were growing. An hour quickly went by exchanging pleasant memories, until the consul glanced briefly at her passport, listened blandly to her tale, and assured her that it would be his pleasure to see to it that her situation was fixed as quickly as possible. It was, in fact, done with unheard swiftness.

Two weeks later, Lily, who, for some reason, had never had her wedding registered in Egypt, was the proud owner of the precious document and was again officially Mademoiselle Leah Mizrahi residing at number 7 Ibn Zanki street in Zamalek. Dumoulin had not stopped there: she also had a Temporary Resident permit valid for two years delivered by the authorities on the strength of her passport and an affidavit by the Castans to the effect that she was renting a flat they owned on the rue de Passy. She had explained to the civil servant "recommended" by Theo that the French entry stamp had been on her old passport, which the Egyptians had kept. Better still, the lawyer had gotten her an authentic driving license to replace her "lost" Egyptian one. She was, in fact, in full compliance with the law. A welcome change after years of illegality and uncertainty. But how had it come about?

"Tell me, Theo," she asked one day when taking him to the grocery store, which was also the clandestine supplier of the fine cognac Julius was so fond of. "Is everyone for sale? Civil servants, elected officials, diplomats?"

"In a manner of speaking, that is more or less true right now. You have to understand that we are going through a period of transition. Though the occupation has ended, the war is not completely over. A new and provisional government is being laboriously installed; however, what is now known as the 'legal purge,' targeting those who collaborated goes on, with more and more people arrested and tried. Some civil servants, whose conduct was not entirely blameless, are keen to help people like you, refugees, Jewish to boot, perhaps calculating that it could help them one day. Of course, they won't mention the discreet financial contribution it's entailed. Keep in mind that, in your case, there was no fraud implied. You were entitled to your Egyptian passport after all; besides, the consul didn't believe for one minute that you intended to go back to Egypt. He knows what goes on in his country. As for your Resident Permit, you are far from being the only foreigner having entered the country illegally when the Germans were there. And you had a driver's license, right?"

"Come on, Theo, that's not what I meant. Without what you call a discreet financial contribution, for which I am deeply grateful ..."

"A simple engagement present from us!"

"And without your contacts, I would never have been received by the consul, or have obtained the Resident Permit."

"Forgive me, my dear, but you are not making sense. Is that a problem for you? Would you rather still depend on the quality of your forged papers to avoid arrest? Are you seriously pretending that it doesn't work exactly the same way in Egypt? That no one there would dream of getting things moving by using contacts or slipping someone an envelope full of cash?"

He began to laugh at the thought, and she joined in.

Lily began waking up in the morning with a curious feeling of well-being. Was it due to her condition? She wished she knew. Then, there was the marriage proposal. She had said yes—it would have been unthinkable to deprive a child of a name and a father, despite her doubts.

"What if I lose the baby?" she asked a few days later.

"Then we shall make another one, now that we know how it works," Julius had laughingly replied, drawing a reluctant smile from his prospective bride.

Something was still bothering her, and she sought out her hostess, who was ensconced in her bedroom, busy examining a perfectly tailored silk dress.

"Tante, I would like to clarify a few things. There is no point in raising the matter with Theo; as the self-proclaimed oldest friend of Julius, he would defend him blindly. You know him just as well. So, tell me: why did Julius marry so young? From what Theo said from time to time, it seems that he was hardly faithful to his wife. That upsets me."

The old lady raised her head quizzically, and Lily felt herself flushing, remembering that her own husband had not been a paragon of fidelity.

"I beg your pardon," she added hurriedly. "I was not thinking."

"I forgive you, as I have forgiven my husband in the past, and still do occasionally. Julius was in a far different situation. I was madly in love when I married Theo. I wanted him so much that I agreed not to have children. I didn't understand the depth of the sacrifice I was about to make. I can admit it today: I was wrong. I should have stood firm. He said that he loved me to distraction. He would have given in." But I ..." she sighed. "I was afraid to lose him. I have long regretted it, and so does he now, though he won't acknowledge it. My dear, as you discovered yourself, it takes children to cement a union. The passion and ardor of the first days do not last. Even if we were well matched in bed, that did not suffice. Soon enough, I became aware that he was not faithful. It shouldn't have surprised me. I had been warned often enough when I was about to marry the most eligible bachelor in town. The same people made a point of keeping me informed of his transgressions. In the beginning, it hurt. Hurt like the devil, and even more so since I had no children to give a sense to my life. Yet I loved him too much to leave him, and he would often tell me, with the greatest sincerity, how much he loved me."

She sighed and blew her nose. "The years went by. We stayed together. Despite his little adventures, we were happy. Because that's all they were. He never had a mistress; I wouldn't have accepted it. Much later, when I could no longer have children, even if we had wanted them, I moved into my own room. That aspect of our lives no longer interested me. We were lucky. Lovers no more, we became friends. I still loved him; his little flings no longer bothered me. Even today, I wouldn't swear to it that he never yields to temptation now and then. A way of proving to himself that he still can. I don't begrudge him that pleasure."

"Tante ..."

"Wait. What you must understand is that it was a different story for Julius. He got married at 18. Young, much too young. She was seven years older, a childless widow, who pretended to be enamored of him. He wanted to be a doctor, and her parents would pay for his studies. His own parents were poor. He was an outstanding student, and yet his only options were to enter a rabbinical seminary, which didn't tempt him in the least, or enlist as a private in the Hungarian army, which would have been pure folly. Since his mother had died in childbirth—that's something that you probably don't know—he was raised by his aunt who doted on him. She said there could be a way for him to study medicine, but it would come at a price. Do you know what he answered? 'To make my dream come true I would make a pact with the devil.' That's how that marriage came about. Magda's father made him swear on the Bible that he would never leave her."

"So, he agreed to the match, his in-laws paid for his studies—and he was unfaithful to the woman who loved him so much."

"That is not what happened," replied Madame Castan. "Soon enough, he discovered that she did not love him, or even care for him. She had married him for all the wrong reasons. He wanted to make a home, but she was not interested. It was a time of great unhappiness. It is no longer relevant. Let me add that she firmly closed her bedroom door to him after the birth of Gabrielle in 1918. He was not even thirty years old. We saw him every week, and we could feel his pain. He was in an impossible situation. I'm not saying this to bad-mouth the dead, but I can assure you that Magda was not a nice person. The things she did … He could have gotten a divorce and left her, taking the children with him. He didn't, because he had given his word.

"When that dreadful war started, he had made careful plans which would have made it possible for them to leave the country and seek refuge in Switzerland or France. She refused time and time again. He could have gone alone; he didn't. He stayed with her to the very end, and if a German soldier had not murdered her, he would have gone with her to the death camps. What I am trying to tell you is that the man you are going to marry is an honorable man. Who could blame him for having looked elsewhere for what he could not get at home? Should he have stayed celibate for decades? Today, you have nothing to fear. Why would he seek someone else when he is already so happy to have found you? He keeps on telling me that he delights in going to sleep at your side in the knowledge that you will still be there in the morning, but nevertheless finds himself waking up in the middle of the night and checking that you are indeed there. He is so happy that it makes him feel guilty—and he lives in dread that you will be the one to leave him.

"Do you mean it?"

"I've never lied to you, and I never will. Lily, you are crying!"

"I don't know why. It's all happening so fast … I'm happy to be with him, I'm fond of him, but is it love? And he's spending so much money on me that I feel like a kept woman."

Zsazsa burst out laughing.

"A kept woman? What does that make me? Theo has been taking care of me for more than half a century and it doesn't bother me in the slightest. Did your mother work?"

"No, but she had a dowry. Besides, it's not the same in Egypt."

"Not the same? Didn't you tell us that you had plenty of money back home? That you were thinking of starting a business?"

"What about his family? His children? Will they accept me? How will they react to such a hasty marriage so soon after their mother's death? When they hear that they will have a little brother or sister younger than their own children?"

"His sister is delighted, and his brother-in-law congratulated him, remember. His children, except Elisabeth, haven't made the least attempt to get in touch with him. Gabrielle has not written a single letter since 1933; we've never seen her since her arrival in Paris. Is she married? Does she have children? In any case, she is in no position to reproach him for anything. André ... he will probably be angry. He was very close to his mother and often took her side. He wrote to tell her about Dr. Gilles. I heard about it from Elisabeth, who was mad at him. Mind you, it was Theo's fault. He had been a little too free in front of the children. Julius had immediately changed the subject, but it was too late. It was particularly wrong of André because he was aware of the tensions between his parents and the fact that they didn't share a bedroom. Still, the news that his father had been unfaithful came as an unpleasant surprise. He was 19 or 20 at the time, and young people can be very sanctimonious. Elisabeth saw it differently, however, and later enjoyed excellent relations with the woman. André, well ... André also blamed us. That's one of the reasons he stopped calling and didn't try to get in touch with his father. Theo never told the truth to Julius. I'm telling you now so that you understand that the meeting with André might be difficult, but it won't be because of you. Better now? She rose from the sofa."

"Wait, I have two more questions. Don't you believe it would be better to tell Julius? And what is more important, are you sure that he no longer loves that Doctor Gilles he was so keen on meeting?"

"Regarding André, you are right, and it's time to inform Julius. As to Doctor Gilles, I am convinced that they never were in love. They were good friends who slept together; they shall probably remain good friends but no longer sleep together. Him, because he loves you; her, because she is in love with someone else and they are getting married."

"One very last question! I can't cook! In Egypt, with my parents, we had an army of servants, and in the Kibbutz we all ate in the communal dining room."

"Did you tell Julius?"

"Yes. He couldn't stop laughing."

"So, what's the problem? You have plenty of time to learn. Just watch me and Hungarian cuisine will have no secrets for you. Stop worrying. Theo and Julius just arrived. Let's go see them."

The wedding was to be held on December 21st, a Thursday. It was coming up very fast. Lily had already had two fittings for the suit she had chosen to wear. It was not white (she owed that respect to the memory of her first husband) but a very pale yellow with a touch of orange, which set off her complexion nicely. She had announced her news to her uncle in Argentina, convinced that he would rejoice, as her parents would have done. She was marrying a doctor, a man with a respectable fortune. Older, perhaps, but that was the way of the world. Everything appeared unreal to her. Would she really become Madame Julius Matthias? Was that what she wanted? Was it love that she felt for the man who had entered her life so suddenly just a few weeks ago, and for whom she felt such a strong attraction? She had no answers to those questions. What she did know was that having a child, and perhaps having more in the future felt so wonderful that she was not ready to think beyond that. Also, through this marriage, the couple's future was set—they would go to Palestine.

Julius was also now fully compliant with French law since Theo's friend got him a Temporary Residence permit valid for two years. The permit had not been difficult to obtain since he had entered France with a proper visa on a legal passport. However, he shared the same feeling of unreality, or split reality. On the one hand, he was a refugee searching for his children and his grandson. He would not relax until he received an answer to the letter sent to Montrichard, saw the child, and discussed his future with the person to whom his daughter had entrusted him. As for Elisabeth, Hans, who was calling every week, was more than ever convinced that she had escaped somehow; how else to explain the complete lack of news despite the best efforts of the Red Cross? Julius didn't share Hans' optimism. Since there was nothing Julius could do, he tried not to think about it.

The other reality was that of a man no longer young who had miraculously escaped a terrible fate and was embarking on a new life with a lovely young woman twenty years younger; a man getting used to the idea that he would be a father for the fifth time. Manny and Anni congratulated him; Paul Zerner had apologized and promised to come to the wedding; so would Hans. Marie-Christine, who rejoiced in her new freedom, would attend with her fiancé, or so she told him during a brief phone conversation, adding, surprisingly, that she would visit him in rue de Passy. He had duly informed the Castans of the date and hour.

Days were now whizzing past at a dizzying speed. Zsazsa's plan to hold a grand reception had been nixed by Julius as being inappropriate under the circumstances. Lily made no comment. The wedding lunch would therefore take place at the Castans. The old lady had lengthy discussions with the caterer, recommended by Grandin. The two erstwhile forgers, who had allegedly abandoned the shady part of their business, were turning to engraving and photography, and would print the invitations as their wedding gift.

One morning, the concierge brought a postcard addressed to "Matthias at Castan" with the correct street number and city. The text was short and to the point: Café du Commerce, Montrichard, 11:00 in the morning, Sunday, December 17. On the reverse side, the ruins of the castle of Montrichard were drawn in pastels. The card was passed from hand to hand. Judging by the writing, consensus was that it had been penned by a woman. It was markedly unfriendly. The lack of the traditional Mr. or Dr. was deliberately insulting. The anonymous correspondent's answer after nearly a month did not give much away. Why not phone? Why this roundabout method? Montrichard and its region had long been liberated, and one could talk without fear. The whole thing was peculiar and did not bode well. Nevertheless, it was a step forward.

At that point, a heated discussion broke out on the question of who would accompany the doctor on the trip. Lily offered to drive part of the way; Julius, not wanting to expose her to what could be a nasty encounter, argued that it would be too risky. To her reply that she would carry her weapon, he simply smiled and would not budge. In the end, it was agreed that Theo would go. He knew the region and the roads, and as a clincher, proclaimed that though not having driven a car for years, he still knew how, and that his driving license was still valid. What neither of them knew was that it was with quite a different companion that the doctor would go to Montrichard.

When Marie-Christine arrived at the appointed time, there was a moment of hesitation. Julius kissed her warmly—too warmly, perhaps? And introduced her to his fiancée. The women observed each other warily. Since her release from Fresnes, Dr. Gilles had obviously taken advantage of the facilities of her establishment and done some judicious shopping. Even with a short and becoming haircut showing no hint of grey and a form-fitting suit showcasing an age-defying figure, she was no match for the youthful glow of the younger woman, whose pregnancy was barely noticeable. After a few minutes of small talk, the visitor turned to Julius:

"I came to bring you and your wife-to-be an invitation to my own wedding. I also thought of what might be a suitable present. Your documents are in order?"

"Absolutely. I have a residence permit valid for two years and renewable."

"Good. You remember that when you came to Paris some ten years ago, I suggested you stay in France and come to work at my clinic; however, you refused because of your family commitments and returned home. I had already put together the formalities needed for you to be able to practice medicine in France. In principle, it would have been impossible for someone who had studied abroad, but I happened to have a very well-connected former patient. Of course, by the time I received the relevant papers, you were gone. But those papers are still valid, and I've kept them. I had a word yesterday with someone in the medical association. All you have to do is go see him right away. His name is on the envelope I brought. He will hand you the proper accreditations without asking questions. My advice is for you to first seek a post in a hospital to familiarize yourself with French practices and medicines. If you wish to do so, phone, when you have the papers, and I shall recommend you to the head of the Salpetriere hospital. Think of it as a wedding gift."

A visibly moved Julius stammered that he was not sure he was going to stay in France.

"Get the accreditation, just in case," she added, turning to Lily, and continued. "My establishment is at your disposal. Julius, don't look so surprised, I have purchased the building next to my clinic and opened a maternity ward. My dearest hope is to see Elisabeth come home and become its director."

"Madame," Lily answered, "I thank you for us both. Now you must have many things to discuss. Julius, why don't you go into the small salon? You will be able to talk quietly."

The suggestion, made with great delicacy, was promptly acted upon.

Even before sitting down in the rather gloomy room, which was rarely used, Marie-Christine asked for news of Elisabeth and the child.

"The Red Cross can't find any trace of her." Julius replied.

"How awful!"

"As long as we know nothing, we can still hope. As for the child, I wrote to Georges the pharmacist, hoping that he would phone. Instead, I got a postcard with no name inviting me to come to the Café du Commerce in Montrichard next Sunday. I hope his mother entrusted him to safe hands; do you have any more information?"

"No, Elisabeth was well aware of the risks she was incurring, and simply explained that she had taken measures for her child's safety should she get caught. She would not elaborate, and I understood. She adores the kid and saw to it he would be well taken care of. As for the card, I wouldn't worry. Georges is obviously a code name. The true recipient of your letter probably did not get it immediately."

"Why not phone? He or she must have realized how anxious I was."

"It's an added layer of precaution. After five years of occupation, one does not change one's behavior so easily. I shall wait for news. Julius, there is something I have to say. Please don't interrupt. I can't find the words to beg for your forgiveness. I bear the burden of having caused the death of your son-in-law and the deportation of your daughter, and it keeps me awake at night."

She wiped away a tear and went on, speaking almost in whispers. "What makes it more unbearable is that I owe you a lot. I was told of your efforts to see me, help me, of your talks with Commandant Duterte, and of the way you were questioned by the police. Yet, you never mentioned my sons, though you must have suspected them immediately."

"It was not for me to do so. It did occur to me that one of them had picked up an extension in an adjoining room while you were planning the rescue with Elisabeth and then acted without informing you. Mentioning it to the police would not have helped; you would have been deemed complicit."

"Let me explain what happened."

"It's not necessary."

"You are probably right, but I need to do it. For me, it came as a terrible shock. You see, my son Wilhelm,—I can name him now, he was killed on the battlefield on October 10 and no longer has anything to fear from the justice of men—has learned of our brief summer tryst from something my secretary said. She also mentioned your daughter perhaps because she disliked her. Thank God she ignored that you were both Jewish. He confronted me. His wife was dead, and, in order to take care of his own children, he expected me to sell the clinic and go back to Austria—to the castle where I had lived with my husband and where he and his brother were born. He insisted it was my duty."

She stopped and wiped another tear away. "Hans, my youngest son, died on the Russian front. He had not been married long and had no children. His wife remarried a year ago. I told Wilhelm that it was out of the question. I had made my life in France, and nothing would persuade me to abandon my profession. He flew into a rage, insulted me, accused me of having lovers and dishonoring the family name. I was in my own establishment, surrounded by my employees, and I thought there was nothing he could do. He came two days later to say he was going back to the front and tried to force me to change my mind. I was on the phone with Elisabeth, and instead of asking him to wait in the reception area, my secretary led him to the office next to mine. He probably wanted to know who was on the line and picked up the extension. When I came to him, he never said a word. Our parting was not cordial. It was the last time I saw him.

"The following day, my driver came back alone, having met, he said, no one at the appointed time. I thought that Benjamin Metzger, who, according to his wife, had been severely wounded, had gotten worse and could not undertake a long train journey. I was not overly upset by the lack of news until the day after the Liberation when two men in civilian clothes burst into my office and started yelling at me. I didn't understand what it was about at first. During all the war years, several members of my staff and myself risked our freedom and our lives to treat Résistance fighters and wounded British airmen. We had turned the coal cellar into a makeshift field hospital. We were very careful. My sons never suspected a thing or realized they were our cover, so to speak. Who would suspect an establishment owned by the mother of two German officers? But then two policemen burst into my office, started yelling at me, mentioned the names and the date, I felt my heart would stop and fainted."

She smiled bitterly. "Being arrested and rapidly taken into custody saved me from the public humiliation of having my hair shorn. I can't believe I survived the first nights in jail. I was insulted and beaten. I didn't even try to defend myself. What could I have said? Who would have listened? I couldn't sleep. I kept thinking of your daughter who had become my friend; I thought about Ben. I was his parents' doctor and knew him when he was a child. I had encouraged him to go to medical school. He was like a son to me—a godson at least. I cried all day long. For her, for him, for myself. I even contemplated suicide. I was lucky. My fiancée, Jean-Michel, came back from London just in time and moved heaven and earth to get me out. The end of a nightmare. My poor Julius, I shouldn't have bothered you with my sorry tale while you ... I haven't even thanked you for your visit at the hospital. It couldn't have been easy, and had you been caught ..."

"Water under the bridge. Tell me, when you last talked to my daughter, did you mention the letter from Kadar?"

"No. It crossed my mind, but it was not the right time, which reminds me, I will have someone bring it to you. In fact, there are two letters. One in German for me and the other in Hungarian. They were in my safe at the apartment. I had it built under the bathtub and the policemen never discovered it."

"Marie-Christine …"

"Say nothing. I came here to invite you to my wedding, not to evoke the past. Please come. Jean-Michel wants our ceremony to be a victory celebration. It will be in the spring. He will be surrounded by dozens of friends and colleagues, while I will have no one. People I thought were my friends disappeared when I was arrested. My parents died long ago, and I have no brothers or sisters. Julius—no, let me call you Yuli one last time—I am more than a little jealous and relieved. Your happiness makes mine possible."

"How?" Julius asked.

"Come on. We were—still are—linked by a strong bond. Vienna, the school of medicine, those were some of the best years of our lives. We made the most of that time, with no thought for what the future held. I was so afraid for you. You're safe, soon to be a husband and a father, and I won't have to worry again."

"My dear, I too feel better knowing that you have found a man you can be happy with. My conscience had been troubling me, and I was ashamed of my good fortune while you were suffering; I felt guilty for having abandoned you, in a way. But what are you going to do about your grandchildren? Bring them here?"

She looked at him blindly. "They died when the castle took a direct hit."

"My poor Marie-Christine!"

"I never saw them. Wilhelm married after France declared war so that I was not able to attend the ceremony. After the 1940 cease-fire, I refused to go to Hitler's Germany. Today, I try to tell myself that had I listened to my son and gone to be with the children, I would have died as well, which doesn't mean I shouldn't have. It was my duty, and had they lived, I would have taken care of them to the best of my ability. I mourn those two innocents, the flesh of my flesh, and my only issue since I obviously won't have more children. Julius, there is worse: the death of my sons makes my marriage possible. Jean-Michel comes from a distinguished and long-established family. He can marry a woman who risked her life to fight the Germans, the widow of an Austrian Count and mother of two enemy officers who died bravely on the battlefield like their father. He couldn't have done it had either son been arrested and tried for war crimes."

"You had nothing to do with it, why blame yourself?"

"I can't help it. At night, I dream of my gloomy room in the castle, the births of Wilhelm and Hans. I wake up sobbing."

"Do you love him?"

"He says he is madly in love with me."

"That's not an answer."

"He is here for me. He comforts me when I have those nightmares that he believes are caused by what happened in jail. Some of them are. He is handsome, intelligent, considerate, and inventive in bed. Since he is about to be given a high-ranking position in the War Ministry in Paris, I shall be able to continue directing and expanding my clinic. I have met his children, and they received me civilly. Julius, we have been in this room long enough. I wouldn't want your Lily to be jealous. Mind you, she has nothing to fear. You no longer have that hungry look of a man who isn't getting enough."

13

ANNI

TWO DAYS BEFORE THE MONTRICHARD MEETING, Anni arrived without warning. Her plane landed in the early evening. Too excited to wait until morning to see her brother, she checked into her hotel and immediately set out for the rue de Passy with her younger son. The concierge admitted them without a moment of hesitation. Not only was Tony wearing the uniform of a colonel in the U.S. Air Force, but his mother also bore a startling resemblance to her brother. They rang the bell at 10:00 p.m. Theo, who opened the door, didn't have time to express his surprise, as Julius quickly rushed to embrace his sister. In the ensuing babble of voices, introductions were made and it became clear that there was not one language common to all. The newcomers usually spoke English, which only Lily knew, or Hungarian, which she did not, which left French, which Anni had learned during her many years in Geneva where her husband had sent her and her children for safety during WWI. Tony, who had been enrolled in a Swiss school, could barely string a few words together. Madame Castan bustled around getting tea and cakes ready while her husband brought out the cognac. Tony looked at it ruefully. He was a handsome man with blond hair and blue eyes like his mother and appeared younger than his forty years.

"Mother will explain," he said regretfully. "I have got to go. My friend Bob, a fellow pilot, is waiting for me in our jeep, and I can't leave him alone any longer. We aim to see the Paris at night that everyone is so excited about. I shall be back in an hour or two for my mother."

"Don't bother," replied his uncle. "Take your time and enjoy yourself. It would give me great pleasure to drive my sister back to her hotel when she wants to go."

"It's our first visit here. We have a rather good city map. I don't suppose you could give us one or two tips?"

"He knows nothing of interest," Theo chuckled. "Why don't I come with you? I shall show you what you really want to see and then take a cab home."

The pilot cast a dubious look at the white-haired old man, searching for how to refuse without causing offense.

"Don't let his appearance fool you. You can trust him. His knowledge of Paris and Paris by night is phenomenal, and he won't tell a thing to your mother!" Julius' reply got everyone laughing. Tony shrugged good-naturedly and bowed to the inevitable.

Lily exchanged a few words with her sister-in-law to be and went to bed on the pretext of the lateness of the hour. Zsazsa soon followed, leaving brother and sister to face each other. Sixty year-old Anna had kept her youthful profile and still golden hair. There were very few lines on her smooth skin.

"What wizardry brings you here?" he asked, taking her hands.

She smiled the lovely smile undimmed by time.

"You ask? My little brother is getting married, and I won't be there? Bad enough that I was not invited when you wed Magda, remember?"

He remembered only too well. Magda's parents had wrongly accused her of having, seven years before, "stolen" the rich young man they wanted for their daughter. They discovered the truth many years later.

"Then, Father Aaron and aunt Donna were present," she went on. "But without me, who would you have? None of your children, right? As your big sister and only remaining relative, it is my duty to see you safely married. Aren't you glad to see me?"

He glanced fondly at his "little sister"—nearly ten inches shorter, though she had always disputed that figure. She was, in fact, his older sister. They were six years apart. Gitte, their mother, had died giving birth to him, and they'd been brought up by her sister "aunt Donna," who married the widowed father, Aaron. But it had been Anni who had held Julius' hand on the way to school or was the one who took him to the park. It was Anni who was tasked to watch over him when they were at Sandor, Julius' best friend's parent's farm. Despite the poverty of their home, Anni had been the symbol of his happy boyhood; together, they had experienced events that shaped their destiny.

Although Julius was extremely fond of the Castans and felt himself falling in love with Lily, the bond with his sister was almost visceral. Like him, she was a survivor from a world which no longer existed. He took her in his arms and placed a kiss on her head. "Anni, you are all I have left from the only family I have ever had, and you can't imagine how your presence here ..."

He stopped, emotion choking him.

"Don't start unless you want us both to start bawling. To tell the truth, I was dying to see you after nearly twenty years, to make sure you were alright. What better occasion than a wedding?"

"To fly across the Atlantic with the war not quite over is not that simple. It is dangerous and must have cost a fortune. How did you manage to convince Manny?"

She made a face. "Manny? Let's talk about him later. You go first. I want to know everything. About Elisabeth, the child, André, and Gabrielle. Then what happened to Magda, to my beloved Madi? It is high time you told me the truth about father's death. The plain truth. I can take it. I want to put all that behind me so that I can whole-heartedly rejoice with you and your newfound happiness. I was a little worried when you told me about that Lily of yours, a girl so much younger than you. A glance tonight was enough to convince me of her love for you. It is the same with you. I can't remember seeing you so … content. At ease. So go ahead."

"There's not much to tell. There isn't even one piece of news regarding Elisabeth. Sunday, I hope to see her child at last. André has not gotten in touch in years. It seems that he learned through Theo's indiscretion that I had been unfaithful to his mother and apparently still bears a grudge, though he must have been aware of the situation at home. I am not looking forward to our next meeting, if and when it happens, and his reaction to being told that his mother is dead, that I am getting married again, not to mention the baby. I have had no contact with Gabrielle since she arrived in Paris. She too could have been in touch. In a perverse way, I believe that the fact that she hadn't tried to contact me means that she is alright and does not want us in whatever life she is living."

He poured himself a glass of cognac. Anni declined and took a second cup of tea.

"Life serves us strange turns," he mused sitting down again. "They have their lives, and I'm no longer part of it, not because I was far away but because that's what they chose. That leaves Elisabeth. I have no more illusions. I believe that when she comes back, because I hope she'll come back—she will need me, for a while. Not more. Painful as it is, it also sets me free. Strange, isn't it?"

Anni shrugged.

"Strange? Who can tell what is strange and what is not? Ten years ago, would anyone have believed the horror that was about to engulf Europe? Now, tell me about what happened to Magda. The truth. Don't spare me."

For the best part of an hour, Julius recounted his last days at home, while Anni listened with painful intensity, shaking her head at times as if to drive away the images conjured by his words. Nothing she had read in the American papers or what Manny had heard through his contacts had prepared her for the stark reality. Julius showed her Sandy's letter, the photograph taken in the cemetery, and she cried softly.

"Yuli, my darling little brother, it is so … horrible, so inhuman. So much hatred. So much suffering. Yet, I have to ask you how our father died. You didn't tell me the truth at the time, and Manny said something in an unguarded moment. Did you tell him everything?"

"Not really. He just connected the dots."

Julius took another sip of cognac and continued his painful tale. The meeting of the Students' League in Oradea in that fateful December in 1927: thousands of students welcomed by the Army Band before going on a rampage, targeting Jewish businesses before vandalizing the largest synagogues. Aaron Matthias was sitting as usual in the Neolog Temple when some thirty students broke in and made for the velvet curtains that protected the Torah scrolls. While the few Jews present fled, Aaron had tried to intervene, but was thrown aside and kicked by a number of booted feet.

"Anni, that is how I found him. I knelt down in the dirt and took his already cold hand. There was the mark of a muddy boot on his shoulder. I closed his eyes."

"We never knew. You said nothing!"

"What for? You were so far away. Why make you suffer? You mourned him; that's all he would have wanted."

"You're wrong. I would have been so proud of him. So would have been his grandchildren. They were old enough to understand. How brave of him to stand up and confront those animals, however hopeless the gesture!"

"Father always did what he believed was his duty. Anni, you must understand that he wasn't afraid of dying. Deep down, he hoped for death. Once Donna was gone, he wasn't himself."

Julius paused and said softly, as if to himself, that it was partly because of his father that his children escaped the fate of the Jews of Oradea. "I understood that day that there was no future for my offspring in their own country, and I decided to send them to study in France. Magda fought me every step of the way, but for once I stood firm. She hoped that Gabrielle would stay and one day make a grand marriage she would arrange for her. Her daughter's defection was a bitter blow. I shall never forget what Gabrielle told me in the one and only phone call I had from her at the time: 'Father, I don't want to die like Grandfather Aaron.' Magda never forgave me, though it was not my doing. You know how she was. She remained deluded to the end, persuaded that because of what she called our social standing we would be spared the fate of others. That's why she steadfastly refused to flee in spite of all my efforts. Anni, what I am about to tell you, I have never told a soul. Some nights, I dream that I am still in Oradea; that I am leaving our flat with Magda and that together we are taken to the ghetto, and from there, to our death. I wake up covered in sweat and my heartbeat is off the charts. I have to reach out to Lily, asleep next to me, to make sure that she is real. And, I secretly rejoice at the death of my wife, which made me doubly free. Free to escape the Germans and flee; free to start my life anew. Pretty shameful."

Wordlessly, his sister poured him some tea. It was tepid but he didn't notice. Absentmindedly, he picked up the last piece of cake.

"Stop talking nonsense" she said. "You didn't cause her death; she did. You could both have been saved if she listened to you. We had a long talk about it when we last came to see you in 1926 for your son's bar mitzvah."

"Yes. One of the last great joys for father and Donna; maybe the last. They understood that they would never see you again. Do you remember how happy father was when he held Isaac, your grandson and his first great-grandson, in his arms? 'Look, Yuli, he kept marveling, he has Gitte's eyes, it's a miracle!' And I kept teasing him that he didn't believe in miracles. Yet, you and your family are a miracle. Thanks to you, the seed of Aaron and Gitte will be perpetuated in America. Enough about me. How are your children? How did you talk Manny into letting you go?"

"Wait. Tell me about Madi. How did she die and how did you find out about it?"

Julius drew his hand through his thick hair. "I have a confession to make. Wait. I have something for you to read first; then you will understand."

He went to his room, careful not to wake up Lily, and brought back the envelope, which still had a faint scent of violets.

Anni read the letter silently and blew her nose. "My poor, poor Madi! Like your wife, she was foolish enough not to leave when she could. What a sad and lonely end, but what courage! So, you had an affair. I suspected it, but you were both such skillful liars!"

"An affair … If only! It wasn't really a lie. What could I have said? That I had fallen in love, as she had, and that it was hopeless? That we only had crumbs of happiness? Two nights in Budapest and one week in Switzerland after the death of her husband, when you'd already gone to America. That is the sum total of what you call our affair. I was left with a broken heart and broken dreams. Lily has made me believe in our future. Can you understand? Please, no more. Tell me how you convinced your husband to let you undertake such a dangerous journey."

"Manny? He didn't utter a word. He simply gave instructions to his secretary to book a first-class ticket to London and a suite at the Hotel Crillon in Paris. Don't stare at me like that. We can afford it; the bank has never done so well. Then, Tony, whose squadron is stationed not far from London, managed to get sent to Paris for a week on some unspecified mission. He is due to go back the day after the wedding. He was waiting for me at the airport, and two hours later, he took off in his plane to bring me here. We dropped my suitcases at the hotel. I was exhausted but couldn't wait another minute to see you. Now, I have to get some sleep. I'll tell you the rest of the story on the way back."

Once settled in the car, Julius asked again if all was well with her husband.

"We have our ups and downs, but are not contemplating divorce, if that's what you mean. I considered it a few years back. Only, it's not done in our circles and the children would have been very much against, especially the eldest. Charles just turned 43. He reminds me of you. Levelheaded. Charles knows what he's doing. Isaac, his son, the baby who so moved father, is fighting in the Pacific, and his eldest daughter is going out with a young man from a very good family. I depend on him and on his wife Katy, who has an important job in a hospital but always finds time to come to see me or go shopping with me. Today, it's Charles who practically runs the bank, though Manny is still the director."

"So, what is the problem?"

"The same. The one you are familiar with. Manny simply cannot remain faithful. It didn't take me long to become aware of that. In the beginning, I thought it was because I was too shy, too inexperienced. He was very patient and never complained; at the same time, I heard that … Listen, I understood or thought I did. Indeed, after a while, he told me how much he loved me, and I thought he wouldn't stray anymore, at least when he was in Budapest. I always suspected that when he traveled to Vienna or Geneva, he wasn't above … Anyway, shocking as it may appear to you, I didn't care, as long as he behaved with discretion. Then, at the beginning of the war he began an affair with a woman in his office who falsely accused him of rape. There was a terrible scandal. That's one of the reasons he packed me and the children off to Switzerland for our safety and remained at home to run the bank. It was a long separation, and I assume he didn't stay celibate, but he joined me after the war and swore that it would never happen again. I believed him. Not long after, our little Julia was born, and he left for America to prepare for our arrival.

Another lengthy separation. Of course, he didn't have to be careful there. In Chicago, far from the tightly knit Budapest community, who knew him? When I arrived with the children in 1926, I refused to see what was happening between us. I was too busy coping with my new life, struggling with English, getting the household and children organized, and finding my way. Manny would leave early for the bank and often returned late. He never came home for lunch as he used to do in Budapest. Then, there were the business trips …" She sighed. "One evening, I found my four children confronting their father in the drawing room. Stories of his infidelities were not new to them, but they had just discovered that his mistress was pregnant. I nearly fainted. He had been in a long relationship with a woman, paid for her flat, gave her a monthly allowance; worse, he was going to be the father of another woman's child! It was an unpleasant discussion. You see, all four children and I are shareholders, and we could have ousted him from the bank. In the end, he had to go along with our decision. In exchange for a huge sum of money, he asked the woman to get rid of the child—I can't believe I am saying this—and leave town. I cried myself to sleep for a week."

"My poor little sister!"

"Life goes on, as they say. Once again, he begged my forgiveness, swore he loved me, that I was the only woman

he had ever loved and that what he called his 'little indis-
cretions' were meaningless. We resumed conjugal life. He
has no mistress, which doesn't mean that he has stopped
sleeping around, secretly. On the other hand, he is seven
years older than me, has put on weight, and has had some
health scares." She laughed bitterly. "Sometimes I wish I had
been unfaithful too. He is the only man I have ever known.
Maybe if I had tried something else, I would have been able
to prevent him from straying?"

Julius stopped the car along the curb and took her in his
arms. She pressed her cheek against him, took a deep breath,
and pushed him away.

"Yuli, pay no attention. It's just that I am so tired ...
I haven't slept for two days. I have nothing to complain about.
Ever since Manny married me, I have never lacked for anything. I have four healthy children and four grandchildren so
far. Manny and I are invited everywhere; I shop at the most
exclusive boutiques. I have my own little circle of friends;
I am the patron of two charitable societies. It would be a far
cry from what would have been my fate if Magda had not
introduced me to Manny nearly half a century ago. And if he
had not married the penniless young girl that I was, Father
would have seen me wed to the widower who pursued me.
I would have had five or six children, and with them, might
have lived through the drama you lived, even the deportation.
It must count for something. I see that we have arrived. I
wanted to hear everything about your charming fiancée, and
all I could talk about were my own problems. I'm sorry."

"Don't be," her brother who had gotten out of the car
to open her door replied. You have plenty of time to know
her. When are you due to leave?"

"I haven't decided yet. I don't want to leave Manny alone for too long. He is unfaithful, but he loves me. And I love him too, after all these years. Maybe not romantic love, but a deep and enduring tenderness. I can't imagine life without him. Goodnight, little brother. See you tomorrow at lunch since the Castans have been kind enough to invite me."

Judging by the well-remembered Hungarian specialties on the table, Anni thought her hostess must have gotten up at dawn. She ate with relish at first, letting conversations swirl around her as others discussed the details of the modest wedding ceremony, which was now less than a week away.

"I can't believe it," she burst out. "Julius, what kind of shabby affair are you planning? As if it's only a formality to normalize the situation? It's been two years since Lily lost her husband, and I fail to see why she should be deprived of a real wedding after all she went through or what you went through. You claim it's too soon? That your wife died less than a year ago? You should have thought about it before fathering a child. Are you afraid of how your children might react? What right have they to object? Did they try to find you? To send you some news? Not poor Elisabeth, the other two. Have you given a thought to your future wife and the mother of your baby? Isn't she getting the impression that you are ashamed, that you want to marry on the sly? Show her, show her family—she told me before lunch that she had an uncle and many cousins in Argentina—show the world that you are proud of her. One day, your children, the children you will have together, will turn the pages of your wedding album with wonder. Don't bother telling me it is too late. Leave it to me and Zsazsa."

"You may be right," Lily sighed. "When David and I got married, it was a very simple kibbutz ceremony. My parents, who were planning a sumptuous reception in one of Cairo's best hotels, never really forgave me."

"It was the same for me," Julius mused. "Fifteen minutes in my father-in-law's drawing room with only Father and Donna. Anni and her husband were not invited. There was no reception."

"There you are" said Anni. "Let's make it happen!"

With the wholehearted support of the old lady, in whom she had found a kindred spirit, Anni got to work with speed and expediency, demonstrating that it was not the first event she had ever planned. There would be no change in the actual civil and religious ceremonies, but the reception would be held in the Crillon Hotel. She would arrange and pay for everything.

The two airmen who had gone to bed fairly late after a rather wild night arrived as coffee was being served. Madame Castan had prepared so much food that there was plenty left and they fell to it with a vengeance. Bob, who didn't speak Hungarian, remembered the French lessons he took in school to please his Canadian godmother and did his best to talk with Theo and Julius. Tony openly admired his uncle's future wife, who apparently found it amusing. Not discouraged in the least, he kept talking in English to her. As she told her fiancé later: "I indulged him because it's only a game for him; his English is far different from that of the British officers in Palestine. I think he's very lonely. He tells me we are very brave to have a child; I didn't have the heart to say that we hadn't exactly done it on purpose."

Before the guests departed, talk turned to the following day and the journey to Montrichard. Lily tried to make Julius change his mind and let her come with him. He wouldn't budge. The round-trip would take five to six hours, and she would be exhausted, not taking into account the fact that they might not be welcome. Who would be waiting for them at the Café du Commerce? Georges the pharmacist? Why all the secrecy? If there was a confrontation, he didn't want her there.

"Why don't you take the boys," his sister suggested. "You should be safe with them! What do you say, Tony?"

When he heard the details of the projected expedition and had a look at the map Theo helpfully provided, the pilot was all for it.

"it's our first time in France. On the ground, so to speak, since we flew over dozens of times accompanying bombers on their way to raids in Germany, and even in France, flying over Orleans, which will be on our itinerary, though I suppose we'd better not mention it. It will be interesting to see it close up. Then, I am sure we can find the time going down or back to see one of the famed Loire castles. I have also been told that the food is spectacular in the provinces."

"No problem, I gladly give them my seat, and will even provide them with detailed instructions." Theo offered.

"Theo, thank you. Since that leaves a free seat, I shall go too." Anni's tone made any argument impossible. "Besides, if there is a problem, I might be able to smooth things over."

Julius willingly agreed to the change of plan, discovering too late that his nephew intended to drive to the meeting in his army jeep and not in the Juvaquatre. "You can't be serious," he had pleaded. "It won't be a pleasant trip. Hours and hours on the road, your friend Bob will be bored to death and all that for a meeting which probably won't last more than a few minutes. My car has excellent shock absorbers, comfortable seats, and heat."

"Yes, but we won't have anywhere to leave the jeep, and if you don't agree, we won't be able to come! We will be sorry to miss the trip!"

The younger man had such a hangdog expression that his uncle relented despite of his misgivings.

"You did right," Theo laughed a little later. "Tony is divorced, and Bob is a bachelor. They may both be forty years old, but they are just two cockerels eager to impress the girls. When I took them around yesterday evening, they were cheered everywhere and women blew them kisses. In your car, who would notice them? Driving the jeep now, that's another story. Don't deprive them of that pleasure. Being a pilot in a time of war is one of the most dangerous jobs there is, and these two risk their lives on a daily basis. Don't forget too, that as your sister says, with them, you have nothing to fear."

Julius agreed. The fact was that he would enjoy the journey in the company of his sister and her son.

They left early in the morning. The cushions they had brought from the rue de Passy to cover the hard army seats did not help much. Four days before winter officially started, the rudimentary covers used for windows were doing a poor job of stopping a cold wind which was made worse by their speed. In the back, snug under an ancient goose eiderdown that Zsazsa had taken out of mothballs, brother and sister were oblivious to the discomfort as they remembered another journey many years ago.

While the First World War raged around them, Julius, who had come from Nagyvarad to check on his sister in

Budapest, had agreed to drive her and her children to Geneva where they would be safe. Madi had been with them, and it had been a merry trip, despite the circumstances. The two thousand kilometers had been traveled in Count von Thüringen's, Madi's "protector" at the time, luxurious Mercedes limousine. On the other hand, today, they had merely some two hundred kilometers on the first leg, and a similar distance coming back. Anni, still not over her jetlag, had fallen asleep almost immediately, secure in the crook of her brother's arm that protected her from the sharp curves.

The plan was to stop in the town of Blois for a hearty breakfast, the first one having been a hurried affair. Blois was not quite on their direct itinerary, but it was chosen so that the two officers could see "a true Loire Castle." Montrichard was close enough, and they would arrive in plenty of time for their rendezvous. There was real coffee in the two vacuum flasks that had been filled in Paris. They found a patisserie facing the castle across the square, with a surprisingly bountiful array of cakes. Julius chose a table with a view as his sister went to freshen up, feeling slightly the worse for wear. A ray of sunshine, which gave a deceptive feeling of warmth, bathed the impressive ruins of the fortified castle. Armed with the pre-war tourist booklet Theo had unearthed, Tony and Bob, wearing their flight jackets and airmen caps, slowly toured the fortifications, taking picture after picture while being admired by a number of passersby. Two bold young women even asked to be photographed with them and kissed them afterwards. Returning to the patisserie, they snagged two brioches and ate happily on their way to the jeep. The mood was decidedly upbeat in spite of some ominous clouds coming from the north. The two friends tried to practice their French, laughing uproariously from time to time. Deafened by the wind and the motor rumbling, the passengers were oblivious. Under the cover of the eiderdown, they managed to converse in Hungarian with no fear of being overheard. They still had so much to say!

There was not the slightest ray of sunshine when they reached Montrichard. Though they had a fairly recent road map, they relied on the directions Theo had given them. The old architect had also drawn them a detailed street map, pointing out with a bitter smile, that to reach the market square where the Café du Commerce was situated, they would have to go through Jew Street, because in the Middle Ages French Jews also used to live in ghettos, though there probably weren't any left. He added a last piece of advice: "Don't be startled if you hear gunfire. Hunting season has begun."

The Café du Commerce was not impressive. Two cast iron tables and some assorted chairs, wet from a recent rainfall, awaited the hardy traveler who would not be deterred by the cutting wind and the prospect of more rain. The grandfather clock above the counter struck 11 as Julius and Tony entered, Anni having remained in the jeep with Bob. The potbellied stove, which did its best to warm the place, belched volumes of black smoke. Several men in hunting gear bantered with the owner at the bar. They all turned around to look at the newcomers. The owner, who had raised his head, was no longer smiling.

"Is that you, Matthias?"

He was being deliberately rude, and his tone was both contemptuous and hostile, so much so that Tony came closer and put his hand on his uncle's shoulder.

There was a pregnant silence.

"Yes. I am Doctor Matthias. I believe you have an address for me."

"I was instructed to tell you that the child is safe where he is, and his location is none of your business."

"Instructed by who? The child is my grandson. I am here because I received a postcard arranging a rendezvous here. Are you pretending that whoever instructed you had me come all the way from Paris to inform me that I was unwanted? He could have phoned; he had my number."

"I have my instructions."

"Which are to give me the address."

The man crossed his arms over his chest and remained silent.

"Is there anyone here who speaks English?" Tony was trying to puzzle out what was happening.

One of the hunters, a tall man with greying hair and an air of authority replied neutrally in the same language. "British pilots have flattened half of Orleans, so they are not very popular around here."

"I am not English. I'm American. I come from Chicago. I came over here to fight for you. You can afford to go hunting, the rabbits are unlikely to shoot back. I, with my fellow allied pilots, American, Canadian, and British, keep on risking our lives day after day by launching raids on Germany to end the war. It's thanks to us that you got rid of the Germans. I was given a week's leave to help my uncle find his grandchild. His father was tortured and killed by the Gestapo; his mother was deported. I believe we have the right to see the child."

Some of the men must have understood English since they exchanged uneasy glances.

"Vincent, give them the address if you have it," said the tall man in the voice of one used to commanding.

Vincent, clearly the owner, scratched his head.

"Could I have a hot cup of tea before we leave? And coffee for the colonel who stayed outside to watch the jeep?" Anni had walked in and was smiling her lovely smile.

"Are you also the child's relative?"

"His great aunt."

Vincent shrugged, accepting defeat.

"Very well. Claudette, tea for madame and coffee for the officer. Turning towards Julius and his nephew, he asked civilly enough: "What will you have?"

Tension dropped at once. One after the other, the hunters came to shake Tony's hand, some engaged him in conversation. In the end, they wouldn't let Julius pay for the drinks, the tall man saying that it was the least they could do. They then left with a lighter heart and a torn piece of paper with some sketchy instructions: "Three Apple Trees Farm," then the drawing of a stream marked "La Chancelle Junction, Luzillé Road." Arrows marked N and S were given for orientation. The two pilots looked at it dubiously, checked it against the larger road map Theo had provided, and they were off.

They crossed the River Cher and followed the road signs toward Luzillé. Shots and hunters' calls could be heard on both sides of the road amidst a medley of barking dogs. After a particularly sharp turn, Bob, who was driving, had to brake and stop on the shoulder to avoid a deer bolting from a hedge. The magnificent animal was followed by another one while the Americans kept clicking their cameras. After a mile or so, they understood they had lost their way. Since a village was nearby, they went there in search of directions.

It was Sunday and people flocked out of church as mass ended. Tony got out of the jeep, paper in hand, and made for the priest who was talking to some of his parishioners. He came back with an urchin of some ten years who was grinning from ear to ear. Perched between the two pilots, using hand gestures, the boy showed them which way to go. In fact, they were very close to their goal. Less than five minutes later, the kid signaled for them to stop by a stone shed. He pointed to a cluster of buildings some two hundred meters away. Smoke rose from the chimney of the larger building. The three apple trees, from which the farm took its name, could be clearly seen, and a brook snaked lazily below, undoubtedly the stream in the drawing. Mission accomplished, the kid departed running in the other direction, clutching in his hand his trophies: two chocolate bars and a pack of chewing gum given to him by the airmen.

The little scene at the café had confirmed Julius' belief that someone didn't want them there, but then why would the person have answered his letter? He thought about the possibility of there being two people. One who had sent the card and was ready, perhaps reluctantly, to meet him; the other, very much against it, had told "Vincent" to turn away the visitor. If Tony had not been with him, he wouldn't have been given the address. He had to prepare himself for a difficult, probably hostile, encounter.

Anni wanted to come with him; after all, that's why she came along on this rather tiring journey. Julius had been all for it, but Tony, fearing for his mother, wanted none of it, unless he also came along to provide physical support, if needed. In the end, it was decided that Tony would walk with them to the farm. If all appeared to be well, he would come back to his friend at the jeep; the two of them would then wait patiently for the meeting to be over. Should it rain, they could take shelter in the shed.

14

EMILE

THE RECENT RAINS HAD LEFT PUDDLES, making the path slippery. Tony held his mother protectively, and she thanked him with a smile. They reached a wide gate which was not locked and pushed it open, triggering a distant bell. The courtyard was empty. There was the sound of a door banging shut and a little boy came running at full speed, stopping open-mouthed at the sight of the visitors. Julius nearly fainted with relief. The child had the blue eyes, golden curls, and angelic face of Georgy, his first born, who'd died tragically at the age of five. They had found Emile, and Julius bent down to hug him.

"Emile, come here now!" came a harsh command.

Julius raised his head and watched with incredulity as a man approached. Wearing hunter garb, limping, far too thin, was it André? By what miracle was he there? Julius smiled and opened his arms to embrace him. His son took a step back to avoid him, glaring at the little group with naked hostility.

"Let's not waste time," the man said in Hungarian. "You came because my sister is dead and you want to take her son. Well, you can't. His parents made me his legal guardian should something happen to them. I have a document signed and notarized to prove it. I want you to leave—now." Then, turning to his aunt, he spat, "After what you did to my mother, how dare you show your face here and try to get hold of her first grandchild to steal his inheritance."

Rooted in place, Julius tried to process what was happening. His son had turned into a hateful stranger. His son, who was Emile's guardian, had known his father was in France and staying in the rue de Passy since he had obviously received the letter sent to Georges the pharmacist. Yet he had not tried to contact Julius. It was beyond understanding.

"You have nothing to say?" André raged. "Get out! Get out with your sister! I'm sure she is the one who talked you into participating in another one of her nasty tricks!"

"Enough!" Tony thundered. "Don't talk like that to my mother and uncle or I'll teach you a lesson!"

André clenched his fists, but Anni, who'd moved to stop the men from coming to blows, missed a step and stumbled and would have fallen if Tony had not caught her.

"What is going on?" An elderly bearded man appeared outside the house and moved towards them, taking the child who had followed the scene with rounded eyes by the hand. "Don't leave her like that, bring her inside!"

Tony carried his mother into a huge kitchen where logs burnt brightly in an oversized chimney.

"Put her down on that couch," said the man.

As Tony followed instructions, Julius kneeled by the couch and checked his sister's pulse.

"Tony, find me a glass of water, please." Julius requested.

When Anni opened her eyes, the old man came close.

"I am Dr. Chamblay, Germaine's uncle. You fainted. Does it happen often?"

"The shock," Julius replied. "And she's still tired from her long journey. She arrived from New-York two days ago."

"Shock? How can you be sure? Are you a doctor too?"

"Indeed. Dr. Julius Matthias. André's father. This woman is my sister. The pilot is her son."

"Where did you study medicine?"

"In Vienna, Austria. I have been practicing for more than thirty years."

"André, you never told us that your father was a doctor."

"What does it matter? Uncle, don't you see? She flew from America the minute she heard Elisabeth was dead, and they came to take the child and his inheritance. Apparently, they don't know that I am his legal guardian."

"Elisabeth is not dead, and my sister wanted to make sure that I was safe. Anyway, what inheritance are you talking about?" replied his father.

"As if you didn't know!" André replied angrily. "What did you do with mother's money? She had plenty, and she left me everything in her will."

"Let's keep this discussion civil," Chamblay said. "Germaine made a pot of coffee before she went out. Sit down everyone."

"It won't be necessary. My sister and her son will go back to the car to wait for me. I won't be long."

Julius felt a white-hot anger, the likes of which he could not remember. André's behavior, his tone, reminded him of his late father-in-law when he'd first met him.

"No, no! There is no hurry," Chamblay insisted. "Let your sister rest awhile. You can leave together. Here, Madame, have a cup of coffee with milk and plenty of sugar, and tell that handsome son of yours to come and sit with us. Please forgive me," he added, turning to his fellow doctor. "If it wasn't to announce the sad news about your daughter and claim Emile, why did you come?"

"It was all in the letter I sent. I was worried about the child." Julius explained.

"Yet, André wrote immediately after his sister's capture to inform you."

"Where did he write? I never saw it."

"He used to write his mother at the pharmacy to make sure she got his letters."

Julius looked at him confused. André wrote secretly to Magda? Gave her news she never passed on?" He shook his head wearily.

"André, Elisabeth was deported in August. When you wrote your mother that letter, she had been dead for more than three months. Damn it, don't you know what was happening back home? The Germans, deportations?"

"You're lying! You ran away, leaving her behind to be sent to the camps!"

"I saw Magda being shot. Only then did I manage to escape. I shall send you the photo of her grave that Sandy sent me."

"I don't believe you."

"As you wish. Regarding your sister, when I arrived in Paris several weeks ago and learned that she'd been deported, I called on an influential friend who contacted the Red Cross."

"She wasn't deported under her own name," the other doctor interjected.

"I am well aware of that. I had a long talk with Commandant Dutertre, who belonged to the same clandestine cell and who witnessed her arrest. My friend found nothing, in spite of all his efforts and the promise of a substantial reward. The fact that there is no trace of her presence, or her death, for that matter, gives us hope."

"What hope! If my sister were alive, she would have written."

"If she could. We don't know where she is, where she might be hidden. I had hoped to find a letter in Geneva ..."

"You have an address there?" asked Chamblay.

"No. That's where my bank is. André knows it and so does she. By the way, did Elisabeth know of the letters you were sending to your mother?"

"No. She always took your side."

"And Gabrielle?"

"I haven't seen her in years and have no idea where she is."

"But why were you writing secretly to Magda?"

"That's what she wanted."

Julius took a deep breath.

"I don't understand any of it. What could she have told you? No. Don't bother answering. There is no more to say. I've been worried sick about the fate of my little grandson, moved heaven and earth to try to find him, but also to find you and assure myself that you were safe. You didn't lift a finger to let me know, and when you got the message sent to Georges, you weren't even bothered to call and waited days before scrawling two lines on a postcard."

"It wasn't me."

"Thank goodness someone did. Your behavior is beyond the pale. Admit that Emile is my grandson, and that it's my right to get news and see him again occasionally. Doctor Chamblay, would you be so good as to give me your phone number? Incidentally, who is Georges the pharmacist?"

"It's my code name; we all had one in the Résistance."

"You fought in the Résistance?"

"Nothing heroic, believe me. They knew they could call on me to treat the wounded when there were clashes with the Germans and sometimes refugees who were in hiding. I chose that name for who would believe that a doctor would pass himself off as a pharmacist?"

"Good point," Julius replied.

Both doctors burst out laughing, drawing a withering glance from a still glowering André.

The bell tinkled, hurried steps followed, and Bob entered, carrying a small suitcase.

"Julius, Anni. You forgot the stuff you bought for Emile in Geneva. Here it is."

Although he was speaking English, they all understood. He left without noticing that his words had been met by a deafening silence. André had gotten madder still.

"You only care for him? Not for my daughter?"

"Your daughter? You are married?"

"He married Germaine, interjected Chamblay. My niece. They have a little girl who is not yet 18 months old.

Julius closed his eyes and breathed deeply.

"I assume there would be no point in my telling you that I had no idea that my son was married, and even less that he had a daughter. Again, you would call me a liar. Listen, in the suitcase there are clothes and toys suitable for her. At that age, there's not so much difference between girls and boys. I will let you decide whether to tell her that it's a gift from her grandfather."

"I'm sorry" said Chamblay. "You don't think that a letter might have arrived while you were away? You visited your friend in Budapest often, didn't you?"

"My friend in Budapest! The last time I traveled to Budapest was in 1927 when Golda, Magda's mother, died. She entrusted me with the task of liquidating the assets she still had in Hungary and depositing the proceeds in an account in André's name in Geneva. That's what I did, and he knows it very well. Since then, I only left Oradea once, in 1933, to accompany André and Elisabeth to France."

"To meet your French friend?"

"My French friend, as you call her, is the owner of a medical establishment, and I hadn't seen her since we both finished our medical studies in Vienna. I barely remained a week in Paris. By the way, she is getting married to a high-ranking French officer. André will tell you that I wanted my wife to come with me on that trip. She refused since she was very much against sending the children to study in France."

"She couldn't have guessed what was going to happen and probably wanted to keep her children at her side."

"In 1933? When we left for France, Hitler was already in power and his men were rampaging!"

"Dear fellow doctor, do you want me to believe that all you've said is true and that your late wife was systematically misleading your son?"

"Facts are facts. If Magda knew of the little girl's existence, it means that she received the news less than 18 months ago. Don't you know what the situation was in Hungary at the time? How could I have travelled anywhere? I couldn't even leave town! We were no longer allowed to take the train, our property had been confiscated, and we were submitted to untold indignities!"

"Yet, you are alive and she is dead. You survived because you abandoned her to her fate" yelled André.

"That's not true. I tried to escape with her when it was still possible, but she refused. She was deluded into thinking that because we were what she called notables, we would be spared. I made another effort when things grew worse and found a way out. It would have been costly, it would have been risky, but there was a real chance that it would have worked. She would have none of it. I could have gone alone; I didn't. How could I have looked my children in the face had I abandoned their mother? The situation became progressively worse. We were treated like pariahs. Patients I had been treating for years, women I helped give birth more than once, would cross the street in order not to acknowledge me.

Magda clung to the hope that it would pass. When we were told to prepare a single suitcase and go to an assembly point, I made one last attempt. I begged her to flee. What could happen? Nothing could be worse than what the Germans had in store for us. By then, we all knew about the death camps. She refused once again. I tell you frankly: I was tempted to go anyway—alone. It was not because of our children that I did not. I didn't have the heart to leave my wife to face what was going to happen alone.

The dreaded morning arrived. May 3rd, a Wednesday. The assembly point was below our house on Teleky Street. We went down with our suitcase, but I came back immediately to leave an address for my neighbor, Dr. Kadar, so that he could write to tell the children … There was an altercation, when I went over to the window, I saw a German officer shoot my wife. I rushed to the door, but Kadar stopped me. He said there was nothing I could do for her and that it was my duty to try to save myself. He went down to close her eyes. I waited as long as I dared, and I left, wearing a suit without the yellow star. Lazlo—Dr. Kadar—made me wear a felt hat, horn-rimmed spectacles, and a cane, which had belonged to his father. The sun was shining, and the streets were quiet. I have never been so afraid in my life. I met two people I knew. Either they didn't recognize me or they pretended not to. Half an hour later, I left the city behind and walked all the way to Sandy's farm. André knows it well. I made my friend promise to find Magda and see she was decently buried, which he did. He sent me the picture. What else is there to say? It took me four months to reach Geneva. Since then, I've been frantically searching for my children.

"I don't believe you" replied André, apparently unmoved by his father's tale. "If mother is dead as you pretend, what did you do with her money? She left it all to me."

"Maybe, but I'm afraid it won't help you. Just like in France, all Jewish property was seized. I had the foresight to 'sell' my clinic to my friend Kadar and the rest to Sandor. Your mother couldn't bring herself to do the same for her pharmacy and the flat in her name. That's what she told me anyway. After your revelations, I'm not sure of anything concerning her."

"You're lying" André had now taken on the stubborn expression his father knew from the past.

Julius shrugged. "Believe what you want. I have nothing more to say to you."

Barely keeping his temper in check, his son strode out of the kitchen.

"Forgive me, but now that the war is over, you will be able to go home and reclaim what's yours?" asked Chamblay diffidently.

"My dear Chamblay, the Germans may have been driven out of France, but the war isn't over in the east. In any case, I shall never go back."

"You can't mean it! What about your property?"

"Doctor, I can't bear the thought of returning to the city where my friends, my neighbors, my patients, who were Jewish, have been deported and murdered and the rest looked the other way. Listen, together with the photograph of his mother's grave and a copy of the letters I received from Kadar and Sandy, I shall send André a note for both Lazlo and Sandy telling them to hand over to my son whatever property they hold for me, in case my son ever goes there. I suppose that you do not believe a word I told you?"

"Matthias, I don't know what to think."

"Never mind. Thank you for your kindness and your patience. Could I ask to see that little girl who is my grand-child too? What's her name?"

"Madeleine. He named her after his mother. We call her Maddie. I'll fetch her."

Julius blinked and exchanged a glance with his sister who was looking better and had left the couch to join the men at the table. Maddie? His granddaughter was called Maddie?

The child, carried in by the old doctor, had just woken up and gazed at the stranger with eyes full of sleep. Chubby and short for her age, she was not very pretty, but her sweet expression gave her a lot of charm. Julius caressed her rounded cheek and she raised her arms trustingly to be lifted. Emile, who had come back, also raised his arms. Their grandfather held them close to his heart, unexpected tears stinging his eyes.

"Tony, will you take a picture? It'll be something at least."

The young man, who had apparently understood a fair part of the discussion in spite of the fact that it was in French, had a troubled expression, but willingly obliged.

"Come on, Anni, time to go." Julius reluctantly relinquished the two little ones.

"Let me accompany you to your car after I put Maddie back in her cot" said Chamblay.

While they were crossing the yard, Julius asked the older doctor how André had arrived at the farm.

"It's a long story."

Tony, who had gone ahead and had a brief consultation with his friend, came back and asked in halting French whether there was a good restaurant and a castle not too far away.

"They came with me in the hope of seeing the Loire region and its castles and so far, haven't managed to do either; they saw Montrichard castle but it hardly counts," his uncle explained.

"You give me an idea. Listen, let me invite you all to lunch. There's a good restaurant in Loches. It's ten kilometers from here, and there's a superb castle. I'm going to take my car, just follow me. No, don't argue. Raymond, my son, was a fighter pilot. In the other war. He didn't make it. He had just turned 22."

He took out his wallet and showed them a small photo. An impossibly young man in uniform, with an open smiling face. One could clearly see the resemblance. Tony, who had understood, put his hand wordlessly on the old man's shoulder, and Chamblay blew his nose.

"He wouldn't have been much older than these two, today. That's why it would be nice to be in their company for a little while and help them enjoy themselves. God knows they deserve it. They are taking incredible risks for a country that's not their own. And we, dear friend, and Madame, will be able to put a number of facts on the table while they tour the castle."

Loches' castle was not as well-known as some other Loire castles, nor was it the most impressive, but it was one of the oldest, and having eaten their roast chicken and mountain of French fries with great appreciation and in record time, it was with enthusiasm that the two pilots made for the castle's massive walls. Brother and sister leisurely finished their meal in the company of their host, who invited them to call him Marcel and told them a little about himself, explaining that he had practiced for many years in Bordeaux, where his daughter still lived with her husband and their two children, only returning to Luzillé, where he was born and had grown up, after his wife's death.

As coffee was being served, he neatly folded his napkin and turned to his guests.

"Here I am, bothering you with my story when you want to know how André came to be at the farm. I'll tell you. He appeared one day, nearly four years ago, looking for work and vowing he could repair anything. He didn't cut an impressive figure: painfully thin, an untidy beard, limping. Germaine, who is my late brother's daughter, was more than a little dubious. Her husband had been killed at the beginning of the war, and she was managing the farm on her own with just one employee. However, her only tractor wasn't working and we were informed that it couldn't be repaired without spare parts, which were impossible to find at the time. So, she told him that if he could fix it, she would give him a job. At the same time, she phoned me and asked me to come with my big pistol, just in case. I wanted to check his leg first. I could see he was in pain, but he wouldn't let me. He worked for two straight days without sleeping, stopping just to wolf down the food he was brought.

"Germaine and I had lost hope, when suddenly we heard the engine running smoothly. A miracle. André just went to bed and slept for 24 hours. Only then did he let me examine him.

"Later he told us that when the German soldiers came knocking at the door of the second-floor flat where he was hiding, he'd jumped from a window at the back and broken his ankle. He managed to run in spite of the pain. It was in Paris. He was given shelter by communist militants operating a clandestine printing press. They found a medic who put the ankle in a cast, but it didn't set properly, and as you noticed, your son still limps. When Germaine gave him the job, he made a point of telling her who he was and where he came from. He soon became indispensable. He is a wizard with machinery. I later understood that he was a qualified engineer, though in the beginning, he spoke as little as possible. He would finish whatever he was working on, take the plate of food prepared for him, and eat in a quiet corner. He slept over the tool shed. After a while … What can I say? My niece is older by ten years, but when she discovered she was pregnant, they married in church. The parish priest is my wife's nephew. He christened André quietly, putting the date as 1914. Nevertheless, it was a local scandal. The parents of her first husband were incensed, and her grown-up children have cut all ties with her and won't even let her see her grandchildren. It's a good thing that she has her little Madeleine and Emile.

"And all the while André had been in contact with his sister?"

"Not at all. If he had, I assume she would have taken better care of him. It happened almost by chance. As I told you, I was doing my best to help those who fought the Germans. They knew that one could call on Georges the pharmacist day or night. A little over a year ago, the "Secret army of the Loire," as they called themselves, launched a raid on a German convoy. Something went wrong, and there were several wounded, though not too badly, fortunately. When I got there, another doctor was already at work. Louis Lenormand was his codename. I'd never met him before. By three in the morning, the wounded were patched up and the farmer in whose barn they had been hidden was passing around mugs of coffee. A new leader, someone I didn't know, accused me of endangering the group by giving shelter to a suspicious foreigner. I replied that the man in question had been born in Hungary but was now a French citizen. 'Give me his name, I need to check,' he insisted. When I told him the man was André Matthias, Louis pricked up his ears but said nothing. I went home by a circuitous route as always and forgot about the whole thing. Less than a week later, a letter to Georges the pharmacist arrived at the Montrichard post office."

"Weren't the Germans monitoring this type of correspondence?"

"We had established a fail-safe routine. As soon as a letter arrived, it was taken out of the normal delivery route and someone would drop it at the church closest to the farm. The priest would hand it over to a randomly chosen choir boy, who brought it to me. In this letter, there was a single line written in Hungarian in the message. I handed it over to André who read it twice open-mouthed and threw it in the fire. He wouldn't tell us what it said. Only later did Germaine and I understand that his sister was making an appointment in Luzillé. When he came back, he informed us that a Doctor Elisabeth Metzger, a woman, would pay us a visit the following Sunday, without further details. I don't know how he was as a child, but today he's withdrawn and rather bitter. Only the little ones can make him smile."

"You don't seem to like him very much."

"You're wrong. He makes my niece happy, that's what counts. Personally, I believe that the farm is not the place for him. I'm sure he agrees. If it were not for his little daughter, and now for the boy entrusted in his care, I'm afraid he would have left."

"How did Emile come to be with him?"

"Elisabeth arrived with him, and André explained who they were. She worked hard to gain Germaine's trust and was soon a frequent visitor. I have to say that I greatly enjoyed talking to her. She has an open mind and an engaging personality, very different from that of her brother. No one in the village was aware that they were related. After the Normandy landing in June, our underground army began harassing retreating German troops. It was at that time that Elisabeth asked her brother if he would be ready to be the guardian of her son should something happen to her. He agreed after consulting his wife. One evening in early August, she brought the child with his suitcase. She wanted him to be safe for a few days. Then we heard that Louis had been captured with his wife 'Donna.' I must add that your daughter had also given Germaine quite a lot of money 'just in case.'"

"Why wasn't Germaine here today? Didn't she want to meet her husband's father?"

"Of course. In fact, she is the one who wrote the card. André was furious and told Vincent not to give you our address. When he heard that you were coming anyway, he ordered his wife to go to a neighbor's and wait until he called her. He intended to confront you alone. My niece urged me to be present. I was going to intervene, but when I saw how much the boy looked like you ... Then, there was your nephew, in his bomber jacket and cap. I couldn't bear to turn him away. Ah, the youngsters are coming back. You have three or four hours of driving ahead so it's time to go. But I was very happy to have met you."

Before they parted, Marcel shyly asked to have a picture taken with the two airmen. Julius promised to send the photos. The rather unexpected encounter ended with warm embraces and hugs.

They had barely taken their seats in the jeep when Anni, visibly fuming, turned towards her brother. "That dreadful woman is still hurting you beyond the grave! There you were, worried sick about the boy, and André couldn't even pick up the phone!"

"I keep thinking about little Maddie, my granddaughter. I might have gone away without even knowing she existed if Bob hadn't arrived with the suitcase. Then, there is the wedding I knew nothing about. How could he have done that? He cut me out of his life without even giving me a chance to defend myself. Anni, I don't think I can forgive him for as long as I live."

"And the way he looked at me! The sheer hatred! The way he talked to me, to us! What could she have told him, and why? Why poison his mind?"

"I made my peace with her when she died, and I won't judge her now. The last years were very hard for her. She was unhappy, bitter, angry at the world, at me, above all. Perhaps it was because, deep down, she was conscious that she should have listened to me, that she'd made a dreadful mistake by refusing to leave when we could. That last night in our flat, when we were both dreading what the morning would bring, she asked for my forgiveness. I understood she meant for not having agreed to flee. I wonder whether it was also for her correspondence behind my back."

"You are being very generous."

"André is the one she truly hurt. As you said, she poisoned his mind to the extent that any rapprochement between us has become unthinkable, at least for now and for the foreseeable future. Yet, he is deeply unhappy. Chamblay feels it as well. He can't be satisfied living like a farmer among people he has nothing in common with."

"How fortunate for you that you didn't bring Lily!"

"It would have been catastrophic indeed. Anni, the main thing now is that I've been freed of a heavy burden. I no longer have to worry about Emile, who seems to be a happy cheerful child. Whatever happens, I know that he's safe."

15

THE WEDDING DAY

ON THE WAY BACK, the traffic was unusually dense and it got worse as they approached Paris and the usual congestion caused by people returning home after the weekend or a day in the Fontainebleau woods. They arrived so late that Tony drove straight to the Crillon. His mother was exhausted. Julius told the two officers to leave; he would take a taxi home and accompany his sister to her suite. She was so overwrought that in spite of her tiredness, she wouldn't let him leave. He phoned rue de Passy, explaining that all was well and that he'd found the child safe and sound. They were not to wait for him; he'd explain everything in the morning. Brother and sister then talked far into the night, but not about the day's events. They reminisced about the past, the poor flat above their father's Talmud Torah where they had grown up. The carefree days on Sandor's parent's farm when they couldn't have dreamed where fate would lead them.

Suddenly, Anni fell asleep, and Julius left her on the sofa, not before taking off her shoes and covering her with a blanket. Even Theo had gone to bed when, at last, Julius put the key into the door and tiptoed to his room, careful not to disturb Lily.

In the morning when he woke up to the smell of coffee, the other side of the bed was empty. He dressed hastily and joined his friends in the kitchen who were considerate enough to let him drink his coffee before pelting him with questions.

"So, you found the child!" exclaimed Theo.

"Thank god. He looks so much like Georgy that I nearly fainted."

"One less worry," Zsazsa said, smiling. "He is safe, then."

"In a way. He is with André. Elisabeth made Andre his guardian."

"André?" Theo raised his eyebrows.

"André and Germaine. His wife. They have a little girl. Maddie. A year and a half."

"But who received your letter," sputtered Theo. "Why didn't he hand it over to André immediately?"

"It was Germaine's uncle, and he gave it to him as soon as he got it."

"Then why …"

"André didn't want to answer me, to see me or even speak to me. He accuses me … let's not talk about it."

Theo swore in Hungarian. "Not talk about it? Come on Julius, you aren't making sense."

"He is convinced that I've known where he was all this time. Turns out he was corresponding with his mother. Says I am lying when I say I knew nothing about that exchange of letters. Theo, there was so much hatred in his eyes."

"So, you haven't invited him to our wedding?" Lily asked drily.

"Invited him? He wouldn't even let us in his house! He sent his wife away so that I wouldn't meet her! He said such terrible things to Anni and me that he almost got into a fight with Tony. If it hadn't been for the uncle, we would have been turned away and would have returned without learning that André was married and had a little girl. I still can't get over it. Please, let's talk about something else. Lily, I need to clear my head. Why don't you come for a walk with me?"

Though the sun had come out, it was very cold, and they dressed warmly. Hand in hand, they strolled along the river Seine, making for a bustling café on the place du Trocadero opposite the Eiffel Tower. They were both lost in thought. Here in Paris, one could feel the beginning of the Christmas buzz. Rationing was still in place, and people were already wondering where they could find the traditional turkey. The upcoming festive dinner would be the first since the city had been liberated. However, the soon-to-be groom and bride had other preoccupations. Decision time was fast approaching. They could no longer delude themselves that the war would soon be over. A daring German counter-offensive in Belgium had been wildly successful. Allied forces suffered more than twenty-thousand casualties. The news from Hungary was bad. Members of the Arrowed Cross, a local Nazi party that had taken over the country, had started a murderous spree, killing the Jews not yet deported.

Russian forces had surrounded Budapest, but it was too late to save them. In Palestine, there was growing anger against Great Britain, a country that had stopped ships in the Mediterranean and set up camps in Cyprus for the survivors and refugees on board. When hundreds of children and youngsters under eighteen who had survived the massacres perpetrated by Romanian troops in Transnistria had managed to reach the port of Haifa, they were immediately jailed. While Jewish paramilitary groups refrained from attacking British soldiers in order not to hamper the British war efforts, Arabs hoarded weapons while those soldiers looked the other way. On every front, the future appeared bleak.

Of more immediate concern to Julius and Lily, was that four days before the wedding they had yet to decide where to live. At the café, Lily ordered a mug of hot chocolate and a croissant she shared with Julius who drank coffee. The Castans were pressing them to remain in rue de Passy. Julius was all for the idea, but he also wondered whether Lily would not prefer to have her own residence. Then, there was Anni's generous offer: go to America and wait there until there was some kind of peace in Palestine.

"Obviously," Anni had told Julius. "you won't be able to leave until you have news of Elisabeth and probably not before the birth of your baby. That would leave me plenty of time to have everything ready for you: papers, a suitable flat, a hospital position—all taken care of. I'd love to have you living nearby. Think about it." Though Julius would also have loved to have been near his sister, he was not keen on crossing the Atlantic.

"Your sister discussed it with me too," said Lily. "I won't say that I'm not just a little bit tempted. I have a degree from Cairo American University where I became familiar with American life. I wouldn't have any trouble integrating there. With Anni's help, we would have a good life. Too good. I fear that once there, we'd never leave. Julius, I want to go home to the sun and the warmth of my country. Tony tells me that it's even colder in Chicago than in Paris. In the winter, it's already dark by three in the afternoon, and still dark at nine in the morning. I feel depressed enough with the greyness of the days here. My kibbutz was never cold, and the sky was blue most of the year. I'd swim in the sea early in the morning before starting the day, or at night after dinner. It's another world. A world of light that I miss terribly. That's not all. I want to raise my child, our child, in a country where he belongs, where no one can call him names because he's Jewish. Tony also says that although he's an officer in the U.S. army, he has occasionally been called "Jew Boy"—though not twice by the same person; he makes sure that doesn't happen. So, I'd rather stay in France and remain in rue de Passy until I can go back.

"Yesterday, while you were away, I sat down with Theo and Tante and we had a long talk. They would never go to America, but they might consider Palestine where they might find themselves among people who shared the same culture and spoke their language. Right now, their dearest wish is for us to stay with them. They don't come out with it openly, but it's obvious that our departure would be painful for them. Being alone once more, seeing us from time to time ... one can sense how much it frightens them."

"What about you? Don't you want your own house?" Julius asked.

"It's more complex than that. Julius, I'll turn 35 soon, and they treat me as if I were a girl of 20. It's touching, but also burdensome. On the one hand, I would like to be independent again, have my own flat and do whatever I want without having to consider others. On the other hand, I owe them too much to hurt them like that. They welcomed me with open arms. That first evening, when we arrived, they didn't know me.

They could have let me go. You would have helped me find a hotel, we would have said goodbye, and, in the morning, I would have taken the train for Marseilles. For all his bluster, my brother-in-law would never have thrown me into the street. He'd have reluctantly taken me in. Some weeks later, I would have discovered that I was pregnant, or, more likely, my sister-in-law would have noticed. Because I'm sure that our baby was conceived on the first night when we were in Saulieu. Can you imagine what would have happened next? Kicked out of their house, alone … Julius, I can't bear to think about it!"

"I wouldn't have let you go like that! I would have checked on you in the morning!"

"You wouldn't have found me. On balance, staying with them is not such a big sacrifice. I've never lived alone. I'm not only speaking about the kibbutz. When I was growing up in Cairo, parents and grandparents lived together with a host of servants. With the Castans, I have found a new family. There is something else. With the documents you got from Dr. Gilles, you may want to practice again, leaving me alone in an empty house. Don't laugh, I'm already planning the birth with Tante. Sometimes I feel that she wants that baby as much as I do! If they come with us to Palestine, it will be different. They will live with us, but in our own house."

"Then it's settled," Julius said with a smile.

Anni had made good on her word and secured one of the majestic reception rooms at the Crillon for the wedding lunch she was giving. It had been agreed that Julius would stay at the hotel for his last two bachelor nights. The day before the wedding, his sister took him aside.

"Yuli, Manny phoned late yesterday. We must have spoken for hours. I'm going home as soon as you tie the knot. He has invited the children and the grandchildren for New Year's Eve. Isaac will have a furlough and be with us. Tony hopes to be able to join as well. I'll have a lot to do. You don't need me anymore anyway. I was happy to have been there for you. I wish you would settle in the States; this new separation breaks my heart. You have your reasons: a wife, a new life, new plans, but the world is changing. Today, a journey which would take weeks can be accomplished in a day. When peace returns, I'll visit you in Palestine. Four years from now, Manny and I will celebrate our golden wedding anniversary. Fifty years! You must promise to do all you can to be there. Meanwhile, write and phone often ... please!"

He promised, and they embraced, trying hard not to cry.

A set of pictures taken by a photographer recommended by Boris, who, invited to the wedding with his companion, could not do the honors, immortalized the day: a radiant Lily on the grand staircase of the town hall in the Sixteenth Arrondissement, Julius at her side; the two of them, seated, listening to the mayor who wore the sash with the three colors of the French flag; the newlyweds sharing a smile. Far more moving were the photos taken during the religious ceremony: Julius, flanked by his sister and her son, moving towards the nuptial canopy; Julius gazing at Lily, advancing slowly between a dignified Theo and his wife, who had taken a dress she'd once worn to the Austrian imperial court out of mothballs.

Doctor Matthias didn't see his old friends; he only had eyes for the girl who'd captured his heart and was about to become his wife. She was stunning, with the special glow of a woman on her wedding day.

What was missing in those pictures was the audience's reaction. Vladimir Malenkov, erstwhile student of divinity in a Cracow seminary, uneasy in this Jewish place of worship, followed the liturgy with interest. He'd willingly donned a Kipa, the Jewish head cover, because it seemed similar to the skullcap worn by church dignitaries. Lena, who held tight to the two sides of her mink coat in an effort to hide her deep cleavage, looked around anxiously and crossed herself several times. Marie-Christine's groom to be, quite handsome in his dress uniform, was surprised to hear that he could keep on his cap instead of the Kipa if he wanted. Entering the synagogue for the first time in his life, he was dumbstruck to discover Colonel Tony Newman, an old acquaintance he'd encountered many times in London. Making good on his promise, Hans the banker was there; he refused the Kipa and instead took an ancient velvet skullcap out of his pocket, something observed with surprise and a great deal of curiosity by his colleague, Zerner. He had also arrived from Switzerland with his mother, who didn't want to miss the wedding of her dear childhood friend's granddaughter. Paul was delighted to meet Anni again, who he'd known very well when she took refuge in Switzerland with her children.

The wedding lunch was attended by people coming from a range of countries and religions. Old Madame Zerner was seated next to the two "engravers"; they spoke Polish and longingly remembered a Poland that no longer existed. She apparently didn't notice that the men were not Jewish but Catholics, however lapsed they might have been. Of course, it could perhaps be because she'd never spoken with people who weren't Jewish. The pair understood that, but went along anyway, happy to be talking about a beloved country they were not sure they would ever see again. Tony and Marie-Christine's boyfriend spoke animatedly in English, which didn't stop the American from stealing interested looks at Lena's sumptuous décolleté. The singer ate moodily, feeling neglected by Grandin, who was engaged in a serious discussion with Theo and his wife. Hans Steuber and Paul Zerner got better acquainted, a fact noted by Julius, who thought his new friend was finding it harder and harder to resist the temptation to reveal his secret. Anni and Dr. Gilles discussed plastic surgery.

Julius felt vaguely remote as he whispered in his wife's ear. She too was lost in thought but turned to him with a sigh of relief. They exchanged an understanding smile.

"I have now gone back to the initials of my youth," she mused. "Leila Mizrahi is now Leila Matthias. But everything else is strange." Her gaze swept the room as she thought: a few months ago I didn't know any of the guests, not even the man I just married. Madame Zerner was just a name at the bottom of a letter of condolences my mother received when Grandmother Vicky died. The people here all helped me in their different ways but will remain strangers, with the exception of my new sister-in-law and the Castans. I have been incredibly lucky, but now I need to go home to Palestine, be myself again.

She turned back to the man who was now her husband, and hand in hand, they got up for the traditional photograph with each of the guests.

16

A WELCOME SURPRISE

JANUARY 1945 WAS THE COLDEST in recorded history, and in the following months, winter showed no sign of abating, even as spring was around the corner. As the days passed on rue de Passy, nothing of significance happened. Out of sheer boredom, Lily decided to learn to cook with her hostess' willing assistance. She was picking up bits of Hungarian, and her efforts to speak that language never failed to have the Castans in stitches. She joined in with them good-naturedly, glad of the momentary respite from all that preyed on her mind. At the wedding Paul Zerner had told her that he had asked his son who lived in Tel Aviv to get discreetly in touch with her kibbutz and check whether she was still wanted by the British police. In any case, he had added, coming back as Madame Matthias, a young mother accompanied by her husband and her elderly parents, she should be safe. So far, there had been no news.

She followed the events in Palestine as best she could, searching the newspapers the concierge brought her every morning for the slightest news about what was happening there. She also tuned in to BBC news on the state-of-the-art radio that Theo had bought for her and which took pride of place on a corner cabinet in the salon. The radio played softly from morning to evening, and once, Julius, returning from a visit to his bank, had found Theo and his wife dancing cheek-to-cheek to the sound of an old tune, vigorously applauded by Lily. He had promptly taken her hand and they had joined the couple. When the song ended, the old lady served her trademark cake while Theo made coffee.

Yes, thought Julius, who had gone for another of his nighttime strolls, staying with their elderly friends was working surprisingly well. The "old couple" didn't complain either. They seemed more than halfway convinced to sail to Tel Aviv with them. Not that the departure would take place anytime soon. Julius wasn't going to leave until he learned something definite about the fate of his daughter. Hans phoned faithfully every week, still confident that the very absence of news was a good sign. Julius wished he shared the same confidence. Assuming that Elisabeth had somehow escaped, however improbable it seemed, he assumed she was hiding or on the run, without any possibility of sending even an innocuous postcard to her father at his bank or to Georges the pharmacist. She would not have written to her brother at the farm, for fear of leading the Germans there. As to André, there had been no reaction to the documents Julius had sent to the farm: copies of Kadar and Sandor's letters and of the cemetery photo taken by the engravers. He would not have minded so much if it wasn't for the two little ones: Emile and Maddie, those two sweet children. He longed to see them again. His only grandchildren. And what about Gabrielle? Was she married, a mother? Had she ridden out the war unscathed? There had been no reply from Monsignor Octavius. Wherever she was, whatever she'd done, she might be in need of help—of money. He had long set aside a large sum for each of his children. Even with his new responsibilities and the fresh path he was taking, he could afford to help her, thanks to Madi. André would demur but would take the money. His wife would make him.

Julius' evening walk ended because of rain, and he hastened towards home. How fortunate, he told himself, that they decided to stay. Lily was never alone, Theo was always ready to keep her company and Zsazsa never stopped fussing over her. Fate, that fickle lady he had never believed in, was letting him live the life he always dreamed of, waking up every day next to the woman he loved and who was going to make him a father once more, then breakfast with his oldest and dearest friends. He would be ashamed to say aloud that it wasn't enough. What he was missing was what had given a purpose to his life. Medicine. His passion. His refuge. For thirty years, patients had flocked to his clinic. People came to consult him from far away. He knew who he was. And yet … his success, his fame, had not protected him. None of the people he had treated for so long, not even the bishop whose life he saved, had stood up for him and tried to help.

He let himself into the house and tiptoed into the kitchen to make himself a hot drink.

In the end, Julius decided he would not work in a hospital in spite of Dr. Gilles' advice. Getting used to a milieu he was not familiar with, to a hierarchy where he would have no status, demanded an effort he was not ready to make, since he didn't intend to stay in France. He had had his first taste of medical officialdom from the man who'd handed over the accreditation needed. It was done grudgingly, with snide remarks about how irregular it all was. He looked for another way to practice, finding a temporary solution in volunteering in shelters for the homeless, of which there were so many, given the difficult times. He would often catch himself searching in vain among the unfortunates waiting to be treated, hoping to recognize a familiar face, a friend or a neighbor who had managed to escape in time.

The mood was as dismal as the weather. While black-market profiteers were openly showing their new wealth, the hunt for those who had collaborated with the Nazi occupiers was not abating. Each day brought new arrests, new trials. The first executions were carried out. Much had been made of someone named Robert Brasillach, author and journalist, executed by a firing squad for having praised German policies and occupation in his writings. Meanwhile, the Allied victory was a long time coming. In what became known as the Battle of the Bulge, the Wehrmacht launched a massive offensive, which was to be the last on the Western Front, targeting eastern Belgium, northern France, and Luxembourg.

In Hungary, German troops wrestled Esztergom, the former capital of the country, back from the Russians. Still, the tide was beginning to turn. In Germany, morale was at an all-time low; daily air raids and restrictions took their toll. The Red Army had routed the last Germans from Poland, and on January 17, they entered Warsaw.

Boris and Vladimir invited the denizens of the rue de Passy to celebrate the liberation of the capital. No one came empty-handed. Theo brought the French cognac Julius liked so much; Lily had, with Zsazsa's help, made the sweet little Polish pastries her mother had taught her to make in Cairo;

Julius unearthed a bottle of Potocki vodka, the oldest Polish brand, drawing a rare smile from Boris. Invited as well, was Grandin who had come bearing caviar and goose liver, but without Lena. The mood was strangely muted. In spite of the news from Poland, the hosts were tense. They loved their country and had suffered for it; yet they were not ready to commit themselves to return. Weary of the Russian bear, as they called Stalin, who had ordered his troops to wait until Germany drowned in the blood of the Polish insurrection and the last pocket of resistance had been crushed before moving in, they wondered if he would so easily let go. Would Poland submit to the totalitarian regime and the lack of liberty which was the lot of the "socialist republics" integrated into the Russian Empire? Would Boris find the medical assistance he badly needed? What would their life be there? They had fought hard to achieve what they had in Paris. Their engraving and photography business was doing well (they swore they were done with the lucrative sideline in forged documents, though their friends were not totally convinced); they had a nice place in a great location.

"They will never go back," Lily later concluded. "They will remain here and keep the memories of the Poland they knew in their hearts, as I shall keep those of the Cairo of my youth, without ever going there again.

As the Russian army swept through Poland, it was hoped that the liberation of the concentration camps would now only be a matter of time. One morning, Julius read that the Hotel Lutetia, situated on Boulevard Raspail on the West Bank, had been chosen to welcome the first survivors. He asked Theo what he knew of that establishment. The old architect had launched into an enthusiastic description of what he called a competent example of Art Nouveau, albeit, in his opinion, vastly inferior to what had been built by the Austrian-Hungarian Empire, and perhaps more notably, the Black Vulture complex in Oradea, where Julius had had his clinic.

"That is not what you wanted to hear, I see. Forgive me, it is one of my favorite topics, and I don't have many occasion to talk about it. Before the war, Hotel Lutetia was one of the leading hotels in Paris, and it was rumored that its wine cellars were the best in Europe. In fact, General de Gaulle spent his wedding night there. In the hotel, not in the cellars," Castan added with a wink. "It was a favorite meeting place for artists, including Picasso, so appreciated by Lily. During the Occupation, German top brass were welcomed there with such an alacrity that the place was requisitioned at the Liberation. That is probably why it was deemed fitting to serve as the first stop for the returning detainees.

Julius went there in early March to offer his services which were readily accepted. Not only was he a trained physician, but he also spoke Hungarian, Romanian, and German, which would make communication easier with the survivors. For him, it was a way to help his people with the unspoken hope of one day seeing Elisabeth come through the majestic double doors. But it was to be the beginning of a long wait. Auschwitz had been liberated on January 27 by the Russians. Hans, who kept on pressing the Red Cross for news, phoned to say that there was no trace of Elisabeth on the registers of the sinister camp. According to the relevant French authorities, due to the complex nature of the health and logistical issues involved, none of the surviving inmates had been repatriated yet. Priority had been given to prisoners of war. For family members and friends who came every day to wait for the return of their loved ones, such a policy was incomprehensible. They barraged people leaving the hotel with questions, but those strangers had no answers to give them.

Inside the hotel, bureaucracy had taken over. Endless training sessions were held on the best way to deal with the newcomers when they eventually arrived. One of the first decisions was to refer to the survivors as being "repatriated" instead of "deportees." Then, a protocol had to be adopted to identify each new arrival. It was feared that war criminals or former Nazis would try to pass for survivors. More prosaically, ingredients had to be prepared and menus devised to include suitable food for the men and women who'd been starved for so long.

All this information was necessary, but of no great interest to Julius. One morning, having listened for two hours to a pompous official from the health ministry detailing how DDT had to be applied to all arrivals, insisting on the fact that "the subjects" had to be naked, Julius left the room. He was well aware of the fact that typhus had been rampant in the camps and that to combat the very real risks it posed, it was necessary to use this new and potent insecticide which had demonstrated efficacy. Nonetheless, he found the thought of the hapless individuals forced to suffer this new indignity unsettling.

A feeling of hopelessness washed over him. He would go home for lunch and check on Lily, nearly six months pregnant. There was no need to call ahead, Zsazsa was always ready to feed the multitude. Outside the hotel, dozens of men and women stood in the cold as always, holding small snapshots of their relatives and clamoring for information. Drawing the collar of his heavy coat closer against the icy wind, he made for his car, parked along the Bon Marche, one of the earliest department stores in Paris, situated on the other side of Boulevard Raspail. He was about to cross the boulevard when he heard a woman's voice yelling "Apa, Apa"—father in Hungarian. He turned around; an elegant young woman wearing a mink coat with a matching cap ran towards him. He blinked. Was he hallucinating? Gabrielle? Here? She threw herself in his arms, sobbing and laughing at once. He drew her closer, his heart bursting with happiness. Raising his head, he met the avid glances of passersby who'd stopped to look.

"Let's sit in the car, we can't talk here," he said quickly, taking her by the arm.

She followed without resisting and entered the Juvaquatre with raised eyebrows.

They faced each other, not daring to believe they could be together. It'd been so long, since that lovely day in August 1933, when he had last seen her waving goodbye as he departed for France with André and Elisabeth. Under the grey Paris skies, they scrutinized each other with an almost painful intensity, searching for familiar traits and marks of time. He found her beautiful as ever, but more mature; she had lost that innocent, almost childish expression that imbued her with a Madonna-like quality, as Monsignor Octavius had once remarked. She was not yet thirty but had the tranquil assurance of someone who is used to giving commands and being obeyed. He wondered what she thought of him.

She was the first to speak. "You came here looking for Mother?"

"No, darling. I'm sorry to have to tell you that she's dead."

She paled. "Poor mummy. Did she suffer?"

"Not at all."

He took her hand. "She was killed by a German soldier on May 3 in front of our house. We were told to gather there with our Jewish neighbors to be sent to a ghetto and then … One of the soldiers started molesting a young girl I didn't know. She looked a little like you, and your mother tried to protect her. The soldier pushed her away and shot her in the head at point-blank range. She died instantly. I was still upstairs and about to rush to her. Kadar—my neighbor, you never met him—stopped me. The Germans didn't check their lists and left without noticing that I was missing. A little later, I managed to sneak out of town without being caught. Not very brave of me, I know. I stopped by Sandor's farm. He gave me some food and promised to attend to Magda's burial. He sent me a photo of her grave, next to Georgy's."

She took both his hands in hers. "Not very brave? Papa, there's nothing glorious or brave in letting oneself be taken and driven to the camps when one can avoid it. At least you are alive. Believe me, you have nothing to reproach yourself for, and I can be proud of my mother. Proud, and relieved that she didn't have to face the horror of the camps. Ever since what happened has become known, I've been torturing myself with thoughts of what you both might have been going through, fearing that you might have died in agony. I almost lost hope and was getting ready to mourn you.

"Your brother is less generous. He's angry at me for having survived when she did not."

"Oh, him! Not me. We all knew what went on at home. You were not sleeping together, you had outside interests, but you never left. Grandmother Golda said it was because you had pledged never to leave, but other men wouldn't have cared and would have gone long ago."

"I tried for months to get her to flee. I stayed with her to the end."

"You don't have to justify yourself to me. I shamefully deceived her! She trusted me and helped me with my dream of studying in that prestigious Budapest school. She was so sure I was coming back, and dreamt of the great match she'd make for me. And I … I let her down, departed for France without a word, without going back to see her. And I never wrote. To her or to you. I was crushed by guilt.

"Water under the bridge. Gaby, we have so much to catch up on! Come to lunch. I'm living at the Castans. I mean the Kahns. I'll take you home afterwards."

"Your friends Zsazsa and Theo? They're here? Alive?"

"Yes, but I am not alone," he replied, starting the car.

"Your redhead friend is with you? Don't be so surprised. Mother knew. Someone saw you together in Geneva and wrote to her."

"My redhead friend is dead. I haven't seen her since 1927."

Gabrielle shook her head. "And your doctor lady? It was André who told me about her."

"Next month she's getting married to a high-ranking French officer." Then Julius took a deep breath. "I … I got married in December. And we're expecting a baby."

Gabrielle burst out laughing. Her reaction was so unexpected that he just stared.

"You are going to give me a little brother or a little sister? At my age? Unbelievable and marvelous. Don't look so worried. You can't imagine how happy it makes me feel. A new beginning, a new life. Are you going to settle in France? By the way, who is she, that new stepmother of mine?"

"It's complicated. Lily was born in Cairo. Her father is Egyptian and her mother, Polish. Both were Jewish. She married a Palestinian Jew and went to live in a kibbutz. Her husband was executed by the British. She is much younger than me."

"Younger than me too?"

"That, no. She was born in 1909."

"I see.

"We intend to go there. To Tel Aviv."

"After the birth?"

"No. I have to wait for news of Elisabeth."

"What do you mean?"

"Her husband was in the Résistance. He was caught and killed by the Germans. She was caught as well and deported. They both had fake identities, and the Germans didn't know she's Jewish. She had entrusted her little boy to André and his wife. In spite of all my efforts and contacts, I have not been able to find out what happened to her, where she is, and what condition she's in. She hasn't written a single letter, and the Red Cross can't find anything.

"My God! How dreadful! My poor Lisbeth!"

"Tell me about you," her father said, deliberately changing the subject. "I see you're wearing a wedding ring. Are you married? Do you have children?"

"I am a widow."

"I am so sorry ..."

"Don't be. That marriage was a tragic mistake—one of the many I've made. Gaétan, my husband, came home from the army after the Armistice in 1940. He admired Germany and openly took the side of the occupiers. Then he blew his brains out at the Liberation when the gendarmes came to arrest him for collaboration with the enemy. I had left him months before and was working for the Résistance. I was shot and lost the twins I'd been carrying. Not a word about that, please. We can talk later. Anyway, I won't be staying in France either. I received a visa for America. I have friends in New York. I was waiting for news about you before setting the date. I went several times to the Lutetia, believing that should you have survived, you might need me. I see that it's not the case. Though, you are living with your friends? Are you short of money? I have more than I need. Gaétan died before the divorce proceedings, and I inherited everything. I can easily …"

"Dear Gaby, don't worry. I have enough money. But thank you. Ah, we've arrived."

"I assume you'll tell me what you're doing in this funny orange car. You must miss the Mercedes. Did you bring it back to Paris? No? Of course, you gave it to André. Did you ever get another one?"

"Yes, I gave it to Vadim. Remember him?"

"Sure! How is he?"

"Married with children and gaining weight."

The first meeting between his wife and youngest daughter went far better than Julius dared hope. The Castans had not seen Gabrielle since they'd left Oradea, when she was a mere child; her unexpected arrival caused quite a sensation. Zsazsa rushed to the kitchen to accommodate her two extra guests while Theo was quick to help the young woman take off her coat before kissing her on both cheeks, adding with a straight face, "as I used to do when you were a child and called me Uncle."

"Funny, I don't remember, Uncle," she replied, stepping back.

Then, she turned to Lily, who was observing her gravely.

"So, you are my stepmother," Gabrielle said, holding both her hands in hers. "How should I address you? Step-mum?"

"Don't you dare! Lily will do just fine."

"Welcome to our family, Lily, and welcome to the little brother or sister you are about to give me."

"Aren't you upset because it's so soon after the death of your mother?"

"Not in the least. I'm happy for my father. I'm in no position to judge anyway. The way I have led my own life doesn't give me that right. In wartime, when one can be wounded, killed, or caught at any moment, conformity and bigotry take a back seat to vital instincts. That has been my experience these past five years."

"You are so right!" Julius exclaimed. "Do you know how it started with us? Lily shot and killed a German officer who was about to kill me. I had never seen death so close. Still, saved by a woman, can you imagine? You fought in the Résistance. Theo and Zsazsa too, they even had a cyanide pill they intended to take should they be caught; Lily has a gun and knows how to use it. And I ... I did nothing."

"Did nothing!" Theo was indignant. "You walked for months on end through hostile territory. You fought with partisan freedom fighters part of the way. I bet you haven't told your daughter about that. Why don't you do so while Lily and I help my wife set the table?"

Father and daughter smiled at that blatant attempt to leave them together.

"She is cute, that stepmother of mine. I am sure we shall get on very well. And you're lucky to have such faithful friends."

"I'm well aware of that."

"What will they do when you and Lily leave?"

"They're coming with us. I shall have part of my past with me in my new country. Lily will have a mother and the baby a grandmother. It's such a miracle that I find myself ashamed of my good fortune. Now tell me about yourself."

"Not yet. Go on, please."

Switching to Hungarian, Julius spoke again of the tragedy that had befallen the town where they had both been born, the slow descent into hell, the last days of the Jewish community, and his wife's death. He went to fetch Kadar and Sandor's letter as well as the photo of her mother's grave. Julius would have stopped there because Gaby was crying, but she urged him to go on. So, he told her about the months on the road, Italy, and his arrival in Geneva. Moved by some unexplained need, he even showed her Madi's letter.

"Poor father! Poor brave father! You did it all alone! I am so proud of you, and so happy that you have found a new happiness with your Lily!"

"You, my children, gave me the courage to go on. I wanted to see you. To make sure you were safe, that none of you had suffered the fate that was almost mine. You see, you were all I had left."

They embraced again, and then followed Theo, who had come to announce that lunch was ready. Zsazsa had done wonders. First her cherry soup with cream, then goulash with paprika, and to crown it all, thin pancakes filled with chocolate mousse and nuts.

"I can see why Father wants to take you to Palestine, that's the best meal I've had in years!"

A beaming Zsazsa thanked her effusively in Hungarian. In fact, the Castans continued to lapse into that language, forgetting that Lily didn't understand.

"Gabrielle," her father suddenly asked. "Do you speak English?"

"Of course," she answered, a little surprised.

"Of course! You put me to shame! Lily, when you feel neglected, talk to her in English!"

"Great idea, Gabrielle replied, getting up. "Lily, let's clear the table and do the dishes together. The rest of you, remain seated. I want to speak to my stepmother."

Lily raised her eyebrows but readily agreed.

Gabrielle closed the kitchen door. "Let's speak English. I want to have a serious talk with you."

"You don't really approve of your father's choice; you just pretend to please him. Don't deny it. I saw how you watched us while we were eating. You believe …"

"Not at all. I don't know you well enough. I like you. I can see that you are fond of him, but not in love."

"Neither is he. Don't be so surprised. He is fond of me, very fond perhaps, as I am of him, but if I had not been pregnant, I'm not sure that we would have decided to get married. Yet, it's a good decision. Each one of us finds in the other something we are missing."

"For you, is it security?"

"If you mean money, I have plenty of my own. What is it that bothers you?"

"Perhaps you're perhaps right, and I thank you for not telling me to mind my own business. In fact, I was voicing my thoughts. My father has suffered enough. It would be a dreadful blow should you leave him when you're back in your country, or in ten years or so, when the age difference will be more keenly felt."

Lily started laughing.

"When I said that each of us finds something he or she is lacking, I meant stability, building a home, a real one. You know, in Tel Aviv, Julius can open a clinic and receive patients who speak his language. We'll make a good team. I hope we have more children. Three or four would be great. I'll need him too much while we bring them up to ever dream of leaving him. I've had several talks with his sister who came from America for the wedding, and she doesn't seem to share your concerns."

"Aunt Anni came? Is she well? Are her children fighting in the war?"

"She's incredibly beautiful, and you would never guess her age. I only met her second son, Tony, squadron commander in the U.S. Air Force, divorced, good-looking, and quite aware of that fact. I had to give him a few polite rebuffs. Julius will tell you more. He'll also tell you about your brother who appears to hate him. That's why he hasn't told him that not only has he remarried but is expecting … He's afraid that Elisabeth will have the same reaction, if they are ever reunited, that is."

"Poor father! He's always done his utmost to protect us and doesn't deserve their scorn. It's thanks to him that we're all in France. Lily, I apologize and am happy for you both. Let's go back, they must be wondering what is taking us so long. Anyway, it's getting late, and father said he would see me home."

17

GABRIELLE'S STORY

GABRIELLE LIVED ON AVENUE BOSQUET in an impressive turn-of-the century building. There was a marble entrance and a wrought-iron lift that took them to a large apartment on the top floor. If this was part of her inheritance, she was indeed well off, thought her father, left alone in an elegant drawing room with a spectacular view of the Champ de Mars while Gabrielle went to change. Fate had dealt him another surprise, a very welcome one. By what extraordinary coincidence had she been there today just as he was walking outside? After André's cold shoulder, the warmth of her welcome had been a balm to his soul. He got up to observe the two portraits hung on the wall. A supercilious cleric on one side and a richly attired wedding couple posing for the photograph on the other.

"Those are my in-laws and a great uncle who was a Cardinal. I barely knew my father-in-law, but as for my mother-in-law … There was also a portrait of Gaétan in dress uniform. I got rid of it."

She extracted a cigarette from a gold case and offered him another, which he declined.

"I forgot. You don't smoke. I started because it helped me appear more at ease than I was."

She lit her cigarette and inhaled, closing her eyes. When she opened them again, she was crying.

He moved to get up to go to her.

"No, please remain seated. I have to tell you my story, and it won't be easy for me. But I must. To explain, to get your forgiveness. Please, listen. In order to be accepted by that exclusive academy in Budapest, to study with girls from the highest society, I abused your trust. I wrote to your friend in Rome and let him think that it was on your advice."

"Come on, water under the bridge. I forgave you a long time ago. Your mother was far guiltier."

"You never told your friend, never reproached him for having neglected to consult you?"

"I would never have done it. It probably never occurred to him that I hadn't known. I only wrote him once, when I arrived in Paris, to ask whether he could get in touch with you and tell you where I was."

"He did try to get in touch. His letter arrived at the castle after I'd already left it. My mother-in-law told me that she'd thrown it into the fire without opening it. 'The Pope's delegate would not want to correspond with a loose woman who abandoned her husband and dares to ask for a divorce,' she explained. But that was later. First, Hungary. When I left home, I fully intended to come back, to make the splendid match which was all mother talked about. But then … Father, for two years I lived a dream. I was studying with the daughters of the greatest families in the country, often being invited to their palaces. My schoolmates were convinced that I was of noble birth as well and that I had enrolled under an assumed name, either for my safety or because I was the illegitimate daughter of a prince. In the end, I met a prince. Armin. Aurica, my best friend's brother. I was a frequent guest in her house. I mean, palace. He was a lot older, neither very tall nor handsome, one leg slightly shorter than the other. Very, very shy and yet always nice to me. He was the only son, and his parents were desperate to see him married and have an heir. He fell in love with me. His mother hinted that they would be ready to consider such a match. I was stunned, and yet …"

"You were tempted?"

"What would have been the point?"

"You were afraid of telling them the truth?"

"Father, what truth? That I didn't have a drop of blue blood; that I wasn't even a Catholic? That I had been admitted to the academy with a fake Christening certificate? Yet I did entertain the idea for a minute. You were a notable, and you looked far more distinguished that they did. I felt they would do everything to make their son happy and ensure the succession. Unfortunately,.."

She got up and went to the window. With her back turned, she went on.

"Mother came to the school with presents she'd chosen just for me: a lovely gold necklace, some clothes. We'd agreed that she wouldn't visit in order not to endanger the story that I was a nice Catholic girl, so she didn't ask to see me, nor did she leave her name. As luck would have it, or fate, Aurica saw her and asked me whether that vulgar Jewess with too much make-up was our coachman's wife. I nearly fainted."

Julius winced. "You said she was?"

"No. I hadn't sunk that low. I replied I had no idea, and we talked of something else. That night, I sobbed for hours under the blankets so as not to be heard. I was ashamed, and I was ashamed to be ashamed. In the morning, I went to see the Mother Superior and told her of the proposition the prince's parents made, adding that I couldn't accept, because if my true identity were revealed, it would cause a terrible scandal in my father's family. She looked at me strangely, and to this day I don't know what she understood, or she thought she understood, but she agreed to help. Two nuns who taught French were going back to their Paris convent at the end of the school year, and it was decided I would travel and stay with them, ostensibly to perfect that language during the vacation. I knew I would never return to Oradea because I wouldn't be able to face my mother."

Julius stood and took her in his arms. "You were very young, child, and were in an impossible situation."

"An impossible situation of my own making! I should never have gone to that fancy school and never assumed an identity that wasn't mine. Ever since I was a little girl, I have turned heads in the street, you remember? People said I looked like a fairy-tale princess. It was the same in Hungary. It went to my head. I had begun to fancy myself becoming a real princess."

"Gaby, it's all in the past."

"You don't want to understand. I don't know whether I was more ashamed of having to lie or more ashamed of my mother. Daddy, I was angry at my mother for having deprived me of my chance to be a princess!" She sighed. "You are right, it's all in the past, maybe I shall make my peace with her in the next world, if it exists."

"That's why you never wrote?"

"Partly. I wanted to forget, start my life anew far from Oradea and my family. It seemed then that it would be easier in France."

"Far from André and Elisabeth as well?"

"We were never close or had much to say. When Elisabeth was not studying, she was going out with that medical student she later married. André was busy too, though not too busy to try acting like a big brother, ordering me to stay with them in their flat, asking me endless questions and refusing to give me money in order to force me to accept his invitation. I had to threaten to complain to you. He couldn't have known that I'd never have done it. I lived with the nuns, giving German lessons to their pupils in exchange for room and board. I enrolled in the Sorbonne and studied literature and learned English and touch typing, all the while keeping my goal in sight: to find a husband, move far from Paris, and cut all ties with the past. Not surprisingly perhaps, I was soon surrounded by admirers, but I kept a cool head. I was no longer looking for a prince, a count, or a baron. I had learned my lesson and I took my time. First, I was going to finish my studies and graduate. Those three years in Paris proved invaluable. I got rid of my Hungarian accent and met people from different backgrounds, all the while taking great care of my reputation. I never went out in the evening, but went straight to the convent after my classes.

It was in my second year that I met Gaétan for the first time. He was studying law. I thought he might do. Tall and handsome, he came from a noble, albeit untitled family with a castle in Normandy and a lot of money. It wasn't love at first sight for me but … He noticed my interest and set out to seduce me, trying to convince me to come for a drink in what he called his 'bachelor flat'. I turned him down each time, hinting that I was not indifferent to his charm but too well-bred to yield. At the end of the third year, he knelt down and produced a ring with a flourish. Am I shocking you?"

"Not at all. So you married him in a splendid ceremony?"

"Not quite. Marie-Paule, his mother, hated me on sight. I had no dowry; I came from an obscure family from somewhere in the back of beyond. Furthermore, she had another bride in mind, someone wellborn, rich, who treated her with what she thought was proper deference."

"Gaétan wasn't interested?"

"He once told me, rather meanly, that the young woman had the face of a broad mare, as well as the laugh. In fact, he said she whinnied when they made love. Anyway, I was luckier with his father who became rather fond of me; when he was taken sick, he decided that the wedding must be held without delay, fearing that should he die before, we would have to wait the full year of deep mourning. The man died barely a month later, in September 1938. We were just back from our honeymoon in Venice. That's when the trouble started. Are you sure I'm not boring you?"

"Certainly not. I worry about you. It must be painful to ..."

"On the contrary, you're the first person I can speak freely with in more than ten years, imagine! Since that August 1933 when I departed for Budapest, I have always worn a mask, always pretended to be something that I was not. I'm yet to decide who or what I shall be in the United States. So bear with me; I need it."

"Gladly. You have a fascinating tale."

"When we got back to Normandy, I discovered that Marie-Paule, now widowed, didn't intend to retire to the smaller manor on the castle's grounds, according to tradition. She wanted to stay and keep on ruling the staff with an iron hand. At first, I didn't object, contenting myself with observing and learning, until I could no longer bear her disdainful ways and habit of putting me down."

"Your husband let her get away with it?"

"She was far too clever to belittle me in front of him; he would urge me to be patient, to understand how hard it was for her to relinquish the place she'd held for so long. So, when I had had enough, I gave him an ultimatum. If she would not move to the manor, I would."

Julius laughed in spite of himself. "Did it work?"

"Not immediately, no. We had a terrible fight, our very first. He wanted to know why I wasn't pregnant yet. I replied that were he to sleep more often at home instead of with local girls, it might happen sooner. That shook him. We had separate bedrooms, as was the custom, and he believed I didn't know about his escapades."

"How did you know?"

"I enjoyed going horse riding, a skill I acquired in Hungary, at Aurica's, more precisely. I was told that the head groom's daughter was sick and decided to bring her some fruit from our orchard. She wasn't much older than I was and was the village's elementary school teacher. Not being married, she was still living at home. We got talking. I came back to visit. I met her grandmother. Everyone called her Mother Jeanne. An impressive woman, a healer according to some, and a witch to others, aware of all that went on in the village and beyond. She decided she liked me and would keep me informed of my husband's little adventures.

"My bluff worked. Marie-Paule moved to the smaller house, cursing me all the way. Mind you, the spies she left behind recounted all I was doing. I fired two, replacing them with village people recommended by Mother Jeanne.

"I soon found my way; the staff started respecting me. We entertained a lot, and I made friends. On Sundays we went to mass, sitting in the family pew on the front row. A model family. Gaétan was proud of my beauty and wanted all his friends to see how lucky he was. He was incredibly attentive; I almost believed him when he swore he was being faithful. I was still fond of him, though some of his less pleasant sides had made themselves felt. Less than a year after the wedding, I became pregnant at last. He was beside himself with joy. That was in August. A month later, he was drafted. War started. My little Julie was born in February. She had your eyes and the smile of an angel. Gaétan, who wanted an heir, was bitterly disappointed and didn't ask for a leave to attend the christening. I didn't care. For the first time in many years, I was happy. I loved that little one beyond reason."

She blew her nose. "Shall I make you a drink? Coffee, tea? Cognac? I remember you liked it so much Uncle Manny never failed to bring you a bottle when he came to see us."

"Cognac, with pleasure, but a small one."

"Your Lily won't worry and wonder what's taking you so long?"

"She knows we have a lot to catch up on. What happened to your little Julie?"

"She caught a cold. It was winter. Night. She coughed, had trouble breathing. Our doctor didn't come immediately. He said he would see in the morning. I held her in my arms. She was suffocating. I felt her desperately struggling for breath. When dawn came, she was dead. Not a word, please, otherwise I shall start sobbing. Let me fetch your drink."

It was the croup, Julius told himself, moved almost to tears by the death of this little granddaughter, of whose existence he'd never known, and that lazy doctor could have saved her.

The cognac was excellent as always, but he found it bitter.

"Later, I blamed myself, you know. I should have called Mother Jeanne, she would've known what to do. You too, you would have saved my baby. After the funeral, I didn't go out for seven days, receiving condolence visits the way we used to do at home. A defeated France signed the ceasefire in June. Gaétan came home a different man, angry at the world, blaming obscure subversive forces for the humiliation of the French Army. When he was drunk, which happened with increasing frequency, he would rant against the communist rabble and the sinister plot involving international Jewish finance. I remained silent, dying inside.

"A German detachment was stationed in the village, and the commandant was billeted in the left wing of the castle. In the evening, he would invite other officers to come drink until the early hours of the morning, ogling and harassing the younger staff who I had to send home in the afternoon and replace them with older peasant women delighted to make a little money. The commandant—his name was Gunther—started courting me. He wasn't aware that I spoke German and made risqué comments to the other officers, detailing what he intended to do to me when he got his way.

I became more and more frightened. In happier times, Gaétan had given me a gun and taught me how to use it. I started carrying it. I had tried to tell my husband what was going on; he said it was nonsense and that I should be able to accept compliments with a smile. He too spoke German and had let himself be drawn a little too close to Gunther, who permitted him to keep his favorite hunter when his men requisitioned all the horses. He began to attend the nightly revels, to speak a little too freely. The other was trying to get information about the Résistance, about smugglers' haunts; we were not far from the coast. People started talking. When I tried to warn him, he flew into a rage and went to bed, slamming the door.

A few days later, he declared that it was not the right time to have another child. I heard that he was seeing Mathilde again—the one he used to call the broodmare. He fought with me incessantly. By then, I attended Sunday mass alone and visited local farmwives during the week; I secretly gave money to those whose husbands were still in German stalags. The daughter of such a woman stopped me one day as I was walking out of the church and whispered that my husband and mother-in-law had gone to see the Bishop of Coutances, the seat of our church district. Apparently, they were trying to get our wedding annulled!

I went into shock. Not at the idea of a separation from Gaétan; by that time, I detested him. I had never realized the depth of his anti-Semitic convictions. I had been granted French citizenship when I married him. Would I lose it? What would happen to me? I had to think ahead. I started leaving money and jewels in Mother Jeanne's care. At some point, it became clear that she was active in the resistance, as were other family members, such as Bernard, our head groom, who'd been discharged from the army like Gaétan, but now was the leader of a local cell. From then on, I reported daily what I heard from the Germans, who talked freely in my presence. I even took to listening at the door."

"Weren't you afraid?"

"Terrified, while coming to realize that I could no longer ignore what was going on: the deportations, the concentration camps. I thought about you, about mother, my former classmates. Yet here I was, safe, and not even reacting to my husband's tirades about the Jews. I started taking incredible risks. When a British plane returning from a bombing raid in Germany was downed not far from the village, everyone saw a parachute opening. Hundreds of Germans scoured the region searching for the British pilot, albeit in vain. I had encountered him by chance the same day while taking a long walk. I can still picture the way he looked. Exhausted, bloody, his leg broken, observing me with haunted eyes. I had to help him to walk, and together we made it to the stables. I hid him in an empty cellar, called on Mother Jeanne, ostensibly to bring me one of her fabled remedies. She treated him, and when the soldiers gave up the search, another cell member saw him safely to the coast. He was the first of many fugitives I hid."

"Your husband suspected nothing?"

"Fortunately! For him Résistance fighters were a bunch of anarchists, communists, or Jewish vermin. When the Gestapo arrested one of his farmers, his wife came begging for help. We both went to Gaétan, who got in a towering rage and told her to get out. Then, he turned to me with such an expression of hatred that I stepped back. It didn't stop him. I'd never seen him in such a state. When he couldn't find anything more to say, he just pounced on me and ..."

"My poor child!"

"Don't worry. I'm getting to the end of my sorry tale. As fate would have it, I became pregnant. When Mathilde discovered it, in February 1944, I was five months gone. She was frantic, yelling at Gaétan that his request for an annulment was based on the fact that I couldn't give him an heir. Apparently having given birth to a daughter did not count. At that point, she told him that it was rumored that I was helping the Résistance. He confronted me; I didn't deny it. He was beside himself with rage, nearly foaming at the mouth. He accused me of endangering him and his precious castle with my treacherous behavior.

"Two days later, he left early, announcing that he had given the day off to the staff because of some local feast. I didn't suspect a thing. When I went for my usual walk, I found two Gestapo officers on the path. They said I was under arrest. I didn't stop to think. I had my gun and fired, downing one. Then without time to fire at the second one, I fell to the ground unconscious. Later, I found out that Bernard, our head groom, Mother Jeanne's son, had arrived in the nick of time and killed the second officer. Somehow, he got me to his mother.

"I hovered between life and death for an entire month. Of course, I lost the twins I was carrying. Boys. I never saw them. By the time I woke up, they had been quietly buried. It didn't hurt as much as when Julie was taken from me. Enraged Gestapo thugs had searched every house, every place they could think of. Upon Bernard's advice, the rumor of my death was floated. It was deemed credible since no one had seen me since the incident. Marie-Paule triumphantly came back to the castle; as for my husband, he was stupid enough to boast of having denounced me and was already planning to marry Mathilde as soon as my body was found."

"My god! How did you manage to stay hidden?"

"At first, I had no idea. Then, as soon as Marie-Paule was ensconced in the castle, I moved into the manor. She had taken her staff with her, and the place was shut down. Who would have looked for me there? People knew in the village, but none would have denounced me. All thought that I was the bravest woman on earth!"

"Rightly so!"

"No. Bernard was the true hero. Someone denounced him. When they came to arrest him, he tried to run and was shot in the back. When I say someone, it was probably Gaétan. He had complained to me about what he called the unseemly way I behaved with Bernard. Don't look at me. Bernard was married. I knew his wife, his mother, his daughter. I might have been tempted. I know he was, but there was nothing improper between us. Sometimes I regret it.

"When I was well enough, I joined the local Résistance cell. Their command post was in a monastery so badly bombed that no one lived there. I knew English and touch typing and I became their radio operator, transmitting information to London. I slept in a different location every night. I was lucky. The Germans never found me. The Allies carpet bombed the region before the Normandy landing. After the liberation, I moved to the lone hotel in Coutances still standing and filed for divorce on the grounds that my husband was being unfaithful to me in the marriage bed. Did you know that France it is the only exception allowing a woman to sue for divorce? I cited Mathilde as a co-defendant.

"Gaétan's lawyer rushed to the hotel. It seemed my husband was ready to grant the divorce and pay all the money I thought I was entitled to in order to expedite the process. I was so surprised. Then I understood. Mathilde was pregnant, and he wanted to marry her as soon as possible. I had to sit down. My head was in a whirl. I went back to my room without giving an answer. I was in no hurry. Mathilde was the one who'd urged Gaétan to throw me to the Germans. She knew what the Gestapo was capable of. I would have lost the children under torture, and maybe died. I'm sure that was her hope."

"You can't believe …"

"I'm convinced of it. That woman hated me. I had taken the man she wanted to marry, and she would have done anything to get him back. Mind you, I might have relented, albeit reluctantly, so that her child could be legitimate. I didn't have time. A week later, gendarmes came to arrest Gaétan. He was accused of collaboration, of having denounced me and denounced Bernard. He asked for five minutes to get ready, went up to his room, and blew his brains out. I didn't attend the funeral; I understand it was a very private affair. I did, however, attend the lawyer's summons. My husband hadn't changed the will he made when we got married, and I was his sole heir, except for some minor bequests. As I told you, I'm very rich. Mathilde soon made overtures through the lawyer. She wanted to buy the castle and raise her child there. You remember that she was also very rich. Well, I was never going back there so I agreed, keeping only a few paintings and some artwork stored in the spare room of this flat."

"What now?"

"Grandfather Aaron was fond of saying that according to the Talmud, the gift of prophecy was given only to very young children and to fools. For now, I'm going to America where I have two or three contacts. That's another story."

"Are you going to get in touch with Anni and her husband?"

"I have no idea. First, I have to decide who I am, or rather, who I want to be. In Oradea, I knew I was a little Jewish girl, the daughter of a respected physician and a pharmacist. I had a father and a mother who loved me but fought constantly. After that, I passed for someone who was not me. There was no one I could turn to. I cut myself off from my family, my roots. I was in daily dread of being found out. My few moments of happiness I owed to my little Julie when she was alive, with whom I didn't have to pretend. I was her mother. I recently saw a doctor, who assured me that in spite of the loss of the twins, there was no reason I couldn't have more children. I do want them. Who shall I be in America? Dare I be Gabrielle Matthias again and stop hiding? Not bear the name of that traitor any longer, though my passport and my visa are still in that name?" She sighed again. "Enough. Forget my unsavory little stories. Go back to your Lily."

"Gaby, we all have such stories in our past; that's called life. You were barely sixteen when you embarked on your Hungarian adventure. Far too young to understand that it was pure folly. Had I been there, I would've put my foot down and you wouldn't have gone. Would it have been better? Your mother would have found the perfect groom for you, you would have had children, but would your husband have been resolute enough to flee in time? I don't know and neither do you. Stop tormenting yourself. You've been granted a new beginning, as I have. Make the most of it. You are still very young, as beautiful as ever, rich and free. There will be other men. My advice would be to tell them the truth. Build your new life on solid ground. Dear child, I don't want to lose you again. Write. Your aunt in Chicago will always know how to find me. Take her address. Why don't we call her together before you leave?"

"Father, the last time I saw aunt Anni was in 1926. I was nine. We would not have much to say. Still, I'll think about it."

"Don't take too long. Over there, you not only have an aunt and uncle, but cousins, not much older than you. Think of it as a readymade family. Meanwhile, I hope to see a lot of you before your departure. When will it be?"

"Nothing is fixed yet. I'll be in Coutances next week. There will be a ceremony at the town hall, and I shall be awarded the Résistance medal. Georges' daughter will be there too, to receive her father's medal. It will be a painful meeting. Then, I'll have to decide: keep the flat, sell or rent it? What would I do with the paintings and the art?" She started laughing. "After weeks and months spent in hiding, waking up at night afraid of hearing the Gestapo approach, I suppose I should be happy not to have bigger problems, especially after today. Our meeting was nothing short of miraculous. Dear Father, let's make the most of the time I have left in Paris."

18

A PHONE CALL FROM AMERICA

ON MARCH 28, Gabrielle came to rue de Passy to celebrate the Seder, the traditional supper marking the start of Passover, the festival of freedom commemorating the flight of Jews from Egypt. The mood was upbeat. American troops had crossed the Rhine and were bringing the war to the heart of Germany, with Allied air forces poundings the capital. Berlin was targeted by one of the largest air raids of the war, receiving five thousand tons of bombs in one day. Russian troops were force-marched to the city before the Allies arrived. The general feeling was that the end of the war was near, though fighting was still going on in the Pacific where the Japanese were fiercely resisting.

There was still no news of Elisabeth. Of course, not all the camps had been liberated despite the advance of Allied forces to the West and Russian troops to the East, but the wait was getting harder and harder to bear. Hans' theory—that Elisabeth had been on a train that had derailed near the town of Weimar and had somehow managed to escape—appeared less and less credible. The lack of the smallest indication after so many months made the worst more and more likely. The banker nevertheless kept on calling every week. He himself had received confirmation that what he feared had happened: only one of his nephews had survived. Sponsored by an American Jewish organization, he was about to leave for New York and had stubbornly turned down his uncle's offers to help.

Julius was slowly coming to terms with the fact that he would never see his daughter again. He tried to convince himself that he should rejoice because at least two of his children were safe. It didn't work. Elisabeth had always been his favorite; she'd known it. He was sure that she'd chosen to study medicine because of him. He remembered the hours spent together when she had come to his clinic to peruse medical journals in preparation for the difficult first year of medical school. It was Elisabeth who kept in touch and had written during the long years of separation. She gave him his first grandchild he probably would never see grow up, perhaps never see again after he left France, as he would never see Maddie, André's daughter. Then he'd sigh and start thinking of his own future and departure which was fast approaching. For the decision was made, and for that, he had to thank Gabrielle. She'd said aloud what the Castans and Lily were afraid to say.

"Father, it is time to face reality. If Elisabeth comes back, as I dearly hope, it won't be to you, newly married to some unknown woman and soon to have a baby that she'll turn, but to André. It's to him that she entrusted her child, who, according to you, seemed to be quite happy at the farm. If my brother hates you as much as you say, you being around will just complicate things. Deposit a large sum of money for her at your bank here and leave with a clear conscience. Can't you see that Lily dreams of having her first child in Palestine?"

He agreed, albeit reluctantly, and preparations were underway. The Castans were eager to leave, as if they were afraid that something would happen to prevent it. Gabrielle asked the old lady what the hurry was when they were together in the kitchen.

"Little one, yes, Gaby, that's what you are for me. At our age, everything is urgent. Theo wants to see Tel Aviv and its white Bauhaus buildings before he dies. I can't wait to be among people who speak like me and don't make fun of my accent. I don't want to lose the family I have at long last. I was afraid, as was Theo, of ending our life all alone. Not having had children was my great regret; now I shall be the new baby's grandmother."

"Aren't you a little bit afraid? According to the BBC, which I used to listen to during my Résistance days, it's free for all there. Arabs against Jews, Jews against Arabs, against the British, and against Jews who don't belong to the same faction!"

"I don't care about politics. Lily says it is not as bad as it sounds and that Tel Aviv is fairly safe. If she's not afraid to go back and bring up her child there, why should I worry? If I have to die, I'd rather be among my people. Listen, when your father showed up six months ago, Theo and I were seriously contemplating suicide. Each of us was desperately afraid of seeing the other die first. If Lily and Julius hadn't so warmly asked us to come with them ... Had we found ourselves alone again, who knows if we wouldn't have carried out that plan. Anyway, if you want to make yourself useful, come shopping for clothes with us. Lily doesn't drive much anymore, and you know how your father feels about shops. I understand that it's hot there not only in the summer but also in spring and in autumn, and we have nothing suitable to wear. According to Lily, one can't find many things in Palestine right now, so we're buying everything here. You know, I've been wearing outfits I brought with me from Hungary for decades. You can't imagine what fun it is to get a brand-new wardrobe. As for Theo, he fantasizes about wearing shorts while lounging on a Tel Aviv beach and ogling the girls in swimsuits."

Less than a week after the Seder, Lily, who was dozing in the drawing room, was startled by the ringing of the telephone. It was five in the afternoon, and she was alone; Julius was not back from the Lutetia, where he kept volunteering, in spite of his approaching departure. The first survivors were at long last expected to arrive any day. Her hosts had gone on an unspecified and mysterious errand. When she picked up the phone, an unknown voice announced that she had a call from the United States. A man then started talking excitedly in Hungarian. She guessed that it must be Manny, Anni's husband. The Chicago banker had to speak English, and it was in that language that she answered, explaining who she was.

"Listen, tell Julius that Elisabeth is free. Tell him not to call me back. I'm leaving for New York, and Anni is at the hospital. She'll call as soon as she has details but it may take a few days. He is on no account to tell André."

"Wait! Elisabeth is in hospital? Where? Is it bad? Julius will be beside himself with worry."

"No, it's Isaac who is in the hospital. Elisabeth just landed in New York. I believe she is fine on the whole."

The conversation came to an abrupt end, leaving Lily confused. Elisabeth alive and in New York? How could such a miracle have been accomplished? She was about to take her coat and rush to the Lutetia to warn her husband when she hesitated. Would she be allowed in? Would she find him? What if Julius was already on his way home? The best thing to do was to wait.

In fact, Theo and his wife had long been back, and dinner was already on the table when Julius arrived at last, tired and depressed after another day of listening to "experts." So great was his relief at hearing the news that he had to sit down. Then, he asked her to repeat what his brother-in-law had said. Why was he going to New York? How had he, in Chicago, been informed? How was it possible that Elisabeth had reached America? Questions, questions, and no clue to the riddle.

In answer to Lily's query, Julius explained that Isaac was Anni's eldest grandson and that he had been deployed in the Pacific. Then there was the next incomprehensible part of the call: why not tell André? Here again, they would have to wait for news from America. Elisabeth was free, Manny thought she was "fine on the whole." Julius was euphoric. The dark cloud hovering over his head lifted; he found himself laughing for no reason and embracing his friends one after the other. Theo fetched a bottle of champagne, and Lily was persuaded to join them in toasting the occasion. She tried very hard not to show her dismay. She was not very proud of her feelings; if Elisabeth didn't want her brother informed, wouldn't she turn to her father after all? Would he feel obligated to help, perhaps delay their departure fixed for May 1st, the first-class tickets already paid for?

The next day, and the one after, Julius stayed by the telephone. Three interminable days after the first call, the concierge from the Hotel Crillon phoned with a message for Doctor Julius Matthias. It was in English, but the man readily translated it. The Newman Chicago bank had booked a suite for the wife of its president due to arrive late the following evening. Madame Newman asked Doctor Matthias to join her for lunch the day after. She wanted him to know that his daughter was doing as well as could be expected.

"I think your sister wants you to come alone," Lily commented after hearing the original message.

"That's not the point. Why is she coming?" Said a perplexed Julius. "Why all the mystery? Why not phone? A call, however lengthy, wouldn't have cost a fraction of a transatlantic journey and a stay at the Crillon. Why wouldn't you come with me anyway?"

"I believe I understand," ventured Lily. "In English, he said, 'as well as can be expected' which can be translated as 'under the circumstances'. That's what your sister came to discuss with you. Face to face, not on the phone. There could be things to be said, measures and decisions to be taken. By you, her father; by Anni, her aunt. Not by me. I don't know your daughter. Don't try to interrupt. I am convinced I am right. You must tell Gabrielle to go with you. Your sister would have suggested it herself had she known you had found her."

"But why keep it a secret from André? It makes no sense."

"No idea. Be patient, she will explain."

Gabrielle, caught up in the final preparations for her departure, demurred at first, reminding her father that she hadn't seen her aunt in years.

"It's not about you," Julius argued. "It's about your sister. And your brother. I may need your advice. Since you're leaving for the States, it's also a good opportunity to renew your acquaintance with your aunt and her family. I'll pick you up at noon."

"In your funny orange car?"

"Why not? It works fine. Why should I change it when we're leaving the country so soon?"

The concierge had phoned to warn Anni of their arrival and she waited for them in the drawing room that was attached to her suite. A waiter was busy adding a third place to a table set for two. She hugged her brother and turned to her niece with bemused curiosity.

"Gabrielle! You were a beauty at nine, and you are even more beautiful today. Come give me a kiss."

Julius observed the two women fondly. They could've passed for mother and daughter. Both slim and graceful, both elegantly attired. The eldest wore a form-fitting purple wool dress with a necklace of twisted gold with matching earrings; the younger was dressed in a soft grey suit over a raw silk blouse, a string of very fine pearls adorning her neckline, the skirt daringly hemmed above the knee. The first had an endearing sweetness, while the second radiated energy.

"Dear Aunt, I see that I don't have to be afraid of getting old. If I have half your charm when I'm your age, I shall be content. You don't even appear tired after such an exhausting journey!"

"I slept all the way … And I had such great news when I arrived! Julius, Isaac is doing much better! He's out of danger, and there is no more talk of cutting off his leg. I was so frightened! For days, Manny and I have been frantic with worry. The poor boy was so scared!"

"All is well now?"

"According to the doctors," Manny told me. "It'll be some time before he can walk without a cane, but for him the war is over."

"I'm happy for you, little sister."

"Little sister! There you go again! Anyway, here I am, running on and on, and must be dying to hear about your daughter. Let's sit down and start eating. It's complicated so let me tell it my way."

Slightly more than a week ago, she began her story, the phone rang in the middle of the night in her Chicago home. Manny was alone; she was staying at Isaac's bedside in a military hospital not far from New York. Manny picked up the phone, his mouth dry, fearing the worst for the boy. The connection was poor, and someone told him he had a call from Germany. His first thought was of Tony, still making hair-raising raids over enemy territory. It took him a few seconds to clear the cobwebs from his brain and understand that it was not about his son. The leader of a motorized unit which had crossed the Rhine three days earlier wanted to know whether he knew someone named Elisabeth Matthias who was saying he was her uncle. She was with two American officers who had escaped their prisoner camp several months ago. The trio had rushed towards the column, the men brandishing their American papers.

Anni stopped to drink and resumed, explaining that the Captain had asked Manny several questions, but when he understood that he had a son and a grandson in the army, he became quite friendly and even let Elisabeth take the phone.

Julius, she begged her uncle to help her come to America; she also made him swear not to say a word to André. Manny promised to do his best. He was as good as his word. He took the name and number of the Captain and spent the rest of the night trying to get hold of Tony and eventually, he succeeded. I don't know how my son achieved it, but three days later, Elisabeth was in New York."

She stopped again and dried her eyes with her napkin.

"How is she?"

"Exhausted, but otherwise all right. Wait." Anni stood up and went to her bedroom, returning with two photographs obviously taken in a hospital. Elisabeth, standing between her aunt and uncle who supported her, was attempting to smile. Her hair, cut very short, framed a gaunt and haunted face. She was wearing clothes far too big for a body which had lost too much weight.

"Aunt, are you sure she is all right? She looks dreadful and can hardly stand." Gaby remarked.

"According to the doctors, and believe me, she has been seen by the best, because we had her admitted to a leading private hospital, she will need time to get over the trauma of spending months in hiding, in constant fear of being caught by the Germans, often with no food and no place to sleep. Yuli, I have their detailed reports in English."

"I will get the gist, don't worry. How is she otherwise? Clear-headed? She understands what is happening?"

"Extraordinarily clear-headed and determined never again to set foot in France."

"Has she described what happened to her?"

"Briefly. Very briefly. She was indeed in the convoy which went off the rails, the one you mentioned. The doors of her compartment opened, and she just ran off without a second thought. A German overtook her, she resisted, wrestled his pistol off his belt, and shot him dead. Then, she took his overcoat and the money in his pockets. Julius, you should have heard her tell it with perfect calm. It was frightening."

"Auntie, she didn't have a choice. It was him or her. Don't worry, she has not turned into a monster."

"You must be right since Tony explained it to me the same way. She didn't say much about the way she escaped. She looked at Manny and I as if she was not seeing us and whispered that she didn't want to talk about it. Then she told us that she had a stroke of luck and met two American officers, who had escaped from their stalag. She seems to have grown fond of one of them."

"Is that why she wants to stay over there?" Julius was still nonplussed.

"Maybe. The main thing is she absolutely refuses to go back to France, mainly because of the way she was caught and what happened to her in jail."

"But they were Germans!

"Not all of them. There were Frenchmen among them. She was tortured and ... Yuli, Gabrielle, you understand."

The younger woman nodded, adding: "Say no more. There were some really awful people among those who collaborated. However, not all Frenchmen are like that, and she knows it well."

"Indeed, and she admits it freely. What she says is that there's nothing left of the life she had hoped to make for herself in France, where everything would remind her of what she has lost. She can't forgive Dr. Gilles. Without expressly accusing her of having betrayed her trust, she is convinced that her former boss was negligent and didn't make sure that she could not be overheard. A lack of vigilance which had terrible consequences. She was captured with her husband who died under torture, and as to herself, only the thought of her son prevented her from jumping to her death through the prison's window. It was what gave her the strength to take the first opportunity to flee and then to use the gun on the German and don his blood-stained coat. It was for Emile that she fought to survive all these months.

Julius, you should have seen how she perked up when I told her about our visit to the farm. Manny, bless the man, had brought the pictures that Tony took. She picked the photo of her child, kissed it, and cried tears of happiness. She was overjoyed to see your photo, to learn that you had made it through the war. She was saddened at the death of her mother but didn't want to know the details. She said she wasn't ready yet. Now she wants to forget the past, look ahead to a new life in America. She'll stay with us until she's better; it will be company for me. Later, Manny will see to it that she gets a post in a local hospital and gets used to the American system. I got the feeling that she wants to see whether her American friend, who is a career officer, will still be there for her when the war is over."

"My dear sister, there is something I don't get. Couldn't you tell me all this over the phone? Was it necessary to come all the way from America?"

Anni looked at him, with a startled expression.

"Someone has to go fetch the child, don't you think?"

It was his turn to be dumbstruck.

"She hates France so much that she can't even come herself?"

"That's not it. First, she's still in hospital. You have seen her. She's exhausted and far too thin. The doctors want to keep her for at least another ten days. The journey would've been too much for her. And not only in the physical sense. Second, it will also be far easier that way."

"Easier! How will you be able to get the child away without his mother?"

"We got him an American passport. Don't ask questions. They used a picture of Isaac as a baby; they look very much alike. Of course we have an official affidavit to the effect that I am authorized to travel with him. Manny arranged everything."

"How?"

"My dears, when I say Manny, I mean Bank Newman. Maybe not the largest in Chicago, but a first-class establishment with contacts at the highest levels. And money. Add the support of Lieutenant Colonel Tony Newman, who was just awarded the Military Cross, and that of captain Mandel, that's the officer whose life she allegedly saved—how? I have no idea, but he shows every sign of being more than fond of her. To cut a long story short, we, Emile and I, have been given two seats on an American aircraft leaving Paris for London in three days. From there, we shall take a regular flight to New York. I must admit that even though the war is still going on, one can still make miracles happen."

"All that must cost a fortune, you must tell me ..."

"Julius, don't ever mention it. Manny told me right away how happy he was to be able to repay you for all you have done. For years, you alone took on the burden of caring for father and Aunt Donna."

"Manny provided ..."

"We're not talking about money. You took care of them, didn't escape when you could because you knew they'd never leave the city where they were born and had spent all their lives. You suffered horribly while we never lacked for anything, were never threatened, and went on with our comfortable existence. Even Charles, our eldest, who wasn't drafted because he was too old, gladly did all he could to help Elisabeth, a cousin he is very proud of. Forget about the money. We have much to do and very little time."

"Anni, you saw the reception we had the last time. Are you sure that André will relinquish the boy that easily? He seemed persuaded that should his sister survive, she'd settle near them."

"There was never any question of that, according to your daughter. She is grateful for what Germaine did for her brother, as well as convinced that their wedding was a terrible mistake. André is not made to be a farmer and has absolutely nothing in common with that woman, however respectable and worthy she may be. Elisabeth told me that If it hadn't been for her pregnancy, he would never have married her. All that is beside the point. Your daughter has given me Power of Attorney and has written a long letter to her brother. There won't be a problem. I am told Germaine is a practical woman and will understand that the law is on my side. Enough. Elisabeth needs her diploma to be able to work in America. You, Julius, will contact Dr. Gilles so that she gives you the relevant documents."

"You have thought of everything."

"No, Manny and Charles did. My part was just to prepare clothes for the trip. Then someone has to go to her former flat in Paris. I have a list of what to get from there. Dr. Gilles has the key as well, apparently. Gabrielle, will you come with me, and then we can go to the farm together?"

"To the flat, gladly; however, I am not on very good terms with my brother."

"When did you see him last?"

"Five or six years ago."

"In six years, people change. Come on, say you'll come? That will give us time to get reacquainted on the way."

"That's a very good idea." Julius nodded in agreement. "Especially since Gabrielle also intends to settle in the States as well. She already has her ticket and visa."

"I have an even better idea, Father. We'll go without you. It makes more sense after the way André received you. This time, not only would you be coming back to take Emile away, but if you don't take off your wedding ring, he'll discover that you remarried. Even if you don't mention the little brother or sister he is about to have, sparks will fly. Me, he will probably end by being glad to see. We never really quarreled. We shall have a frank discussion and settle our differences while Anni packs the child's suitcase. Father, André will be very bitter, and rightly so. It is to him that Elisabeth had entrusted her little boy. He took good care of him. Suddenly, not only it is his aunt who announces that his sister is alive and in the States, but also that she was tasked to bring Emile back. He won't simply be bitter; he will be furious. Who could blame him?"

"I tend to agree with you," said her aunt. "Manny and I suggested that she phone André. She became agitated, stating that it was beyond what little strength she had left. She wrote a long letter, which I am to give him, but I'm afraid it will only make things worse. The way he insulted me the first time! He and Tony almost went to blows."

"Yes, Auntie, but you have to be there. You are the one who will bring the child to his mother. You are the one with the Power of Attorney and the affidavit."

Julius shook his head.

"You don't know the way, and Gabrielle doesn't have a car. And should André turn violent …"

"Yuli, she is right. The car won't be a problem. We can hire a chauffeur-driven limousine. No, don't interrupt. I shall phone Dr. Chamblay—you have his number, right?—ask him to break the news to his niece and come to Montrichard to guide us to the farm. André will calm down when he sees the photo of his sister and reads her letter."

"Not a bad plan. However, I won't let you go along with a chauffeur you don't know. What if Chamblay doesn't show up? I'll come with you. Gabrielle, wait, just listen! I'll ride with you to Montrichard and your rendezvous with Chamblay. If he doesn't come, I'll drive on. I believe I remember the way and will plan to remain in the car to avoid a confrontation. If he does come, I will hand over the car keys to Gabrielle, and wait in a café until you come back. I will bring a book to keep me company."

"A book? Some heavy medical tome?"

"Not at all. *The Perfume Of The Lady In Black*."

Gabrielle burst out laughing.

"Father! Where on earth did you find it? I adore Gaston Leroux."

"Well as you see, so do I."

"Seriously, Father. Won't you consider hiring a comfortable limousine? You expect us to travel in that strange-looking orange vehicle?"

"That strange-looking vehicle has an excellent heating system and great shock absorbers. And we can take turns driving there and back."

19

A BITTER PARTING

HISTORY DOES REPEAT ITSELF in a curious way, Julius thought as he drove on. I'm on my way to see Emile for the second time, and Anni is with me. Of course, the mood is quite different; I am no longer apprehensive; I feel a tremendous sense not only of relief, but of release from pent up stress. I see the end of my worries and can now serenely await our departure for Palestine. What is astonishing is that Lily was positively euphoric at the news that Elisabeth would settle in America. She took me in her arms, beaming. "See," she said, "how wrong you were to blame yourself for having sent your children to France? In spite of the war and of all they went through, they made it!"

She was right. Perfectly right. And she hadn't made the slightest push to be included in their expedition.

As had been agreed, he took the wheel on the first leg of the journey. His daughter was seated next to him while Anni, more tired than she would have cared to admit, was napping in the back. They changed seats at Orleans to let Gabrielle familiarize herself with the car. She soon admitted grudgingly that it handled nicely. They were in no hurry. According to the arrangement established after a call to Dr. Chamblay, they were to meet a little before noon at the Café de la Gare opposite the Montrichard train station. He was already there when they arrived and stood up to welcome them. They had a quick lunch. Seeing Gabrielle proudly wearing her Résistance medal, the retired doctor asked many questions.

When they left, Julius ordered some coffee and settled in for a long wait, albeit not an unwelcome one. He had rarely been alone in the past months and was happy to be able to gather his thoughts. So much had happened since December! The arrival of his sister, the discovery that he had not one but two small grandchildren, the hatred in André's eye, the wedding, taking the hand of his new wife, the mother of his child.

March had brought Gabrielle back into his life safe and sound. To crown it all, with April had come the great gift of Elisabeth. She had survived, had been spared the horrors of the camps, and was slowly being reborn in freedom. Was he beginning to believe in a benign fate, which, having made him fear the worst, was now beaming on him? Not quite. The children he had found again, the grandchildren he had discovered and were already tugging at his heart strings—he was going to lose them all, separated by the Mediterranean or the Atlantic. Of course, he could have accepted Anni's offer, settled in the United States where his two daughters were going to live; he could have persuaded Lily to go along, but the cost would've been too high and broken the hearts of his old friends who had set their sights on going to Palestine, and Lily would not have been happy. No, it was for the best. One day, he told himself, he would be able to take the plane and visit his growing American family; his daughters could also come to visit him. He smiled happily, ordered another coffee, and was soon chuckling at the antics of Rouletabille, the feisty sleuth imagined by Gaston Leroux. Two hours later, he started to check his watch every few minutes, wondering what was taking them so long?

Eventually they came. Gabrielle stopped along the curb. "All is well. Emile is asleep in the arms of his great-aunt. Get in, I'll tell you how it went."

It had been a difficult meeting, she told him. André, taken off guard when he spied her arriving with their aunt, had embraced her. As for his wife, she met them with naked hostility.

"How is she?" Julius interjected.

"Fortyish, not precisely handsome. Someone used to be in charge. Forewarned by Chamblay about the purpose of our visit, she had called on the village priest and the Mayor's assistant. At her request, the latter had brought a notarized affidavit signed by Elisabeth Metzger granting André custody of her child. I politely explained that Elisabeth had tasked her aunt with fetching Emile, giving her Power of Attorney, to that effect, which had been attested to by the French Consulate in New York. I added that her husband, being deceased, left her the sole guardian of their son, and that the new document cancelled whatever provision she might have made in the past. While the man perused the document, André yelled that it was a fake, that we had come to kidnap his nephew and steal his inheritance. Were his sister alive, he argued, she would have come in person to thank them and hold her son.

"Anni opened her purse and handed the hospital pictures to Germaine, who passed them onto the others. She then gave André his letter. He read it, his chest heaving, and then threw it on the ground, vilely cursing in Hungarian before stomping out. The priest and the Mayor's assistant left soon after, shaking Germaine's hand who then went to fetch Emile while trying very hard not to cry. I can understand her. Emile is adorable. He looks so much like my little Julie. I was getting teary myself. The kid cast frightening glances all around, sensing that all was not well in his small world. Aunt kneeled down in front of him and told him she was going to take him to his mother. You should have seen how his little face lit up! 'Can I fetch my teddy bear?' is all he said. By that time, Germaine had regained her composure and told Anni to choose what she wanted to take. You know, Father, I rather understand my brother. He and his wife had accepted responsibility for the child and were ready to raise him as their own, yet Elisabeth could not bring herself to phone them or even send a telegram to say that she was alive. Then there is Mother's alleged wealth. Chamblay explained that André and Germaine were really counting on that money to pay their debts. When Germaine married André, she had to give her children from the first marriage their part of their father's inheritance. They had not demanded it before because they did not want to force her to sell the farm. She took loans, which she cannot repay. They are hurting."

"You are right to tell me," Julius consoled. "I'll take care of it. I intended to leave money to each of you before I left. You don't need it, but he does. Elisabeth too will need help in settling in America."

"When you are through plotting, can we stop?" came Anni's voice from the back seat. "Emile woke up and we have to stop to let the child relieve himself."

After such auspicious beginnings, April was bringing good news by the day. Germany was reeling after suffering one setback after another. Russian and Allied forces were still making an all-out effort to be the first to reach Berlin. One after the other, the camps were being liberated and the first survivors were arriving at the Lutetia. The fate of the returnees was no longer first page news in France. People wanted to turn over a new leaf. The talk was of the local elections due to be held on April 29, it was to be the first popular consultation in nine years, and the first time women had the right to vote. A record turnout was expected. Zsazsa, who acquired French citizenship long ago, was set on voting, something she had never done before, without quite knowing for what or for whom. She was not the only one. Dozens of new political parties were clamoring for the women's vote. Indeed, *Le Figaro*, the daily paper, had issued "A Short Guide for the Use of Parisian Women Voters."

Meanwhile, Lily and Theo attended to the last details of their departure, with the welcome support of Gabrielle, who postponed her own trip to be with them until they left. She had also worked hard at bringing father and son together. A seemingly mission impossible was crowned with success after she called her sister-in-law and hinted at the financial assistance her father was ready to give them. After hearing that, André's wife pressured him to go to Paris where he stayed with Gabrielle in Avenue Bosquet. They had a painful discussion.

"André," Gabrielle finally said. "Father is alive and mother is dead. Do you truly believe that he is lying when he says he did all he could to persuade her to flee, that he stayed with her to the end, that he would have gone with her to the ghetto and the camps? Because everything else is secondary. You don't want to answer? Now he has gotten married again. He has his life; you have yours. You have suffered, so has he. Doesn't he have the right to another chance at happiness? Next month, he is going to Tel Aviv with his new wife and old friends. He wants to give you enough money to pay your debts, help you make a new start. He will give you that money whether you agree to meet him or not. André, we are talking about your father, the grandfather of your child. Make up your mind. Let him go, knowing that you may never see him again, or remember that he has always been there for you? You feel you would be betraying our mother's memory? Have you forgotten how she fought to prevent you and Elisabeth from going to France for your studies? The false accusations she leveled at father? You accuse him of having been unfaithful? Come on! I am younger than you are, but from a young age I was aware that they slept in separate rooms, and that it was her decision. I remember hearing Grandfather Emile reproaching her. It's all in the past. We no longer have to take sides."

Somewhat begrudgingly, André relented. Julius had come to meet him at Gabrielle's flat. André let his father speak of the last days in Oradea, of his mother's death, and his escape. He then asked for his forgiveness and gave a tentative peck on his father's cheek. With lowered eyes, he thanked him for his generous assistance. The farm would be clear of debts, and there would be enough money to hire more workers, leaving André free to look for a job as an engineer once more. He promised to write and send photos of his little daughter.

Elisabeth had phoned her father a week after Anni's return, to thank him for the generous sum he had transferred to Bank Newman for her. She said nothing about her ordeal, didn't ask about her mother, but spoke haltingly about the new life she hoped to make in America and promised to write when she felt better. Anni had then briefly taken the phone to tell Julius not to worry. His daughter was getting better by the day and was beginning to smile again now that her little boy was with her. He had ended the conversation with an aching heart. After months of anxiety and desperate efforts to learn what had happened to his beloved eldest daughter, then rejoicing at her miraculous escape, he had not been able to hold her in his arms even once and would not be there for her in her arduous path to recovery. Then he shook his head ruefully. Life is made of choices, he chided himself. You have made yours. Be thankful with what you have.

On Sunday, April 22, Doctor Julius Matthias, accompanied by his very pregnant wife, attended the grand wedding of Marie-Christine and her general at the Saint Philippe du Roule church. In the evening, Julius went alone to the reception, which was given at the prestigious Cercle Militaire. Lily said she was tired and used the age-old complaint that she had nothing suitable to wear. He had not pressed her, wanting to be alone for that last time with a woman who played such an important part in his life.

Leaning against the paneled wall of the great ballroom, he watched the bride waltzing in her husband's arms to the strains of the Blue Danube. She wore a sumptuous lace creation in a very pale rose; he was in dress uniform. A handsome couple, it was murmured. Not in the first flush of youth but facing the future with confidence. He didn't intend to stay long, but just waited for his dance with her. When she finally came to him and he took her in his arms, he could feel his heart beating. They were both trying very hard not to show how deeply moved they were; it was an emotion they could not afford to show. She asked about Elisabeth, he told her she was doing fine. She did not quite believe him but went on to enquire about Lily's health and wanted to know when they were leaving for Palestine.

When the music came to an end, someone else came to claim her. Julius bowed, kissed her hand, and left. Walking slowly home under a fine drizzle, his thoughts turned to the other woman, who had, for so long, held him in thrall: Madi. Madi, tender and vulnerable, whose last thoughts had been for him; Madi, whose unbelievably large fortune had set him free and would provide for his new life and that of his children. Madi, who was fading from his memory. He shook his head in the darkness and blew her a kiss.

Then came his last week in Paris and time to say farewell. Paul Zerner had promised to come and see them in Palestine, and Hans hinted he might come with him. A visibly moved Jerome Grandin had come one last time to see his old friends the Castans. He was going to sell the flat for them, promising to get them the best possible deal and make sure that the money reached them in Tel Aviv where, he said, he had contacts. There had also been a last dinner with the engravers in a recently opened Polish restaurant.

On the last evening, Anni phoned to wish them good luck and told them to let her know about their safe arrival. Manny joined her on the phone, reminding Julius that he had pledged to Anni to come to Chicago in four years to attend the celebration of their jubilee wedding anniversary. Elisabeth cried a little but already sounded much better; she even joked that she was in danger of getting fat with the bountiful food she was getting and was looking forward to seeing her sister, who had promised to come visit her.

Gabrielle explained that she would be leaving for the United States in the morning. She had decided to sell her Paris flat, symbolically cutting her last tie to France after having lived there for ten years. She would, she told her father, take her time about deciding her next steps.

EPILOGUE

THE MOON WAS FULL, as it had been on his first night on the arduous road to freedom. Julius was awake. He crept noiselessly out of his first-class cabin, careful not to wake his wife who was sound asleep, a smile on her lips, and made his way to the deck. Leaning on the railing, he watched the dawn beginning to color a cloudless sky over a profoundly dark sea. It was not the perspective of embarking on a new life at nearly 55 that kept him awake.

A year ago to the day, on May 3, 1944, his world fell apart. His wife was murdered, his neighbors, his friends, were herded off for deportation. Fueled by the need to connect with his children again, he had made a desperate bid for freedom. Now, he was leaving them behind with a heavy heart but no qualms. They were safe; he would see them again, somewhere, sometime. It was up to him to shape his new existence with the woman fate had thrown into his path and the child who would soon be born.

With him, he was taking his old friends, his last link to the world he left behind and he felt ready to confront whatever difficulties awaited him across the sea. He rendered silent thanks to Madi. She had ceased to trouble his nights, and he no longer saw her in his dreams but would never forget how much he owed her.

Doubts and last-minute hesitations were left behind. He would not look back. Fittingly perhaps, the previous evening, the ship commander had made a surprise appearance in the first-class dining room, followed by an army of waiters carrying champagne bottles. In a voice which was not quite steady, he said that the BBC had just announced the death of Adolf Hitler. Three days earlier, according to the report, the German dictator had killed himself in his bunker in order to avoid capture by the Russians entering Berlin. This announcement was met by thunderous applause and the popping of the corks.

Julius found it hard to rejoice. Germany had lost the war, but its troops were still battling the Soviet Union in the East. The *Times of London* was already speaking of what it called the fall of the Iron Curtain countries "liberated by Russia," including Hungary and Romania, cutting them off from the rest of Europe. The West, shaken by reports of what happened in the death camps and reeling at the sight of the starved inmates slowly emerging from hell, was nevertheless not in a hurry to help survivors or offer them asylum. The gates of Palestine were still firmly closed to desperate Jews. One needed to have a lot of money and be able to show it to obtain a visa, which was fortunately the case for Julius, Lily and the Castans, quietly sleeping below. Yet, alone in the darkness, Julius silently pledged not to forget the plight of his less fortunate brethren, consoling himself with the thought that he'd find ways to help.

Suddenly, a small hand sought his own. His wife had come to join him. Hand in hand, they watched a new sun emerging from the dawn mist as the ship plowed its way to the promised land across the sea.

www.ingramcontent.com/pod-product-compliance
Lightning Source LLC
Chambersburg PA
CBHW030635020726
47493CB00006B/1724